Praise for Faith O'Shea

Faith O'Shea is a contemporary women's literature writer who loves writing about romance, magic, conviction, and loyalty, with strong women and the friendships they build. She has created many series of stories to make us laugh, cry and feel empowered and writes in a voice that speaks to women of all ages. Faith believed there were subjects and life that needed to be written about. ~ Loyce M.

I truly love the Everyday Goddess series. The strong, leading women characters, in this day and age, are inspiring to me and keep me coming back for more! The books are light, fun, extremely relatable and I can't put them down! ~ Kathryn B.

I just finished the Fire and Ice series. It had romance, strong friendships between the women characters and complex stories that were clearly very well researched. Loved all of them and looking forward to the goddess series next! ~ Gail N.

Oh wow! I just finished reading the *Magic Bean Café* and I must say that I was hooked from the first chapter and loved every page. The characters were full and believable. The child, Willow, had my heart with her wild imagination, gift of laughter, and the way she melted Aisin's heart and helped him to realize that you can love a child that wasn't yours. Thank you for gifting me this awesome read. ~ Your newest fan, Carol F. ♥

Magic Bean Café is a fantastic book of compassion for others with realistic characters. Plus a generous millionaire to help fulfill dreams. ~ Belinda

Books by Faith O'Shea

The Greenliner Series
Four baseball players, one team on the rise

Thrown for a Curve
League of Her Own
Clutch Hit
Out in Left Field

The Scalera Family Series
Five boisterous Italian siblings, five ways to find love

Cold Sweat
Edge of Forever
Thin Blue Line
Coming Home to You
Finding Joy

SCALERA FAMILY

Five boisterous Italian siblings, five ways to find love

Cold Sweat

Johnny's the oldest, drummer for the heavy metal band Raging Thunder. The man knows how to rock and roll and thinks he's just the one who can teach Letitia Jones, a classically trained pianist, everything there is to know about life but when the tables are turned, he runs scared. Will he come to realize that settling down, isn't the worse thing in life that can happen?

Edge of Forever

Rissa's sketches of Luca Caroli, bassist for her brother's band, are uncovering edges, and revealing things meant to stay hidden. He's not what he seems and she's beginning to think he might be her forever. Problem is, he's stuck in the past. What can she do to align the stars in her favor?

Thin Blue Line

Lana, the youngest, never got over her father's death, and swore she'd never marry a cop. Her mother had paid the ultimate price for loving such a man. So how did she find herself married to Zachary Taylor, a cop, who's more than willing to put his life on the line every second of every day? If she sacrifices him now, will it save her grief in the end?

Coming Home to You

Tony is his father's son, with a badge and a gun, but he's not going to leave a widow behind like his father did. When he takes Tansy McPhail under his wing, and gives her shelter, he thinks he's just doing some community service. How long will it take for him to see, that his place isn't a home, without her?

Finding Joy

Dennis has been married before and has no plans on walking that aisle again so when he meets the sexy diva Artemis, under protest, he has no illusions. But as he works to produce her new record, he finds she's more than the tabloids have led the public to believe. She's warm and funny and down-to-earth, but she's still Artemis to him, not Joy Munroe. Does he have what it would take, to win her love?

THE EDGE OF FOREVER

Scalera Family
Book 2

FAITH O'SHEA

Cover Design by Jaycee DeLorenzo at Sweet 'N Spicy Designs
Formatting and Interior Design by Woven Red Author Services, www.wovenRed.ca

The Edge of Forever/Faith O'Shea- 1st edition
ISBN eBook: 978-0-998-7229-4-8
ISBN print book: 978-0-998-7229-5-5

www.faithoshea.com

To My Readers

Writers must love their characters. You spend so much time with them, whether it be six months or ten years, that you'd give up their story before the end if you didn't. Johnny and Tish, from Cold Sweat, stayed with me way past the final chapter. So much so, I decided to tell the story of each of the Scalera siblings. The family is of Italian heritage, and I've lived the Sunday dinners, the sibling rivalry, the close-knit community. My grandmother always had something to feed me whenever I visited. It was her way of saying she loved me, and she said it well. I remember being a little girl and watching her roll out the dough for the home-made ravioli, crimping the edges with her crimper, fingering the cavatelli with just the right amount of pressure to make perfect drops of pasta. And her escarole pizza? I miss it as much as I miss her, now that she's gone. I've tried to duplicate it, but it's not the same.

Missing ingredient? Nana love.

The Edge of Forever came out of a sense of curiosity about Reject's name. Where did it come from and why was he still using it? With Rissa's help, I began peeling away his defenses, and discovered a sensitive soul who was looking for love, the same way Rissa was. He is far more complex than the name suggests, and I hope you enjoy discovering who he is. I sure did.

Next one in line is Lana and it's in draft form with a lot of work yet to be done. Thin Blue Line will be available next year sometime, and I can't wait to get back to it.

Thrown for a Curve is off the market due to editing changes, but I hope to have it back on Kindle by mid-fall.

Feel free to contact me at www.faithoshea.com. You can also follow me on twitter and Facebook.

CHAPTER ONE

Marissa Scalera was reeling as she tried to grasp what had just happened. It had been so sudden it had cut the legs right out from under her. Nausea curdled in her stomach, and a frightening sense of disorientation only added to the crippling sensation. Her breathing was erratic, coming in shallow spurts, so she put her hand on the kitchen counter to keep her legs from buckling. The retching convulsions began, and she stumbled to the toilet just in time. She wiped her mouth and leaned her head against the cool ceramic bowl, trying to regain her bearings.

This isn't working. I want you to cancel the wedding.

She should have seen this coming, but the disquieting sense of alarm came too late to make a difference. It was over.

You need to be gone by the time I get home. Leave the keys to the condo and the car on the counter before you leave.

Did he expect her to eliminate every trace of herself from his life?

Wipe her prints from every surface, eliminate any telltale sign that she had ever lived here?

Not that there was much to pack. He had stripped her life down to a few inconsequentials so most everything of value was already at her mother's.

It was final this time. He wouldn't change his mind. He'd found someone else.

She hadn't even noticed.

With the bile settling, and as feeling came back into her fingers, her mind cleared, and she finally swallowed a dose of anger. She scrambled up from the marble tiles, ran into the kitchen and flung open a cabinet. The box of green garbage bags sat on the shelf, the thick plastic peeking out from the slit and she ripped two of them out. With jerky movements, she stripped the closet clean of her meager possessions, and stuffed them in. Then into the bathroom, removing toiletries, feminine products, shower cap, towels. With two bags filled, every shred of what she owned cleared out, she wrestled the diamond off her finger and flung it on the quartz counter, along with both sets of keys. Finally, she stood in front of her most prized possession, the Monet print her parents had framed and given her for Christmas, and gently lifted it up off the hook, carefully wrapping it in another bag. The last scan of the room alerted her to the picture of her family resting on a table in the stark and sterile living room. She swept that into her backpack, shrugged into her coat and went out to the front stoop to wait for her stepfather Paul to arrive. The snow was falling lightly, the air chilly, typical for March in New England and drifts of snow enveloped her feet.

Her head dipped as one of her...former neighbors passed her, and she could feel the inquisitive eyes take in the small pile around her before she disappeared behind her door. The shame covered her more thickly than the accumulation of snow.

She was alone again, staring out into the distance.

What the hell was she going to do now?

Before long, a car pulled up along the sidewalk, the headlights illuminating the white powder, but she was frozen in place and couldn't move.

She felt the warmth of her stepfather's body as he wrapped his arms around her, helping her to her feet. The anger emanating from his solid form seeped through her as well.

She felt bedraggled. Or maybe it was shell shocked.

"Come on sweetheart. I've got your bags."

Paul supported her weight by taking her by the arm as she let him lead her to the back door of his car, his partner from the homicide unit in the passenger seat, a captive audience to her humiliation.

Making sure the seat belt was secure, he offered her soft assurances.

"It's going to be all right Rissa. I'm going to take you home."

Her arms snaked around her middle to keep herself from spilling out.

Once he was back behind the wheel and pulling out from where he double-parked, she said in a raw voice.

"I'm sorry. I called Ma but she didn't answer."

She could have called one of her brothers but it was Paul's calm demeanor she needed right now.

"I'm glad you called me, Rissa. I've always told you I'd be there if you needed me."

She had given him only a brief rundown of what had happened when she'd called him but even with as little as he knew, he looked like he wanted to pummel her ex-fiancé, his eyes dark and dangerous. She might only be his step-daughter but he'd always made her feel loved, even as a baby. Her father's partner for over twenty years, Paul Catalano had taken over full responsibility for her family not long after her father's death. And he'd worn the mantle of protector better than his predecessor although she'd never said that out loud.

She heard the jab as he punched the button that controlled the heat, the full thrust of hot air reaching her in the back. When she noticed his eyes in the rear-view mirror as if to check on her, she asked so softly he must have read her lips to understand her question.

"How could he have done this?"

She didn't mean the break-up but the callous way he'd gone about it. To drop in, drop his bombshell and then leave was the height of cruelty.

Paul's expression was tight, his answer held a bite.

"Jude is a certified asshole. That's why. It has nothing to do with you. And if I hadn't sworn to protect and defend there'd be a bloody murder on my hands."

Choking back the sob that threatened, she sat silently until they pulled up to her childhood home where her mother came racing out to meet them.

Celia Scalera Catalano brushed away the clinging snow off Rissa's head. "I'm sorry I didn't get your call. I always have my phone off while we're serving.

Celia was catering a wedding reception that night, something Rissa had forgotten, her brain too numb to process thought.

Paul got the bags out of his trunk along with a large rectangular package and deposited them in the front hall before kissing both women goodbye.

Rissa leaned on her mother as she helped her out of her coat and threw it over the banister.

"You go on up. I'm going to heat up some soup. That will make you feel better."

She felt like a decrepit old woman as she struggled up the stairs, her grip on the wooden banister taut, her shoulders curling in.

After taking a few steps along the landing, Rissa came to a stop at the threshold of her old room, the twin beds on either side of the window like they always were. The walls had been repainted a pale, soft blue but she could still see the bright pink walls of her youth, the coverlets white eyelet, hers covered with her softball uniform that had never made it to the wash after her last game, a pair of sneakers peeking out from under the duster ruffle skirt, her muddy cleats sitting on the mat her mother insisted she use. A pitcher's glove sat on the floor, along with her roller blades. Athletic apparel was strewn around the room, and on the table against the wall were her brushes, small canvases and tubes of paint.

Lana's side was more girlie than hers, stacks of cooking magazines on her nightstand, a glass mirror tray on the bureau where she stored earrings, bangles and necklaces, a picture of whatever current boyfriend she had in view. It changed every month.

They had always been so different. Today it was more glaring than ever.

Lana was living in an apartment, totally self-supported. Although she didn't have the kitchen of her dreams, she could go home at the end of her working day to her own personal space. No one could kick her out, no one could tell her what she could leave out and what had to be hidden. Her cookbooks were all over the place, taking up a good portion of the little counter area she had, and they sprouted little tabs where she could easily find her favorite recipes, spiral notebooks filled with a list of ingredients for the new cooking experiments. She had a steady boyfriend, but she refused to be bogged down with restraints of any kind.

While Lana didn't mind living alone, it scared her to death. No matter how hard she tried to escape her feelings of loneliness, they always found her.

Would everyone she loved, abandon her?

Rissa crossed over the threshold into her old life, sank onto the new duvet, dropping her head into her hands wanting to cry but her nervous system and all her senses had shut down leaving her numb.

Her body swiveled to take in the woman standing at the doorway, a bowl of soup in her hand. Her mother was petite and round, with curly brown hair and an apron around her waist, she felt her mother's love wash over her. Love in Italian meant food, so she knew she'd be coddled and fed for as long as it took for her to get back on her feet. If she ever did.

The anger had seeped out and the tears were finally ready to fall.

"Oh, Ma. How could he have done this to me?"

Rissa looked to her mother for an answer, the tears falling in big, fat drops.

Celia took a step into the room and gently placed the oversized cup on the nightstand before she plopped down beside her daughter.

"I don't like the way he did this any more than you do. But it was the best thing to happen. You know this."

"What I know is that I wasted three years of my life. How can I be back here with you and Paul?"

"We love having you, you know that. I miss the noise, the life you kids brought to this house. It will be nice having you here for a time."

She patted her daughter's hand.

"I'm going to have Paul clear out the back landing so you can paint again. The light is good there and I think it's the best spot."

It's where she used to paint when she was younger, the space small but adequate for her needs. And the light spilled in from the double window. She found it difficult to see herself at the spattered table again.

"I haven't painted in ages. I'm not sure…"

"You gave up who you were for him. I never liked that."

Celia's lips curled and her voice held hostility, something Rissa rarely heard from her.

Her eyes shot up to meet her mother's.

"You never said anything."

"It was your mistake to make. I just prayed…a lot."

She thumbed the moisture off her face and a weak laugh broke free.

"It seems your prayers were answered."

"I had always hoped it would be you who broke it off, not him."

Celia clasped her hands and squeezed.

"Marriage today is different than it was when I was your age. Back then, women stayed home, had kids, smothered their own needs. Today women have choices. Jude took them away from you."

"But I wanted kids…"

She pulled Rissa close with an arm around her shoulder, she admitted, "I know. I did, too."

"You know I loved your father."

Rissa went on alert. She nodded and said, "Of course."

Celia hesitated, glanced up, before going on.

"Well, there was a time I resented my life. Five kids in seven years is a lot to take on. Don't doubt that I always loved you with my heart and soul. You know that, right?"

Rissa sat up. What was her mother trying to tell her?

"Your father expected me to live his life. Be home when he got here, have supper waiting, cook, clean, take care of him. I lost myself. It's hard to remember who you are when you're someone's wife and someone's mother. I got restless. I needed something that was mine. But he never encouraged it. I had to fight him when I opened the catering business. And then he was killed, and it was up to me to support you all. So, in the end my decision was a good one."

"You're so good at what you do. Cooking is your life."

"No, Rissa. Cooking is a part of who I am. It is not my life. No one single thing should be. I have a good one and it includes you kids, Paul, the Italian Club, my movie nights with my friends."

Rissa stared at her mother. Understanding was beginning to dawn.

"Paul never made you give any of that up."

"No. He wanted me to find those things that made me feel good about myself and do them without guilt or consequence. It was one of the reasons it was so easy for me to fall in love with him."

Her eyes grew wide, and she stammered, "Were you and Paul..."

"Absolutely not. We didn't even look at each other that way for over a year after your father died."

As if to make sure Rissa believed her Celia measured her facial expression before going on. "From where I'm standing today, I know it's important to find a man who values your passions as much as you do. One who doesn't want to mold you into someone you're not but gives you the freedom to be exactly who you are. Jude was not that man, my love."

She let her mother's words permeate her mind and took them to heart.

"I guess I was trying so hard to be who Jude wanted that I forgot what I wanted, that I was important, too."

"And you are. Very important to a lot of us. I say good riddance to someone who was never right for you. Now you can start being you again."

She hugged her mother tightly, like she had when she was younger.

"Thank you for sharing that. I would never have guessed that you had a hard time with Dad. You kept it hidden well."

"I fell in love with your father when I was sixteen years old. What does a person know at that age? And it was right for me at the time. All I wanted was a family, lots of kids, like my own mother and your father gave me that. Ten years later, I wanted more. I was the one who'd changed."

"Do you think you would have gotten a divorce if he hadn't died?"

With a measured response, her mother assured her, "No. I would have muddled through, fighting him more often than I'd want but doing what was important to me in spite of it."

She gave her mother a knowing look.

"It takes so much energy to fight all the time."

"When you try to be someone you're not, you waste a lot of energy. Don't hide who you are my love. Let it spill out."

Rissa embraced the woman who had always seemed so wise. "I love you Ma."

"I love you, too, Rissa."

As panic came back to assault her, she asked, in almost a wail, "What am I going to do now?"

"You're going to go to work tomorrow as you always do, putting one foot in front of the other."

"But it's so embarrassing."

"There would have been more shame in marrying the wrong man."

She studied her mother and thought maybe she was right. But it would still be hard going to work and telling everyone that the wedding was off, only one-month shy of the event.

She should have called his bluff when he'd postponed it the first time.

Or gotten the message that it was doomed.

Celia placed her hands on either side of Rissa's face and looked her straight in the eye.

"This will always be your home. Take some time to heal and to remember who you are."

"I got a little lost. I'm just not sure how to find myself again."

"I think that will be easy enough. The hard part will be growing into who you can be. And finding someone who can encourage you to get there. And that isn't Jude."

Celia got up to leave.

"I'll be in the kitchen if you need me. Lana will be here when she's finished up with the event."

"I'm sorry you had to leave because of me."

"I'm not. My children have grown, and they don't need me as much, which is the way I wanted to raise you. But it's nice every once in a while, to truly be a mother again. You have your family behind you, and we'll be there for you, Rissa, whenever you need us."

When she exited the room, Rissa lay down on the narrow bed, curled into a ball, sobbing until there was nothing left except exhausted sleep.

CHAPTER TWO

A few days later, Rissa had all but raced into the house, dumping a box of her belongings on the kitchen counter. Her mother's kitchen counter. She was still here in her parents' home, still undecided about her future. As of an hour ago, it looked even bleaker.

Her voice didn't hide her distress.

"I quit today."

She'd gotten written up for rubbing medicinal ointment on one of the kids, per parental instruction. The requisite forms were never filled out, a big corporate no-no and the director was not happy. It didn't matter that it wasn't her responsibility because it wasn't her student, or that every teacher in the afternoon school program had been doing the same thing; she was the one caught and all but suspended.

After weeks of frenzied thinking, agonizing over whether she could leave the students she'd grown to love, all her anger and frustration coalesced into a split-second decision. No notice, no backward glance. Vanessa would have to be in a classroom until closing but she didn't give a double chocolate shit-on-a-stick.

She stood waiting for a reaction, both her mother and sister sitting at the table, papers spread out before them as if this were just another day, another Rissa dilemma. The house was the home base for their catering service and whenever they were in the planning stages of an event, she would find them huddled together, mapping out strategy and menu. They had a bond that she found hard to infiltrate.

Celia turned her head, her eyes peering from above her glasses.

"I had a feeling it was coming."

"You what?"

Celia flicked her glasses off and gave Rissa her attention.

"You've put so many dings in the pots and pans at the kitchen from all your banging, I was ready to order a new set. What happened?"

Rissa told her about the afternoon events, the humiliation, the shock, and the anger.

"It was the last straw. I should have quit when the others did. It didn't take more than a month with Vanessa at the helm for them to read the signs."

"You should have."

Flipping her glasses back on her head, Celia went back to the task she was working on.

Lana's eyes never reached hers, her fingers busy shuffling options.

"What are you going to do instead?"

Rissa all but glowered at her. Lana never had an indecisive moment, wouldn't know what it was like to be grasping for a place to fit in, someone to hold on to.

It was a good question, but she didn't have an answer.

Her mother apparently did because without missing a beat, Celia said, "She's going on tour with your brother's band."

Sucking in a breath, so caught off guard by the pronouncement, Rissa blurted out, "What? Why would I do that?"

Her day had been teetering but this pronouncement just whirled it off its axis.

"I talked to Tish this afternoon. The woman they hired to nanny got engaged and she's moving to Illinois. They are in desperate need, and this couldn't have come at a better time."

Rissa all but stormed over to the table, bent down, and glared into her mother's face.

"What if I don't want to go with him?"

The tone serene, as if Rissa wasn't in her face, Celia responded.

"Have you other options? You weren't planning on sitting around the house, were you?"

That was the intention, for a week or two anyway. Her mother just took it off the table.

"I was going to look for another job."

Eventually.

"Rissa, I love you to the moon and back, but this is your third job in six years. What's left to try?"

With a hopeful smile, she said, "I can work for you."

"We don't need any more workers. We just hired our summer help."

Rissa dropped into the vacant chair, deflated. What the hell?

"But I'm family."

"Which makes this perfect. I'll call your brother and tell him you're available. Tish will be quite pleased. She was a bit skeptical about leaving Rosie with a stranger. Now she won't have to worry."

"They're leaving in a few days. I can't possibly be ready by then."

"You throw some clothes in a suitcase and drive to Tim's. I don't understand the problem."

She wouldn't. Her mother never had problems, only solutions. Celia's head snapped up, her eyes wide in disbelief.

"You don't mind spending time with your niece, do you?"

She felt a smile creep onto her face. The small wonder all pink and perfect might be just the right medicine for her burgeoning depression. Crying in her beer at the bar probably wasn't the best solution to her problems.

Shaking her head, she admitted, "You know I love Rosie. I just don't like being forced into something before I can think it through."

"Did you think before you quit?"

She was back to glaring at her mother.

"No."

"Then it's settled. You can take the next three days to...rest. Rosie might be young but she's a handful."

All the fight went out of her. Maybe she should let her mother make this decision for her. The last couple of big ones she'd made weren't the best.

She pulled herself up out of the seat, and retreated to her room, box in hand.

After placing the box of her personal things on the bed, she began unpacking the contents. She marveled at how things had changed in just a year. She'd won employee of the year under her old boss, had taken on a couple of odd jobs like decorating the bulletin board in the entryway. It was the first thing the touring families inspected on entering and she'd been complimented on how colorful, yet inviting it was. Lifting some of her art books out of the box, she sifted through them. She'd spent some of her money on resources for different art activities for preschoolers. The one on top looked like one of Lana's cookbooks, a profusion of purple tabs sticking out, keeping the place of some of her favorites. After tossing the pile on the floor, she dug out the coffee mug one of her students had bought her for Christmas. It read LIFE IS GOOD IF YOU'RE A TEACHER. After fingering the rim, she set it down on the dressing table. She unpacked the pom-poms, ribbons, and other notions she kept on hand for spur-of-the-moment projects and rainy days and put them away in the closet. After taking the empty carton and tucking it under the table, she dropped onto the edge of her bed.

How had she lost control of her own life?

She should tell her mother that she refused to do it, but when she got around to the process of thinking, she knew there was nothing better on the horizon.

It wouldn't be too much of a hardship being with her brother's family. They were some of her favorite people, and the seasonal job would give her time to figure out what the hell she was going to do with the rest of her life.

⌒

Reject Caroli waited for Johnny to get off the phone.

The band was just finishing up one of the last practices before heading out on Raging Thunder's summer tour, which was only three days away. He was feeling good about it. Exhilarated. It was a relief knowing he'd soon be with his buddies again on a regular basis. He missed the frenetic energy of a tour, the endless traveling, the companionship, the freedom. Playing bass had never been part of his future, but once the nightmare of his life had become intolerable, he'd turned to the instrument, and it'd saved him. Raging Thunder had become his home, and this year, the band was riding the crest of a wave. Every venue was sold out and the critics had lavished praise on their newest CD. They had their mojo back, in no short measure due to Johnny and Tish's dynamics. He hadn't seen that relationship coming. Johnny had been set in his ways, his conviction that family meant pain and suffering such an ingrained part of who he was that when Tish had come into his life, he'd fought it and lost, and had never been happier. The band had won, coming alive again with the classical pianist at the keyboard, or maybe it was Johnny's return to his role of leader to help her that created the new buzz. All he knew was that they were back on top and the tour would be a welcome change from the monotony of day-to-day life. He was still hitting the clubs, but now that

Johnny was married, it wasn't the same. It was the drummer who could lure women to their table with a smile, his looks and personality a lethal combination that women seemed to love. Honey and flies. It was something Reject lacked, had always lacked. He was analytical, serious, less engaging, unless he had a couple of drinks in him. Then the light was switched on and he'd become gregarious, his inhibitions lower, his confidence heightened.

But drinking alone wasn't fun. Once he lost his best friend, it was more work than pleasure to get out there and socialize. He had never fit in anywhere, until the band, until Johnny offered his friendship.

Out on the road was another story.

As the only remaining member of the band who was single, he was sought after without having to do a thing.

He was looking forward to getting back out there where women threw themselves at his feet and he could pick and choose at his leisure. It offered the acceptance he craved, the popularity that had always evaded him.

He glanced up when Johnny gave a whoop.

"What a relief."

There was a big smile on the band member's face.

"What is?"

"My sister is going to nanny for us. Tish wasn't sure what she was going to do."

Johnny's wife, Tish, a classical pianist in her own right, had played keyboard with the band last year and Johnny had somehow convinced her to play with them again this summer. The problem they faced was who would watch their three-month-old daughter while she did. It seemed like their problem was solved.

Cautiously, he asked, "Which sister?"

"Marissa. She quit her job and Ma offered her services."

Reject grimaced. A dark rain cloud appeared casting a shadow over the upcoming tour. Rissa wasn't one of his favorite people, but if it meant Tish could play with them, he'd have to suck it up.

Some of his initial excitement seeped out. This would put a major crimp into his plans to be with the guys, but he knew how to hide, and he'd use his finely-honed skill to stay outside her reach.

Once home, he kicked off his boots, and gravitated towards the kitchen. His sister would have stocked it with all his favorite foods, and he was famished from all the energy expelled earlier.

After rooting around, he heated up the container of cavatelli and sat at the bar, his laptop open. As he ate, he roamed his fan page and the band's website. He loved to read the comments people left, relishing the approval that had been so hard to come by.

A name popped out at him as he scrolled down.

His finger worked the pad, and he went back, his heart all but stopping in his chest.

Paige.

It couldn't be his Paige.

Not that she'd been his for long.

It was their break-up that had caused the dominoes in his life to fall, and it had taken him a long time to get them upright again.

He was sitting here right now because they had gone in very different directions.

He peered at the screen, willing his eyes to focus.

I'm looking for Luca. If this finds him, please let him know I've been thinking about him lately and would love to connect. I can be reached at PChung@Columbia.edu. I'm sure he'll remember who I am.

Paige. At Columbia.

It seemed *her* future hadn't blown up after their dating debacle. A professorship required not only a master's degree but a doctorate as well. It meant she'd been in school most of the ten years since he'd last seen her. Her life should have gone off the track, like his, at least for a little while. Although in her case, it didn't matter how long she took to finish college; her parents had the funds to waste on a lost semester or two. He hadn't had that luxury.

He reached for the bottle of white wine and uncorked it, his hands unsteady as he poured himself a liberal dose and swallowed it down in one gulp.

There were a lot of memories stuffed into the short message. They were exploding in color, each spark defining one of them, bringing him back...to a place he'd thought was lost forever.

His curiosity was piqued, and he read the missive again, questions racing through his head.

What was she doing on Thunder's webpage?

Did she listen to their music?

She'd been more into soft rock, listened to it when they studied, shut it off along with the light before they went to bed, before the end had come.

A heavy weight settled on his chest when he thought about those last few months. After it was over, he'd closed the door on that type of relationship even though it had been nice being part of a couple. He hadn't opened it since.

He sat staring at the screen, too numb to think or feel, trying to wrap his brain around what this could mean. Had she missed him? Was she at a point in her life where she wanted to revisit the past for some reason? At a crossroads?

Did it matter?

He snapped the laptop closed.

He dug his fingers into his eyes.

He didn't need this shit right now.

He'd gotten over her, moved on.

The day he'd woken up and didn't once think about her had been a long time in coming. He'd felt the same strange sense of relief, the day he walked off the stage with his diploma from high school.

He'd made sure that no one touched him again, no longer the target of small lives.

He'd have to think long and hard about whether he wanted to go back there, even for a visit.

It was a jar of pain he wasn't sure he wanted to open, even if it resulted in a return to when it had been good between them.

He poured more wine into his glass, swirled it around, anxiety thrumming in every nerve cell, his stomach churning with ambivalence.

Columbia was in Poughkeepsie, which wasn't far from New York City. The band would be there for a couple of nights. He could probably schedule a visit, invite her to a concert. See what she was up to, what she was doing.

Maybe he could take a small trip to hell, see what that was like.

As they used to say, been there, done that.

He moved to the sink and washed his dinner bowl.
He decided he'd be crazy to go there.

CHAPTER THREE

A tornado whipped through the open garage and careened through the door.

Appearing flustered, Rissa, rushed out, "I'm so sorry I'm late. I got a flat tire halfway here and had to wait for Triple A to come and change it."

Reject watched her entrance and took her in with mild distaste.

Olive complexioned, with a soft, curly chocolate-brown bob and matching eyes, she was almost a ringer for her older brother Johnny. Lean and thin, her muscular frame indicating athleticism, she was half dragging her suitcase with one hand while her pocketbook, roller blades, and jacket were hanging precariously from the other.

He noticed the smile on Johnny's face.

Someone's glad she's here.

"This is the Rissa I know and love."

"Scattered?"

"No. Energy in motion."

Reject had other descriptive words for the woman who'd just arrived but they weren't as nice. The last-minute nanny switch had come as a mild shock. The part about Rissa getting dumped a month before her wedding didn't surprise him in the least. Her surliness hit the top of the offense meter. He'd been the object of her derision for as long as he'd known her.

The thud as she dropped everything in her hands onto the tile floor gave him a start. It's when he noticed the expression on her face.

It appeared she wasn't any more thrilled than he was that she was here.

"I don't know why I let you talk me into this."

Johnny gave her one his most disarming grins.

"It wasn't really me and you know it. Ma didn't give either of us a choice."

Her shoulders stooped.

"Didn't we grow up? Can she still tell us what to do?"

"Seems she can. Cause you're here."

Johnny put her in a headlock, kissed her head. The way Rissa slapped him away, a smile almost breaking through, made it seem like a familiar gesture, one they might have started as kids.

Celia might have forced the issue, but Johnny wasn't bummed at all. He'd have his small family with him, and it had become his top priority.

Reject guessed it was a win-win for both their sides.

Just not for his.

Leaning against the doorjamb, Reject watched as Johnny took her paraphernalia and placed it on the bench in the mudroom. Rissa petted and hugged the dogs that had come running at her arrival before following her brother into the kitchen.

"Welcome aboard the traveling circus."

He watched Tish, her sister-in-law follow suit, wrapping her arms around her and squeezing. "I'm so glad you're here."

That made two.

What he saw was a woman who took pleasure in putting people in their place. He'd been stung by her barbs before, but as he took in her pale face and weak smile, he tweaked that opinion a bit. Maybe the take-down had softened her edges.

He watched as she pushed a hand through her hair, her eyes darting around the room taking in the scene. Her appearance spooked him. She stood at the edge of the chaos as if afraid to become a part of it. She had appeared spunkier than this in the past, and her vulnerability touched something inside of him when she mumbled, "Thanks, I think."

He took in the frenetic activity around him, trying to see it from her perspective. Craziness was as much a part of the entourage as the people. Members of the band and some of the roadies were eating, milling around, talking, joking, and laughing and even though the kitchen was huge, there always seemed to be a lack of air. The house belonged to Tim Matarrazzo, the band's lead guitarist and singer, and it had become tradition for the band to stay here before the kickoff of a tour. They'd do a final run-through in the recording studio Tim had built on the property before the equipment stored there would be loaded on the truck, and they'd head out on the road. Palatial in size, the house accommodated the inner sanctum of the band quite comfortably.

Some unknown element pulled his attention back to the slim figure, who looked uncomfortable, a bit self-conscious, and was inching back towards the garage instead of into the flow.

Her eyes darted around the expansive space.

"Where's Rosie?"

He heard Johnny's deep laugh.

"Sleeping but that shouldn't last long. She hasn't learned that sleep can be a good thing yet. If we're lucky, we'll get an hour before she's howling for attention."

She rolled her eyes in panic and asked breathlessly, "Are there always this many people?"

Tish laughed, the sound making her husband smile. "It gets worse, trust me."

Unable to hold his tongue any longer, still aggravated that she was even here, Reject expressed his opinion. "I still don't understand why you offered her the job and didn't hire another nanny."

Rissa looked at him aghast.

"Have you seen how many men have affairs with the nanny? Who can blame Tish for wanting a member of the family?"

There was the tart tongue. He wasn't surprised it didn't take long to surface.

John put his arms around his wife, his head leaning on hers. "Couldn't happen here. Tish still has the Glinda spell in place, and it's got an impenetrable shield. I don't even see other women."

Rissa asked, "Is that where the song came from?"

"Yup. *Glinda* was written in defiance."

It had become one of their top hits.

"I wrote it right before she left. Sang it for the first time the day she headed back to Boston. Realized pretty quickly I had to get her back."

Johnny had fought the blatant chemistry with Tish for weeks, and Reject had been right there by his friend's side, insisting it was only infatuation. Finally seeing that it was deeper, that her talent was huge, he'd come around, accepting he'd lost his playmate to a higher cause.

His lingering reservations prompted him to ask, "What happens when the spell wears off?"

With a rueful shake of his head, Johnny said, "I thought you'd figured it out. The spell is Tish herself."

He had no desire to insult the muse who'd inspired it. He countered instead, "Some of us can deflect that kind of spell, my man."

Johnny merely said, "Some of us don't want to."

"My plan is to sidestep that indefinitely. All it takes is discipline and intention."

Although in the last few days, he'd been rethinking that. Since the email from Paige, he was toying with the idea of being part of a couple again. He'd been alone for so much of his life, and the loneliness was beginning to gnaw at him.

In a voice that vibrated with venom, Rissa threw him off guard.

"And a well-deep supply of ego. Do you really think you do womankind a favor by staying in the game?"

Rissa's retort and the accompanying glower reminded him that the dislike went both ways. It had always been like this, as if they rubbed each other the wrong way.

He wasn't going to let her get the last word in.

"I haven't heard them complaining."

Rissa had folded her arms across her chest, her chin jutted out.

"Of course, you wouldn't. Too busy whispering nothings in their ear."

Leaning back against the kitchen counter, he replicated her stance.

"That would be sweet nothings."

"No, nothings, words without meaning or value."

He straightened, his hands going to his hips.

"Hey, they're in for the same reason I am."

She flashed him a look of disbelief.

"Doubt it. They want a night of flash. You want a night as demi-god."

"I don't disappoint."

He could hear his voice raise a decibel.

Rissa looked down at her curled fingers, as if inspecting a nail.

"I'm sure you honestly believe that."

He took a step toward her, which got her attention.

"They all wake up with smiles."

"You actually let them stay that long?"

Her unruffled manner, the smug look was infuriating.

"Well, they leave with smiles."

Flicking her eyes up to his, she asked, "For a game well played?"

"For a game well served."

"Do you charge a stud fee?" Her voice dripped with sarcasm.

He spun away, frustration spilling out in a heavy sigh. He'd had enough of her viper tongue.

This was the type of person he'd vowed to stay away from since he picked up the pieces of his life.

"No wonder you got..."

The sharp look that Johnny gave him stopped him cold.

A high-pitched scream filled the air as Rosie decided she'd been ignored long enough. Reject heard, "Whatever," as Rissa hurried down the hallway in search of her charge.

Reject stared at the space she had vacated, his distaste souring into something akin to extreme dislike. The spunk was back. It hadn't taken more than one sentence before she launched the antagonism. She had dismissed him with a wave of her hand.

It had become a pattern.

The same thing happened when they'd both attended Tish's return to the concert stage. The famed pianist was back in the spotlight after a summer spent on tour with Raging Thunder because of a meltdown. With Johnny's help, Tish had regained her foothold in the classical world, and family and friends had all shown up to support her.

While milling around with the band before the concert had begun, hanging out with his buddies, he'd studied the conservative patrons in their evening wear, noses in the air, glasses of champagne held in fingers littered with diamonds. Chatter had echoed in the hallowed vestibule, subtle put-downs of the woman who'd soon take the stage. He had wanted to defend her but knew that Tish would win them over as soon as her hands touched the keys. Instead, he'd ignored them, making small talk with his own group. Wearing a tuxedo had been a first for him, and he had felt like the proverbial penguin. It was a far cry from his usual mode of dress but from all appearances he'd fit right in.

When the lights had flickered, announcing the concert was minutes away, they'd found their way to their plush seats, family and friends intermingled, Tim and Annie in front of him, Terry, the band's guitarist, and his wife, Marci, behind. He had taken the end seat in the auditorium to accommodate his long legs, knowing when Johnny returned from backstage, he'd have to shift over one, putting him beside Rissa. She had ignored him right up until he leaned over to ask John which piece Tish was playing, complimenting her in the process. Before John could answer, he'd heard a hiss from his left.

"Don't you have any manners? You should never talk while someone is performing like this."

He'd snapped back in his seat, ready to defend himself, but she'd already gone back to complete absorption in Ravel's concerto. She'd dismissed him that night as well, and her condescending attitude had put him firmly in his place.

Johnny had whispered back, "Ignore her."

But he couldn't.

His past was a patchwork quilt of ripped jeans and narrow escapes. When your focus was on survival, the niceties of life passed you by. Nothing in his past could have prepared him for a night in this kind of landmark, during this kind of a concert. He might be dressed for the part, but his lack of genteel manners had told another story. After Rissa's comment, he'd listened to the underlying silence, felt the music cascading over them. He could have heard a pin drop and knew she was right. He was more comfortable with Thunder's fan base, where everyone screamed, applauded, and shouted during the concert itself.

That night was another in a long list of times, he'd fallen short of expectation.

He might have come a long way from the run-down neighborhood that had been his home, but it seemed he still had a long way to go.

When Johnny had told him that Rissa would be on board the buses this year, he'd sworn he'd stay as far away from her as he could. Who needed a prickly pear for company? Or someone who could send him through a time warp to the days when he hadn't fit in?

Taking several steps into the hallway, feeling his insecurities sliding back into place after the public rebuke, he stopped at the mirror hanging there, took out his comb, and started dragging it through his waist-length locks.

He liked what he saw. Different than when he was in high school and college with his buzz cut and glasses. Reinventing himself, he had given up the nerdy looks, the short hair, worked out at the gym and taken up the bass. His abs rippled; his biceps bulged. He was a celebrity. Something that might have eluded him if Johnny hadn't taken pity.

When Raging Thunder had been looking for a bass player to replace the one they'd kicked out of the band, he'd shown up for the audition with no real hope of being hired. Introducing himself, using his given name, there hadn't been a flicker of recognition. Neither Johnny nor Tim had placed him as one of their high school classmates, so he'd re-introduced himself using the nickname that he was known by, a moniker his peers had given him that had stuck. With a wide-eyed expression and what looked like guilt, Johnny had given him the job after he'd plucked out one short song. Disbelieving his luck, he'd given himself over to it with a vengeance, wanting to prove to Johnny he hadn't made a mistake. That was almost six years ago and today he was popular with the women, tight with the guys, and rated one of the best bass players around.

A blur of images took hold as he gazed at his reflection in the mirror.

Had he changed or was he wearing a mask, one that covered up the insecurities of the past?

What if Rissa could see through the disguise?

What if he was the same man he'd been when he was younger, just better at deception, at playing the game?

A niggling worry planted itself.

⌐

Between the number of people filling the kitchen and the disturbing energy coming from Reject, Rissa had been rattled. Large gatherings usually didn't bother her, so she didn't know why she felt like this. With a family as large as hers and the weekly dinners that pulled everyone home, she was used to rowdy and loud. Everyone talking over each other, voices growing in volume to be heard, hands fighting over bowls of food, arguments over anything from politics to whether the new recipe was one they should keep. She loved the activity, the loving atmosphere. Growing up in an Italian household had been a curse and a blessing. From the time, she was old enough to stand, she'd been given an apron and a wooden spoon. A pot of sauce was always simmering on the burner. There was always bread and pasta to fill any empty stomach. With four siblings to compete with, she had learned to be quick and cunning, beating them all back for a piece of the ricotta pie.

And she'd been part of so many teams, group dynamics had become her area of expertise.

But her skills were deserting her here. She felt overwhelmed and underprepared for what the tour would mean. The banging noise just outside her window was a small indication of the disorder that would govern her life for the next few months as the truck was packed, instruments and gear being secured in with hammers and nails. And the voices, a cacophony of yells and hoots, whistles and shouts, rushed down the hallway to find her.

She guessed the term discordant symbolized her life right now.

Thinking she had found a better head space over the last three months she hadn't been prepared for these feelings of vulnerability. She had wanted a change and the tour would certainly provide that. She just hadn't realized it would feel so...scary.

Rosie had stopped her crying as soon as Rissa entered the room, her gaze riveted on her aunt, watching as she got closer. With one scoop, Rissa picked the baby up from the makeshift crib and held her close, the sweet baby smells a welcome diversion. As Rissa held Rosie in her arms, a sense of peace came over her. The turquoise eyes were awake and alert and they watched her every move. The top of the bureau had been transformed into a changing table for the night, and she laid her niece down on the surface, Rosie's fist stuffed in her mouth. She spoke in soft whispers as she cleaned and changed Rosie. As she tossed the used diaper away, she thought about where her life was headed.

Nowhere.

"I sure would have loved a sweetie like you."

She would have to wait now and it was the most disappointing part of the break-up.

At twenty-seven-years-old, she had to start all over again. Three years with that a-hole down the drain, wasted.

She nestled Rosie in the crook of her arm, began to rock and croon, using her niece as her sounding board.

"It seems like we'll find out together what kind of crazy life your father leads, won't we?'

Rosie continued to make slurping sounds as her fingers pulsed in and out her mouth.

"Yeah, there are a lot of people here. Different is good sometimes, though. At least that's what Nona says."

When Rosie didn't respond, Rissa continued with a thought that snuck into her consciousness.

"I can't believe someone is okay with being called Reject. What's wrong with his real name?"

The gurgling gave her answer.

"You're right. Luca Caroli does have a bit of an international flavor to it, but Nona would say it's a nice Italian name."

When Rosie gave a pucker look, her legs jerking up then out, Rissa smiled and said, "You're right again. Reject does suit him better."

She gave Rosie a pucker look of her own.

She hadn't liked Reject since the day they'd met. Knowing his dating history probably skewed her opinion, but he even looked the part of serial lover, smug and arrogant.

Anyone fitting that description was listed under the asshole column in her book.

What she couldn't wrap her head around was the difference between the kid she'd known in high school and the man who was a member of the internationally famous Raging Thunder.

Not that she really knew him back then. They were never friends or even acquaintances. She would see him walking the hallways, his head down, never a hello or smile to anyone. Sure, other kids gave him a hard time, but he was so unfriendly it wasn't surprising. When Johnny had told her that Reject had joined the band, she couldn't understand why he had chosen someone so anti-social.

Over the years, she'd heard about his complete transformation. He'd become Johnny's sidekick, both enjoying the sexual component of their celebrity. Not that she ever asked or really wanted to know about it.

She'd met him for the first time when she attended a Thunder concert a few years back, but he hadn't given her the time of day, distracted by all the female attention. He'd barely said two words to her since. Until today.

He was so fucking full of himself, although she didn't know why.

She'd seen the socially awkward side of him at Tish's concert last year, and he had just proven he was obnoxious as well.

She couldn't understand why Johnny liked him so much, treated him like a brother.

Then again, nothing made sense to her anymore.

She must have started giving off bad vibes that the infant picked up on because Rosie was becoming a little fussy, so she rejected any further thoughts of the bassist. She pushed back in the rocker, began to hum, quieting them both

She heard a slight knock and when she looked up, Tish was standing there smiling at her.

"Hey. You seem to have everything under control."

"There's something about holding a baby. The smells, the soft skin, the total trust. I offered to go into the infant room at work whenever they needed coverage. I was hoping that I'd be holding my own soon. I guess I'll have to live vicariously through you for a while."

Taking a seat on the bed, Tish said, "I want to thank you for coming with us. I know your mother was behind it, but it's hard to find someone you have faith in to take care of your most valuable possession."

"I still find it hard to believe this is Johnny's daughter."

She looked up sheepishly. "And yours."

Tish laughed.

"I know what you mean. When I found out I was pregnant, I wasn't even going to tell him. He was so adamantly against having kids."

"And a wife to go with them."

"There was that."

"You don't know how much we love you for bringing out the best in him again. He was such a jerk for so long."

"He wasn't really. Just lost, I think, like I was."

"Well, whatever it is between you, I want some. I still can't believe I let something so bad go on for so long. I should have broken it off with Jude after the first fall off the fidelity wagon."

"Why didn't you?"

With a strong need to feel the soft skin under her fingers, Rissa stroked Rosie's cheek while she considered the question.

"I figured if I just tried hard enough, everything would be okay."

"There are some people you can never please, no matter what you do."

Rissa knew Tish must be referring to her own mother. She'd heard about Madeleine Jones from Johnny and there was no love lost there.

Curiosity prompted the question. "Do you ever speak to her?"

"No. She's tried to get in touch here and there, but my boundaries are still in place. Maybe someday it will be worth the effort, but for now I don't want to put Rosie in that kind of a toxic relationship. Rosie's got your folks, and they love her in healthy ways. I want her to thrive, not wither."

Tish's mother had a mental disorder that made it almost impossible to connect in any real way. A bully who kept Tish under lock and key, she was charismatic one minute, then cold and calculating the next. Feeling entitled to Tish's genius and money, she had sucked the life out of her. Getting out from under her influence had taken all of Tish's courage and determination, but her escape had driven her right into Johnny's arms, and it was a pretty happy ending for both.

Rosie seemed quite content, so Rissa asked something she'd been wondering about.

"What's it like out on the road?"

"Crazy. Poor Reject thought we'd be flying again this year, finances being as good as they are, but I can't put Rosie through that. We'd be hopping a plane every day and it's not good for her ears. After a lot of discussion, the band decided to go the bus route, although not unanimously. With Marci and Annie pregnant, there'll be three small kids on board next year. It means we won't see the skies for a while."

"It doesn't surprise me Reject had a problem with it. He seems to have a problem with everything."

Tish was studying her.

"That's not fair, Rissa. You don't even know him. He's a great guy."

"I don't see it, the great guy thing, but then again, I don't need to."

Everyone was in his corner and before this member of his cheering section got going, she asked,

"When will I have Rosie with me? While you sleep? Perform?"

"Sleep? That's a foreign concept these days. We don't get much. We won't expect you to be with her twenty-four-seven. Just while we're on stage, which should be six or seven hours a night."

The rocker came to a standstill, Rissa taken off guard by the answer.

"You play for that long?"

Tish laughed at the thought of expending that much energy.

"God, no, but we need to be at the arena beforehand for setup and sound checks, and it takes some time getting back because the guys always do a meet and greet. I'll be doing my own practicing during the day, but Johnny will take over for that. I'll make sure he gets some shut-eye, or he'll nap with Rosie."

"When's your tour coming up?

Tish had her own series of concerts throughout the year, but she staggered them so they wouldn't interfere with her husband's.

"First part of November. We'll be back in time for Thanksgiving. Just a few cities, New York, D.C., San Francisco. I refuse to miss your mother's turkey and stuffing, so I kept the concert series short."

Rissa pictured the large dining room table in her childhood home, which had accommodated the family but as the numbers swelled...

Where was her mother going to put everyone this year?

"We might need a bigger house soon."

Tish had gotten up and began folding some of the scattered clothing lying around the room.

"We've offered to host at ours, but no way could I handle cooking that kind of meal on my own. I've got years of catching up to do. She's thinking about it."

"She likes her traditions. I'm not sure she'll move it anywhere. She'll squeeze us all in like sardines if she has to."

"I'd rather be squished in her house than be alone. I've had enough of that to last a lifetime."

Rissa's head dropped to lean against the chair as she continued to rock Rosie in her arms.

It wasn't that she wanted to be alone but...at her age, she should be on her own.

"I can't believe I'm living at home again."

Tish glanced over as she continued to pack away her daughter's garments into the suitcase lying open on the bed and said, "It won't be forever."

"I certainly can't afford an apartment on what I make. Cancel that. I don't have a job anymore. Unless I count this one and its only seasonal employment."

"Where did you live before Jude's?"

"In Melrose with a couple of roommates. One was a high school friend, the other a member of my volleyball team."

She blew out the words, "They're both married now."

It looked like she was never going to walk down that aisle.

It was a bitter pill to swallow.

Tish picked up the lightweight blanket Marci had made Rosie and began to fold it.

"Maybe you can live at our house while we're gone. Keep it running. I'll talk to your brother and see if he's all right with it, although I can't see him saying no to you."

They wouldn't need her for that run. Johnny would be Rosie's caregiver.

"That would be cool. But it's so big I'm not sure I won't get lost in it."

"There's a room on the third floor, on the other side of Johnny's music room, that you could use as an art studio. Lots of sunlight and space."

"I've worked on a couple of canvases at Ma's, nothing great. I've had to start all over again. I hadn't picked up a paintbrush in... ages."

Even though Paul had given her a bright space, she hadn't put as much time into her art as her parents had hoped.

"Why haven't you been working at it?"

She laughed it off as if it was of no consequence.

What she kept secret, was it hurt like hell.

"There was really nowhere for me to do it. Besides, Jude didn't like the mess it made."

"Just one more reason for me not to like him. Did you bring your sketchpads and pencils?"

"I did. I have to have something to keep my fingers busy."

"You and your brother. He doesn't go anywhere without his sticks. It drives most everyone crazy."

They were never out of his grip, and he was always tapping away on something, just like he had when they were younger.

"And for us, it's a necessary evil."

"There'll be lots for you to draw out on the road. Landscapes, tourist attractions, people."

"Yeah, I know. I've visited the website called urbane sketching and they've posted some impressive artwork. Getting out on the street to capture life will push me to try different things."

Rissa had never been outside a two-hour perimeter of Boston proper, so she was excited about seeing different parts of the country. She was also impatient to get rid of the hurt still festering inside. Not so much for Jude anymore but the way he had made her feel about herself. His disregard for her feelings, his subtle put-downs, his pretentiousness had whittled her self-confidence down to a splinter.

Looking at her sister-in-law, her blonde hair and sparkling aqua eyes making her look fragile, knowing the steel that lay beneath, she was glad she had agreed to this. If anyone could make her feel better about things, it was Tish.

Anxious to be on the road, Rissa asked, "What time are we leaving?"

"In a few hours. Rather than starting on the West Coast, we're starting local and working outwards. Portland's our first stop and it won't take long to get there."

Rosie had started fussing so Tish got up and walked over to scoop her daughter into her arms. "It looks like it's time for her to eat and I'm the only one who can satisfy that need. Why don't you go back out and join the gang? Get to know everybody. Have something to eat."

Not wanting to leave the safety of the room but wanting to give Tish some privacy, she agreed with a simple, "Okay."

With empty arms that longed to be filled, Rissa quietly shut the door and walked slowly out to find her brother.

CHAPTER FOUR

As Rissa stepped out into the sunny day with Johnny, her hunger satisfied at the buffet lunch Annie had served, she surveyed the scene in front of her. Huge black buses lined the driveway, the equipment truck just pulling out along the winding curve. People swarmed like ants in every direction.

"Crazy, huh?"

Tish had come out just behind her with Rosie in her arms.

All their personal belongings had been stored on the bus, and all that was left for them to do was to board and be off. Ralph, the bus driver in his second year with the band, came up to them, the newly packed suitcase in his hand, and all but laughed.

"Rosie has almost as much equipment as the guys."

"I'm sorry, Ralph. You might want to quit at the end of this tour cause next year there will be two more babies on board."

"I love it. Don't worry. It'll keep me from missing my own too much."

She couldn't help but smile at him.

"I hope you can say that...I don't know...forty-eight hours from now. I don't know how Rosie's going to react when she doesn't find either John or I in her personal space."

Rissa was still glancing from one end of the yard to the other.

"I can't believe they have to bring so much."

"It's a real caravan. The truck leaves first and goes at its own pace. The buses pretty much stay together. It'll only take us a couple of hours to get to

Portland and we'll go right to the concert hall. Maybe you can come in with us, see the set-up, before you have Rosie to yourself."

"I'd love that."

She smiled a real smile for the first time since arriving. The prospect of the trip was beginning to excite her. Her mind and body were adjusting to the activity going on around her, her nerves weren't as much on edge, and she wasn't as disoriented as she'd been at first.

And then a voice cut through her, asking, "Who the hell's car is that? Wait. Don't tell me. I think I already know."

When he reached the spot where the women were standing, Reject asked, "How can you drive that thing? It's an accident waiting to happen."

A 2000 Honda Civic with rusting paint and a tire that looked as if it was about to collapse was keeping company with Mercedes, CRVs BMWs and a Saab.

Bristling at the arrogance of a man she didn't like, she said indignantly, "Thanks for your opinion but I'd prefer it if you minded your own business."

Glaring, his hands on his hips, he answered, "That thing is ancient and probably none too safe."

He turned to Johnny, who had been listening intently, and barked, "How can you let her drive it?"

Before John could answer, his sister barked back, "It's not his job to support me. He offered, I declined, so don't go off on him."

Without taking his eyes off his friend, he informed them both, "I would have had it delivered without asking."

"Well then you would have been out some money because I wouldn't have driven it."

He fingered his hair back as he turned to look at her, his eyes burning chips of amber.

"That's just plain stupid."

Johnny gave him a signal that he agreed but wouldn't do it in public.

"Paul checked it out and it's in good running condition, just not easy on the eyes, and my sister isn't stupid."

"I didn't say she was. Not taking you up on your offer is, though."

Rissa, her cheeks flushed and warm, informed him, "I take care of myself in the world, you jerk. No one pays my way."

She had to force that lie past her conscience and out because it wasn't true. Jude had supported her for a long time, her paycheck inadequate for the type of place they'd lived in, the lifestyle he wanted for himself, and she had gotten used to it. Taken it for granted, really. His condo was nice, had an open floor plan, which was great for entertaining, over eight hundred square feet in Boston, beautiful windows, two bathrooms. He'd bought it before he met her, so it was decorated in his style, with his furniture, and it was his friends they entertained. Hers were not socially mobile enough. He'd covered all the bills. Her paycheck was so paltry he'd refused to call it a contribution. Told her to keep it for pocket change.

The day Jude had forced her out she'd promised herself it would never happen again. She was still feeling the shockwaves of that backward step.

"What happens when your spare goes flat? What if it blows while you're driving?"

The snarky voice was back, and she scowled.

"I'll get another one when I get back. It doesn't concern you."

Their eyes met and latched. She put every hateful thought into the glare and Reject backed off.

"Your life."

And with that he stomped away to board the bus second in line, his backpack hanging from his hand.

Rissa watched the tall bassist hurry away, his temper easy to read.

They had gotten into another pissing contest, and she shook her head, wishing he didn't get under her skin this much. But then again, maybe she did understand.

He reminded her of her ex-fiancée.

Not in looks.

Reject was tall, dark, and...brooding. Muscular, rough around the edges, where Jude was blonde, blue eyed, and a true Millennial. Phone in hand, always dressed flawlessly in a suit and tie, impeccable manners, his ambition had ambition. But neither one could pass a mirror without gazing at their reflection, totally absorbed in themselves, with a similar proclivity for nighttime activities. She'd read enough about the bassist to know he loved the women, and Jude had proved to her more than once, he was aligned with what the night could bring. Both thought they were God's gift to the ladies. She should have known one would not satisfy Jude, especially one who so poorly resembled what he looked for in a female partner. Over the last few months, she'd come to the conclusion that Jude stayed with her because she was malleable, wouldn't ask questions, let him come and go as he pleased, allowed him to control every aspect of their lives. In the end, it wasn't what he wanted or needed. As he so eloquently stated, she had become a non-entity. She was grateful that he had saved her from a lifetime of grief, and it was no longer sorrow for the failed relationship that haunted her. It was who she'd become.

As the middle child, two older brothers in front of her, two younger siblings below, she was usually odd one out but never felt an outsider in the big rowdy family. Things had changed after her father's death. Johnny had started the band, Dennis had stayed away from the house, burying himself in school and his afternoon job, Lana had attached herself to their mother and Tony had begun acting out, taking the narrow slice of attention that was available. The trauma of the murder was deep and invasive but there was no one around to help her through it. She hadn't known what to do with the loneliness that fermented in the aftermath. Cut off from the family that had sustained her, she began to surround herself with friends, teammates, anyone who could fill the feelings of isolation and emptiness. To this day, she didn't like being alone.

It was the reason she'd stayed with someone so bad for her.

Not a good basis for future happiness.

She was determined not to find herself in the same situation next time around. That meant learning to be on her own and liking it, learning to trust herself to find what she wanted.

First, she had to figure out what that was.

She might not know that yet, but what she did know was she didn't want an ego-driven man, womanizer, or control freak who found fault with her at every turn. Reject would get the full wrath of her vengeance because he represented all she had lost of herself.

Spinning around, she asked her brother, "That's not the bus we're riding in, is it?"

Johnny was busy cooing at Rosie, so he didn't see the look of apprehension on his sister's face, only her finger pointing in the wrong direction.

"No, we're first in line."

Under her breath, she mumbled, "Thank the stars."

She hoisted her carry-all over her shoulder and made her way towards the vehicle that would be her home away from home for the next few months, climbed aboard, and claimed a bunk smack-dab in the middle.

Reject threw his backpack down on the bunk at the back of the bus. It used to be Johnny's space, but once the drummer made the transition to married status, he had taken it over. He could look out the huge expanse of window and watch the stars as they made their way to their next destination.

Pushing the thick mass of hair off his face, he almost growled again.

He didn't understand why he cared that Rissa Scalera was driving a piece of junk. It certainly wasn't any of his business but if she were his sister, he'd make sure she was safe behind the wheel. Would have if he'd had the money to do it back then. Instead, he'd been witness to an accident caused by bald tires in the middle of a bad winter. Val hadn't been badly hurt, had just broken a few ribs, but he'd been scared shitless when she lost traction. The car spun out of control around the curve of a rotary and been flung into the concrete barrier sitting to the side. His seat belt had kept him in his seat, but hers had been defective, so her rib cage had taken the brunt of the steering wheel. Today, she drove a brand-new Volkswagen, thanks in part to the jobs he paid her to do: financial manager and personal secretary. She answered his fan mail, took care of all his personal errands, invested his money, and looked after their mother. She would never lack anything again, not if he were alive.

With their father being out of the picture and their mother, Elana, working all hours and two jobs to support the family, they had clung to each other as kids and had each other's backs as adults. It was his sister, older than him by a few years, who had helped him with his college finances. After she had graduated from Bentley, she had gotten a job as an accountant, living at home so she'd be able to pay some of his schooling expenses. His scholarship had helped, but there were so many other financial constraints, she had given up her life to make sure he would have a future. When he'd dropped out, she had been so angry, she'd stopped talking to him for a few weeks. Even though he had lifted a heavy burden off her shoulders, it'd taken her a long time to forgive him for deserting what she thought was his dream. The night she'd come to her first Raging Thunder concert had been a step in the right direction. She had seen how much he enjoyed performing, and that he had finally formed lasting relationships with the guys in the band. That she continued to live at home had confounded him, but she'd always been close to their mother, and she had told him that she liked living there. Soon, she'd be moving but only next door. She was engaged to a sales analyst for a large car dealership. He'd be giving his sister away to a man he knew would love and protect her. He'd have to start thinking seriously about who he'd take to the wedding. His sister would be merciless if she thought he didn't have anyone to share the day with him.

He liked Val as well as loved her and was glad she'd agreed to meet them at the concert in Providence. That was only a week away, but he'd spent so much time with her on the off months, seeing to their mother's healing, that he already missed her.

With cell phone in hand, he punched in a number.

"Hi, Luca."

"Hi, Val."

"You on the road yet?"

"In about five minutes. Can you do me a favor?"

"Sure. Anything you want."

"I want to buy a car for someone. Maybe a Honda. It has to be safe, so it has to be new."

"Luca. You can't keep doing things like this."

"I haven't bought a car for anyone in a long time. This one is for...a friend in some financial trouble. Have it delivered to Tim's house but make sure you have a set of keys."

"You have a friend at Tim's house in financial trouble? One of the roadies again?"

"You could say it's one of the staff."

"You can't change the past, Luca, no matter how much you want to. I was fine and you take very good care of me and Ma."

"This has nothing to do with the past. And soon, it will be Ken taking care of you. Although I hope you keep working for me. I'd hate to find someone else to keep my life in order. You do such a good job."

There was no way he'd trust a stranger with who he was.

"You know this job is perfect. Why would I leave it?"

"You'll have your own life soon enough. You might not want to be so closely attached to mine."

"I work out of the house. So even when I start having kids, I'll be making sure you stay divested."

Not that anyone outside his circle would believe it, but he couldn't wait to have nieces and nephews underfoot. He'd grown up with such a strong sense of family, it was something he always wanted for himself. Now, he refused to open to that possibility. There was no way he was going to invite someone in to break his heart.

He sat stunned for a minute. Wasn't he considering doing just that?

It took him a minute to come back to the conversation at hand.

"That'll be fine by me. Did you talk to Ken about the condo?"

Reject owned a duplex that he had turned into two condos. His mother and sister lived on one side; he lived on the other. At his sister's insistence that he invest in real estate, he'd just bought a house not far from them. It needed major renovations, but he had already had plans drawn up and contractors hired so they could work on it while he was gone. His sister would do periodic checks to make sure they were following the specs. The goal was to move into it when he returned, and he had offered his part of the two-family to his sister as a wedding present.

"I did talk to him. He wants to buy it from you. Says it would make him feel better."

"It's one of the reasons I like him. He'll always take good care of you."

They spent so much time taking care of each other that it had been hard letting someone else in. Ken had been patient, and he loved Val. It had given Reject a reason to expand his constricted circle by one.

"So? Will you let us? Buy it?"

"Of course. I'll give you a good price. But I'll keep Ma's in my name. That way I'll absorb the cost of repairs and updates. By the way, how is she?"

"Good. She's been busy in the garden this week. Those raised beds you put in are exactly what she wanted. We'll be eating pure organic food soon."

"You always eat that kind of stuff. It'll just cost you less now."

He heard her laugh across the line.

"That's true but the garden gives her something to do that gives her pleasure."

"I like that she doesn't have to work so hard anymore."

"She's waiting for grandchildren to spoil. Yours as well as mine."

"Well, she shouldn't hold her breath on that one. Yours will have to suffice for now."

"Luca, you can't let the past..."

Images of Paige filled his senses when Val mentioned the past. He could take the step that might bring resolution to the past Val spoke of. If he could find it in him to respond to the email, he'd know what kind of resolution he was facing.

"I'm good, Val. For now, I'm good."

They exchanged good-byes before Reject disconnected the call, pulled out one of his books, and reclined. He delved back into a world where a grid had been hacked and part of the world was in blackness when he picked up the book he'd left off this morning.

⌐

Rissa took in the activity that hadn't stopped since they'd left. Annie and Tim were at the back of the bus, playing cribbage, a bag overflowing with odds and ends sitting on a seat beside them. Terry was up front talking to Ralph while Marci was reclined on their bunk, reading a baby book, calling out possible names for the boy that was scheduled to arrive a couple of months after the tour ended. Tish and Johnny were busy keeping Rosie occupied with books, taggies, and rattles. Some of her toys were spread across a small sofa, along with all the bags and pails they'd need for diaper duty. A laptop was resting on one of the chairs; books were lined up on shelves over beds. A TV hung from the front of the bus; a shower and toilet were tucked in a corner at the back. Baggies full of trail mix, cookies, popcorn littered the space. A refrigerator stocked with cold drinks and fruit pops, Johnny's favorite, sat at the front beside the driver who would make sure it was refilled every day with the sundries the passengers requested.

This was a traveling office, home, and studio all wrapped up in one location.

She was glad they would be staying in hotels along the way. For as much as she thrived in a crowd, here there was no respite from other people, nowhere to hide, no place to escape to if things got overwhelming. And if someone was occupying the lav, there was no place to wash your hands if they got sticky on a cinnamon bun. She laughed as she licked her fingers like her mother's cat licked her paws. With a heavy sigh, she'd reached the conclusion that everything was going to be a novelty and she had to quickly learn the tricks of the road if she was going to survive.

She swiveled the seat so she could watch the scenery on the edge of the highway, trying to block out the noise that came with seven people living in a small, confined space. She was glad that the windows weren't tinted. Instead, there were night blinds that pulled down if anyone wanted to get some shut-eye.

She let the steady motion relax her.

Although as soon as she thought again of the sabbatical she was taking from her life, and the why behind it, her shoulders tensed.

She didn't have to ask what had gone wrong anymore.

She hadn't miscalculated the depth of her relationship.

The numbing conclusion was that it was her own stupidity that had doomed her future. There had been glaring signs along the way that she'd closed her eyes to, undermining herself, subjugating her needs to the point that she was no longer part of a partnership but merely a shadow hiding behind the larger force. Focused purely on keeping Jude with her, she'd all but given up herself. Her art had suffered because he didn't like the mess she created, the brushes drying, the charcoal smudges, the smell of paint and turpentine. She should have found someplace else to create instead of giving it up altogether.

He criticized her Italian meals, not liking the thick red sauce she'd grown up with, preferring the refined fare of French cuisine, something she couldn't master. He'd caused her to miss more than a few Sundays with her family, and so many league volleyball and softball games her teams had replaced her.

The things he had loved about her, her quirkiness, her athleticism, her creativity, had prompted the proposal. As soon as the ring was on, he'd become strident in his attempts to change her, and she'd foolishly followed his suggestions. One was that she apply for a teller's position at a local bank, which meant leaving a job she loved at a retail store. He felt finance was more in line with his status, even if it didn't pay much. When she was fired after her probationary period due to an inability to balance her drawer on a regular basis, he'd retreated with obvious disdain.

How inept did she have to be, not to be able to add and subtract?

Her self-esteem plummeted.

When she'd accepted a job as pre-school teacher, a position she became passionate about, he'd stopped coming home for dinner. She loved working with the kids, loved working on art and crafts with them, enjoyed creating vibrant bulletin boards. She never felt alone when she was surrounded by their unconditional love.

"How can I tell my friends you work at a day care center? It's just a glorified term for babysitter."

She was never able to convince him otherwise.

His friends were accountants, financial advisers, doctors, lawyers, professionals, with spouses and partners who matched, who dressed up every day to go to work, talked to adults, made good money.

In the end, she couldn't hold him. He wanted someone intelligent, a bit more professional. She was neither of those things and the harder she tried to please the more distant he became.

Until the postponement and ultimate break-up.

The eviction from the condo was a traumatic shift, but once she moved back to her childhood home, and as she cleaned out some of her old things from closet and bureau, she could see all the flaws in the relationship clearly. It had only taken a few days to find comfort in her belongings, and realize it was a relief not to have to watch what she said all the time. She'd forgotten what a loving environment felt like, and if her mother hadn't become so excessive in...mothering her, she might have relished it. Paul had become her father over the years, in every sense of the word and in him she found love and caring. Work still occupied her days and when she got out, she'd drop by the commercial kitchen to see if there was anything she could do to help her mother and sister. Once home, she'd eat and crash. Those were the worst hours, when all she could think about was how she'd lost herself so badly.

She let her eyes follow the cars zooming by, becoming almost hypnotized by the action.

What would have happened if she'd broken off the engagement when he'd suggested they postpone the wedding?

For one thing, her parents wouldn't have lost thousands of dollars in deposits, including the additional ones they'd had to put down to hold a new date. Secondly, she'd be further along in the healing process, perhaps far less bitter because she would have been the one to end it.

She was better off without him. She knew that now.

But it didn't take away the sting of the rejection.

This last one being the grand finale in a long line of rejections throughout the relationship.

She was too busy trying to please, to prevent him from leaving her, that she hadn't seen what was right in front of her eyes. He'd spent years trying to shove a square peg into a round hole, trying to mold her into his perfect mate, and she'd let him, even helping him along in his efforts by sanding down the edges of herself.

She didn't need to ask why anymore.

The disturbing conclusion was: she'd turned into a pretzel, an emotional contortionist, to fit both situations.

She needed to find what fit her now.

The first two steps were taken.

Jude and the job were gone.

But what would replace them?

School, as her mother suggested a few weeks after the break-up?

Another job?

She issued a small groan.

What would she do if she had to live at home forever? It might be better than living alone.

What if she never found a man who wanted her for herself, whoever that turned out to be?

Her track record proved she wasn't very astute at choosing that kind of person.

She knew she wouldn't find it on the road. There'd be no time to form that kind of bond with someone, but she could enjoy the freedom she'd been offered.

She was glad her mother forced this respite, was beginning to see it as a fresh start.

A chance to take short bursts of alone time to reconfigure her life. She could handle those.

The sign, "WELCOME TO MAINE" told her it wouldn't be long now before they reached their destination. If she could just sit back and enjoy the journey, she might find out what was missing in her life and figure out how to fill it.

Maybe she'd follow whatever urge struck her fancy and go with it.

She shivered at the thought.

CHAPTER FIVE

The bus rumbled, the brakes squealed as they pulled up alongside the venue in Portland where the band would be playing tonight. She glanced out the window to see a brick building right in the middle of the city, and the buses had to pull up one at a time so as not to disrupt the flow of traffic, theirs still first in line.

"Are you going to join us for a while?"

Johnny was standing at Rissa's bunk with Rosie in his arms.

"I'd love to. I can't wait to see what happens with all that equipment you've packed away."

Jett boarded the bus and asked, "You ready?"

There was a bodyguard for each of the band members who assured a safe entry into the building and Jett belonged to Johnny. Even hours before show time, fans lined the street hoping to get a glimpse of their idols and maybe a little something personal in the process.

"Good to go."

Johnny handed Rosie over to Tish. "Be better if you carried her in. Don't want her jostled."

Rissa understood the swap as soon as she disembarked. There had to be close to one-hundred people lining the sidewalk, reaching hands out to touch the guys, pull their hair, throw them a souvenir of their own. She looked around, not quite believing what she was seeing, all while being hustled into the venue in her brother's wake.

When she stood just inside the vestibule, she whispered hoarsely, "That's kind of scary."

She noticed the others being led in, Reject accompanied by his own personal guard, Lou.

Rissa watched him outrace the hands that pulled at his clothes. He stumbled into the lobby, almost knocking her over.

Breathless, she asked, "How do you stand it?"

"All part of the game. Besides, it's better to be adored than shunned."

"I'm not sure about that."

Proud eyes met hers before he said, "I've been on both ends of the spectrum and trust me, it is."

Without elaborating, he made his way to the steps that led to the stage, where his bass stood, having already been unloaded from the truck.

Johnny led the way up the carpeted stairs and she stayed behind him until she reached the edge of the platform.

Then she stopped and stared.

It was huge but empty, voices echoing off the high ceilings as the band discussed positions and where to set up the instruments. She was mesmerized by the transformation, as the roadies hauled amplifiers and guitars into place, began to set up the drum kit, roll the piano to its mark. Lights flashed and flickered as Joe worked the lighting. High-pitched squeals were heard as Rambler worked the soundboard. Chappy directed the traffic as roadies built the Thunder setting right in front of her, which would resemble the sky during a summer storm.

Her eyes settled on Reject, who was hooking up and plugging in to his amplifier, before they moved to Johnny, who was putting the finishing touches on his cymbals. Tish was making sure the piano was in tune after travel.

Cords were everywhere, a multitude of effect pedals placed where the musicians would stand, and she could feel the excitement build as the band prepped for upcoming show.

She'd never seen this phase of the performance. The few times she'd attended a concert, she'd been in the audience, caught up in the frenzy of the fans, never knowing what it took to create the stage. The art behind it fascinated her.

She took her sketchbook out of her satchel, and sat on the dusty floor, crisscross-applesauce style, her hand working furiously with a stub of charcoal to capture the action. Joe at his station, Johnny at the drums, Tim and Annie talking as the guitarist worked on his multi-amp wall, Reject working with Chappy, Terry checking the strings on one of his guitars, Tish at the piano, her toes bare, working the pedal.

Her brother told his story through music. Her form of expression was art. Her media was sketching.

She was working with captive subjects, people standing in one spot while performing an action. Each impression she made began with one rapid stroke, and she swept through each figure without getting bogged down in the detail, the egg of the head, the hand positions, gestures, and direction of limbs to remind her of how they were posed. Engrossed in what she was doing, she didn't realize someone was standing over her shoulder, watching the scribbling.

"Those are pretty good." The unexpected voice jolted her and the line she was drawing ran off the page.

Her head shot up, and her eyes met his. She couldn't tell if he was sincere or being sarcastic.

Lost in his amber orbs, she had no conscious thought. The feeling, though, was visceral and her breath held. Electricity flowed the circuit along her spine when she noticed how seductive his eyes were, so she shifted her gaze sharply back to the work at hand, losing control of the charcoal in her fingers as it began to tremble. Reject had a high forehead, his hair parted in the middle, the long strands reaching his waist. His eyes were penetrating bits of amber tucked away under the ridge of his eyebrows. His nose was broad, but it was in proportion to the rest of his face. His lips were full and looked oh-so-kissable. Three buttons of his chambray shirt were undone and she'd caught a glimpse of his chest. Her stomach did a flip and spin.

There was a quiver inside at the thought of touching it.

What the hell?

Her, "thanks," was mumbled into her chest.

She was completely off-balance, and she wanted him gone. But he stood his ground and asked, "You've got some talent for that. Have you ever thought of sketching as more than a hobby?

Still unwilling to look back up, she said, more bite in her answer than she'd planned, his presence doing strange things to her, "No. I *was* just enjoying the moment."

In a steady voice, the tone determined, he suggested, "You should be promoting, selling your art. Why were you teaching instead?"

She snapped at him, not wanting to admit this was what called to her soul. Her voice was thick with the resentment she held for all the people who'd told her it shouldn't be, her instructors included. They stressed oils and watercolors as true art. Sketching was just another word for doodling, in their book.

"I was good at it. Like you said, this is a hobby. It holds nothing of consequence."

The blood was pounding in her ears, his presence having an electrical effect on her body. If she hadn't been so tuned in to him, she might have missed his words and meaning.

"Some hobby."

Before they could continue the conversation, Johnny was carrying Rosie over to where they were. "Think it's time. We're going to be doing the sound check soon and it gets kind of loud."

"Okay, sure."

After packing away her materials, she wiped her hands on her running shorts, took the infant from her brother and with Jett by her side, returned to the bus wishing she could figure out what had just happened.

⌒

Infant screams that were ear-splitting were coming from the bus.

"What the hell is Rissa doing to her?"

Johnny left Reject's question in the dust as he raced forward scrambling up the steps, giving Ralph, their driver, an apologetic expression. Striding down the aisle, Johnny reached out to take Rosie and asked, "Has she been crying long?"

"Um, off and on for maybe a couple of hours."

Reject had climbed the steps of the bus to take in the scene, curious to see what the problem was and how it was being handled.

Johnny looked back at Ralph and winced.

"Maybe this wasn't one of my better ideas, but there was no way I was going to leave Tish and Rosie for months."

Turning back towards his sister, he wore a worried look.

"Are you going to ask me if you can leave? Cause the answer is no."

Rissa smiled at him. "No, I'm not going anywhere, except maybe to my bunk. She's all yours."

He fingered the tears off Rosie's face, admitting, "We weren't sure how she'd be without one of us here."

"She'll get used to me. It'll take some time."

"How can you be so calm? I'd be pulling my hair out."

"None of my textbooks suggested that particular strategy. I think I'll go with the ones that have worked for me before."

Tish had entered at a more moderate pace and smiled at her sister-in-law, asking, "It doesn't bother you at all?"

"Not really. I can put up with a lot, as we all know. And I'm used to it. The babies at work cry all the time when they first enroll. Rosie took her bottle, she's got a dry diaper on, she's not sick, so I wasn't worried. I took her outside for a bit and she could hear your music. It settled her down. You guys sounded great."

"Maybe you could play our music for her when we're gone. Mine or Tish's."

"That's a good idea. We can try it tomorrow. Being on the bus wasn't ideal. It should be easier when we're in a hotel room."

Reject took Rissa in, the unruffled expression on her countenance in the face of the ungodly racket and almost lost his balance. She was glowing in quiet confidence and it drew him in. There were no creases of tension on her forehead, no arched brows in annoyance, no pursed lips in displeasure. Only an earthy groundedness that made him question his perception of her. She looked almost like a goddess, a modern-day one, with cropped hair and basketball shorts. He had thought she lacked femininity but had to reassess it in this light. Her demeanor was calm and the smile she gave her brother was genuine. It was becoming obvious that the only one she took pleasure in torturing with her tongue was him.

And he couldn't fathom why.

Not that it mattered.

It wasn't like he was out to get her into bed and faced a serious challenge.

There were enough women out there who wanted him and he wasn't going to waste his time on a woman who didn't. It was like walking across burning coals and he'd done that once, and it was one time too many.

An image of Paige came into his head.

Wasn't that exactly what he was thinking of doing?

He wasn't even sure the email wasn't a joke, a tease, to see if he'd respond, to see if she could reel him in again. Would she laugh at him if he did?

He glanced over to Rissa, her expression a glower, her eyebrow arched as if to ask him why he was there.

He took her up on her invitation to leave.

Shaking off her censure, Reject bounded up the steps onto his own bus and took a seat up front behind Dave the driver. The ride from the concert hall to the hotel was a short one. This was the shitty part of the tour this year, as it had been last year. They were going the bus route. There had been a few years when they'd chartered a private jet and flown everywhere. It was the best way to travel. They'd be at their destination in short order and have much more time for the things that mattered. He had a sinking suspicion it was a thing of the past. With most members of the band settled with wives and children, his vote on mode of travel had been cast and discarded. He'd finally resigned himself to grabbing sleep on the road, being stuck in a small space for hours on end, limited bathroom facilities and crowded spaces. The real problem was he liked his privacy. Not only because of the women but because he liked things orderly. The guys on the bus didn't seem to care. The place was usually a mess, with beer bottles, candy wrappers, clothes, video game pads, and shoes, strewn all over. At least he'd claimed the bunk at the back of the bus, where he could shut himself away from the craziness. The one perk of their success this year was staying in more upscale hotels. And with Johnny married, he'd have a room all by himself. No sharing. For as much as he loved the guy, he was a total slob.

When the bus pulled up to the four-star hotel, he wanted nothing more than a shower and some action. He'd let the line to Paige grow cold. She might be playing one of her silly games, tease and switch, and he didn't want to fall for it again. What he needed was a woman he could trust to accept him for who he was.

He jumped off on arrival, got his key and was ready to go in record time.

He couldn't seem to shake the image of Paige in his head, and it followed him down to the lobby where, he met Joe and Rambler. He needed to eliminate her from his consciousness. Nothing good would come of it except maybe a whole lot of bad. He'd be able to fix that soon enough. The club they were headed to was a good one. They'd been there before and he was relishing the idea of winding down, good music and a whole lotta love.

Thirsty from the pepperoni pizza she'd had earlier, Rissa tiptoed down the hallway to get some ice. The whoosh of the elevator signaled that some member of the band was getting back, and from the giggles that echoed, she knew he wasn't alone. Hiding in the alcove, her back to the wall, not wanting to intrude, she curiously peeked around the corner to see who was out there.

"Keep it down, okay?"

The male voice registered.

A woman was literally hanging on to Reject, her hands roaming his body freely, coming to rest on his ass, which Rissa had to admit was one of the best she'd ever seen. His back was to her, his head dipped as if he was kissing the woman in question, and she was startled by the high voltage of electricity that shot through her. She watched with a thudding heart as the action heated up, female hands caressing a part of his body that should have had him a bit more excited than he seemed. Extricating himself from the lip lock, he said with a curious lack of emotion, "Let me get my key out."

The woman didn't seem to get the message, so Reject fumbled the key from his back pocket and the woman all but shoved him in the door.

Once Rissa heard the click as it closed, she just stood mute, letting the adrenaline course through her. She wasn't surprised at the scene. She knew Reject scored with the groupies quite regularly. What she was surprised about was the way she'd felt while she was watching it. Not usually such a voyeur, she hadn't been able to take her eyes off the man, wanting to see the way he kissed and needing for some reason, to feel the pressure of his lips on hers. Yet all she'd been able to witness was the woman's physical possession, arms around his neck, biting his shoulder, holding him closely. The urge to jump forward and rip her arms away from him had ended only with their disappearance behind closed doors.

Shaking off the insidious need to see for herself what he felt like, she swore and asked herself,

"What the hell are you thinking?"

After stomping back to her own room, she opened her door and threw herself on the bed, the pulsing in her body a sure sign that she'd lost her mind.

Throwing her arm over her forehead she tried to block out the scene but as she did, another stole into her consciousness. It was a year into her relationship with Jude. They'd gone to the wedding of one of his college roommates in New York and had stayed over a couple of nights. Giving her the excuse of wanting a night with his buddies, he'd left her alone to go club hopping. Coming up from the bar after a couple of hours, hoping to alleviate the loneliness of being in a strange town with people she didn't know very well, she'd returned to their floor only to find Jude in a compromising situation with the wife of his friend. Startled into incoherence, she'd watched the foreplay from a distance, until the hurt became too much. The sense of betrayal too intense to confront him, so she had packed her things, rented a car with his credit card and gone home to her parents. It had taken him only a couple of weeks to get her to move back in with him, promising it would never happen again, proclaiming his undying love for her and weakening her defenses with his romantic gestures of apology. But it hadn't been the end of his nighttime activities, although she hadn't found that out until recently. She had been a fool for forgiving him, for trusting him in the aftermath.

The two incidents blurred in her mind, becoming one.

And she swore at Reject and his inability to keep his hands to himself.

Yet the situations were completely different.

Reject might not favor monogamy, but he didn't promise something he couldn't deliver. He might flaunt his sexuality in a way that was troubling to her, but her heart certainly wasn't at risk. He was single, and free to do anything he wanted.

A slow burn of desire grew in her belly along with an unhealthy dose of curiosity.

She pulled the covers over her head to muffle the words that echoed.

So are you.

⌒

Luca stood by the open mini fridge, studying the contents.

The night hadn't gone exactly as planned. The music was mediocre, the drinks were weak and the woman he'd showed to his hotel room door a little after four a.m. was like all the others.

Exhausted, totally spent from the concert and what was required of him in the sack, he fingered out a nip of vodka and drank it down in one swallow.

This had stopped being fun. In fact, it wasn't even satisfying him anymore. Helen something or other had been all over him, touching places that should have come alive with feeling, but her hands hadn't had any effect other than him wanting it done and her gone.

Maybe the lure of Paige was too strong. It might be time to answer the call, see what she wanted, see where it would lead.

He retrieved another shot and swallowed it down.

What the fuck?

He'd sworn he wouldn't do this again, with anyone, wouldn't go looking for permanent.

He'd protected his heart for too long to drop the shield. There were vampires out there ready to suck him dry.

Paige had been the first in a long line of them.

After removing his jeans again, he slid into bed and put his arms beneath his head. He needed to get some sleep, needed to find a way to fill the aching loneliness. This life that he thought would bring the acceptance he'd coveted had brought adulation instead, and he found it was even more difficult to cope with than rejection. He was beginning to think maybe he'd gotten his fill.

Were the old scars healing?

There were ghouls that still haunted him but they were becoming fainter and fainter each year, each city, each bed.

Being belly up in the grass with kids pelting you with fists and sticks, being taunted walking down the hallway at school for being different, finally falling in love, or so he thought, and having it blow up in his face had taught him to be very careful in exposing the real him.

It wasn't safe.

Better to be alone than to run that gauntlet again.

Better to keep his identity hidden than to expose who he was.

That was the problem with intimacy. It required openness and sharing, something he'd done once only to find the recurring hurt and pain.

He had worked hard to recreate himself, to rebuild his self-esteem, to find acceptance, to prove to the world he wasn't a loser.

Could he trust Paige? Did he have to?

Another loss might wipe out everything he'd accomplished, and he was determined not to let that happen.

All of it didn't matter in the long run. The urge to respond was too compelling to put off any longer. He pulled his computer off the nightstand and opened it. He spent over an hour drafting and editing before he was satisfied. Staring at the finished product for longer than was necessary, his growing frustration with himself reaching a peak of ridiculousness, he hit send.

It was too late to turn back now.

CHAPTER SIX

Rissa was at loose ends. And scared.

She had no idea what she'd do to pass the time, and an unexpected feeling of trepidation shot through her.

She didn't want to admit it, but she was afraid to go out into the unknown.

When she'd agreed to nanny, she hadn't given much thought to how different each place would be, or that there would be such resistance to go out and explore, jog, or Rollerblade. Comfortable in her own community, she knew exactly where she could find a path or a trail, the roads to take to keep her away from traffic and madness. It was a bit unnerving to be in such unfamiliar terrain.

It was also a startling revelation.

Her confidence wasn't a natural part of who she was, like she'd thought. She only felt safe with people around her, only felt secure when she was part of someone else's life.

Her parents, siblings, friends had called her reckless for skiing down the most treacherous mountain slopes, fearless when facing a batter or charging down the soccer field before scoring the intended goal.

She was neither and it was one more flaw that was surfacing, muddying the reflection of who she was.

Who she'd thought she was.

She straightened her posture, glared at herself in the mirror, refusing to give in to the apprehension. She was going to force herself out, otherwise she'd be spending her days in the hotel.

Just not this morning.

There was a fitness center here, which gave her the excuse she needed to stick close. She donned some leggings and a tee, grabbed her iPod and her earbuds, and made the elevator ride down to where the gym was located.

Consumed by the movement and the music, Rissa didn't see who took up the exercise machine next to her until he had worked up to match her speed.

She glanced over to see who was running next to her and was surprised to see Reject keeping up. She was also surprised to see he had his hair tied back, a bandana around his forehead, and had dressed in running shorts and a tee, as if he did it regularly.

Between breaths she commented, "Didn't think you had it in you."

"How do you think I keep my body in shape? Playing guitar?"

"I don't know, maybe lifting women in your spare time, using them like a big barbell."

For some reason, she felt honor-bound to take him down a peg. His body was having an undesirable impact and the effect was unnerving her.

"I don't mix business with pleasure."

"Such a shame. I laugh at work all the time."

Well, maybe not lately but she needed to support her position.

"I laugh at work, too. Have you met the guys I hang around with?"

"Actually, I have. I love one of them in particular. You know, my brother."

He glanced over and probed her eyes.

"You look a lot like him."

She managed to even out her breathing so she could continue talking, not wanting to slow her pace. She said, "I don't see it."

"You're kidding. The eyes, nose, shape of the head, lean body angles."

"I've got short hair that curls every which way, our eyes are the same color but not the same shape and I've got boobs. Or haven't you noticed?"

She knew they were only orange-sized but there was still definition.

He made a show of studying the firmly insistent boobs in question before saying, "First thing."

She ignored the tingle that roused her nipples.

"You're a breast man?"

"That among other attributes."

She bit her lip, her legs now beginning to tremble. It wasn't from the running. She'd been doing that her whole life. There was something else causing it, but she didn't want to look too closely at what it was. With an exaggerated sigh, she said, "It's too bad. There are so many other qualities that should come first like, oh, I don't know, brains, personality, nature."

With an indifference that annoyed her, he responded, "Brain power is overrated."

"You'd rather have someone dumb and buxom than smart and perky?"

"Most of the time."

She was half the equation. She wasn't buxom, she wasn't bright. Her high school grades would prove the point.

With that thought came a sour expression and a bitter retort.

"Boy, and here I thought my opinion of you was as low as it could go."

He slowed the machine down, took a towel and wiped off the sweat that had accumulated on his neck and face. Rissa did the same.

While stepping off the treadmill, he said, "It's a good thing your opinion doesn't mean much to me," before walking in the direction of the weights.

He checked the weight amounts before adding another layer. After reclining on the bench, he began to press the bar over his head as if it weighed nothing at all.

Rissa was watching the play of his muscles as he worked the barbell, saliva pooling in her mouth and in another part of her body she'd thought had dried up.

"Say I did give a shit. It would be interesting to hear what else there is about me that you don't like."

Caught off guard by the question, she gave him the first thing that made its way through the fog.

"You spend too much time thinking about who you'll get in your bed tonight, or any night. There has got to be something more that interests you."

She waited for him to release the bar for an answer.

"What I do for a living suits me fine."

"Aren't you curious about the world?"

"Not particularly. It'll keep spinning with or without my attention on it."

Reject lifted and released between each answer.

She became acutely aware of each rippling muscle, the zing in her retorts losing energy.

"What do you believe in?"

He grunted out, "Having fun."

"That's juvenile, don't you think? Especially at your age."

"I didn't have much of a juvenile period in my life, so I'm making up for it now."

It was said so casually that Rissa stopped to wonder and then asked outright.

"What do you mean?"

"Let's just say I didn't have much of a social life. Besides, I needed to work to pay bills. Save for college, all the good that did me."

She gasped, the barbells in her hand becoming dead weight.

"You went to college?"

"Don't sound so surprised. I am actually quite intelligent."

A memory flashed. She knew that. He was valedictorian his senior year, gave the speech at her brother's graduation.

How had she forgotten?

"Where did you go?"

"MIT."

A mouse squeak came out of her mouth as well as the question, "In Boston?"

"Is there another one?"

She asked, after regaining control of her vocal chords, "What did you major in?"

He hesitated, did another curl before finally answering, "Particle physics."

What the hell is that?

She was unwilling to show her ignorance, so she pretended she knew what he was talking about. "Why would anyone major in physics?"

"Million-dollar question. It's one of the reasons I dropped out. How about you?"

"Huh?"

She was too busy shifting her perspective of him from pretty party boy to someone who'd majored in physics at one of the most prestigious schools in the country.

Finally finishing his routine, he tried again.

He wiped his forehead with a towel already soaked from sweat and asked, "Did you go to college?"

Rissa had been using the light weights but could never find a rhythm, stopping periodically to assimilate all this new information.

"Three courses, community college to get my certification and lead teacher qualification in early childhood."

"How come you didn't go further?"

She glanced up, his amber eyes taking on a glow that almost glinted. She had the impression he was somewhat disappointed.

"It's all I needed to be able to do my job."

"You only do what's required?"

It echoed Jude's sentiment about ambition, and she was irritated by his mocking tone.

"I don't make a lot of money doing what I do. It was more a question of what I could afford than whether I wanted to pursue a higher degree."

"Seems to me Johnny would have been happy to help you."

"Jude, my ex and I talked about it. My going back once we were married. It made sense to wait."

"How's that working for you?"

She finally gave up working the weights, placed them back on the shelf, her voice edged with a bite.

"I didn't count on him dumping me."

She mindlessly followed him to the ab benches and slipped into place beside him.

In between crunches, he said, "From what your brother told me, it was just a matter of time. Were you the only one who didn't see it?"

She'd seen it but was stupid and ignored it. Jude could be so charming at times. He'd always be able to worm his way back into her good graces. She didn't want to let on she'd been a sap so she inferred that there had been one area of their lives that didn't suck.

"No one knows what goes on behind closed doors."

"He was good in bed?"

It sounded more like an assumption given what she said, rather than a question.

"That's so none of your business."

"Well, why else would someone stay with an asshole?"

"He was quite nice at times."

"Did he make you feel loved?"

She looked at him then, surprised at the depth of the question, and answered him honestly, "Not all the time."

"Then you're lucky to be rid of him."

They both settled into their routine, silence allowing each to be with their own thoughts.

When Rissa was finished, she slipped out and finally said, "That's it for me. I guess I'll see you later."

"Maybe. Maybe not."

She gave him a long stare before moving away, towards her room where she'd shower and change. When she boarded the bus just behind her brother, her insides were still humming, her heart still pounding a syncopated rhythm.

⌒

Rissa sat on her bunk, paper and charcoal in her hand, taking in her surroundings. They were headed to their next destination which was a few hours away.

Johnny was asleep, Rosie lying atop his chest, his arm protectively around her, Tish cuddled next to him. She couldn't stop her flying fingers from putting the scene on paper and once captured, flipping the page and starting again. Memories of her brother taking care of her when she was younger flooded her mind. There was a picture in their family album that captured the same scene of him at five years old with her lying atop him and it made her smile.

She allowed the flashbacks to snap out in sequence.

Him bandaging one of her skinned knees when she went chasing after him down the driveway and fell when she was four, the time he got her out of the tree she'd climbed recklessly when she was six, the days he'd hit her fly balls when she was trying out for the youth softball league when she was ten, braiding her hair when their mother had left for work too early to get it done when she was twelve. How he'd held her after their father was killed during a domestic dispute he and his partner had been called out on, let her tears spill out onto his tee shirt, let her pummel his chest in anger and grief. She had been almost as devastated when Johnny had left as when they had buried their father's body, after his fight with Paul over parental control, which had driven him out of their lives for years. Never understanding how he could turn his back on them all, because he had loved them so deeply, she had been unrelenting when it came to keeping their connection. She wasn't going to let another member of her family disappear. She visited him at his apartment weekly and, over time, watched the progression of the band from amateur to world famous. Thankfully, he had kept his door open to her although she knew where he'd draw the line. She'd kept Paul out of their conversations allowing the connection to remain strong. She'd visited as often as she could.

Her friends had been only too happy to accompany her to the practice sessions, so enamored of the boys in the band who acted so cool, whose looks could turn on females of any age. Reject hadn't been part of the band yet. He had come on board later when one of the original members developed a drug habit and had been voted out, although it was more of an intervention that turned ugly. Within a year of Reject joining, the band had become famous and Johnny was endlessly on the road. She'd made sure to call him once a month, fill him in on all the family drama, unwilling to let go of the big brother whom she had adored. They were the only two in the family who had never lost touch.

But she'd grieved for the loss at holiday gatherings, Sunday dinners and birthdays, never understanding why he couldn't just get along with Paul for the sake of the family.

She would be forever grateful that he had found Tish. Fatherhood had come easily to him, and she loved the picture of his small family so comfortable at rest.

With her back against the wall of the bus, she let her thoughts drift back to the conversation she'd had with Reject.

He had gone to MIT, the Massachusetts Institute of Technology. She was sure it wasn't that easy to get in. A person probably had to have a megawatt brain, something she would never have expected of him.

She had to give him credit for being so unassuming. There were a lot of people who lorded it over you if they had a modicum of intelligence.

Like Jude had?

She forced her ex out of her mind and thought about the nerds she'd known in school, so brainy that they had no social skills at all, a lot of book knowledge but no common sense.

That certainly didn't seem to be Reject's problem.

He had it all.

A veritable social calendar filled with names and numbers.

Not that she wanted to be one of them.

Her interest had been piqued, was all, and she'd like to get to know him better.

Her original perception had been off.

What else is new?

Irked by her lustful thoughts, she leafed through the sketches. The lustful thoughts intensified. There was an overabundance of the man taking up too much space in her head.

She picked one of them up and brought it closer.

And stared.

It captured a certain essence that she hadn't even been aware of. A seriousness about life that his actions didn't quite convey, a thoughtfulness that appeared as melancholy. Who was he beneath the façade of sex-loving tomcat? Egomaniac? An alternate version was clearly expressed on the page. There was vulnerability in his eyes, something she assumed he didn't want anyone to see, and it captivated her. A tiny spark flared, a spark that she had to douse, and quickly.

Her fingers fumbled the sketch back into the stack, began leafing through the others. They were good, even if she said so herself. She was drawing from the outside in, with more maturity than she had in the past, more detail and better technique. This art form had always been her favorite past-time. She loved observing people and things, was driven to reproduce the subject material that resonated with something within. It also answered the need to keep busy and this medium scratched that itch. If she kept up her pace, she'd have a whole catalogue of life-on-the-road pictures. Maybe she could put it together to give Johnny and Tish for Christmas this year. They'd appreciate it, had always encouraged her to do something with her talent. But she never thought it would amount to a career.

Had it been her teachers in art school who'd initiated that mind set?

They were always pushing her to go into oils but it was a medium that didn't speak to her. It was time-consuming. She'd begin with a layer of oil paint, then needed to wait until it dried before adding another. Sometimes it would take weeks before the canvas was ready. Her fingers weren't satisfied with that kind of attention to detail. They itched for quick strokes, frenetic activity and she'd known that there would be nothing for her at the end of the two years, so she'd dropped out.

The teaching assistant job at Kiddie Kare was supposed to be temporary, but she had enjoyed it so much she'd taken the required course work to get her certification. It lent itself to all her skills, creativity being the strongest suit.

Her dream job would have to use some form of creativity.

Maybe...

She was shifted forward as the bus lurched to a stop.

Ralph swiveled in his seat and announced, "Up and at 'em. We have arrived."

Rosie opened her eyes and lifted her head unsteadily, instantly curious, and as if he felt the slight movement, Johnny came awake as well.

"Will wonders never cease. I think I got a whole two hours of sleep at one time."

He raised his daughter up over his head, Rosie smiling at him, her head well supported by his fingers.

Rissa smiled at the picture.

Johnny looked over. "You know you are free to do whatever you want until tonight, right? We've got it covered till then."

"I do, although I have no idea what to do with all the free time. I used to work eight to nine hours a day."

"I think there are some parks. You might be able to rent a bike, Roller blade. Tish always looked up things to do on the computer. Found us some places we enjoyed. I'm not so sure we can do that as easily this year, but it might put you on the right track. We'll be at the hotel overnight, then it's off to Burlington. Just make sure you're back by late afternoon."

"What are you going to do?"

"I have an interview later. Other than that, not sure. We'll check in, get Rosie settled, fed, and then decide."

Johnny gathered up the diaper bag, the backpack, and Rosie's blanket before asking, "You've got the credit card we gave you, right?"

"I do. You didn't need to do that."

"I know but I wanted you to be able to do what you want without worrying about expenses."

"You're paying me a lot of money, more than I'd make in a year at my job, so I should be fine."

Johnny kissed her on the temple and said, "Use it and that's a direct order."

She watched as they all exited the bus before packing away her materials. She picked up her backpack and followed in their wake.

As they were checking in, Chappy deposited all the overnight bags in the lobby, so when she went up to her room, she had everything she needed.

Her room was small but homey. The bed, covered in a white and red cover, was already turned back as if waiting for her to climb in. It beckoned, but sleep wouldn't come until after the band's concert, when Tish returned home for the night.

CHAPTER SEVEN

Still anxious about going out in a strange place, Rissa stuck close to the hotel. She had her own room, which was great, but it was also a bit lonely. Not wanting to invade Johnny's privacy, she didn't feel comfortable knocking on his door to hang out. And the routine hadn't gelled yet, so she didn't know the sleep cycle, the practice cycle, or the Rosie cycle. Used to being active every minute, she was finding it difficult having nothing to do until late in the day.

She was relieved when she heard her brother's voice.

"You're still here?"

"Yeah, I was waiting to see what you're up to."

She was sitting on the rocking chairs out on the veranda the sun warm on her skin, as John and Tish came walking out, Tish holding Rosie, John pushing her stroller.

"While Johnny's at the radio station for the interview, I thought I'd go downtown with him and then wander around. It'll be nice to get some fresh air. Annie's coming with me."

"Can I come along, too?"

"Sure."

As they headed toward the bus that would transport them into town, Annie, Tim, and Reject got off the elevator and walked over to join them.

It irritated her that she noticed Reject immediately. He was dressed up in a pair of white pants and a tucked-in shirt, which was a surprise. His style was more jeans and tee shirts and she had to admit he cleaned up well. He'd been in a tux the night of Tish's concert, but she hadn't appreciated the package at the time.

He'd unsettled her back then, but she hadn't wanted to explore the why at the time.

She'd been engaged, planning for a wedding that was six months away.

Now she wasn't.

He must have noticed her perusal because the slow smile radiated heat. "Something you want?"

She tried to squelch the flicker that had sparked, found it impossible, so her voice was shakier than she would have liked.

"Not a thing. But thanks for asking."

He gave her a mocking look and said, "I'd rethink that. It might put you in a better mood."

They were back at it, insults being flung, only more discreetly this morning.

"My mood will improve as soon as you're gone."

He simply admitted, "So will mine."

"So why are you here? I'm sure there's someone willing to keep you company."

"I'm sure there is."

Rissa had been overwhelmed with the numbers of women who hovered nearby and what they'd do to get the attention of the band. She couldn't blame Reject for taking advantage of all those raging hormones or the treats the women were willing to share with him. Especially considering what he'd told her yesterday, that it could ease the loneliness, but for some reason, she didn't like the fact that he was enjoying it quite so much. There was no way she was letting him know that, so she gave him her most disdainful sneer.

"I guess, if you're into the sex trade."

Tish took Rissa's arm and lead her up the stairs of the bus.

"Okay, children, it's time to go."

Not meaning to, Rissa proved the point by sticking her tongue out at the bassist.

The chuckle did nothing to make her feel any better.

⌢

After the women dropped the guys off at the radio station, they meandered along the route, the air warm with just enough of a breeze that made it a perfect day. The park was in colorful bloom, the flowers a riotous array of yellows, purples, and pinks. There were sun worshipers on towels or in folding chairs, joggers, walkers wearing backpacks, toting briefcases. Tish was pushing the stroller, just ambling along, when she asked Rissa, "So have you gotten used to us yet?"

"It's crazy. I don't understand how you can do this every year."

There were so many people around them. Not only the entourage itself with the merchandise crew, publicists, roadies, manager, accountant, and stylists but the hundreds of frantic fans all wanting attention and dozens of journalists snapping pictures and asking questions.

"The guys used to do it non-stop until they realized they were slowly killing themselves and their creativity. They decided to only tour on a limited basis, which works for all of us."

Tish asked, a smile on her face, "So what's up between you and Reject?"

Rissa felt the tingling that was becoming too familiar when her thoughts strayed to the bassist.

She cleared her throat along with those pesky thoughts.

"Nothing. Why?"

"Because you don't talk to each other, you zing each other. It seems to be a Scalera trait."

There was a flicker of apprehension at Tish's observation.

Setting her straight, she said, "I don't particularly like him."

"You've mentioned that but the air charges up every time you two are in the same space."

Peering at Tish, she saw a wide-open smile as if she were onto something.

"It's just the undercurrent of mutual distaste."

Tish gave her a speculative look that suggested there was more to that than she was implying. Rissa refused to go down that road.

She changed the direction of the conversation.

"Did anyone know him when we were in high school?"

When Johnny told her they'd hired him, she'd had a vague recollection of who he was. Since they'd been juniors when she was a freshman, there'd been no interaction. If he'd been into sports, it might have been different. Every team she'd been on had a variety of grade levels.

"Most everyone did. I think he tried hard to stay under the bullshit radar, so he became almost invisible by the time we got to senior year. The guys didn't recognize him when he showed up for the audition. He'd changed significantly. No more short hair, glasses, or nerdy looks."

"He said he went to MIT. I guess that's not surprising."

Tish stopped in her tracks. "He told you something about his past? Most of us don't know what happened to him between high school and his audition. He somehow always changes the subject when we ask."

"It was kind of in passing."

Rissa finally asked something she'd been wondering since meeting him.

"Where did he get that awful name?"

Annie's voice was filled with contrition.

"Some of the kids called him a reject and the name stuck. He was taunted with it even though he was just minding his business, going to class. I'm ashamed one of us didn't stop it. He's such a good guy and it's hard knowing we didn't lift a finger to make him feel like he belonged."

Rissa thought about that.

Was that why he looked so sad all the time?

Annie added, "He didn't really fit in anywhere. I was in some of his AP classes and heard he'd transferred in from Roxbury. No one wanted to hang around with him. Since he was new, smart, poor, and not very good-looking the kids at school were pretty rough on him."

Rissa looked askance.

Not very good-looking?

The guy was gorgeous. She was going to have to get a hold of that yearbook to see what Annie was talking about.

Still thrown by the description, she asked, "Why hasn't he dropped the name?"

Annie pushed her glasses up on her nose.

"I don't know. I guess that's how the guys recognized him, and then when they got famous, the fans got a hold of it, and it stuck."

"He's certainly not a reject anymore."

Rissa must have put too much emotion into the statement because Tish was studying her, a slight smile on her face.

Annie responded with words, not some wily implication.

"No, he's not. Contact lenses, bassist for a popular rock band, and ripped body make him a target for the women awaiting a night with a celebrity."

Under her breath, Rissa murmured, "And he doesn't disappoint."

"What was that Rissa? Why the frown?"

Her sister-in-law was teasing her again or baiting her. She wasn't sure which, but she wasn't biting.

Which gave Annie the opening she needed to offer, "In my own humble opinion, I think he can't get enough attention. Sort of like in-your- face people. Look at me now."

A bell rang in Rissa's head. Like *ding-ding-ding*, right answer.

Is that why he hooked up so often?

Was it giving him what he wanted?

It sure hadn't seemed that way the night she spied him in the hallway. He was more detached than into it.

Annie explained further, "It's one of the reasons Johnny insisted they hire him. Felt bad for all the grief he got in high school. But it was a great decision. Reject has an intrinsic quality that complements the other instruments. If you listen closely, you can almost hear him playing another song beneath the melody. And he's gotten better with age."

Tish had obviously been thinking about the observation regarding his name because she insisted, "Rissa is right. It's horrible we still call him that. He has a name and we're going to start using it. Anyone who doesn't is going to get fined."

"And how much will this fine be?"

"Five dollars, no ten. The more it is, the less time it will take everyone to drop it from their vocabulary."

Rissa grumbled, even though she was the one who'd pointed out the need for change.

"There goes my spending money."

Tish led them to a few benches to sit and enjoy the day.

A refreshing breeze rustled the new leaves as Rissa thought about Reject's life, and she lifted her head to feel it on her face.

She felt bad Reject had been bullied. Several horrible scenes of her own played out when she stepped back into the past.

Had things changed for him in college?

MIT was probably full of nerds, so he must have fit in there. So why had he dropped out? Why hadn't he finished and done something that required brains? Found a cure for something, discovered another galaxy, or...what did a person do with a degree in physics?

It was possible he couldn't afford to finish. MIT had to be expensive. Where would he have gotten the necessary funds to pay the tuition? He couldn't have had anyone helping him with that either. Not if his father wasn't around.

In the long run, he'd found something else that called to him.

He didn't need to use his brains to play bass, but he still excelled at what he did.

Was that why he worked out so much? Wanted to make sure his body stayed toned, acceptable to the world, or maybe just solid enough to protect himself?

With every layer of his personality, she was peeling away, she was beginning to see other facets to the man. He certainly was not what he seemed.

Pulled out of her thoughts when Tish's phone rang, she heard enough in the one-way conversation to know the radio interview was over and they were meeting the guys for a late lunch.

CHAPTER EIGHT

Reject sat looking out the window of the radio station, thinking about the interview while he waited for the guys to join him. He was tired of getting all the questions about being single. He wanted to be respected as a musician, not a player, but the media didn't touch on that. The groupies were great for easy sex, but it was the performing, expressing their myriad of songs, delivering it to an audience who appreciated them that he thrived on. It was the energy, the tight-knit relationships he had with the guys that made touring worth it. And it wasn't as if the women had stopped baiting the other members. They still threw themselves at John and Tim but soon realized it wasn't going to go anywhere. Marci never let Terry out of her sight. No one even got near him. When the reality of mission impossible struck, Reject had even more women clamoring for his attention. It was getting to be too much, and he was beginning to think that maybe Johnny had been right. The women got younger every year and he was beginning to miss conversations, or rather, intelligent conversations, connections that lasted longer than a few hours in bed.

When he'd told Rissa, he didn't care about the world, he'd outright lied. She had preconceived ideas about who he was, so nothing would have altered her opinion, not even the truth. Being a scientist at heart, he was always reading to expand his understanding of the nature of things.

As to what he looked for in a lover? He'd learned through the years that having expectations in that area caused a lot of pain. It was better for sex to be a diversion rather than a form of acceptance and approval.

Wasn't it?

He was beginning to understand that he was getting neither. Adulation had its downside, and it was getting a bit boring.

Johnny plopped down beside him, taking him away from his musings.

"We're meeting the women for lunch. Gonna join us?"

He had nothing better to do, and although he'd made the decision to stay away from the snark queen, he had to admit the sparring he did with Rissa put a spark into an evolving dissatisfaction with life.

"Why not."

The women were already seated in the back, Rosie asleep in her stroller, when they arrived.

Johnny took the seat beside Tish, Tim beside Annie, which left him sitting opposite Rissa, who was looking over the menu and ignoring him completely.

Reject became somber, unable to understand why Rissa disliked him so much. But then again, most of his life, he'd wondered the same thing about everyone. He had begun to think it was purely his way of being in the world that people were uncomfortable with. He must give off a vibe that was offensive, like a stink bug. For as much as he'd changed himself over the years, there was still an intrinsic quality that defined him. He was still the boy who'd been boringly studious, lacking all social skills.

Tish checked on Rosie, making sure she wasn't too hot under the blanket while asking, "How'd the interview go?"

Johnny tapped his fingers on the table in drum speak.

"Same old. Reject gets the questions about the ladies, Tim and I get the questions about the music."

Reject pushed his chair back, stretched his long legs out, his arms tucked against his chest.

"I guess they haven't realized that I'm actually part of the band and not just an appendage."

Tim's hand went to Reject's shoulder and squeezed.

"They should be asking you questions like how do you get the bass to talk to the other instruments so well?"

"It's not exactly my musical skills that I'm known for."

"It should be. You're a friggin' genius."

His head came up and he smiled. That these guys appreciated him should be enough.

"Thanks. You've never said that before."

"I haven't?"

Johnny's eyes narrowed as if in thought.

"We don't tell you. Ever. I'm sorry. Like Tim said. You're a friggin' genius. We wouldn't be half as good without you."

"Okay, that's enough. I'm going to blush soon."

It felt good, being included. Part of the group. He could get used to it. His nighttime activities had been pulling him outside the circle, entrapping him in the fan snare that no longer served. It was time for a change.

The meals soon arrived, and he was enjoying both the meal and the company.

Tish leaned towards him, her eyes glittering with humor.

"Oh, and by the way. You are no longer going to be called Reject. As Rissa pointed out, it's a horrible name. You'll be Luca from now on."

He gave Rissa a look of utter disbelief.

Tish looked at John and said, "Right, babe?"

"Um...sure. It might take me a while to get used to it."

"Well, it will cost you ten bucks every time you get it wrong."

"That's highway robbery."

Johnny's voice echoed in the tiny corner of the restaurant.

"That's right. If you have a problem with it...tough."

Reject was oddly touched, leaned in and asked, "This was your idea?"

She dipped her eyes, took a bite of her meal, and said with a caustic tone,

"Tish is the one who came up with the fine. I don't care what you're called. Luca, Reject. It's all the same to me."

He wasn't sure he believed her, but he'd take her at her word.

When he got back to the hotel, an hour before they had to leave for the venue, he pulled out his phone and checked his email. He'd shut it off during the interview and lunch.

Had Paige gotten back to him yet?

He stared at it before turning on the power, his gut churning.

Why was he so anxious?

If she'd reached out as a joke, so what? He didn't need her anymore; didn't need the acceptance and love she'd showered on him those first few months they were together.

He'd proven to himself he could get it from other sources.

When the screen flashed on, his heart stopped. There was a new message. He held his breath, telling himself he cared even though he didn't want to.

Opening it, he braced for disappointment.

Luca:

I'm so glad you got back to me. I didn't get the email until today. I'm attending a week-long conference and I've been busy with back-to-back-to-back seminars. I'm on the faculty at Columbia, and although I didn't fulfill our dream of working at an observatory, it's fulfilling. I get to work with so many fine minds and I get to share my passion about the Earth with my students, passing along critical information to a new generation about the future of our planet. I was surprised you took another path. You were so caught up in the field of physics, hungry to learn all things cosmos. I've imagined all these years that you were doing the work you loved. When I found out you were part of a band, well, let's say I was dumbstruck. One of my peers introduced me to Raging Thunder. I've never been interested in that kind of music, classical is more to my taste, but she showed me one of your CD jackets. I became speechless when I recognized you, so different, but then so very much the same. From what I understand, you'll be playing in New York City, which isn't too far from Poughkeepsie and I thought that maybe...you might want to have dinner, or a drink after the show. I'd love to see you again. I understand if you can't. But I will remain ever hopeful.

Paige

She wanted to see him.

It amazed him now, the same way it had amazed him when she'd said yes to their first date. Without equivocation.

It had gone better than he'd anticipated. They'd lingered over dinner for hours, learned about each other, what their hopes and dreams were, where they'd come from, where they were going. In a lot of the same classes that freshman year, they began to sit with each other, sharing notes, discussions, opinions, until they were together all the time, each savoring the profound emotions that came with first love. While they were dating, she'd introduced him to a different world. Many of the debutantes she'd been cloistered with at a private, all-girls school in upper state New York were attending Boston-area colleges, the best educations money could buy. Spending weekends and breaks with the affluent crowd set had set him on a new learning curve.

When it was over, it'd turned upside down.

The suffering that had come with it was not something he'd ever forget.

He sat back against the headboard, his eyes rereading the missive over and over.

Now the question was: did he want to see her?

The past washed over him, the ecstasy and the agony.

He didn't know because he didn't dare believe they could go back.

He wasn't going to respond until he knew for sure, but when he hit the stage in Guilford, memories flooded him.

As he looked out over the sea of faces, all nine thousand seats filled in one of the best venues in the country, he saw Paige's face in every one of them. They had come to Lake Winnipesaukee one weekend. Her roommate's family had a summer home here. They'd stayed overnight, swimming in the lake, enjoying the spread Nan's family served to the filled house. He'd been a passive observer as some of the guys water-skied, played volleyball, his lack of sporting prowess on full display. Paige didn't seem to mind, staying behind with him, holding his hand, making him feel part of the rowdy group. When they got back to the dorm the next day, they'd made love for the first time.

It had been a long time coming and he couldn't get enough of her. She'd seemed just as obsessed. It had lasted longer than he thought it would, which had given him hope that it would last a lifetime. It hadn't.

Since then, he'd taken advantage of all the pleasure women brought him, but he was tired of the pretense, the meaningless interactions.

What he had wanted was a lightning bolt to strike him, for love to take him by storm.

It never did. He never gave it a chance to. Not since Paige.

Would he invite her to see him play or would he let the past lie in its fallow field?

By the time he got back to the hotel, he'd made his decision.

Better to try and fail...than wonder for the rest of his life if he'd let something of import pass him by.

He sat at his laptop, practicing the words out loud before putting them down.

Paige:

It sounds like you've found your niche. You always did have an intimate connection with Mother Earth. I remember how we used to argue about whether she was a sentient being. You believed firmly that she was, and it didn't take long to convince me you were right.

Every time I see a picture of Gaia from space, in all her beauty, I think of you.

After I quit school, I didn't go back. That doesn't mean I lost my wonder about the sky or universe. I still read, keep up with all the new discoveries but my life took a turn and I am grateful. I found good friends, a loyal following and a way to express myself without words. Words, as you know, were never my thing.

I'm not sure there would be a purpose in seeing you. We're light-years away from where we were when we sat on the bench outside the lecture hall. I live in a foreign place that's more chaos than divine order and I'm not sure you'd be comfortable here. If you decide you want to come to one of the concerts, let me know how many tickets you'll need and which night works best. I'll leave them at the box office in your name.

Until then,
Luca

He read it over, leaving it open so that if she was planning on bringing a boyfriend, significant other, husband, he wouldn't look like a fool.

And hit send.

⌒

Rissa's fingers were getting tired from texting.

She'd made the decision that the cancelled wedding costs should be divided equally.

If Jude thought he was going to get away without paying for anything, he was sadly mistaken.

Before leaving on the tour, she'd gone over the outstanding bills with her mother and had been trying to reach Jude since. She wanted him to pay half, and she'd promised her folks she'd somehow pay back the rest. With what Johnny was giving her in salary, she'd be caught up by the time the tour was over.

He was ignoring her. He was good at evasion. She'd have to hit him with a barrage of messages before he knew she meant business.

"Hey, whatcha doin?"

Johnny and Tish had gotten back from the concert a little while ago and when she looked up, she noticed her brother had changed into sweats and a tee.

With the phone in her hand, she raised it.

"Shock and awe."

"What?"

"I'm shocking the dick and it's awesome."

Tish had come out yawning but managed to ask, "Whose dick are you shocking?"

Rissa chuckled. Tish looked like she was sleepwalking. Was she even awake?

"I don't mean dick the way you're taking it. I mean dick as in a-hole, not dick as in...dick. Jude is not going to believe my persistence. It's my small way of making his life a living hell. I'm so enjoying it."

Tish curled up into Johnny's side, her head laying in the crook of his shoulder and within minutes was snoring softly.

"She's got a lot on her plate."

Pulling his wife into his lap, he nodded.

"Too much, I'm afraid. She told me earlier that she's not sure she's got the stamina for this."

"Are you listening?"

Johnny usually needed a two-by-four to get his attention. Her expression softened as she glanced at her sister-in-law. He was different with his wife. More in tune, more attentive.

"I am. If it gets to be too much, we'll adjust. She doesn't want to give anything up until the routine sets in. She thinks it might level out at some point and doesn't want to quit until she knows for sure she can't manage it all. Just make sure you pick up the slack. Okay?"

He gave her one of his broad smiles. She returned it instead of the pillow she was going to throw at his head. She didn't want to disturb Tish, so she held her hand.

"No problem. I need more slack. Never get enough of it."

He slid his legs onto the coffee table, careful not to jostle the sleeping body in his arms and burrowed back into the cushion.

"Are you okay? I know Ma forced you into this and I didn't give you much of a choice. I hope you're not too unhappy with the arrangement."

She leaned her head on the back of the chair, tucked her legs under her.

"I'm actually enjoying myself. Now all I need to do is get up and out."

"You'll find your way."

He had such confidence in her, she wished she could borrow some.

"I think I'm a little old to be wondering what I'll be when I grow up."

"You've been busy sketching. Every time I see you without Rosie, you've got a pencil and pad in your hand."

"I have to admit I love nothing better than scribbling."

"I wouldn't call it that. You're talented, Riss. Go with it. It's one of your strengths."

She studied her hands, smudges of charcoal embedded in the swirls of her fingerprints. It was why she'd switched to pencil. It was neater.

"It's one of those useless things that comes naturally."

"You've been practicing since you were a kid. You're good and need to accept that."

He laughed and asked, "How many times did you ask me to change your book covers to give you fresh space to work on?"

Those brown paper shopping bags had come in handy. It was a good thing the school wanted the textbooks covered because she had an unquenchable need to scribble.

"I asked Ma once. She couldn't get the sides folded right. You were the best book coverer on the planet."

"Is that why you used to come to my place once I left? Make sure I didn't give up the title?"

"You know why I came over. I needed you in my life."

He rested his head on Tish's, and admitted, "I needed you in mine, too, sis. More than you needed me. You had the rest of the family, I would have had no one if you'd given up."

She got up and went over to kiss his cheek.

"That would never have happened. Good night. And thanks, Johnny. For this. For everything. I love you."

"Love you too, Riss."

She closed the door to her room and stripped off her shorts.

After she climbed under the covers, she looked at her phone one more time. She'd take up the battle cry again tomorrow, up the number of texts and see what happened.

Jude would have to get back to her at some point.

The longer it took, the more pleasure she'd get from driving him crazy.

A smile took over her face.

I'm no longer a doormat Jude. Get used to it.

CHAPTER NINE

They arrived in Burlington around noontime the next day. Rissa was determined to go off on her own.

She couldn't continue to count on her brother for entertainment.

Jude's accusation that she was needy was also a great motivator. She was going to prove him wrong.

Her plan for the day was to rent a bike and cruise south. She heard there were a couple of great breweries. She might stop at one so she could sample some of the craft ales. The paths were all mapped out, making her less nervous about the excursion.

Dressed in a pair of white shorts, tee, and sneakers, she hopped off the bus.

With Rosie in his arms, Johnny exited right behind her.

"Have you decided to have some fun today?"

"Yes. Biking and beering."

"Um, the beering might be a problem."

"I'll grab lunch first, I promise, and no more than two for the road."

Reject must have overheard the conversation because he asked, "Mind if I come along? The stationary bike in the gym just lost its appeal."

Ready to say no, Rissa glanced up and into iridescent amber.

The smile curved up; his eyes gleamed.

"Afraid you won't be able to keep up?"

The challenge wasn't lost on her, and she changed her mind completely.

"Ha. It'll be the other way around."

He took a step in her direction.

"Okay. Come this way."

Over his shoulder, Reject called out, "We'll be back by five."

"Thanks for going with her. Now I won't have to worry."

Reject took the spot to her left, on the edge of the sidewalk, and she kept pace as he walked north towards the town.

The silence they shared was comfortable.

It was a surprise.

She usually needed to fill the quiet. She'd ramble on about inconsequential things, afraid there might be nothing of importance to say.

She kept pace with Luca's long strides. He seemed to know where he was going so, she was more than happy to let him lead the way. His male presence was palpable, and she was stirred by it. When his arm brushed hers, her skin prickled, and she thought about the scene she'd witnessed the other morning outside his hotel room. She peeked over at him without moving her head and gauged him to be four or five inches taller than her five-eight frame and wondered how she would fit in his embrace. The prickles became shooting points of electricity when she thought of kissing him, his lips so soft and full. Her eyes fluttered closed for a moment, her memory so clear and vivid of what it felt like watching, imaging herself in his embrace.

In a flash, her eyes flew open, and she tamped down the embers starting to flame.

What was she thinking?

She was ready to buy another one-way ticket to disappointment.

Hadn't she learned anything?

Putting some distance between them without missing a step, she felt a bit more in control.

The rental place sat on the edge of Lake Champlain, and Rissa stood admiring the view while Luca paid for the bikes, at his insistence. After she climbed on, she followed him down a path that was dedicated to bikers, walkers and joggers, matching his pace. They pedaled in tandem, the sun warm, the breeze a balmy one.

"You're more athletic than I gave you credit for."

"You being a super jock back in high school, you think you own the playing field."

Her disbelief showed in her voice.

"How do you know that?"

"That you were a super jock? I might have been a loner, but I didn't live under a rock. Your exploits were legendary. All-star pitcher as a sophomore. A gold in states for track. That news was all over the school."

Her athleticism was one of her strengths. It wasn't about the medals, it was about the students who swarmed around her, offering companionship. She'd never lacked for friends back then.

The thought of his solitary existence made her squirm.

"Why were you such a loner? I never saw you with anyone."

"Let's just say I tried to stay out of trouble."

"What kind?"

"The kind where you get stuffed in a dumpster."

Her foot faltered on the pedal, and she almost lost her balance.

"Who would do something like that?"

"Jocks. They got away with just about everything. No brains, all...dicks."

Her body stiffened.

"You must not have liked me by association."

He looked over and gave her a half grin.

"I never saw you play the mean-girl routine. Back then."

She looked out into the distance, her cheeks heating.

"Then you missed a chapter."

It was a bit disconcerting to say that. No one knew about those first few months after her father's death when she'd been angry, grieving, mean. It hadn't been her finest hour.

He glanced over at her, a cynical twist to his lips.

"You mean to tell me you were just like the others after all? I should have known you'd practiced it before me. Was I the victim of that evil tongue back then?"

"I wouldn't have dared. You were an upper-class man. Bullies stick with the ones weaker and more vulnerable."

"Are you saying I was weak and vulnerable?"

She scowled. That wasn't what she meant to imply.

"No. Maybe. I don't know why they picked on you. I tormented kids because I was angry, feeling left out. I guess I needed to feel better and that was something that did it for me."

"How long did it last, this chapter in your life?"

"Until my brother Dennis gave one of my victim's hell for retaliating. He missed the first foul, my part in the interaction. He didn't know I'd started it."

The shame had done what nothing else could have.

"Then?"

"I stopped."

She studied his expression, but he was giving nothing away. She, on the other hand, was feeling dismayed at the confession.

As they reached the asphalt that wound a path through the lake, she relaxed, and they found a companionable rhythm. Time seemed to melt away. They stopped to admire the beauty of the landscape at different spots, looking out over the placid lake, his presence making everything more vivid, more sentient.

Afraid it was becoming too magical, she let her competitive edge kick in. Arching over the handlebars, she pedaled faster and faster, hoping to outrace him. But she was never able to leave him in the dust. In seconds, he caught up with her and she laughed like a kid, her eyes twinkling in playfulness.

Dryly, he quipped, "Nice try."

"I should have known."

"Do you and your brother compete at everything?"

"Usually, it's just with each other. He wins a lot. But every once in a while, I come out ahead."

"He's got the weight and height, but you have the finesse. And you're sneaky so you also have the element of surprise on your side."

"Sorry. Couldn't help myself."

She gave him an open smile and the look of surprise on his face, as if he didn't think she had one in her, struck her in a strange way, right in the pit of her belly.

After the silliness of the race, they began talking to each other in earnest, each pointing out scenes of interest as they wound south.

"I didn't realize it would be this beautiful."

It was symbolic of the Earth from space, green and blue everywhere, trees along a path that dissected the water. The sweeping views of the Adirondacks with their steep hills, were the reward for her burning muscles.

"I've biked in a few different places across the country. This is one of the best."

THE EDGE OF FOREVER

They were coming up to a more residential area and Luca led her to the bike rack just outside a pub. "Want to stop and sample?"

"This isn't Switchback, is it?"

"I don't think we have the time to get there, back, and stop for something to eat. The food's good here and they'll have the Vermont brews you were talking about."

"How do you know?"

"I was here last year."

With her stomach growling for the last mile or so, Rissa was glad they'd finally be able to eat.

They locked up the bikes and entered.

Seated at the bar, they each ordered a specialty beer and their lunch.

Rissa closed her eyes and licked her lips after taking a sip of the murky golden brew.

"It's good."

Rissa felt the spurt of electrical current shoot from his seat to hers and she looked over at him, agitated by the way it hit her. His eyes were burning chips of amber and she squirmed in her seat before asking, "What are you looking at?"

"You. You're enjoying this, aren't you?"

The heat was prickling her again and she felt her cheeks flush. In a pique of annoyance that he could make her feel this way, she quipped, "Well, don't get so involved in that. I'm nothing like those women who swoon over you."

"I know."

"I don't fall into anyone's bed."

In a split second, she was envisioning just that, the bed being his, but she reined in her feelings when he said, "I don't believe I asked you to."

"Well, good. I stay away from men like you."

The bartender placed their sandwiches in front of them, and with trembling fingers, Rissa lifted her turkey-style Reuben and took a bite.

She picked up her pickle, biting into the crunchy, garlicky treat and Reject grinned.

"You Scaleras certainly like your pickles."

"Actually, it's only me and Johnny. We have them with just about everything."

"Annie brought a jar of them to Tish's concert last year."

"I remember. What was that about?"

"He didn't believe that Tish would ever reach the concert stage. Annie said she'd make sure he'd have pickles when he ate his crow."

Rissa couldn't help but laugh.

"Did he? Eat the pickles with the crow?"

"Didn't you ever notice the jar sitting on Tish's piano?"

"Oh, my God. Yes. I thought maybe he'd just left it there for his late-night snack or something."

"He said he never wanted to forget what a moron he was once upon a time."

"Do you think he needs a reminder?"

"I think he gets one every time he looks at Rosie."

She looked up. Luca had just taken the last bite of his pastrami sandwich, wiped his mouth, and pushed the plate toward the edge of the bar. His words had shaken her a bit. He could be so serious at times, with a surprising depth of understanding. It just didn't jibe with what she knew about him, and it unsettled her.

As did his baritone voice.

"Are you enjoying the tour so far?"

"It's nothing like I could have imagined."

"Is that a yes?"

"I love being with Rosie. As for the tour itself, I don't get to see very much from your perspective."

"You probably wouldn't want to."

"I've always loved going to concerts. All that energy. I used to love hearing Johnny play the drums when he was younger, at least when he knew how to play. Up till then it was just crash and bang. Kinda hard on the ears."

"He said he was relegated to the garage."

"Summers, yes. In the throes of winter, my mother refused to give that up. He moved them to Tim's. The Matarazzos' had a two-car garage and his dad let them play there. Until dark. Then Johnny would have to take the kit apart and redo it every afternoon."

"I wish I had been with them then. It sounds like they had fun."

"Not if you heard Johnny grumbling about it. Were they the first band you joined?"

"No. I was in another one for almost a year. They did mostly covers, and I knew they were going to stay second-rate. But it gave me the experience and practice I needed for something better."

"You certainly got that. The something better."

The smile he gave her was delicious and she was back to wanting a taste.

"Even I didn't realize how big we'd get."

"You seem to enjoy the notoriety."

She tamped down the hunger, knowing how many women had already lapped up all that gorgeousness.

"Most of the time. I've learned that you can't have it both ways. You can either take it for what it is or quit. I'd prefer to take it."

She dipped her head and gave him a lopsided smile. "Or get it. Whatever the case may be."

She straightened as he became serious and gave him her full attention.

"I know you don't like the lifestyle, but it can get pretty lonely out on the road. Every now and then, you need a connection of some kind."

The comment stung.

She knew what lonely was. Even when she was living with Jude, she'd felt it. His admission told her something about why he did it. It wasn't as ego-driven as she'd thought. He was nothing like she'd thought, and it was disturbing her equilibrium.

"Ready to go?"

Snapped out of her musings, she said simply, "Yes."

She reached for her credit card, which was tucked in the backpack she'd brought along.

"I got this. It's a thank you for letting me tag along."

Not knowing what to say, she slid off her seat and headed to the exit.

Who was this man?

Solitary but a good companion. Smart but down-to-earth. Serious but with a dry wit that made her laugh.

A dichotomy of contrasting personalities and she was more than intrigued.

It was an unwelcome surge of excitement thrumming through her that frightened her. He was way out of her league. A one-night disaster waiting to happen.

Could she curb her curiosity now that she was getting to know him? He still wasn't a safe bet.

She was afraid of the answer because the afternoon had been more than enjoyable.

Rosie was finally asleep although it had taken lots of rocking, soothing and finally a dose of Tish's piano music to lull her into the land of slumber. Restless, Rissa paced the small area, picked up the novel she was reading, looked at the cover, then dropped it quietly down on the coffee table, not in the mood for it tonight. She turned to the television as a diversion, channel-surfing for something to take her mind off the afternoon's outing with Reject and found an old movie to watch. She had read *Wuthering Heights* in school but had never seen the film version. Curled up on the sofa, she became engrossed in the unfortunate tale of Catherine and Heathcliff, a love story that could only end in disaster. As she watched, she remembered the brooding male character, and the image she'd had of him back in high school seemed to bear a strong resemblance to Luca. He looked so sad, as if longing for something he couldn't have. Not the thing he wanted. Catherine's love.

Acceptance.

Was Luca longing for the same thing?

The love of some woman he'd lost? Acceptance?

But surely, he could have anyone he wanted.

She felt the tingle return, the one that hit her when she caught him watching her at the bar that afternoon.

If she were anyone else, she might go for it.

A night with him would probably be...?

Out of the question.

She jumped up, flicked off the movie, and began pacing again.

Her body felt a nervous energy that demanded release, was palpitating a few various points on her body, and she didn't know how to get rid of it.

Snatching up her pack, she roughly pulled out her pad and started furiously moving the charcoal across the page. When she was done, a shiver of fear ran through her.

Page after page of Luca's face, brooding eyes, sad mouth, sensuous lips, slight smile sat before her.

An alarm was sounding a dire warning because that wasn't the root of the problem.

She wanted to kiss away every shred of his melancholy.

CHAPTER TEN

Going down to the restaurant for breakfast the next morning, Rissa was sleep-deprived as was becoming habit. It wasn't that she needed to eat, just that she needed to hear conversation even if she wasn't contributing to it.

Connection.

Everyone needed it and she more than most.

She'd never felt plugged-in to Jude. It was as if they lived in parallel worlds, walking in the same direction but without an affinity to each other. She'd spent a lot of her energy trying to merge their paths, but it had been impossible. Next time around she'd look for what was important.

Choosing a table near the huge glass panel, she sat in the light that filtered in.

Soft conversation flowed around her, forks scraped, glasses clinked, and she drank it in.

Luca's solution to quell loneliness wasn't something she was willing to duplicate. She couldn't just climb into bed with someone. It had to come from a deeper place. It might be sexist, but she thought that was one of the differences between men and women. Men were fine with getting it where they could.

Or maybe it was just her. She wasn't made that way. She had to be in a relationship for it to mean something. Maybe that's why she had stayed too long at Jude's fair.

Dawdling, she knew she had a couple of hours until she watched Rosie so Tish could practice. There wasn't a concert tonight, so they were free to do what they wanted and she thought she'd get out and enjoy the beauty of the place.

As she finished up her breakfast, the lunch crowd began to straggle in. Just as she was about to leave, she glanced up to see Rej...Luca enter.

He looked over at her, gave her a brief smile and went to sit at a table on the opposite side of the room.

She felt a sting of rejection.

He was shutting her out, even after the time they'd spent together yesterday. It was like it had never happened and they were still trading insults, keeping their distance.

She was losing sleep, restless in the dark of night, more than mildly curious about how his lips would taste, wondering at the insane attraction. Their time out on the bike trail had only heightened it.

It seemed he did not have the same type of fantasies about her.

She peeked up to take him in.

He had a haunted face, beautifully sculptured lips and those deep-set eyes held a look of vulnerability. Studying the features that set her heart to beating in a pounding rhythm, she thought maybe it was just a purely physical thing. Her mouth watered at the way he looked, even now in his jeans and tee shirt. She admitted, if only to herself, she had a powerful urge to see how he would fit. She'd never felt such a magnetic pull to anyone before.

Ignoring the warning bell in her head, balancing her coffee, plate, book, and utensils in her arms, she walked the distance between them and asked tentatively, "Can I join you?"

He paused, his expression one of mistrust.

"Sure."

Taking a seat across from him, laying down all that she transferred from one table to the next, she noticed the apprehension. "You don't trust me. I can't say I blame you. It's because you remind me a little of my ex."

"Thanks. Still sticking with the insults, I see."

Her eyes widened in surprise. "You don't even know him."

Taking a swig of his Coke, he revealed, "I've gotten an earful from Johnny."

"Well, my brother's a bit...over-protective."

"The jerk should have just cancelled the wedding to begin with instead of postponing it and stringing you along before he dropped that bomb."

She didn't want to tell him Jude had postponed it because he had grave reservations about their future and that she had all but begged him to give her another chance. In hindsight, she hated the fact she'd groveled, knowing it had come from the insidious fear that if she couldn't hold him, she wouldn't be able to hold anyone and she'd end up alone. She'd thought she had done a better job at accommodating him so the breakup had still come as a shock.

"Can we talk about something else?"

"Sure."

Silence settled uncomfortably around them. She sneaked a couple of peeks at him, but his expression told her he was mentally in another place.

"Do you want me to leave?"

His eyes shot up, a startled look on his face.

"No. I'm sorry. In my own thoughts."

Taking a bite of her eggs, she asked, "So what was it like growing up so smart? School was never easy for me."

"Not great. I never quite fit in so I never had a lot of friends."

"Not even the nerds like you?"

"In the movies, the nerds sit with each other at lunch. Not reality. Socializing wasn't our thing."

"You were alone by choice then."

"I wouldn't say that. I don't think anyone likes being alone but when you're trying to be invisible, it's a solo act."

She would have guessed he liked his solitude, he seemed so good at it. Apparently not. He'd chosen it over the alternative. She'd fought against it with everything she had, going to the extreme of staying with someone even when it wasn't in her best interests.

The waitress came over with Luca's hamburger. Placing the ketchup on the table, she asked if there was anything else they needed. When the two shook their heads, she moved away.

As Rissa swallowed another bite of the cold toast, she picked up her line of questioning.

"Was it any better in college?"

"A little. It took time to build some friendships but I improved with age. It was easier because my classmates were a lot like me."

After squirting the ketchup on his bun and fries, he took a bite and began eating. Rissa pushed her plate away but stole one of his fries and began chewing on it before asking, "You have a sister, right? My brother has mentioned her. What's her name?"

"Valeria."

"Older, younger?"

"Older by five years."

"What's she like?"

He took a bite of his burger, wiped his mouth, and gave her his answer.

"Loyal. Just what a big sister is supposed to be I guess."

"Do you see her a lot?"

"As often as I can. She's coming out to Providence with her fiancée."

"I hope I get to meet her."

"You will. She knows the guys really well and we always hang out for a while after the concert."

"When's the wedding?"

"Late summer."

"Have a plus one?"

"A what?"

She smiled. He was still a bit socially underdeveloped.

"A date?"

"Are you interviewing for a job as my social secretary?"

After stealing another fry, she snickered, "Don't have the experience. There would be far too many women to sort through. I wouldn't know where to start."

"There aren't as many as you'd think. Not the serious kind, anyway. She told me she wants to look at her wedding pictures years from now and have people who mean something in them. I haven't found the right fit yet. But like I keep telling her, I've still got plenty of time."

When she snuck another fry into her mouth, he asked, "Do you want me to order you some or will eating all of mine satisfy?"

"Oh, sorry. I have a problem keeping my fingers still. The rest are yours. Promise."

She sat back in the seat, grasping her hands in her lap to still the urge just as Johnny and Tim came in and joined them.

"You're here. Why didn't you go out exploring?"

"I'm planning on it as soon as I leave here."

She called the waitress over to ask for her bill, signed her room number, and excused herself leaving the guys to whatever it was they did.

As she walked away, she couldn't help but admit that as she got to know Luca he seemed less and less the kind of man she'd pegged him for.

Getting to know him any better would be a mistake. He was sneaking under her skin and she didn't like the feeling. The fact that he loved women and what they could give him certainly wouldn't change. If she'd learned nothing else from Jude, she'd learned that. Variety was their spice of life and they made sure they tasted as often as they could. Jude was successful at the infidelity game. Rej...Luca was in a class all by himself. Rich, gorgeous, smart, and talented.

And thanks to the band, he had a never-ending supply of willing flesh.

Wasn't he exactly the kind of man she'd promised herself she'd stay away from?

It would be pure stupidity to think she could worm her way into his heart for any length of time. He'd discard her, just like all the others.

And she was through with getting dumped.

—

Luca hadn't gotten a response yet to his last email, and a new set of worries were taking space in his head.

Paige was at a conference and entrenched in seminars with renowned scientists from East Coast universities. She was a geoscientist specializing in predicting the behavior of Earth systems, having completed a doctorate in earth and environmental science from Columbia. She'd been an intern during her graduate program and they'd offered her a full-time position once her thesis had been approved.

He'd read her school biography. The university had an acclaimed faculty, she not the least among them.

The resentment that she'd gotten to pursue her academic career while he hadn't was an unexpected new pill he had to swallow.

He spent a minute reviewing his years with Thunder. That's all it took for him to know the resentment he felt had nothing to do with the band. He was happy there. It was at how easily she'd picked up the thread of her life when it had taken him years to find his own, years to find the acceptance he craved. That his personal life had been a series of highs and lows since she left him had more to do with him than her. He'd chosen to fall into bed with anyone, rather than risk rejection again. If he refused to open his heart to the love of a woman, he'd get what he could on another dimension.

Now? Was there a chance they could re-connect?

He had to decide if he even wanted to. There was a push-pull going on inside of him, and until he could find the balance point, he was staying away from clubs, drinking, and other women. He'd hole up in his room, where no one could touch him, and finish the book he'd started the first day on the bus. On his way to keep the date with his reading material, he heard, "Hey, Caroli," and turned to see Johnny hurrying down the hallway toward him.

"Yeah."

"Can you do me a favor tonight?"

"Sure. What is it?"

"I want Rissa to have some fun while she's with us but I don't like the thought of her going out alone. You two seemed to enjoy the day cycling. Can you take her out tonight and show her a good time?

Luca smiled. It'd be a better way to spend the night than holing up, thinking of Paige and her life. Although being out with Rissa might have its drawbacks. He wasn't sure yesterday wasn't an anomaly. They'd had fun in between those awkward moments.

A crackle of energy shot through him as he envisioned her tongue sliding over her lips as she tasted the foam from her beer.

Where did that come from?

Rissa was in no way the kind of woman he was attracted to.

So why was she taking up room in his head? Shouldn't Paige be the one occupying most of the real estate?

He snickered to himself at the irony. Rissa probably wouldn't even want to go out with him.

"I'm still not one of your sister's favorite people."

"What do you mean? My sister likes everyone."

"That could very well be true but you know she's not crazy about me. Seems I remind her of her ex."

Johnny's eyes widened; his hands went to his hips.

"What the hell are you talking about? You are not anything like that jerk."

He shrugged, the comparison bothering him more than he wanted it to.

"Her words, not mine."

"I'll talk to her, see if she'd be willing. If she is, would you do this for me?"

"Anything for you, bro. You know that."

Johnny shifted as if to leave but hesitated. He turned back, a frown on his face.

"The family thinks of Rissa as a daredevil but I'm beginning to realize she's kind of not. It seems she's fearless only when she's feeling safe, comfortable. You'd kind of have to stay with her, make sure she got back okay."

"Not a problem."

"You're sure. No bigger and better plans?"

"Hey, there'll be plenty of nights to play catch up."

Johnny gave him a punch in the arm.

"Thanks. I appreciate it."

"I'll be down in the bar waiting. Just text me if it's a no-go."

Johnny nodded and headed off to his room.

Luca watched him slip into his room.

He'd bet his life Rissa would turn the offer down flat but took the elevator down to the lobby.

Was hope following him?

CHAPTER ELEVEN

Rissa spent a part of the afternoon at the Church Street Marketplace, people watching, sketching, and drinking in the ambiance of the college town. Later, she took Rosie for a walk along the main street while Tish was occupied with her piano. Johnny and the band were at one of the radio stations, an interview scheduled.

Back in the sitting room of the suite she was sharing with her brother and his wife, she was hunkered down, flipping through a magazine when Johnny came in.

"How about a night on the town?"

Tossing the magazine on the coffee table, the excitement easy to read on her face, she answered, "I'd love it. But what are you going to do with Rosie?"

"Tish and I will stay with her. I asked Reject if he'd take you out."

Tish's voice came across the threshold of the sitting room and landed in her husband's ear.

"Ten bucks please. In the bin on the table."

He pulled some cash out of his pocket, a scowl on his face, and stuffed the bill in.

Yelling back, "I'm going to start calling him Caroli. Will I get charged for that?"

"That's his name so it'll save you some money."

Rissa flopped back and said in answer to his question, "No thanks."

Her voice went up a decibel so her sister-in-law could hear her.

"I don't want to go anywhere with Luca."

Tish's voice echoed into the room, "It's about time you got it right. Most of the money in there is yours."

Raising her head, projecting her voice toward her sister-in-law, Rissa called out, "You'd think that seeing it was my idea, you could cut me some slack."

"Seeing it was your idea, I should charge you more than the others."

Rolling her eyes, she was brought back by her brother's cold tone.

"Why?"

She grabbed for the magazine, and flipping pages again, she gave a plausible explanation.

"I don't like him much."

That wasn't true anymore. She was beginning to, way too much. And she had made a solemn promise to stay away from the temptations he offered.

Johnny was flabbergasted.

"Why the hell not?"

More than a partial truth fell off her tongue.

"Don't like the way he lives his life."

He had moved closer to where his sister sat, his hands on his hips as he glared at her.

"That was my life until last year. It seems you wouldn't have liked me much either then."

"You're my brother. I knew who you were, deep down."

"Maybe Luca is worth getting to know. Maybe there's something worthwhile in him, deep down."

She knew that to be true and it scared her to death so she brushed Johnny off the only way she knew how.

"Don't want to do anything more than scratch the surface there."

"Marissa Scalera, I'm surprised at you."

Tossing the magazine down on the table, she leaned forward, a look of astonishment on her face.

"Oh, my God. You're doing your father routine. I didn't like it then and I certainly don't like it now."

Johnny had tried to get her and her siblings to toe the line after their father's death. She'd resented his authoritarian ways and was relieved when Paul came into the picture, even though it had driven Johnny away.

He backed off a bit at her accusation.

"All I'm asking is that you go out and enjoy yourself tonight. He's just going to keep an eye on you. I'm not asking you to marry him."

"I don't need anyone keeping an eye on me. I'm a big girl now or haven't you noticed?"

"You can't stay in every night. I know you're here because of Rosie but I had hoped you'd get out and enjoy yourself, to help you get over...that guy."

She was over him. Wouldn't have to call or text again. He'd caved and she'd won. He'd sent several businesses checks for the balances owed for the cancelled wedding.

"His name is Jude, and I am getting over him just fine without partying."

He was glaring at her now and she didn't like the feeling. She didn't like it when he was mad at her and she was ready to acquiesce when he said, "Okay, what if I can find someone to watch Rosie for a couple of hours? Would you tag along with me and Tish, then just hang out with Re...Caroli if you want to stay?"

"Nice catch, babe." Tish's voice now held a tinge of laughter.

Rissa smiled as well and reluctantly agreed.

"I might do that. But you don't have to change your plans to keep me busy."

"Gia has been hounding Tish to babysit. She's trying to convince Chappy the time is right for them to get pregnant. A couple of hours with the Rosebud might change her mind."

Rissa laughed because she knew how her niece could be on any given night.

"If everyone agrees, then I'm in, but like I said you don't have to force anything to make it work."

He hadn't had to force a thing.

Gia was ecstatic, Tish was grateful, Johnny was looking forward to a night out with his wife and...Luca seemed more than willing to play babysitter to the babysitter.

She slid into some jeans, pulled on a simple racerback top and some matching flats, and was ready to go.

Luca was waiting for them in the lobby, in jeans and a black silk shirt although the buttons were done up higher than usual. She didn't like the fact that she'd noticed and refused to admit he looked hot.

Or that she could be bothered by it.

She scampered ahead of them and climbed into the cab, hoping that she'd be sitting beside her brother, but when Luca pushed into the interior to give the others room to get in, he was pressed tightly against her. The rush of heat was immediate. Clasping her hands in her lap, she turned her head to look out the window into the night, wondering why she'd agreed to this.

She felt his breath tickle her ear when he whispered, "Don't worry. This is as close as you'll get to me tonight. Grin and bear it. The club's only ten minutes away."

The resonance of his voice washed over her and she closed her eyes against it.

She sat there, mute, still feeling the tingles shooting through her at such close proximity to the rangy body. His scent was subtle, and as she inhaled, she thought she could smell a combination of cucumber and melon. It was clean, light and deeply arousing, creating a sensation that pulled at all her vital organs.

As soon as the taxi emptied, she scooted out onto the pavement and scurried away from the tantalizing aroma.

When she heard the deep chuckle, she glanced up and fell into eyes filled with amusement.

As Johnny and Tish moved toward the entrance of the Chinese restaurant, her brother grabbed her hand to pull her along in their wake.

"Why haven't we ever done this before?"

"Maybe because you've only been back in the familial fold for the last seven months, and I've been somewhat...preoccupied."

"I'm glad we never double-dated with you and Jude."

"Why?"

"I wouldn't have liked him and I would have had to tell you."

Luca was waiting, his hand on the door pull, and as soon as Johnny gave her a succinct assessment of Jude, he opened it, letting everyone precede him in.

He was right behind, and the static electricity of his aura was emanating out and surrounding her, creating no shortage of sparks. She stumbled as she sought to get away from him, but he was there, grabbing her hand, helping her regain her equilibrium.

The hostess led them into the darkened lounge of the Chinese restaurant and sat them at a round table at the edge of the stage. The music was playing in the background as one of the customers was belting out a rendition of "Ain't No Mountain High Enough." The singer wasn't half bad. You never knew what kind of sound the participants would make. Sometimes it was pure noise.

The waitress hustled right over and took their drink orders.

The smiles on the other faces, combined with the energy of the place kicking in changed her mood completely. All she'd have to do was stay away from Luca and she'd be fine.

The guy who had taken over the microphone was dressed in a collared shirt and dress pants and seemed way out of his comfort zone. He was attempting to serenade a woman at the table to the left of them with "You are the Sunshine of my Life." The woman looked more embarrassed than impressed.

Why hadn't he chosen something more upbeat, fun, rather than one of the old standards? It might have brought a smile to the woman he was trying to impress.

There had always been music in the house, Thunder's music, all kinds of rock, country, blues, although their mother leaned towards classical, so that was the genre that came through the sound system Paul had installed most often. It'd made Celia Scalera Catalano euphoric when Johnny had married one of the most renowned classical pianists in the world.

He hadn't heard Johnny's question to Rissa, only noticed that she was shaking her head.

"Come on. Just one."

Johnny was trying to convince Rissa to get up and sing. "Tish will go with you."

Tish looked at him with a stunned expression. "I can't sing at all. You go."

Johnny answered, "No, then everyone will recognize us. Have another glass of wine. It might help you overcome your inhibitions."

"Are you trying to get me drunk?"

"Don't have to. I know how the night will end whether you're sober or tipsy. Doesn't matter to me which it is."

Rissa got up and tossed out, "You guys should get a room. The only reason I'm agreeing to this is to get away from all this heart-warming affection."

Luca was thinking along the same lines. Johnny and Tish were still so obviously in love it was almost ...sickening? He wondered if Rissa was just envious.

He wondered if he was.

He studied her movements as she walked to the edge of the stage, and couldn't help but admire her lithe grace. She might think of herself as a tomboy but her movements were very feminine. The sway of her hips wasn't overt, but worth a look.

He dedicated the next few moments to admiration. His body was appreciative and nagging him to take it further.

While she was looking through the catalog, Tish got up, scraping her chair back.

"I'll join her for solidarity. I can move and pretend."

As soon as Tish joined her up on stage, Rissa smiled. It reached her eyes, lighting up her face.

There was a flare of response in his body and he tamped it down.

Stepping to the microphone, she seemed a bit nervous, her voice shaky for the first few lines but then it smoothed out. Her voice was silky but had depth, with a wide range, hitting the higher notes with ease. The audience was having some fun, singing along to the Taylor Swift classic. Upbeat, about sparks flying, something reckless that should send her running and being on guard.

Her eyes met his more than a few times.

There was heat there, something he couldn't ignore.

Was she flirting?

He pushed the question away. He needed to guard against what he was feeling. He'd already committed himself to see if something clicked with Paige, and he didn't need anything to cloud his judgment. She was more in line with what he was looking for, a woman who was intelligent, aloof, independent. Rissa was none of those things.

His mind kept repeating the phrase, but his body seemed incapable of grasping that fact whenever Rissa's eyes landed on him. Her eyes were filled with a curious kind of longing, and there was a twinge of disappointment he wouldn't be able to satisfy it.

Enthusiastic applause filled the air when Rissa finished the song. The timbre of her voice, the way she moved, and the infectious smile were like a solar flare, a combination of energy that suddenly flashed in blinding light.

As Tish dragged her off the stage, the crowd called for more.

He couldn't blame them.

As she picked up her purse, Tish looked at John and said, "Okay. The clock is near the stroke of Rosie. We'd better get going."

Looking at Rissa, she asked, "Do you want to stay or come with us?"

He caught her peeking over at him, as if trying to figure out whether she should go.

It caught him completely off guard when she said, "I guess I can stay a bit longer."

"You okay with that?"

Johnny had a hopeful look on his face.

Taking a swig of his beer, he nodded his head, not knowing how he felt about Rissa's decision.

As the couple was threading their way through the crowd toward the exit, the DJ came over to the table and asked, "Could you please do another? There's a woman who is up for the sixth song and she gets worse each time."

Licking her lips, Rissa said, "No, thanks."

Leaning in, Luca encouraged, "Go ahead. Give the audience a break."

He personally didn't want to suffer through another off-key rendition of anything.

When she pushed her chair back and stood, he thought maybe it was a pesky spark that shot between them that had made the decision for her.

He watched as she strode up to the microphone, her jeans defining her ass, the racerback showcasing her muscular arms and shoulders. He anticipated another song that would showcase her range, one that could rival the most talented.

The song she chose was a Disney classic. It played on the radio ad nauseum, which is why he listened to his iPod more often than not. Her eyes were closed, her facial expression matching the aching loneliness of the words and melody. So consumed by the music she didn't seem conscious that the club had grown still, everyone as intensely involved in the performance as she was. And only when she sang the last note, her eyes now wide in understanding, did she realize what she had just done: put her heart out there for all to see.

Handing over the mic to the DJ, she raced out through the front exit, her face flushed, her movements shaky.

Luca threw some money on the table, grabbed her purse and went chasing after her, his senses reeling from the incredible expressiveness and Rissa's mezzo-soprano voice. She had given Menzel a run for her money.

He found her leaning against the outer wall, her head in her hands.

Stopping abruptly in front of her, not knowing what to say or do, he lifted her chin and gazed into her eyes.

"That was some song."

Pulling her face out of his hand, she growled, "Go away."

He knew if there was anyone she didn't want to see how vulnerable she was right now, it was him.

"Look, I know I'm not the one you want out here but I'm the one you've got. Talk to me."

When all Rissa did was dip her head again, saying nothing, Luca threaded his fingers through her hair, as if to soothe her. The jolt backed him up and he stuffed his free hand into his pocket.

More gruffly than he wanted he said, "I don't know why you're so upset. You brought the house down."

He waited patiently for a response, becoming convinced she was going to keep freezing him out. With a soft voice, she finally said, "I didn't know that was in there. And to come out in front of all those people. It's embarrassing."

"Are you kidding? You rocked it."

She hiccupped out a weak laugh.

"That was far too revealing. Everyone in that room now knows..."

"That you're taking your life back? That's not something to be ashamed of."

"But I let every drop of emotion out. You didn't find that...awkward?"

"I found it powerful. Tim reaches out like that on a good night. It's magic when you can connect with an audience like that. I don't have that kind of courage."

"You sing back-up on some songs, don't you?"

"Yeah, but that's far from being in the spotlight."

Trying to laugh it off, she admitted, "I've been told it's ego-tripping."

"By whom?" He rethought the question. "Obviously, by someone who can't sing."

She dipped her head, not able to look him in the eye.

"Jude stopped talking to me for a week once for doing that."

"What?"

His voice registered not only surprise but something that sounded like hostility. She was caught in the burning intensity of his amber eyes and he was drawing her in. It provoked her to tell him a secret, one packed away with all her other ones.

"We went to a club with his friends one night. Everyone got up at some point, except me. I was afraid I'd get carried away but they insisted. I made the mistake of belting one out. It didn't sit well with him. He told me I made a fool of myself and humiliated him in the process."

"And after a week?"

"He called, told me his friends had been impressed but he didn't like my being such a show boater. I stopped singing, in the car, around the house, in the shower."

"Stopped singing, stopped painting...what else did he get you to stop doing?"

"Breathing, I guess. I was trying so hard to please, I...Why am I telling you all of this?"

Gathering his courage, he touched her hair again, tucking some loose strands behind her ear. "I don't know why. It doesn't sound like he appreciated you. At all."

The velvety softness of her ear sent out a warning, one his mind latched on as his fingers continued the caress.

Then her eyes met his and he knew instantly what the expression "time stood still" meant.

She broke contact first, cast her eyes down. It was when she noticed he was holding her bag.

She reached out for it and slung it over her shoulder. "Let's get out of here."

As they started walking down the street, she kept some distance between them and he didn't blame her.

This was dangerous.

With a mere brush of his fingers against her skin, a spark had ignited that didn't seem to want to end. And it was spurting whenever she was around lately. And he didn't understand it. She wasn't who he wanted. The woman calling to him was from his past, his first serious love, and he wanted to see where that went. But he couldn't deny he wanted something from Rissa that had nothing to do with any of that.

⌒

Standing by the window, looking out into the night, Luca felt...good. He'd been part of a couples' night, even though he hadn't been part of a couple. Tish and Annie didn't usually want him around if he was with one of the nameless women he picked up so it was a rare event to be included.

And Rissa's song had boggled his mind.

But before he could process his emotions that had come with it, he heard a light rap at the door.

Without asking who it was, he opened the door to find Johnny standing there.

"Hi. What's up?"

"Can I come in?"

"Yeah, sure, sorry."

"Are you alone?"

Johnny couldn't know just how alone he felt sometimes.

"No women tonight."

Crossing the threshold, Johnny scanned the room and joked, "I must have driven you crazy with the messes I made."

Luca smiled, admitting, "A bit."

Johnny became serious and he waited to hear what he'd come to say.

"What happened after we left?"

"What do you mean?"

"Rissa came back and all but ran into her room and closed the door. I was just wondering if something happened that I should know about?"

"You think I..."

"No, of course not. I trusted you with her for a reason. But something must have happened. Usually she sits with us before turning in."

Johnny must have noticed the hesitation on his face, and added, "This is between you and me. Whatever you tell me will stay with me. I just need to know if something upset her."

Not comfortable sharing something that had affected Rissa the way it had, he knew that Johnny would do what he'd promised and keep it between them.

"The DJ asked her to sing another song. There was a woman who couldn't hit the right note if she tried, wanting another turn. I think she agreed, more to get away from me than anything."

Johnny waited for Luca to continue.

"And then?"

"It was as if it was just her and the song. I've never heard anything so powerful. When she realized what she'd done, she raced out of the place. I followed her to make sure she was all right."

"And she wasn't."

It wasn't a question.

"No. She was totally embarrassed, looked like she was going to cry over it."

"She's such an idiot. If she hadn't been so young when we started, I would have dragged her kicking and screaming into the band with us."

"She certainly has some voice."

"I'm convinced Jude has something to do with the way she reacted."

"He does."

Johnny wore a look of incredulity.

"She told you that?"

"Yeah. I think part of her problem right now is that she told me things she doesn't want me to know."

"My mother sensed that's what happened. It was one of a few strange changes that came over Rissa during their engagement. She stopped singing, stopped painting, started reading the *Wall Street Journal* and the *Times*, tried to discuss the stock market with Paul. Very out of character for her."

"You think Jude discouraged her from...being her?"

Luca couldn't imagine anyone wanting to do that. She might not be his ideal woman but she had a lot to offer. Her heart had a child-like quality to it that was appealing. She knew how to play when she let her guard down, and she brought others with her.

"I tried to get her to go back to art school after he-who-shall-not-be-named cancelled the wedding, but she said she thought it would be a waste of time. If you think she can sing, you should see some of her paintings."

"I've seen her sketches. She's definitely got talent."

Luca looked up in surprise as soon as he processed that information, and asked, "She went to art school?"

She had told him she'd only taken a few courses to get her certification in early childhood.

"For a year. Someplace in Beverly. She dropped out, telling the folks she could never earn a living from it. I could never see her as an art curator or working in a museum. She has too much energy, so I knew she wouldn't use her education for that. We all let it go. But my mother said that she was a great teacher. Ma volunteered to read to the kids periodically and said the classroom screamed Rissa's talent in every corner. She had them singing songs, and the art projects they'd complete were displayed on every bulletin board. My mother thought she might have found her calling."

Luca had amended his opinion on her nurturing skills.

"She seems to be good with kids if Rosie's any indication."

Johnny laughed. "I can't believe how patient she is with her. She sings to her all the time, dances her around the room, gets down on her level and makes her smile. She'll make one hell of a mom."

"I can see that."

Without anything left to say, they let silence fill the space.

"Look, it's late. I'll let you get to bed. But thanks for being there for her. I appreciate it."

"I think she would have preferred to have anyone other than me. I'm not so sure I made it better."

"I can guarantee you didn't make her feel as if she did something wrong. Am I right?"

"She didn't do anything wrong. Why would I have made her feel as if she had?"

"You wouldn't because you're not an asshole."

Luca hoped Rissa's ex died a slow and painful death.

CHAPTER TWELVE

After crawling into bed, curling into a ball, she hugged Luca's words to her like a teddy bear. She might not be a kid now, but she needed his reassurances. She had once felt powerful, able to do anything. Then...an infectious need to please.

It had been all about her once- her athletic competitions, her wins, her friends, taking advantage of her brother's good nature, making demands on her parents about where she wanted to go, what she wanted to do.

Then on an ordinary day, she was pulled out of class, escorted to the principal's office, where she was told about her father's murder, the shock syphoning the blood from her body.

Her life had never been the same. In a heartbeat, she learned about grief and abandonment.

The slow-growing virus took hold when her mother began to work so many hours that she was never home, no longer attending soccer matches, softball games, track meets. It had always been her claim to fame, the one thing that drew praise and had given her a sense of accomplishment. When her cheering squad was no longer available, when sole support of the large family fell on Celia's shoulders, Rissa had shifted from grieving over her father's death to being angry about it.

She'd carried that anger around in her backpack for months, becoming the mean girl who bullied and taunted.

When her brother's intervention had shamed her into backing off, she hadn't known how to release the pain so she'd bottled up the hurt, never let anyone know about it. It was another secret in a long line of them.

When Johnny had left, the fragile hold she had on her emotions broke. The anger distilled into outright fear. But she'd fooled them all, appearing confident outwardly, while inwardly she was freaking out, unable to deal with the dramatic changes taking place in her life.

When she'd met Jude, at an inter-league softball game, she was primed for a relationship, hoping it would take away some of the desolation. Her anxiety and insecurities about being alone had prevented her from standing up to him, so she'd accepted his coldness, his indifference, the few crumbs of kindness he threw her way.

Her willingness to sacrifice herself like that was her undoing. Her flaws were of her own making.

Luca's voice came to her, telling her how good her sketches were, how she'd killed the song.

She laughed but it merged into a sob.

There was a man who would leave her in the dust.

Not that it mattered; she wouldn't dare tempt that fate.

She shivered at the thought of tasting him.

The gentle caress of his fingers against her ear had touched something inside of her, that she'd never felt before.

It was a feeling she wished she could explore, experiment with.

But science had never been her thing and she knew she'd fail as miserably as she had in chemistry lab class. No matter how carefully she followed the procedure, she would never get the suggested results.

This would be no different.

The embarrassment hadn't faded the next morning, so she hung back wanting to be the last one on the bus. Hoping to outwait everyone, she stalled until Johnny's text sent her racing down and onto the vehicle that would take them to Albany.

"What the hell took you so long? We're the ones with all the crap to pack up."

"Sorry. I got up late."

She noticed Johnny's suspicious look but ignored it, claiming her seat and swiveling to take in the parking lot.

Then she heard booted feet charging up the steps, a voice that was beginning to affect her far too much, and she closed her eyes in resignation. She hadn't escaped after all.

"I got the bags from Ron. Can I ride with you guys and go through it here?"

Johnny was laughing when he asked, "What? You don't want to make a mess in your space?"

The dry wit was evident when he replied, "Yeah, that's it, Scalera. I like pristine. That's why I'm here."

Rissa took in the bus with his eyes and understood what he meant.

It wasn't exactly neat.

In fact, the garbage bags didn't seem out of place.

Luca parceled them out, each one labeled, then shifted some of Rosie's things off one of the bunks and sat down.

She was watching, mystified but refused to open her mouth.

What was in them?

Tish's voice was filled with surprised delight.

"It's almost full."

"You up for going through it?"

"Why not. It's as good a time as any."

Luca had already opened the twist tie and was reaching in.

She was trying to be as unobtrusive as possible as she watched him extricate his hand, holding on to a card as he read it.

Finally, her curiosity getting the better of her, she asked, "What is it?"

Tish responded. "Stuff from the fans. Notes, gifts...personal effects. Can I borrow one of your pencils? Not a good one, one I can throw away after."

Leaning over, Rissa gave her a Ticonderoga, which Tish used to pull out a pair of men's briefs.

There was a look of distaste on her face.

"Why do they do this?"

Johnny quickly took the offending article of clothing and dumped it in one of the bags used for Rosie's soiled diapers.

"That's not for you, babe."

What was Johnny saying?

"They're not for her?"

"We're going to say they're for me. I don't want to think about a man giving my wife his underwear."

"Oh, so are the bras mine?"

"No. We're going to throw them away and get to the notes and the gifts."

Johnny finally lifted the bag up and dumped the contents onto another one of the unclaimed bunks that held Rosie's playthings.

The pile covered the whole surface. Rissa couldn't imagine the time it would take to go through everything.

"Do you read all of them?"

"We try."

"There has to be hundreds."

Johnny was pointing to where Luca sat.

"His bag is usually the biggest."

Luca was being much neater about it, taking out one thing at a time so she couldn't tell whether Johnny was correct or not. But she had to assume....

She watched as Tish and Johnny attacked the envelopes, the single scraps of paper, the pictures and drawings, overwhelmed by her brother's popularity.

She had seen the crowds, had heard the screams, but she still hadn't grasped the reality of who he was. Or rather, who he'd become.

She was proud of his success, loved that he was being rewarded for all the hard work he'd put into the band.

And what Tish had, that had drawn him in and away from the adulation.

Sweet smile?

Talent?

Innocence?

Witchy eyes?

If she was honest with herself, and she was going to make the effort to be from this day forward, she didn't have any of that to offer a man.

Her smile certainly wasn't sweet. It was more tomboy than femme fatale and the only compliment she'd gotten was that her smile was infectious.

Her real smiles came when she'd pitched a good game, or won a track meet, or brought the kids she taught to an aha moment.

It wasn't something that would catch a man's attention.

She didn't have those kinds of wiles, but that was on her. She'd never wanted to hone them.

Her talent lay in squiggly lines and dramatic effects. She was one hell of a softball player but that wasn't exactly the kind of skill that could win a man's heart.

And she couldn't claim to be innocent.

She swore like a trooper, got in your face if you were trying to steal her soccer ball, would hurtle over you if you slipped on the track, her competitive streak strong. Most men didn't like it. Didn't like it when she won.

But she couldn't seem to back down. Once she was in a competition, she went all out.

As she had proven so well with Luca while they were cycling.

She'd never learned the art of flirting, was more comfortable in a pair of leggings than dress pants or a skirt, didn't wear much make-up, didn't ooze sex appeal.

What would it take for a man to notice her? Want to stay?

She had no idea, but if she found the right one, all those things would work for her. She was taking herself off the shelf and letting what was inside spill out. If it made a mess, she really didn't care.

She was going to learn to live by herself, if she could ever get out of her parents' home, rebuild her friendships, and find a way to be happy on her own.

No more adaptations.

No more becoming what someone else wanted.

It didn't do any good anyway.

Glancing up to see Luca seriously reading every note he took out of the bag, she pulled out her pad and charcoal.

Then he was smiling, and her hand scribbled across the page, needing to record it for history.

He looked up just as she did, wanting to get the curve of his lips right, not that she couldn't do it blindfold by now.

"What are you doing?"

Without lifting her hand from the page, her fingers stayed busy, capturing the moment.

"What does it look like I'm doing?"

"You're making me self-conscious."

Too engrossed in what she was doing, she ignored him.

Johnny joked, "We're all captive subjects on the bus."

"More like objects."

Her hand stilled and she scrutinized him.

Did it really bother him? She'd already drawn him hundreds of times. It was apparent he hadn't noticed.

Not letting that thought bother her, she felt the beginnings of a smile tip the corners of her mouth.

"If you want me to stop, you'll have to let me see some of the stuff in the bag."

His eyes narrowed as if he didn't trust her with what was in there.

She couldn't really blame him.

"I won't make fun. Honest. I'm curious is all."

"Fine. I get to choose what you see, though."

She heaved herself up from her seat and sat next to him as he handed her one of the note cards.

His steady gaze bored into her when she took it from his fingers. The electric shock didn't surprise her; it was becoming the norm.

What wasn't was the way his eyes darkened in anticipation.

She took the card with trembling fingers, her eyes falling deeper into his.

"Is this a good example of what you get?"

"I don't think we want to go there. Some things are best left to the imagination."

She got the gist.

Women. Pictures. Probably naked. Beautiful. Lusty.

She didn't really want to see them anyway.

She opened the card and began to read.

Hey Reject:

You don't know me, but I just wanted to say thank you. You've inspired me more than anyone else in my life to chase my dreams. Because of you, I picked up the bass and played, hoping one day to be as good as you. You taught me with enough dedication and hard work, that you can do anything you put your mind to. Anybody who plays an instrument has an idol and you are mine. When I can't learn a fancy new trick or a song, I just say to myself, "Well, if he can do it, so can I." Thank you for inspiring me to pick up the guitar, and to follow my dreams. Once I've shown people to chase their dreams, I'll know who to give credit to. Once I'm on stage, doing what I love, know it's because of you. Thank you and

Rock on!
Jakob

Rissa handed it back, her eyes meeting his.

"That's a great letter. How does it make you feel?"

"Humble."

When he didn't say anything else, she asked, "Did anybody do that for you?"

"Influence my playing? I guess. All the great ones I listened to while trying to master the bass played in bands of the sixties, seventies and eighties. Bands like Cream, The Who, Paul McCartney. I downloaded all their music and would listen, play, listen, play."

"What drove you to pick up that particular instrument?"

"I didn't think of myself as musically gifted and it only had four strings. I figured it'd be the easiest one to learn. It wasn't. Not if you want to do it well."

"You were wrong twice, then."

"How so?"

"You are musically gifted. You'd have to be to get fan letters like that one."

He didn't respond in words, but he placed the note in a separate pile as if it would find a home somewhere other than back in the bag.

"Can I see another? I'm glad I read that one, but it was on the tame side."

"That's all you get."

Her hands found their way to his shoulder and she pulled him close so she could whisper in his ear.

"One love letter. Just one or I'll go back and start sketching you again."

His muscles bunched as if tensed, his eyes finding hers, filling her with a need that had nothing to do with the love letter.

She pulled back.

What the hell was she doing?

It had started out as simple inquisitiveness but it had turned dangerous. Although from his reaction to her touch, he didn't seem to feel the same way. He'd tensed as if she were an unwanted distraction.

She scampered back to her seat, grabbed a bag of trail mix, and started munching. Anything to keep the nervous energy at bay.

When a pang of longing shot through her, she swiveled to watch the scenery, her eyes not really seeing anything but the illusion of heat in his.

He felt Rissa crawl off the bunk, saw her head to a chair some distance away and he had a feeling she'd misinterpreted his reaction to her touch.

When her fingers made contact with his shoulder, he'd almost come out of his skin. Heat had rushed through him, and it was like nothing he'd ever felt before. A deep sexual hunger burned in his gut, a hunger that could never be satisfied.

He was relieved when she moved away, although he missed the subtle fragrance that he'd come to think of as hers. It wasn't perfume or lotion. It was part woman and something indefinable.

She usually smelled of fresh air, or sweat or charcoal. Maybe it was the mixture of all three that was her personal scent.

Strangely, it was the sweetest smell in the world.

He had no business feeling like this.

Rissa was not the woman of his dreams.

He needed someone who saw the world like he did, who could dissect a scientific thought clean through to the core, who was logical, professional. He needed someone with enough in common to cement the relationship.

So why was his body reacting in such strange ways?

It was insane.

He stuck his hand back in the bag, his eagerness in reading his fan mail fading with each glance he shot her way.

He managed to wade through it for the remaining hour they were on the road, but as soon as they arrived, he collected his correspondence and slipped off the bus.

Her heart skipped a beat when she heard his footsteps bounding down the stairs, as if he couldn't get away fast enough.

The fireballs that shot through her when Luca merely looked at her had been unnerving. After she moved away, she continued to watch him go through the bag of fan mail although she kept her gaze discreet. He was pulling her in and she was becoming more intrigued than she wanted to be. He made her feel something she didn't want to feel and she wanted to be as far away from that as possible.

She'd been excited about their arrival in Albany. Now it seemed even more imperative to seek out the solitude she craved.

After dropping her overnight bag in her room, she scooted down to the coffee shop, grabbed a coffee and muffin to go. She was looking forward to spending hours in the one place that drew her. A cab was sitting outside, Luca standing by the passenger door. Shifting her backpack over her shoulder, she nodded to him, telling him without words she'd wait for the next one.

"I think the two of us will fit. He can drop you wherever you're going, then it'll be my turn."

This was not what she wanted. Her main purpose for going off was to get away from him.

But here he stood, looking mouth-wateringly good.

The urge to get under his skin was still strong but it had altered in color and texture. She no longer saw red or felt hostile. Now she was looking through a lens that offered softer shades, a more complex composition.

He shifted from one foot to the other, waiting for her decision.

Not wanting to hold them up any longer, she took small steps, trying to sidestep him, avoiding the temptation to get too close.

As soon as her bum hit the leather, she slid as far over to the other side as she could. He folded his body in behind her, asking, "Where to?"

His expression was serious, as if he wanted to stick to the data.

She found it hard to think with his eyes on her.

"Museum."

The cab driver asked for clarification. There were several in the environs.

"History and Art, please."

Luca's long fingers fiddled a strand of hair behind his ear. There was a small diamond stud glistening, which she hadn't noticed before. She could have laughed. With that one adornment, he wore more jewelry than she did.

"Museum. Makes sense. What's special about this one?"

As their gazes locked there was a sizzle that had nothing to do with the topic and everything to do with the man.

Her throat was parched as if all moisture was pooling into one place. The words were stuck and she had to force them out.

"The Hudson River School collection sounds like an interesting one. The art follows the history of the area."

"Art mixed with some history."

"Yeah, I guess that's why they call it a history and art museum."

Her smile was tentative.

"I looked it up on-line and it seems they have work by a sculptor from Albany, an exhibit called Wampum World and on the Erie Canal."

When the cab pulled up to the curb, she breathed a sigh of relief. The remaining silence had been deafening.

The driver pointed to the pay slot, where she pushed the ten-dollar bill. The museum was a short distance from the hotel, and even though she was sharing the fare, she wanted to make sure she left enough.

She hopped out, came around the side of the cab, and stood staring at the building. It wasn't what she'd expected. It looked like it belonged on a college campus. Two brick buildings were connected by a modern glass structure made of steel and concrete which added a futuristic rendition to the original Beaux-Art architecture. The Museum of Fine Arts in Boston was more impressive, with a granite façade, the grand rotunda adorned with paintings by the master John Singer Sargent. It had several wings that held its comprehensive collection. She'd been spoiled. It was the fourth largest museum in the world, and she'd spent as much time there as she could.

"Nothing like Boston's MFA."

Her gaze jerked to the left.

Luca was standing there, his hands in his pockets, studying her.

Her words sputtered out.

"This isn't where you were going, is it?"

His eyes met hers before moving back to the edifice.

"No. I think it might be more interesting than what I had originally intended. Do you mind?"

"Ah, I wasn't just going to look around, I was going to work while I was here."

"That's okay. I can watch you here as well as anywhere else."

They were moving as one up the steps, her legs not as steady as she would have liked.

After entering the large main foyer, he proceeded to the counter and paid for the tickets before she could argue, then waited for her to choose a gallery. After taking a few minutes to decide whether to talk him out of this, she finally headed down one of the exhibit halls.

"Can you give me a running commentary? I know next to zilch about art."

A whisper of unease teased her senses. He was standing close, his scent a familiar one, his eyes gleaming with curiosity, the light casting a shadow of uncertainty over the interaction.

She cleared her throat and offered, "The works here focus on the history, art, and culture of Albany and the Upper Hudson region. This is one of the oldest museums in the country."

His hands were behind his back as he followed her down the aisle, his head tilted back as he examined each painting they passed.

"What do you see, feel when you walk into a museum?"

She let her eyes explore the marble statues that adorned the vestibule, each work of art an expression of someone's soul.

"Like a priest walking into a cathedral."

She walked up the curving staircase, her hand light on the iron rail. When she reached the upper gallery, she breathed it in. The majesty always astounded her, the detail of the work enthralled, and the beauty amazed. She always felt small in the stillness.

CHAPTER THIRTEEN

He was captivated by the look on her face.

Her eyes were shining, the love for what surrounded her reflected in them.

"That's how I feel when I look through a telescope. The grandeur of the heavens, the planets pinpricks in the cosmos, the stars bursting into light, the colors and musical harmony of the whole remind me true beauty exists. It helped when my world was in chaos."

His eyes flashed up.

Why had he said that?

She seemed to have a way of pulling things out of him. He had to stop giving them over without thought. He'd been on his way to the state science museum when he bumped into her and he didn't know why he'd changed course.

She went back to her examination of the exhibit, scrutinizing the swirls of paint on the canvas.

He was studying her more than the paintings, unable to read what she was thinking. Her profile had lost the tip of the smile and her mouth was tilting downward.

She turned to look him in the eye. "I lied to you."

His eyes searched her face, the expression one of guilt by deception.

"About what?"

"I went to art school. For a year."

"Why did you feel the need to lie?"

"I didn't finish. I quit. I already felt your disapproval about the teacher thing."

He stood gaping. He longed to pull her close and make it right. It was a powerful urge that he didn't give in to. Instead, he reached out his hand to touch her cheek. It felt hot, as if the admission had colored her opinion of herself.

"I quit school, too. It would be hypocritical of me to put you down for it."

She stepped back, began to amble toward the end of the gallery, leaving his fingers hanging in mid-air.

"I don't seem to finish anything I start."

When he caught up with her, he contradicted her words.

"You've finished lots of sketches. I've seen them."

"That's easy for me. My discipline is on the lower end of the scale. I don't push for more."

"Maybe you've found the spot where your soul rests lightly. You don't need to push for more."

She flushed but remained silent.

"Too metaphysical for you?"

"I don't know what that is."

"Metaphysics examines the fundamental nature of the world and our place in it. Through your sketching, you might have found yours."

She shifted her backpack off her shoulder and hung on to it by the strap.

"Where is yours?"

Good question. Today he felt it might be right around the corner.

"I'm almost there. Just a bit more wiggle room to get comfortable."

Her chocolate eyes seemed to melt into him and he felt a smile tilt his lips up.

"Didn't you say you wanted to work? Don't let me keep you. I'll wander around and meet you back here in say, an hour?"

"Are you sure? I can always come back next time."

His fingers took her chin and held it.

"You don't have to try to please me. You want to sing, you sing; you want to sketch, you sketch. If I get bored, I'll come back and watch you."

That never got boring.

"If you're sure."

"That's not what you should be asking."

"What should I be asking?"

"Where's the best light? Which painting do I want to work on? How much time do I have left?"

Her eyes closed at the way he was making her feel.

"All good questions."

"Then answer them and I'll see you later."

She followed him with her eyes until he went around a corner and disappeared. Then she wandered.

The art hanging in the hushed halls was significant, which pleasantly surprised her. An entire exhibit of her favorite style was being displayed in one of the galleries and she sat on many different benches scattered throughout the space to take in each piece. While attending art school, the courses covering Impressionistic art were her favorite. Learning that the masters were revolutionaries of their time only added to their appeal. Painters like Monet, Degas, and Pissarro went against the established form of fine finish and detail and depicted in its stead the momentary sensory effect of a scene. They took their brushes and canvases outside, to capture their impressions of life on the streets, or by the seaside, using an interplay of color and light, with short brushstrokes that barely conveyed form. In Rissa's opinion, academic form was one dimensional, abstract form too busy and chaotic. It was the vivacity of color and the play between light and shadow that impressed her.

Her parents had one of her favorite Monet prints framed in faux gilt, and it had been her only real possession at Jude's. She'd carefully packed it up before leaving but hoped that it would one day grace the wall on another home. Hers.

Envisioning a wall of her favorites, she planned on having her own version of the Louvre right where she lived.

She pulled out her sketch pad in front of one of Lilla Cabot Perry's masterpieces and began to duplicate the form and substance expressed on the canvas. It was the perfect style to study as a sketcher because of the unfinished appearance and the blunt strokes.

Her fingers flew furiously over the page, faithfully duplicating dimension and proportion on the paper, promising she would add watercolors to enhance the replication when she returned to Boston.

"You are very good."

She looked up from her work and then glanced back down, wondering what he was seeing.

"Thank you."

The man sat down next to her, studying her lines in more detail. Rissa would have to put him in his early fifties, his hair just beginning to grey at the temples, his eyes kind, his fingers tapered.

His voice was a deep alto.

"Do you do this for a living?"

Rissa laughed at the thought of that. "No. I kind of do it to keep my fingers busy."

"The construction of elements is well done and perfectly proportioned on your paper. You have a very good eye."

He seemed to know what he was talking about and that was confirmed when he told her, "I teach drawing at Oswego. I would love to have you as a student."

She could feel the blush as her cheeks heated.

Was this a come-on or for real?

She hoped for the latter. He was a bit too old for her taste but very gracious.

"I attended a school in Massachusetts for a year. I enjoyed it but never thought I'd use what I learned in the real world."

"So you decided to let your talent go to waste?"

"I don't think I'm wasting it. I use it all the time."

At least she was beginning to, again.

"But does the world get to share it?"

"The people in my world do. My mother has some of my paintings hanging on the walls at home."

"It's becoming more commercial these days. You might want to rethink that. What medium do you use?"

"Watercolors. They seem to go better with my style."

"I can imagine they would."

He pulled a business card out of his wallet and handed it to her.

He was for real.

"Please, if you ever change your mind, call me. I'd help you go through the application process; help you procure a scholarship if you need one. You have promise."

Glancing down, the gold of his name gleaned up at her.

"Thanks, Dr. Aalmers. I appreciate it-and your appreciation."

"No. Thank you. I enjoyed watching you work."

She watched him walk away, but not before he stopped to admire a painting by John Leslie. He gave her a backward glance and a brief smile before moving on.

Staring at the card in her hand, she felt a hint of pride surface. After spending so many years with someone who belittled her art, it felt good to have a second person offer a compliment, an accomplished one at that. It seemed she was getting praise from unexpected sources and when she looked back down at her still life, she smiled.

"See? I'm not the only one who thinks you've found your calling."

Luca had returned and it appeared he'd heard the whole conversation. Ignoring his input, she packed up her things.

"It's time to go."

Slowly, she stood, glancing around her one last time before her companion led her to the exit and they stepped out into the late-afternoon sunshine.

"You want to take a cab back or walk? It's not that far."

"Let's walk."

She slung her backpack over her shoulder, and they strolled along the sidewalk.

"What did I pull you away from today?"

"The science museum."

"I'm sorry."

"For what? I think it's a good idea to expose yourself to new things."

"You're right, it is. I'm finally getting out of my own way. It feels good."

"I think we should celebrate. You up for an ice cream cone?"

"My taste buds just did a happy dance."

"There's a shop up the street. We can eat it on the way back."

⤳

"Tutti-frutti?"

He was shaking his head as he took in the swirls of ice cream, the chunks of fruit.

She licked her lips.

"Mm-hm. Bananas, cherries, pineapple, oranges. Lots of colors, lots of taste."

He was winding his tongue around the vanilla in his cone to catch the drips before it melted in the warmth of the day.

"Yours is kind of boring."

"That must be why it's the best seller."

"It just goes to show that there are too many boring people in the world."

"And I'm one of them?"

She gave him a piercing look, as if studying him, trying to decide.

"No. You are definitely not boring. Just in the ice cream department."

"You're sure? I think I remember you calling me boorish once."

The expression on her face was grief stricken and then her eyes fluttered closed.

"Yeah, sorry about that. To this day, my mean streak comes out every now and again. That was uncalled for."

"Why?"

"Was it uncalled for?"

"Why the mean girl?"

She paused, as if not wanting to hand him some truth.

"It's when I'm scared, or angry about something. I pay it forward, just not in a good way."

"Why were you angry that night?"

"Jude was supposed to attend the concert with me. He cancelled last minute. I should have expected it. He didn't like socializing with my family."

She gave him a half-smile.

"He thought we were boorish."

He popped the last of the cone in his mouth and wiped it with a napkin.

"Your family's great."

"We're your typical Italian family. Loud, boisterous, loving. He comes from a place where you keep things tucked inside. Night and day."

She was inspecting her hand that was saturated with multi-colored glop, so he snagged a clean napkin from his front jeans pocket and handed it over.

"Thanks."

She began to wipe the stream of melted cream off, finishing off the cone with a pop to her mouth.

He watched with humor. Until her tongue gained traction, licking off what the napkin missed.

A shot of adrenaline hit, and he whisked his eyes onto the street scene. He'd been indifferent to the sights and sounds, the noise and street traffic, so caught up in the way she looked, acted. She had the heart of a child. Open, curious, playful.

His eyes sought her out again.

"Don't take this wrong, but I still don't understand why you stayed as long as you did. He had so many problems."

She gave him an impish grin as she balled up the napkin and dropped it into one of the trash receptacles that lined the street.

"I was controllable. That suited for years, then it didn't. From what I've heard, he's going out with a friend's wife, one whom I think he's been seeing for some time. She doesn't take shit from anyone. He seems to respect her. Go figure."

"Go figure."

His thoughts streamed back to his last days with Paige, when he'd become a liability. She had wanted studious, complex, and then she didn't. She began to hunger for the forbidden: motorcycle rides, smoking weed, dancing at a frat party until the wee hours of the morning.

He had no longer suited her.

What made her think he would now?

Did she think that he'd changed?

His persona out in the world today was much different from who he was back then.

Today he appeared outgoing, popular, with a reputation for being a ladies' man.

Hidden beneath the façade was the same vulnerable nerd he'd always been.

Something, it seemed, he'd have to keep buried if he wanted her back.

⌒

When they returned to the hotel, Luca dropped down on the sofa in the lobby, not wanting to go back to his empty room yet. Rissa gave him a small wave as she entered the elevator, her backpack slung over her shoulder. She didn't seem to go anywhere without it. Her supplies were always at the ready and he saw her take them out whenever the setting pulled at her. He'd never thought of sketching as an art, but to watch her fingers move over the canvas, or the notebook, was to watch a master at work. She created expressive drawings that were spontaneous scribbles, her hand moving rapidly across the page, the result an artistic adventure where daily life was expressed for appreciative eyes.

Her tools were impressive as well.

She not only used pencils and charcoal, but fountain pens, with nibs and liquid ink. Thinking that kind of instrument had lost its importance with the introduction of the ballpoint pen, he'd watch in fascination as she wielded it. She communicated ideas, captured moments, dipping the quill, barely skimming the surface with ink, in a variety of colors and textures. Her mind was always at play, in sync with her fingers, speaking a language all her own.

He wasn't sure why he'd hopped out of the cab and run after her. Curiosity about her world might have prompted the diversion. He didn't know much about art; only what Val and his mother had introduced him to. He had flown them to Florence to attend one of Tish's performances and they had spent three weeks in other parts of the country. It had been an insightful trip. The old Renaissance city had been magnificent, and it had filled him with a true appreciation for paintings of any era. When the cab had stopped in front of the museum, he'd had an urge to see her world and how she fit in it.

Unsure about what kind of reception he'd get, he was pleasantly surprised when she acquiesced.

Now that the snarkiness was gone, she was easy to be with. He'd spent more time with her than anyone else since college.

Sadness coursed through him because he couldn't keep hanging out with her.

He had to put it behind him.

He had a future to look to.

Paige.

She was living the life they'd talked about. They had things in common.

Or did they?

He wasn't looking at the stars for a living, wasn't sure he'd fit academia any more than he'd fit high school. He loved what he did and if he had the ability to go back and change things, he wasn't sure he'd pick differently.

Agitation churned at the thought of her.

She'd been everything to him once, the only foray into a committed relationship. The only woman he'd lived with. When it was over between them, he hadn't been tempted to replicate it.

It's why he stuck to one-nighters. He refused to be seduced into dropping his guard, making another mistake.

He clenched his teeth. His will had been undermined the moment she reached out.

After dragging himself up, he headed to his room to change.

He was supposed to meet the guys back down here for the trip to the Palace, the place they were playing tonight, and he was running late.

Maybe he'd rescind his furlough. He'd get back in the game, get back in the sack. Cross Paige off his to-do list. It was the only way he knew to stay safe, keep from getting too close to a fire that could burn him alive.

⌒

Just as she was closing the door to her room, Thunder's "Gonna Get Me Some Lovin" signaled a call, so Rissa looked at the phone in her hand to check the number before answering it.

Dropping down into the swivel chair at the desk, she clicked on.

"Hi Ma."

"I waited a few days before checking in. How's it going?"

"Seeing that you've already talked to both Johnny and Tish, you know how it's going."

"I want to hear it from the horse's mouth."

"So now I'm a horse? What happened to the gazelle?"

"Four legs, they both run, same thing."

Rissa laughed into the phone.

"Things are good. I've been sketching nonstop and I'm having a very interesting time."

"I'm glad to hear that. What are you drawing?"

"Street scenes, the band, yesterday some buildings, today some paintings at an art museum. I've been not only using pencil and charcoal, but I've been experimenting with fountain pens. It's all coming back."

"I want you to think seriously about going back to school. Meet some new people, make friends."

She bit her tongue, almost spilling the news about Dr. Aalmers. If she knew her mother, Celia would take the ball and run with it, not even asking if it was what she wanted. She needed to make the decision herself, with no input. Then she'd know it was hers.

"I've got plenty of friends, Ma. I just didn't see them much. But I'll think about it."

"How's my grandbaby?"

"Adorable. Still getting used to the routine but she's so curious, just looks and stares. I've taken her out most days after the guys leave for the stage and we've walked around, grabbed a bite to eat, enjoyed the scenery and the weather. How's it going with you?"

"Since the article in *Northshore Magazine* came out, we are swamped. I've had to hire two new waitresses and we're thinking of renting space somewhere, bigger kitchen, more room to work."

"That's great."

"I actually liked it better before. I'm thinking about handing it over to Lana and just working the hours I want. The idea to expand was hers not mine."

"She goes after what she wants."

"She certainly does. Which is in direct opposition to Dennis, who dropped by yesterday morning before work. He's taking Delaney to New York to see a concert."

Dennis was working as a producer for a local radio station. Having graduated from Columbia College in Chicago, he came home instead of landing in a small, nondescript town to gain experience. He wasn't going anywhere fast, but his dream was to produce for record labels and he'd been talking to John about the possibility of him handling their next CD. A musician in his own right, he'd have the skills on both sides of the album to get the job done. John was mulling it over, not sure Dennis had the experience yet but not wanting to say no outright.

"I think Tony's coming to one of the Boston concerts. Is he dating anyone yet?"

"No. Still hanging out with his friends. He called Johnny to see if he could have a half a dozen tickets."

Tony had graduated from the police academy, finally admitting he wanted to carry another generation into law enforcement. Only after his therapy, finally dealing with how his father died was he able to take the step that he'd wanted to since he was a kid. Paul said he was a natural and was proud that he'd joined the royalty and was on his way to being a true blue blood.

"You sound good. I can stop worrying."

"Good. Because I'm fine."

"I'll see you in Boston."

"Yeah. It'll be an opportunity to see the band. I'm kind of excited."

"Then I'm glad I turned down your brother's suggestion I go to one of the concerts. Too loud. And from what I hear I wouldn't like seeing what those women will do to get—some attention."

Rissa laughed. She could just see her mother reprimanding anyone who came too close to John.

"You wouldn't, trust me."

"Who knew he'd be this famous? If I had, I probably would have given up my garage for him to practice."

"No, you wouldn't have. You would have told him suffering would make him stronger."

"Well, if things come too easily…"

"We don't appreciate them. I know."

"I love you."

"Love you, too. See you soon."

CHAPTER FOURTEEN

The next morning, Luca threw on some sweats and a tee. Any inclination he had to start up again in the love department had burned away quickly, so he'd hit the sack early. He'd awoken with tangled cobwebs of long and lean limbs that were off-limits and it unsettled him.

He needed a run to clear his head, but before he could think it through, he found himself knocking on Rissa's door.

It was just a few doors down from his and his feet had a mind of their own.

About to spin away, cursing himself for his lack of conscious thought, he heard her voice through the door.

"Who is it?"

He took a deep breath, giving in to the urge to be with her.

"Me. I'm going jogging. Wanna come?"

She opened the door and he looked at her lazily, knowing this wasn't his best idea. She had a pair of leggings that only reached her trim calves, and an oversized Thunder tee that looked well-worn.

His eyes took her in hungrily.

There was something about her that appealed to him. Maybe it was the openness, maybe the athleticism. Johnny was right. She was energy in motion. If it wasn't her fingers moving across a page, it was her body that seemed to keep an inner beat. It was a beat he wanted to listen to even though he knew it wasn't smart.

It probably didn't matter anyway. She'd probably tell him to get lost, but her face registered surprise, and the smile that replaced it was warm and inviting.

"Actually, yes. I'd love to. Let me throw on my sneakers and I'll be ready to go."

The hotel was central to downtown Albany, which made for a good place to run.

When they reached the front entrance, she began to stretch, and he watched her out of the corner of his eye.

She was limber, her ass round, her legs long, and he could almost picture them wrapped around him, his hands roaming the curves in a way that made him sweat, and he hadn't even gotten out in the heat yet.

His body was beginning to invest in that image in a big way, and he was glad when she snapped him out of his X-rated daydream.

"Do you run often?"

"Not really. Just when I have down-time and I'm looking for a way to expend some energy."

She laughed as if he'd just told her a joke.

"I would think this is somehow mundane for you. You expend lots of energy at night in ways that can't possibly compare."

"I've taken a sabbatical. Need to find a replacement."

"I was talking about being on stage but FYI, people are asking why."

Her features were animated, her smile open and infectious, so he told her the truth.

"I haven't hung out with the guys like this before and I'm enjoying it."

"To the exclusion of everything else?"

He shrugged and returned her smile.

"It would seem that way."

Her arms were extended as she stretched them into the air, her legs centered to balance herself.

"Just think of how many women you're disappointing."

Touching his toes, his own stretching routine in progress, he said drily, "They'll live."

He noticed her watching him as he did some crossovers, raising his blood pressure in the process. He'd better get this going or his legs would lose their ability to run.

They began at a sedate pace, so conversation was easy to maintain but he knew it was only a matter of time before she'd push him, and he was right. A couple of miles in, she pounded the pavement with fervor even though the humidity was higher than he'd like, but he kept up, his heartbeat rapid, his breathing labored. Why he hadn't brought water with him confounded him. It was usually the first thing he thought of.

Today it had been the woman beside him.

He seemed to be off his game.

They covered another couple of miles before she asked, "Do you have any money on you?"

He huffed out his answer.

"Yeah, why?"

"I'm thirsty. Can we stop for a drink?"

"Yes, please. I don't know how much farther I can go."

She slowed down, and eventually stopped in front of a pub-like building.

"No beer. Just a tall, cold lemonade."

"Sounds good."

He wiped his forehead with the edge of his tee, then opened the door for her and stepped into the cool interior, dim but welcoming.

They sat at the bar, where she ordered her lemonade. He ordered an iced tea and asked for seconds when he drank it down in one long gulp.

His elbows rested on the wooden bar, as he finally gained a semblance of normal breathing.

"Do you do everything all out?"

"Yup. Can't seem to help myself. A curse from being surrounded by brothers. I would have been left in the dust if I didn't."

"You ran like your feet were on fire."

"Sorry. It felt good."

"I can see now how you won a gold medal for running."

After taking a sip of her drink, she asked, "You never played any, right? Sports?"

His eyebrow arched up an inch.

"I was never really good at anything physical."

She skipped the joke about nerds being too top-heavy. It was one of the mean girl things she would have said once upon a time. She hoped those days were behind her.

After taking another sip of the cold drink, she admitted, "You kept up pretty well."

"Grit and determination. Nothing more. There was no way I was going to let you show me up."

His phone had pinged, letting him know he had a message. Taking it out of his pocket, he checked the screen.

Email.

He glanced up and his breath hitched when their eyes held. His pulse accelerated and for the briefest of moments, he thought she must have felt what he did.

Relief flooded through him when she asked, "You ready to head back?"

His heartbeat took its time slowing and he didn't have the energy to resume the run. "Yeah, I'm ready to walk back. Or better yet, find a cab."

"I guess I can suck it up."

"Good to know. Otherwise, I was going to have to stuff you in the cab kicking and screaming."

"I might balk just to see that."

Her laughter sounded good and he took a moment to enjoy it.

He dropped her at her room and made his way to his. After sliding the key through the pad, he entered and threw the piece of plastic on the bureau. With phone in hand, he flopped down on the bed and opened the email.

Dear Luca:

I understand your reticence at seeing me. I'm not proud of my actions back then and it seems they provoked you to quit school for good. I always assumed you'd pick your studies up at another university like Cornell. Sagan's work is such a prominent part of the curriculum and I know how much you admired him. It appears I was wrong. And I am deeply sorry for the part I played in your change of direction. My rebellion brought consequences I didn't anticipate.

My friend, the one who told me about the band, is quite impressed that I know you. When she found out we'd dated, she was nonplused. She couldn't fathom why I had let you go.

Since seeing the CD, I wonder why as well.

It was light-years away, and it's just catching up with me now.

How many times did you explain light-years, what they meant, what they measured? If I remember correctly, if Andromeda blew up today, we wouldn't know it for another seventy-five years. The information, traveling at the speed of light, would take that long to cross the interstellar distances.

Physics was never my strength but you made it understandable. The Earth held all the wonder for me, while the stars called to you.

You were the brightest among them.

If you agree to see me, I would love to come into the city for the first show. I will be coming in alone, so one ticket will suffice.

I sign off hoping...
Paige

He put the phone down.

An old frustration began to rise.

She had no idea of how the real world worked.

She'd thought he'd pick up his studies, possibly at Cornell. Did she know how expensive that school was? It was his first choice when applying for admissions senior year and he'd been accepted. But the scholarship covered only partial costs. MIT had offered a full one. That had finalized the decision. How the hell did Paige think he could have just picked up his studies at a school like that? She knew his limitations with money. She never made him feel like it made a difference, but he found out over time that she never fully understood the implications. Her true colors had come out at the end when she'd chosen security over emotion.

If she had felt any emotion. Today he wasn't sure it had been what he'd thought it was.

He could have been the vague beginnings of her rebellious phase.

Now?

She'd have to assume there'd be security with him.

Was that the attraction?

Did it matter?

She was a scientist, not a groupie. She had her own small fortune and would never be looking for his. He didn't want to end up with someone who wanted him for what he had. That meant either his bank account or his celebrity. One of the biggest draws in seeing her? Intelligent conversation. He hadn't had that in a long time. The members of the band were great guys but none of them had the cognitive skills for that kind of mental exercise.

Plumping the pillows against the headboard, he stretched out, still not sure this was smart, and began to type.

Paige,

No one knows what kinds of consequences our actions will yield. I can't deny I was pissed when it happened, but it all worked out. I took some time to regain some perspective and decided not to go back. I was lucky and found something else that I was passionate about. I've done well for myself. I'll never make it onto a who's-who's list in a scientific journal, but Thunder has hit the top of the charts with a few songs so there's a slight chance I'll make it into the Rock and Roll Hall of Fame.

Celebrity is celebrity, right?

I'm impressed with your credentials, and I've already ordered the book you wrote a few years back. It didn't surprise me it's on climate change and I'm interested to see if you are a skeptic or believer. Man-made or cyclical. I know it's more complicated than most people think. With the earth changes that have taken place over millions of years, it could just be the earth rotating her crops, so to speak. I'm hoping to read it by the time we swing into New York City just in case...

The truth is, I'm puzzled by the request. So many years have gone by without a word and I'm curious to know why the sudden interest. I'm not sure what to expect. A drink for old time's sake, to catch up? I tend to doubt you're in it for a night with a rocker. Unless of course you never outgrew your rebellious stage.

I've already talked to our manager, and he'll have the ticket ready and waiting.

Luca

He rose from the bed, pulled a water out of the mini-fridge and drank it down in one long gulp.

Still dehydrated from the run, he had sweat running in rivulets down the sides of his tee shirt. He didn't usually go all out like that, liked a more moderate pace, but whenever he was with Rissa, she insisted he step it up.

There was life there, right down to the bottom of her feet. There was also the beat of something forbidden that was unrelenting.

He stripped off his tee and shorts and headed for the shower. A cold one.

It was the only way he knew to curb the desire for a woman who just didn't suit.

~

Rissa went to her room, the tingles still shooting through her.

When they'd fallen into each other's eyes, it'd seemed like the earth stood still.

Gone were the wise-cracks and insults and in place was an overriding curiosity of who he was under all the flash.

Showered and changed after her run, she sat on her bed, laptop in front of her, and pulled up his Facebook page.

When she clicked the word *photos*, he was there, on stage, with the band, playing with others at a charity event. There were videos, posts from friends and groups that included guitar magazines praising his fretwork, *Billboard* citing his talent.

Bass Guitar Magazine stated in bold letters: Reject Caroli dishes on his band.

Another listed the top ten bass players of the age. He was listed among them, ranked number four.

She scrolled through them all, watching every video, reading every article and quite a few of the public posts his fan base published. There were a few websites that were highlighted, all scientific in nature, notably cosmology and particle physics.

He was still a nerd.

But it didn't sit uncomfortably with her.

Still not tired, she spent some time Googling the websites listed as favorites.

PNAS was the National Academy of Sciences. She reviewed the table of contents of the newest issue and considered which category he'd be drawn to. She ruled out biology, social science, chemistry and engineering which left planetary science, part of the cosmology field. When she clicked to the subject, the title alone intimidated her. With words like lability and particulate matter causing brain cramps, she closed out and proceeded down the list hoping she could navigate through one of them with some sense of understanding.

She couldn't.

Closing the laptop, she put it to the side.

Who the hell was he?

There were so many sides to him he was like a mosaic, all chips of different-colored glass glued together to make a whole.

She'd been to a couple of museums that featured that kind of art. One in Boston while she was in art school. The Director of the Brocton facility had brought together extraordinary objects for viewing, and she had attended the opening with another student who she'd befriended during her year there. She'd previewed artists she'd never heard of before and was impressed with the quality of the work. The pieces were showcased to highlight refracted energy, and the characteristics changed with light or from different angles.

Different perspectives.

She was coming to see Luca as a work of art.

And art was her specialty.

She could break down the attributes of a picture with a keen eye and she was beginning to break him down, one glass shard at a time.

And what she saw was much different than what he led everyone to believe about him.

⌒

The bus ride to Concord, New Hampshire, was a smooth ride without much traffic but they had cut it close. The band didn't even have time to grab something to eat before the concert. Ralph had dropped all the passengers off at the Performing Arts Center, including the wives. Sitting backwards, her knees against the seat, Rissa had followed the movements of one member who seemed to draw her eyes more than she liked. Luca was laughing along with Chappy and Terry about something and she was mesmerized by what the smile did to his face. She was strangely attracted to him, and her body shivered at the thought of taking it to the limit. He didn't have a clue about what she felt, her delivery of sarcasm like FedEx, quick and efficient. When they disappeared into the building, Ralph pulled away from the curb. She made the lonely ride to their accommodations with only her niece for company. The hotel they were staying in was just a couple blocks down, so as soon as she settled in, she took Rosie for a walk along the main street. Old brick buildings lined the walkway. Hundreds of years old, they had a New England feel to them, something she loved about the area. For all the traveling they'd done so far, they were only an hour and a half away from Boston, close enough to feel like home. A pizzeria called to her growling stomach. After placing her order, she put a few toys in front of Rosie, perusing the clientele, a strategy she was employing again, now that her art had taken over. When her food arrived, she ate as people chatted around her. It sounded as if some were making a pit stop before the concert and she envied them. She had watched the troupe charge off the buses, only a handful of fans waiting to greet them. The venue held less than two thousand people and the fans would be enthusiastic but less rowdy. Customers were filtering out and when she checked her watch, she knew the concert would begin soon. Mechanical Devices would be the opener, Raging Thunder waiting in the wings for their turn on stage. Getting up and exiting the pizzeria, she made her way across the street to the where the center was located. The music thrummed through the air and she stood outside listening, Rosie waving her arms as if she were keeping the beat to the drummer. Little did she know her daddy wasn't playing yet.

With Rosie as content as she to enjoy the show, she sat on a bench to take in the area. She'd been here before. For a concert in her younger days, days when she'd had friends. Friends to play with, friends to party with, friends to hang with. That had all disappeared during her years with Jude. Or maybe she'd let them go all on her own.

When she'd left art school, her dream had died, the dream that she could fill her life with something she loved. Once that was gone, she seemed to settle, had settled for the teaching job, not going further with her education because it didn't set her heart on fire. Had let a man take over, a man who needed to be in control.

She'd been lonely.

Now that she had picked up the stubs of charcoal again, she was re-energized. Couldn't wait for the next outing, the next street scene, the next jam session when she could capture life, the pulse of movement, activity, and bustle.

Wiping Rosie's drool with one of the cloth diapers she always had on hand, she gave the infant a sad smile, lifted her head to let the warm breeze ruffle her hair.

"What do you say we wander, Rosebud?"

Turquoise eyes crinkled in response, so Rissa got up and began to push the stroller along the sidewalk, watching the people as they strolled down the street, laughed with their companions.

Coming up to a bookstore, she hesitated only a minute before opening the door and going in.

The clerk was behind the counter, a man wearing glasses, a bit disheveled who gave her a half smile before going back to his task. Moving around was awkward and there was no rhyme or reason to the way the books were organized. History was mixed with fiction, biographies with mysteries, but with her head at an angle, her finger running along spines, she found a mini-section that held a variety of science books. Then the task was finding one whose title wasn't intimidating. She flipped through a half-dozen books, until she found one that she thought might hold her interest. The pictures drew her, a form of art in a higher dimension. She knew the natural world was filled with wonder, the basis for may works of art, but these were numinous in nature. They had a touch of the divine. The title was another hook. The one word sounded profound. *Cosmos.*

After taking it up to the front of the store, she slid the credit card her brother had given out of her back pocket and waited to swipe it on the keypad.

"You're into science?"

"Um, more curious than anything. I'm hoping this isn't Greek."

"It's actually the definitive book on the universe. Sagan was a master at explanation, and it reads as prose rather than scientific treatise."

"That's good to know."

The man put the book in a plain brown paper bag, had her sign the slip. Rissa placed it in the bottom compartment of the stroller with reverence before heading back to the hotel. It was getting late, and it was time to put her niece to bed.

And once she was down, the universe beckoned.

⌒

She escaped to the lobby once her brother got back.

Her brain was having muscle spasms from all the heavy reading. If that was the definitive book and Sagan was a master, then she was never going to understand the workings of the universe. Her fingers itched to sketch, and although she didn't have a subject, she knew she'd have to doodle at something. Getting out her materials, she sat visualizing, hoping to pull some memory out of mental storage. Luca was embedded, so an image floated up. Putting charcoal to paper, she began to scribble short, quick lines. The face that emerged on the page was a boy with short hair, glasses that did nothing to hide the amber in his eyes and a brooding expression.

What was she looking for? Some resemblance to the man who existed now.

It was still the man who could satisfy the quivering that had taken hold.

Absorbed in her work, she didn't notice that someone was standing behind her until she heard the expletive.

Turning her head, looking up into the angry eyes that touched her soul, she was unable to get her voice to work.

"Getting your kicks at my expense?"

He spun around and began to walk back to the bank of elevators. His shoulders had slumped, and he fumbled his steps. Jumping up, she hurried and took her place in front of him, putting her hand on his chest.

She licked her lips nervously.

"No...I...It was...to satisfy my own curiosity."

He stepped away and held her at arm's length.

"If you wanted to do that, there's a million of them on-line."

He was scrutinizing her, and her cheeks heated with color.

"I know. I've seen them. It's where I got the template. But..."

There was more than fury in his eyes, there was also a sadness that was chilling.

His next statement held the same effect. "I would think I'd have to be a better subject than that freak."

She met his glare. Her explanation might do nothing to make him forgive her.

"I wanted to get a sense of you. When you were younger, before your transformation. When I sketch, some things appear that previously went unnoticed. I know it's weird, but it's true."

The pause made her uneasy, but she waited him out.

"Did you find anything?"

"Maybe."

His amber eyes turned cold and translucent.

"What?"

Careful to phrase it in a way that didn't increase his hostility, she said, "Your hair might be longer, and you might not wear your glasses anymore, but it's still you."

His hands went to his hips, his hair floating in wisps around his face.

"It is not. I've changed—"

"No, Luca. You haven't. There's still the intelligence, the integrity, the kind heart."

"That guy was a loser."

Her hand found its way to his face, and she cupped his cheek. It was smoother than she'd imagined, and she wanted to trace it with a finger. Able to control that lunacy, she explained, "No, he wasn't. The one's who bullied you were the losers. I know that for a fact, being a mean girl myself for a time."

"Tell that to the kid in the picture."

"I wish I could. I'd tell him he was the kind of friend I would have wanted. But then again, he wouldn't have listened. I was a lowly freshman when he was a junior. He wouldn't have given me the time of day."

She had tried to make him smile and she studied him for some sign she'd been successful. His posture was straighter, but the smile that was dangerous to her heart didn't appear. The melancholy was back.

"I don't think you ever shake off the feeling, no matter how successful you become."

She ached for him as she tried to picture an even younger version being taunted, hurt.

"It's like you're covered in a thick sludge, and even though you're able to peel away layers of it, there's still the residue that sticks. Anyone who tried to stick up for you was tainted with it as well. That's why not many people did."

"I wish I had. At least tried."

His eyes took on an iridescent warmth that she felt to the marrow of her bones, and her heart flip-flopped in response.

"Thanks for that. It shouldn't still bother me."

Beginning to relax now that his anger was gone, she noticed he had a fresh tee shirt on, but the jeans looked like the ones he'd worn on stage. The ones that had a rip at the knee and she'd bet were soft to the touch. If only she had the nerve...

Her head snapped up.

"Big brother sent you to check on me, didn't he?"

"You know him well."

Shaking her head, wondering what kind of trouble Johnny thought she'd get into, she asked, "He didn't interrupt anything important, did he?"

"Nope. Just hiding in my cave."

"Your cave? Why?"

He gave her a casual shrug.

"It's nice and cool and quiet."

"You don't get lonely?"

His expression shut off the smile that had emerged.

"Except for the bats clicking, not so much."

He was hiding behind the joke. She could read lonely. She'd felt it often enough.

Well, she could hide, too.

"Is that what that noise is? I thought it was crickets."

He dropped down onto a bench by the elevator, his arms hanging loosely between his legs.

"It could be. Every cave is different."

"True. And even when there's another person living there, it can still be a cavernous hole."

His head came up and he looked her right in the eye.

"Are you implying that you can be lonely even with another person in the space with you?"

She sat down beside him, close to the edge so they weren't touching.

"It's not an implication, it's a fact. I never felt so alone as when I was living with Jude."

He leaned back, his arms tight against his chest.

"Then why the hell..."

How could she explain the stupidity?

"Because there was another voice that bounced off the ceilings. It wasn't only my own."

"It has to be the right voice, Rissa. One that's in sync with yours. Otherwise, it's chaos, not cosmos."

Her eyes flicked up.

Weird coincidence that he used that term. Did it have a larger meaning?

"Cosmos?"

"The order of the universe. The laws of nature that govern it. It's in direct contrast to chaos."

When she looked up and into his eyes, the two-by-four hit her.

He had gotten too far under her skin.

She'd have to talk to Johnny tomorrow. If he wanted to know where she was or what she was up to, he could text. He didn't need to send the cavalry.

When they got off the elevator, Luca made sure she got into her room safely.

Such a gentleman.

Wishing he weren't, she huddled down for a night of what ifs.

CHAPTER FIFTEEN

They arrived in Mansfield, and after settling in, Luca headed off to meet up with the guys. Holed up in one of the hotel rooms, they'd work their way through riffs and lyrics, polish off some songs near completion, and figure where they'd introduce them and where they'd fit in the play-list.

Last night, after his run-in with Rissa, he'd begun fiddling with some lyrics and had added a melody.

What had come out had surprised him.

It revealed too much about his past, and was extremely personal. Johnny never had a problem expressing his feelings in his songs. "Glinda" was about Tish and pretty much told the world what he was fighting, those demons that prevented him from accepting the inevitable.

Luca's song spoke to the destructive forces of bullying, the need for acceptance and social connection. Not something he spoke about, although Tim and Johnny knew that much about his past. His name would be associated with the song, probably listed first as the lyricist, which meant people would know...

He had never talked about it before.

Too ashamed that he'd been targeted.

Shoved into lockers, tripped in hallways, verbally threatened. No one had physically assaulted him after middle school. He'd made sure he had the muscle to thwart attacks that had resulted in ripped pants and bloodied nose when he was younger. Not wanting to spend all his time defending himself, he'd found places to hide, developed strategies to become invisible. It lessened over time, but he'd never healed completely.

Maybe getting it out and in the open would help.

He knew it wouldn't hurt any more than it had and maybe he could speak to the millions out there who were going through it now.

He titled it "Word Darts."

Words were a tool for torment in the same way darts were a tool for a game.

Word darts
a game
to shame
the weak and undefended
different and unfriended

Barbs prick
a skin too thin
to withstand the words that pummel
worse than sticks and stones they humble
us all.
the bullies are protected
their kills go undetected
their pronouncements are respected
the defamations are deflected
by all.

You sharpen your pencil
your message is clear
words that can't be unwritten
from the wall of my fear.
Rejection results from the slander and lies
the potential within goes unrealized
insults are hurled, but it's no big surprise
that they come from the mouth of the popular guys
So, I'll sharpen my pencil
so the message is clear
We were far better off than those bullies we feared
No longer a victim, I now realize
they were the one's immature, undersized

the power they sought at other's demise
was only their fear masked in stunning disguise

He clutched the wrinkled papers in his hand, sure Johnny could even it out, make it less dorky, more compelling.

He thought of Rissa and her sketch of him. She had seen him clearly, had replicated the facial expression, better than the physical features.

She'd nailed it.

Had it made such an impression that he was willing to feel the pain again?

He didn't like her knowing he was the same person. He'd hidden it from everyone else. She said her sketching uncovered things, and although it sounded farfetched, he couldn't argue that she'd been right.

Putting it out there for all to see was a bit of a risk, but maybe it was time for him to take one.

He didn't know what he was worrying about. The guys might not even like it, so the point would be moot.

When he entered Tim's room, the other band members were already there. Tim's and Johnny's heads were together as if they were putting the finishing touches on another new song. The two of them wrote non-stop and their partnership was one of the best in the business.

Johnny looked up and smiled. "Where you been?"

"I went to the bus to get my bass. I...um...Got a minute? I have something to show you."

Johnny stood up, hands on hips and said, "Yeah, what?"

Luca's stomach ached. He still wasn't sure this was smart but what the hell. He'd come this far.

"A song."

"You wrote a song?"

"Don't congratulate me yet. You haven't seen it."

"In seven years, you've never once let on you wanted to write. Have we hogged the spotlight?"

"No. I...Last night the lyrics just came tumbling out. I've got a tentative melody but I'll let you decide if it works."

Johnny was the one who could see the larger picture, and he studied the words, started humming a tune.

"This is powerful stuff, Caroli. Why have you been hiding your talent from us?"

Luca's eyebrows arched and he scoffed. "You've got the talent for this kind of stuff. I figured you could work your magic on it."

"This makes me feel even worse, you know. I should have had your back."

"Hey, it's in the past. Let's leave it there, okay."

"If I'd been less of a shit, you could have been with us from the start and we wouldn't have had to go through that mess with the drugs."

"I was still planning on college. It had to work out the way it did."

"I guess everything does. I still regret it though, okay?"

"You're a good man, Charlie Brown."

"I hope you keep writing. It's good to hear a different voice every now and then."

"Well, if the mood ever strikes again, you'll be the first one to know."

The next couple of hours were spent refining it, adding music and making plans to reveal it.

The only problem was, they wanted him to sing it.

He wasn't sure he wanted to go that far out on the limb.

Rissa sat with the rest of the women in lawn chairs, a blanket spread out before them, appetizers and a cooler of drinks at the ready. It was the perfect June night, the sky clear, the temperatures moderate. She'd been to the Xfinity Center, located in the western part of the state before, under a guise of other names when she was younger and into the band scene. Her friend Kathy had just gotten her license and they'd driven out to see Pearl Jam, Eric Clapton and Phish, whoever happened to be playing during the summer. The outdoor amphitheater was meant for fresh air, warm nights, and picnic-style pickings. With great acoustics, the wail and whine of the guitars, the pounding beat of the drums pulsed through her. There was another good memory associated with the place. It's where she'd seen Raging Thunder for the first time, as an opening act for a group she couldn't even remember. It was when the tickets were affordable, and she had lots of friends to party with.

She glanced at her companions and thought it was nice to be back in that place with friends and music. She'd missed this part of her life and was glad she'd been given the opportunity to be here. Tish had stayed with Rosie tonight. The baby had come down with a slight fever and needed the kind of comfort and soothing only a breastfeeding mom could give. It gave her the opportunity to relax and enjoy the tour in a different way and she was taking advantage of it.

Caught up in the musical style of the opening band, Mechanical Devices, she knew they'd become the main event one day soon. Suzy, the lead singer, had an amazing voice and the band knew how to wow a crowd. Sipping a beer, Rissa half listened to the conversation going on around her. Annie and Marci were talking about upcoming motherhood, rubbing their bellies, discussing name choices. There was a connection between the wives that was nice to watch, participate in on a peripheral level. They all dealt so well with the success of their spouses, the women who were blatant in their attempts to get them to bed and they were confident in their ability to prevent it.

Here were women who could hold a man.

Even Gia. Almost brash, totally honest, with a bull shit meter that was always on, she could zero in on an interloper and back her off without a word. It hadn't surprised Rissa to hear about how she'd ended up married to Chappy. She was a bartender in one of the local pubs that Chappy frequented and hadn't put up with his big talk about Raging Thunder. She'd cut him down to size when his oversized ego made him sound like an asshole. When he began spending time there, just to talk to her, she'd concluded he wasn't as bad as she'd thought, and they fallen into bed, love and marriage. The whole thing had only taken a couple of months, but they seemed happy. Maybe a person just knew who lit up their world. It didn't take years of analysis to determine if it was right or not.

She was enjoying their company and wished she could soak up their composure by osmosis.

Gia took a swig of her beer and asked, "How come you haven't hooked up yet? Not your scene?"

Looking out into the distance, Rissa told a truth that was becoming clearer every day. She'd considered Luca a reject, moody and frivolous. He was not any of those things.

"I've been burned pretty badly so until I can tell the treasure from the trash, I've sworn off men."

Crossing her legs, the small beach chairs low to the ground making it a challenge, Gia settled back.

"Speaking of trash, are you over him yet?"

Annie gave Gia one of her shrink looks. Gia grimaced as she shrugged her shoulders.

Rissa gave her a contemplative look. Uncoupling was hard even when it was the right thing to do.

With a heavy sigh, she admitted, "I'm over him. I'm having a hard time figuring out why the hell I spent so much time and energy there in the first place."

Now she had to filter out what she thought, needed, wanted. It had become a lost art in her case.

Annie, holding her bottle of water with one hand, nibbling on a cookie with the other, said,

"I didn't think it would take long. You were never really into him."

Rissa's eyes narrowed.

"What makes you say that?"

"He didn't seem to set off rockets. You were detached, never openly showed your affection."

Fiddling with the neck of the beer bottle she held between her legs, Rissa explained, "He didn't like public displays."

Gia swore under her breath.

"If Chappy didn't let me kiss him wherever and whenever I wanted, I would have flattened him."

Rissa gave her a small smile, knowing she'd do it.

Annie asked, "Did he ever touch anything inside you?"

She instantly thought of Luca and how he touched her with just a look.

"I...Not really. I guess I was too busy trying to be someone I wasn't to notice. Being who he wanted. That takes a lot of energy."

"So intent on getting him to love you, you never asked yourself if you loved him."

Annie had counseled many women over the years and had been the one to help Tish find herself again.

Rissa asked Annie, her friend the therapist, "Why do women do that?"

"I don't know. Conditioning. The love and marriage thing. Self-esteem. Wanting it so badly we'll take it where we can get it."

Rissa asked pensively, "What makes a person love someone?"

Annie gave her words of wisdom. "It's different for everyone."

Gia gave her perspective. "I think it's the things you can put up with rather than any one good trait. Chappy might drive someone crazy with his practical jokes, something I can deal with, even one-up him every now and then. I couldn't deal with Luca's neatness. Such pressure."

They laughed at her implication.

Gia added for good measure, "I also think it's the chemistry. It's there or it's not."

Marci agreed. "There are plenty of women who want to get our husbands into bed and will go to any lengths to see if they can. The sex for mating needs to be combustible."

"Like burns you to the core."

"Incinerates you."

"Makes you want to rip his clothes off when he's anywhere in your vicinity."

Rissa listened and her heart sank. She hadn't felt that with Jude on any level, but the ripping clothes off and the incinerate part was a close match to someone else. And she inwardly groaned. Did she have the courage to feel that kind of heat, knowing it could only be a flash in the pan?

She could be replaced as easily as him crooking his finger.

She still wasn't sure about taking that leap. Or maybe she was but was merely postponing it until the end of the tour. Then she could return to the safety of her family and not spend weeks wishing it could be something else.

⌒

The stage had gone black, but there was no hush in the audience as it geared up for the main event, women screaming, applause thunderous, and the excitement was starting to sprout in Rissa's belly.

Then the frenzy of the electric wail of the guitar and the pounding rhythm of the drums attacked them from the stage.

The opening song was one of her favorites and she moved to the raucous beat, feeling the music pulse along her nerves, simple joy spurting in her soul.

She loved this.

She watched her brother for a time, his energy so explosive she was mesmerized by his moves, proud of the way he held the entire band together with his strength. He defined the way they played, all power and heat, and it was engrossing to watch. Tim played well but it wasn't what he was known for. It was his voice that held the crowd spellbound, soulful and resonant. She had to admit Terry was very good, but he seemed stiffer than the rest, staying in place and leaving the explosiveness to the others. Finally, she gave up all resistance and her eyes sought out the bassist, the heat there almost palpable. He moved with a gracefulness that she wouldn't have thought possible, and she could hear his underlying melody keeping time with the drums. Johnny and Luca were the foundation that supported the energy building around them. And she couldn't for the life of her let him go once she had him in her sights, the deep bass chords striking in harmony with the beat of her heart. He plucked the strings, his fingers and thumb controlling the vibrations, balancing consistency and tone. He made a huge impact on the totality of the music. She was impressed. Tim had been right. Luca did not get enough credit for his style and interpretation nor his contribution to the band's sound.

Her body matched the strums with a hum of her own, and it didn't fade as the night wore on but increased in vibration. And heat.

It was over before she was ready for the finale. She had loved every minute of it and was more than excited that she'd be able to catch a couple more in Boston.

As soon as the encore was finished, Annie started gathering their belongings.

"We're going backstage, hanging out during the meet and greet and going back to the hotel with the guys."

Rissa hesitated; not sure she could even talk to Luca without letting him know what she was feeling. It hadn't dissipated in the least and she could still feel her body betraying her. Annie must have sensed her hesitation.

"Come on. This is another part of the experience that you just can't miss."

Backstage was a mob scene. There was a swelling of people after each concert. The media, anyone with a backstage pass, peers who'd happened by to see the concert, venue management all crowded the space.

"Geez. It's crazy."

Rissa's eyes jumped from one spot to the next, members of the band signing autographs, reporters asking questions while they did so, women hanging on, wanting some personal mementos like hair or articles of clothing.

Johnny came over when he spotted his sister and gave her a huge hug. "What'd you think?"

He was so sweaty she pushed him away, laughing as if it didn't bother her as much as she made it seem.

"No words to describe it. The energy was exhausting."

"That's why we keep coming out."

Tim came over to give Annie a kiss and with his arm around her asked, "Were we up to snuff without Glinda?"

"Just like the old days. Pure thunder."

"Luca was especially on. He picked it up for her."

"What did I pick up?"

Luca had sauntered over to where they stood, giving her a quick appraisal.

She wondered how she stacked up against the bevy of beautiful woman in every corner.

She had worn a skirt, although it was blue-and-white-striped cotton, nothing fancy, with a white tee shirt. Compared to how the others turned out, she looked homespun.

No way would he ever pick her out a crowd, at least not this one.

Which kind of pissed her off enough to say, "It's who. Who did you pick up?"

Johnny flicked her on the head, telling her without words she was at it again.

"Great job, Luca. You picked it up for Tish big time. A very big thanks."

The roadies were already beginning to dismantle the stage, packing up the instruments and loading them on the truck for the next stop. Joe yelled over, looking directly at Luca, "You sticking around?"

"Yeah."

She glanced around the stage, the women impatient, waiting for him to make his selection, and she almost wanted to wait around to see who tonight's winner would be.

Looking up at her brother, a bemused smile on her face, she asked, "Could you flick me again? I need to get a thought out of my head."

He did and then wrapped his arm around her neck as she sputtered, "You stink. You're soaked. Let me go."

He didn't. Instead, he laughed and hugged her all the way back to the hotel where Tish was waiting to hear about the night.

CHAPTER SIXTEEN

As soon as Tish and Johnny had gone to bed, Rissa went down to the lobby, unable to sleep after the frenetic energy of the concert. It was becoming habit. It gave her some peace and quiet after time spent with a three-month-old who didn't like to sleep. Rosie was a happy girl, as long as you were giving her lots of attention.

After sitting down on one of the couches, her sketch pad on her lap, she tried to draw elements of the concert from memory. The one that seemed to be the most insistent, at least as far as her fingers went, was Luca moving to the music, totally in sync with the beat and the drums. His solo had been almost mournful, the bass reverberating outward to capture all in attendance. The spotlight picking up glints of brown hair, showcasing his tall frame, his magical pull of the strings.

Hearing voices, she raised her head to see a foursome entering the interior of the hotel. As Luca ambled over to where she sat, she fumbled with the pad, not wanting him to see her drawings, the ones with him covering the page.

"You're up late."

"Yeah. My body is still vibrating from the music. I'm trying to settle down."

They exchanged a look that held a suggestion, his eyes deepening to almost a bluish amber that held her captive. She gulped. There was a driving urge to inspect them more closely.

Plopping down on the sofa, Luca extended his legs and sat back.

She had to flick off the feelings, so she went right to her strength. Mean girl.

"Too tired from your exertions to make it up to your room in one trip?"

"I swear you're Sybil. I never know which personality I'm going to be talking to."

He started to rise but she put a hand on his leg to prevent it.

"I'm sorry."

She didn't remove her hand and he looked over at her to see what it meant.

As soon as his eyes met hers, she grabbed it back and placed it in her lap, the tingles shooting up her arm.

Taking a breath, she stated the obvious. "You're back kind of early."

With a lop-sided smile, he said, "Sometimes I feel like the candy in a candy store."

Rissa couldn't help but laugh.

"You are."

"I'm trying to decide if I like it anymore."

"Is it that much of a science?"

The smile spread across his face and he was downright gorgeous.

"It's all about the physics."

After shifting to the corner of the couch, wanting to get a better view of him, she said humorously, "I bet you didn't think it would come in handy that way."

He moved into the other corner, his leg bent at the knee, so they were face-to-face with just a slight distance between them.

"That's for sure. It has to do with energy, force, space and time."

Putting her fingernail between her teeth, Rissa gave him a thoughtful expression.

"The energy expended, how forceful the women are, the time it takes to satisfy them, and the space...you need between them?"

"Not exactly. Sometimes the force is not in balance with the energy needed and sometimes you need space and time away from all of it."

Her eyes danced at him. "It must get pretty exhausting."

Sobering up, he admitted, "Actually, it all gets a bit boring."

That was the kind of information she didn't know what to do with, so she circled back to their original topic.

"That the reason you passed on all that lusciousness?"

"I'm the candy, remember?"

She peered at him, thinking that he certainly was. The gooey chocolate, caramel-kind. Her favorite.

Her smile disappeared as Suzy came over to them, as if waiting for a cue.

When Luca noticed her standing there, he got to his feet and asked Rissa, "You coming?"

Something pricked at her...heart.

"No. I'm not ready for bed just yet."

Rissa saw Luca place his hand on the small of Suzy's back as they walked over to the elevator and waited for the door to open.

His stride was confident, his ass nearly perfection.

A little twinge of green pulsed. Where were they going and would they be together when they arrived?

She shook the thought off as soon as they disappeared into the elevator. Pulling out her sketch pad, she studied the profile etched on it. There was no way she could have let Luca see what she'd been working on. It was way too embarrassing and he might get the right idea entirely.

⌒

The next morning, she awoke to find her brother pacing the hotel room, his expression concerned. Pulling on the sweatshirt she used as a robe, she stood waiting, but he just continued to move from one point of the room to another. She walked over and put her hand on his arm.

"What's wrong?"

Pushing his hands through his hair, he said, "It's Tish. She's overwhelmed. There's too much on her plate. Remember, we talked about this as a potential problem?"

Looking around, she asked, "Where is she?"

"Trying to grab some sleep."

Dropping to the edge of the chair, she vocalized, "She doesn't seem to have much downtime. If she's not taking care of Rosie, she's off practicing, or doing sound checks, more practice, concert..."

"I know. And Rosie's not being the trooper I thought she'd be. We're up half the night with her, or I should say Tish is."

Looking up at him, the worry etched on his features, she gave a half-smile.

"You always slept pretty soundly. When your alarm went off in in high school, it would continue to buzz until one of us ran in to shut it off. You never even stirred."

"Yeah. Nothing's changed there. I told her to wake me up, but she doesn't."

Noticing the coffee maker was plugged in, she got up and got it ready to brew, then turned it on. As the dark liquid filled the plastic cup she said, "I can keep Rosie with me a night or two."

He went back to pacing.

"That's the thing. Tish wants to be with her. She feels like she's missing so much because she's gone a good part of the day and night."

Taking a sip of the sugared and creamed coffee, she asked, "Does she want to quit the band?"

Giving his sister a sad smile, he said, "We certainly make enough she could be a stay-at-home mom if she wanted to. My forcing this issue about her staying with the band is a selfish one, but I love having her on stage with us. Love being with her all the time."

"But if it's too much for her..."

He stopped and dropped to the chair she'd vacated.

"I know. I'm being selfish."

"What are the alternatives?"

He began tapping his fingers on his thigh, and she knew that meant he was thinking.

"We could get another keyboard player or let her sit out some nights. But then we'd have to change the play-list every time."

Looking up, he met her eyes.

"Or we could drop the keyboard completely."

She came over to sit opposite him on the edge of the couch.

"She's not a member of the band, Johnny."

"I know. She's only playing with us because she doesn't want to disappoint me."

"What are you doing to do?"

"I'm working on it."

Her brother was always so in charge it seemed funny to see him out of his element.

"What do you think the guys will say?"

"Not sure. But I guess I'm going to have to broach the subject. We never had keys before, so they may want to go back to being a foursome. It's just our sound does have more depth with it. And Tish has written some impressive scores to go along with what we write. I'd hate to see them wasted. I've set up a meeting later. See what they think."

His look of concern showed as he asked, "Whatever we decide, you'll stay, won't you? I want her to have as much help as she needs."

Taking a breath, Rissa responded.

"I hadn't even thought about what that would mean for me. Are you sure? I'm enjoying the change and it will help me avoid any decision regarding my real future. I could give a seminar on procrastination in action."

"I'm sure. Tish will still need to practice her stuff, and if we have a new keyboard player on board, we'll have to work with him to get him up to speed. Besides, I'd still like her to come to some of the concerts. If I don't get to see her, she might as well have stayed home."

"You can pay me less—"

"I'm not paying you less. Forget about it."

"But Johnny, I won't—"

He interrupted her again. "The prospect of paying you less is not on the table and I'm not wasting my energy on it."

He leaned forward, his arms hanging between his legs.

"There's something else I wanted to talk to you about. Tish is the one who mentioned it. Luca thinks it's a great idea, too."

Apprehension fluttered up her spine.

"What?"

"Those sketches you do. We thought they might make a good book. One we can sell at the merchandise table. It will showcase your work, you'd get most of the profits, and it would give the fans an idea of what we do out on the road when we're not performing."

"Absolutely not."

The answer flew out her mouth before she'd even thought about it. It wasn't the first time. She'd done the same thing when her mother had informed her she was going to tour with the band.

She didn't like being thrown off-balance like that. It was as if she was being cornered. She needed time to process the request, or directive, in the case of her mother.

Johnny's brow furrowed.

"Why not? It's a great way for you to earn some money doing something you do very well."

While untangling the skein of thoughts that were becoming twisted, she asked, "Who'd buy it?"

"A lot of our fans. I've already talked to Jessica, and she'd love to see them, get an idea of what we're talking about."

She fiddled with the haphazard curls she couldn't tame this morning.

"Johnny, I'm not sure about this."

He stood, his hands on his hips.

"I am. Like I said, Tish suggested it and Caroli's on board. He's the most private one of us, so if we don't get flak from him, there are no excuses."

Luca was on board? Why?

The she looked up, startled, "Does Luca think I know about the offer?"

"I don't know. We talked about it a few days ago. Why?"

"He saw one of the sketches of him last night. He wasn't happy with it. Now I think I understand why."

She'd have to talk to him, reiterate it wasn't for the...proposed book, that she hadn't even known about it.

Then she thought about some of the pictures, the more intimate ones of him that she'd drawn. She'd kept them hidden so he wouldn't think she had the hots for him.

Even though she had the hots for him.

And they were getting hotter by the day.

It wasn't only her privates telling her that, but her tongue was still cutting him to pieces on occasion. It was the only way she could think of to bury the urge to jump him.

The perfect defense mechanism but it was doing nothing for those privates.

"Let me think about it. Go through them."

"Okay. Some of your time can be spent collating them."

The thought was daunting but interesting.

"Maybe I could add watercolors."

She was getting excited about the project. It would give her something to do in her down time and she'd love enhancing what she'd done so far. But there were some that would never see the light of day.

She couldn't do that to herself.

Or him.

"Get working on it and talk to Jessica."

Needing time to digest what Johnny had asked her, she headed down to the lobby, hoping it was quiet so she could think.

She'd never imagined she could make money doing what she loved, but Johnny had given her the opportunity to see if she could. The book would be personal. Sketches offered a fresh perspective and a direct impression of a moment in time. Her own personal expression of that moment, which would offer the audience a glimpse into the daily life of someone they cared about.

Most of them were drawn on the spot, calling for spontaneity, a passion for the subject, getting it down as it unfolded in front of her.

She had started sketching in grammar school. Back then it was called doodling.

Her textbook covers were covered in her scribbles all through high school, the doodles becoming more detailed as the years went on. It was Paul who had noticed the emerging talent and talked her mother into paying for lessons.

She had a natural talent for drawing and the more she experimented with textures, tools, and washes, the more she enhanced the pictures so they came to life.

Only when she'd been told by her professors that it was a secondary art form had she given up any idea that she could make a living doing it.

That's what school had given her.

A flawed view of her passion.

Then Jude had added another layer, another dimension by calling it a waste of time.

The result? She'd stopped altogether.

Now that she was scribbling again in every spare moment, her love for the medium had grown even more consuming.

CHAPTER SEVENTEEN

Luca made his way to Johnny's room. His band mate had called an impromptu band meeting for noon, and he was a couple minutes early.

Would Rissa be there?

The first one to arrive, he discretely scanned the area, disappointment hitting when she was nowhere in sight.

And relief.

He never knew which Rissa would show up, which one he'd talk to. Not that it mattered. She was provoking some dangerous feelings; whichever personality was present.

As soon as his curiosity was satisfied that she wasn't here, he noticed Johnny pacing.

His concern was heightened by the look on Johnny's face.

"What's wrong? Is it Rosie?"

"No. Maybe in a way. She's fine...Let's wait for Terry and Tim before we get to it."

Luca breathed a sigh of relief. They had all come to think of the little girl as their own.

When the other two band members came through the door, Johnny wasted no time and blurted out, "I've got something to run by you guys."

Tim glanced over at Luca, as if to ascertain if he knew what was going on. He shrugged his shoulders in response. Taking seats, Terry and Tim put their attention on Johnny's fidgety form.

Seconds went by before Luca said impatiently, "Tell us what's wrong already."

Rubbing his temple with his free hand, Johnny stopped and started before getting to the problem.

"Tish has been spreading herself too thin. Rosie takes a lot of time and energy, and with her own practice ritual, she's running on empty. She's informed me that she can't keep all the balls in the air, so with her permission, I've taken her off the keyboard. We have to decide what we want to do—go back to being a four-piece band or add a keyboard player."

Tim looked at Luca again, his eyebrows arched in question.

Luca answered it.

"Tish was behind the keys when we recorded the new CD last year. I liked the depth it added. I'm not sure we should let it go."

Terry sat biting his thumb nail. "I tend to agree with Luca."

Tim got up and began to pace the same path Johnny had just moments before.

"This is a big step. We only added the keyboard because of Tish's predicament last year. We'd never thought of adding it to the mix before that. Could she do it periodically?"

"No. She's running herself ragged and I don't want her doing it anymore. I don't know why I didn't realize Rosie was going to take so much energy and work."

Luca was the first to cast his vote, wanting to be there for Johnny like he'd been there for him, ignoring the wave of unease that hit him.

"Tish is one-of-a-kind but I think the keys still add a dimension we need. I say bring someone else on board."

Terry said, "I'm in, whatever you guys decide."

He knew Terry's contribution would be acceptance.

Johnny swiveled around to face Tim.

"I didn't expect the resistance to come from your direction. It's Caroli who doesn't like change."

Luca opened his mouth to contradict that statement and then closed it.

Sure, he liked routine. It kept him safe. It was the only way to control what went on around him.

He pushed the twist of anxiety into a knot.

"We should give someone a try. See where it goes." He glanced over to Tim. "Right, bro?"

Tim paused before nodding in agreement.

Johnny breathed out a sigh of relief as he looked each one in the eye.

"That leaves the question, who?"

Tim and Johnny went back and forth, discussing the merits of different people they knew might work.

Luca was sitting back in the chair, his legs stretched out, his arms in his lap, thinking.

About Rissa.

"Luca, what do you think?"

Johnny's voice had risen as if he was asking for a second time.

He took his mind out of the gutter and offered a suggestion.

"Do you remember the keyboardist from the opening act last year? His name is Lenny Grey. He might be available because, as you know, his band fell apart when the lead singer imploded from drugs."

"Is he into them? Drugs?"

"Would I even mention him if he was?"

"Are you sure?"

"Yeah, we hung out a lot after you took up with Tish. I got to know him pretty well and he's clean."

"Do you know how to reach him?"

"I have his number. I can see if he'd be willing to audition."

"We can have him step in some night. But we have to give him some lead time to get familiar with our music."

"Being with us last year, he's got a good handle on what we do and how we do it. He also knows how crazy it can get, so I'm not positive he'll agree."

Pulling his phone out of his back pocket, Luca scanned for the number and let the call go through. Putting it on speaker, he responded to Lenny's "Hey, Luca. What's up?"

Luca cut right to the chase.

"Want to ask you something?"

"Okay, shoot."

"Have you hooked up with another band yet?"

"No. I've auditioned a few times, but I don't want to get involved in the same kind of situation as last time."

Luca, along with the rest of the band, could hear the sardonic laugh before Lenny added, "That gives me a very limited group to choose from."

"How about us? Would you be willing to audition for us?"

"Are you kidding? Man, that would be my dream job. What happened to John's wife?"

Johnny took up the thread here. "She had to choose between her music or ours. Hers won. Thank goodness. She's too good to give it up to play keyboard."

Johnny heard his own words and added, "I didn't mean it the way it sounded."

"No offense taken. She is in a class by herself. I would love to give it a shot though. When did you want me?"

"We were thinking you could come right out. Rent a car. We'll reimburse you."

"I'll get on YouTube, listen to what Tish has done, add my own take if it suits, and see where it goes."

"Great. I hope this works out, Lenny."

"Me, too. I really do."

Luca picked up the phone again and shut off the speaker.

"You'll hit the road tomorrow? It'll be good to see you."

"Yeah, I will. Thanks, Luca. I figure you're the one who put in a good word."

"No problem. If it's not Tish up on stage with us, it might as well be you."

"I'll be bringing my girl. Is that okay?"

"Why not? This party has become a real family event."

"Okay. See you tomorrow then."

"Bye, Lenny."

Johnny was up and pacing, his fingers clicking the sticks still in his hands.

"That was too easy. It's got me worried."

"Relax. If it works great. If it doesn't, we'll find someone else."

"He's a good guy. That's a plus. He won't bring any drama to the scene."

"I wouldn't have mentioned him if I thought he'd bring anything but a talent for the keys. We had enough drama last year to last us a lifetime."

Johnny sank back into his chair.

"Now, the next question is, where are they going to ride? Our bus is full, but so is yours. We could probably fit one person but two more...I'm not sure where we'd put Rosie's things."

Johnny glanced up and stared at him.

"What?"

"Can you swap? And before you answer you have to remember the rules."

"I do. No women, no mess. Although I don't know why you have the second rule. Your place is always a mess."

"Yeah, I don't either, but there it is. The women set them. We just follow."

He stared back, his mind processing the request. It might be nice to ride with the band for a change. He was the only one who rode the second bus and he was enjoying how tight they'd become over the past week.

"I can follow the women's rules as blindly as you guys. Besides, we're staying in hotels. There'd be no point on having a woman on the bus."

He didn't mention that he'd taken a sabbatical. Rissa had insinuated everyone had noticed.

"It would make it easier. You're family. No matter how close the others are, they don't fit that description."

That thought only increased the feeling of connection.

"I'll move my stuff before we leave."

"Thanks, bro. I owe you."

"No problem. I'm more than glad to do it."

And he was. This would give him an opportunity to see Rissa in more personal space. See her true colors. They were blinding him, and he needed to remember what his end goal was. Nothing like proximity to get that job done.

⌒

Luca stood at the top of the stairs scanning the space. From this vantage point, it was obvious he'd have to take the only bunk left, which was at the front. It didn't suit his need for privacy, but it offered him a great view of Rissa, so he wasn't entirely bummed. Throwing his bag, his blanket and a pillow, along with a couple of books on top of the bed, he began to organize the items around him. Tim and Annie had the spot in the back and were playing cards, Marci and Terry were next, with Tish and Johnny halfway between. John was asleep, Rosie lying on top of him. Tish was sitting in Rissa's space, and they seemed to be chatting. It was a lot more subdued than his bus, the quiet a nice change.

Tish looked up and smiled, "Welcome aboard. Sorry, that's all that's left. We kind of take up a lot of room. We cleaned it off as well as we could."

The bus was supposed to sleep ten but with all of Rosie's paraphernalia it had condensed down to eight.

"No problem."

"Come on over and join us."

Tish was patting a seat to the right of the bunk as she said, "I don't get a lot of time to just sit. It's nice."

"Johnny's turn with the Rosebud?"

"Yes. I didn't get much sleep last night. Rosie didn't want anything to do with the pack and play. She wanted the big-girl bed but I'm not going that route."

He was going to turn down her offer but found himself dropping into the bus seat and asking, "Tougher than you thought?"

"Not in theory but definitely in actuality. I put too much on my plate. It was tipping precariously. Thank you for coming up with an alternative that just might work."

"No problem. Lenny's not you but he's a good guy."

"I remember. He's got some finesse, and that took work considering who he was playing with."

"He needs the gig so it's a win-win."

"Where's he meeting us?"

"At the hotel."

"You'll probably be practicing most of the afternoon then."

"We will."

"That means I can practice whenever I want. I'm going to love this."

When Tish repeated her name, he looked up to find Rissa staring into space.

A small frown slipped across her face when her name finally registered, and she stared at Tish for a moment as if she were coming out of a fugue state.

"Huh?"

"Will you be able to watch Rosie this afternoon? I want to put in some real time. I can completely immerse myself in my love affair with Rachmaninoff."

"Yeah, sure. I'm planning on exploring Springfield, but it probably isn't the sightseeing capital of the world. What time will you need me?"

The bus had pulled up to the hotel, travel time just over an hour, and they all got up to disembark, Rissa waiting to hear Tish's answer.

"Say two p.m.?"

"Okay. I'll be back by then."

"Just out of curiosity, where are you going?"

"I don't know. Just wandering around. I'm beginning to feel comfortable out there in the unknown."

Alone.

Shrugging her backpack over her shoulder she stepped off the bus and headed into town.

⌒

She breathed in the dry air that was warm on her skin.

They were still in Massachusetts. She could tell for some reason, and it felt good being so close to her hometown. Walking through the busy business district, she studied the people as she waited for lights to change, looking for differences, similarities to those she'd see on the streets of Boston. Everyone was rushing somewhere, scurrying into shops. Cars beeped and sped past on their way to work or running errands. It wasn't unlike a late-morning walk along the North End. The sights and smells were familiar. Almost laughing to herself that she seemed to gravitate towards the Italian part of town, she peeked into some of the small storefronts, checked menus, and when she peeked through the window of a bakery, she couldn't help but be drawn in. She was sure it was due to the scent of freshly baked bread and her mouth began watering before she got to the counter.

Knowing that her brother would love some of the homemade goodies, she placed an order that would feed fifty people. Italian sticks, one of which she knew would be gone before she even reached the hotel, along with cookies, biscotti, napoleons, cannoli, pastries filled with whipped cream and fruit squares of all kinds. When the boxes were bagged and handed over, she wondered if she had the strength to carry them back with her. With arms laden with goodness, she finally entered the hotel, her arms trembling under the weight.

Luca was just coming off the elevator when he saw her, rushing over to give her a hand he began, "What the...?"

She looked up at him with a grateful expression, "I guess I got carried away."

Taking the bag with the loaves of bread, he asked, "Um, did this come half-eaten, or did you meet a mouse along the way?"

Giving him a small smile, she admitted, "The bag was right under my nose and only a few inches from my mouth. What else could I do?"

Luca raised the bag to his nose and inhaled.

"I see your point."

Ripping away part of the white wrapper, he bit in where she'd left off.

"It's still warm."

"I know."

Taking another bite, he smiled back. "There'll be one less stick to share."

"First come, first serve."

"Should we bring it up to your brother's room?"

"I guess we can start there."

"We could go room to room handing them out. It looks like you got enough for a small army."

"I don't mean to be stingy, but I thought I could throw some in the mini-fridge for the ride to Worcester."

"As long as I get some to throw in, too, I won't tell."

He had an open, easy smile on his face and it sent shock waves through her system. Dipping her eyes away so he couldn't see the growing need there, she mumbled, "Deal."

He passed her the dwindling loaf for another bite.

"I don't want to be greedy."

Her eyes meeting his, she filled her mouth with the gooey texture, wishing for a taste of his lips.

She'd bet her life they'd be even more delicious.

⌒

As soon as Johnny saw the bounty, ripping box after box open to see what his choices were, he dug right in, his first bite leaving a whipped cream moustache he let Tish finger off. It was more intimate than a kiss and Rissa's heart took a slight dip.

Whining, she said, "Oh, come on. It's too early for all that sharing."

Tish laughed. "Sorry. Can't help it."

Luca grabbed a corner of the couch, tore off another chunk of the bread.

Moving over, he patted the seat next to him and although she hesitated, Rissa eventually gave in. It put the two of them in a bubble, away from everyone else.

As he lifted the two-inch slice, he admitted, "I could eat this stuff all day long and never get sick of it."

"My downfall as well. I was hoping the walk used up some of the calories but if I keep this up..."

Closing her eyes, she took another bite before saying, "I wish we had butter with it."

Luca smacked his lips together.

"Or some sauce to dip it in."

Her eyes opened wide at what seemed to be a shared memory.

"Yeah. While Mom would make her Sunday pot I would sneak in and dunk. Paul learned to get an extra loaf just for me."

"My mother would fill a little bowl for me after the sauce was done, hand me a chunk of bread, and sit me down at the table. I might have been five years old. It was my favorite part of Sunday."

"I don't know where they got the phrase Wednesday is spaghetti day. Sunday was ours."

"Yeah, ours, too. My grandmother was always around to help in the kitchen. Sometimes she'd make cavatelli. I'd watch transfixed as she'd use her thumb to curl the pasta. Sometimes veal parmigiana, before we found out where veal came from. I miss our ignorance."

"My mother still has the edger that my grandmother used to crimp the ravioli. No store bought for us. Is your grandmother still alive?"

His head dipped as if the memory of an old Italian woman hurt him. He must have loved her.

Looking back up at her, he said in a solemn voice, "No. She passed away right after I left college. She was living with us by then."

"Where did you grow up?"

Luca's eyes searched the room as if he didn't want this to be a public sharing. She was still the only one within earshot so he gave her a bit of his background.

"Tough part of Boston until I was in my teens. My mother worked two jobs to afford the rent. When my sister was in college, she worked as well, made enough money so we could move to Melrose. That's the only reason I got to go to high school with Johnny and Tim. She took the pull-out couch so I could have my own room. She wanted me to be able to study without distractions. I don't think I'll ever be able to repay her for everything she did for me."

"That's what family is for, isn't it? I bet you've made up for it in spades."

"I moved them both out the first year we hit the stage. When we started making serious money."

"Where do you live now?"

"Winchester."

She whistled through her teeth.

"Nice town."

"It's got good schools, which is what my sister was looking for."

"Your sister lives with you?"

"Yes and no. The house was a duplex that we turned into condos. I'm on one side, she's on the other with my mother. I'm selling her mine, per her fiancée's request, before they get married. I wanted to give it to them for a wedding gift but he nixed it. I respect that. I'll give them a good price."

"Where will you live after that?"

Johnny walked over to where they sat. Done with the cream puff, he was eating a cannoli, smiling between bites as if he were in heaven.

"Same town, different house. I like being close by."

"What's it like?"

Johnny intruded and dropped down into the empty spot next to her.

"You should see the place. It's going to be great once it's updated. When was it built? Nineteen eleven?"

"Around there."

Tish asked, "What are you going to do with all that space?"

"Good question. I bought it because Val said it was a good value and I could make some money on it. Maybe I'll just flip it and find something smaller."

Johnny brushed his hands together to clean off the powdered sugar.

"Keep it awhile. It'll be another hangout for the band. I do get sick of driving to Acton."

Tish offered, "You can keep Rosie overnight occasionally."

"Only when she's older and eating solid food. But thanks for the offer."

His booted feet were leaning against the table, he was smiling and Rissa noticed how relaxed he seemed with the people here. It was different than when he was surrounded by women, journalists, or strangers.

Even when the rest of the group straggled in after getting Johnny's text about the goodies, Luca's body language signaled he was in a comfort zone.

No one had refused to partake of the pastries, and a dozen or so people filtered in and out of the room. As Rissa bit into her ricotta cannoli, her eyes closed in anticipation of the sweet creamy taste. When she opened them again, they met Luca's.

His smile melted something inside her and then he winked, playfully and a shade conspiratorially. They not only shared the secret of the hidden stash, but an ethnic past as well.

That night she dressed carefully for the concert. A skirt and scalloped shirt, lip gloss, and flats completed the outfit. With Lenny joining the band soon, she was going to get to go to a lot more of them. Tish had asked Gia if she'd watch Rosie.

"I want you there, Riss. It's my last night in concert with the guys."

She hadn't seen Tish on stage with them before and wouldn't get the chance again, so she didn't argue.

When Luca met them in the lobby, he was more dressed up than usual, his fitted black pants and button-down shirt showing off his well-sculpted body. Taking more than a quick look, she studied the way he moved, his posture, his muscles so well defined at the shoulders. And the part of her that was becoming insistent to sample the whole package broke into a five-sense-luscious Riverdance.

Her body had never betrayed her like that before.

Sex with Jude was good at first but over time had become inconsistent. His largesse had depended on how well she had behaved, especially on the weekend when they might have the time to fool around. He'd worked so many hours that she'd barely seen him during the regular workweek, and Saturday nights had found them at some dinner party with his peers or entertaining them at the condo. Her look might be offensive, her conversation dull, her ability to deflect his backdoor compliments poor, and they all played a role in their lack of true intimacy. And when she'd finally won some small measure of praise and he'd take her in his arms, it would still be about how well she performed.

Becoming horny as soon as someone walked into a room was a new experience.

What was it about Luca that had her ready and oh-so-willing whenever he appeared? Maybe it was the vulnerability that she sensed just beneath the surface.

She just didn't know what to do with the feeling.

Taste the decadent morsel, knowing it would only be just that, a taste?

Wasn't she done with unfulfilling relationships, men who took it whenever they could?

She wanted a serious commitment, and she wasn't going to find that in any candy store.

His voice cascaded over her, filling her with more need than sense.

"All dressed up. What's the occasion?"

Getting defensive, unable to admit it was her attempt to get him to notice her, she stammered, "Does there have to be one?"

"No. You're usually dressed more casual, so I thought you were finally going to get out there and find some action."

The detached manner told her he didn't feel the same kind of desire for her as she felt for him.

It was going to be another long night of look but don't touch.

The venue the band was playing was an indoor arena, and she was front row, center, the crowd surrounding her showing their appreciation as they always did. Loud and strong. Much closer to the stage than last time out, Rissa concentrated on the figure that seemed to draw her attention once Thunder took the stage. Now that he was riding the bus with them, the space had shrunk, the air had evaporated, and she'd been almost breathless the hour it had taken to get from one town to the next.

As he stood in his spot, his head down, only rarely lifting it to look out over the crowd, she thought how humble he was. More than she'd given him credit for. The only time he became arrogant was when she pushed him to defend himself. Otherwise, he was quiet, almost reserved, with a keen sense of observation, a critical eye, and a dry wit that had people laughing. Herself included. As she watched his performance, her focus on his play, she had to admit that he wasn't the crazy exhibitionist the newspapers had often described. The same couldn't be said about the women in the audience. She could hear them calling out his name, the one she'd finally given up for good, and she wanted to slap every one of them. How could they think he was that? Of course, they probably didn't think. The cries were all filled with emotion, as if they could win his heart with such telltale signs of love and adulation.

Candy in a candy store.

And they all seemed to want a taste.

She did, too, if she was honest.

They went after it as soon as the show wrapped up.

It was tough watching Luca fending off so many amorous females, and she kept waiting for him to pick one out of the crowd. Instead, he handled them with aplomb, respectfully, but declining every offer outright.

And then he was gone.

Disappointment snuck in.

Drawing a glaring conclusion, she retreated to her room, wondering who, what, when, where and how, the how in capital letters.

CHAPTER EIGHTEEN

She picked up that thread when she saw a taxi pull up in front of the hotel just as she was returning from an early-morning run with Gia. Luca stepped out, handed the driver some cash, and headed for the door. He must have seen them from the corner of his eye because he waited and pulled it open for them.

Gia smiled and said, "Thanks, Re—Luca."

Rissa noticed the grimace on Gia's face. The fines Tish instituted had done the job even if it was a delayed response.

She gave him the evil eye because she was pissed at him. He'd shared his sweet treats with another woman. While she'd spent long hours into the morning thinking about him, he'd been busying himself in other ways, ways she'd thought, hoped, wished he'd taken a break from. She had to assume he hadn't spent just a couple of hours in the sack but the whole night.

And she bristled.

In her snarkiest voice, she asked, "Just getting in? Must have been a wild night."

Luca smiled with stiff lips but offered his assessment, "I enjoyed it completely. I'm beginning to think you're too tightly wound. What you might need is a good...—"

"I don't just jump into bed with anyone."

"Only assholes and the like. Good for you."

With no zingers left, she huffed through the door that was waiting open and all but stomped to the elevator, her arms folded across her chest, her foot tapping as she waited for it to arrive.

She was still pissed as she packed up her things and flung her bag over her shoulder to head out to the parking lot. Standing by the bus, waiting for Ralph and the ride to Hartford, her brother in deep conversation with Luca, she couldn't help but overhear where the bassist had spent the night.

And her stomach flip-flopped.

She'd done it again. Thought the worst only to find out that he'd spent the night with his college roommate and his wife, not in the arms of some faceless woman.

Luca had a real smile on his face as he explained to Johnny, "It was good seeing them and they really enjoyed the show."

"They're good people. How old is their daughter?"

"Almost a year. She spent the night with Trevor's parents, but we picked her up this morning and went to breakfast before I left."

When Luca finally noticed her, all she could say was "Ouch."

"Don't worry. I'm used to it."

"You got used to people insulting you?"

"I didn't say I liked it. Only that I got used to it."

Johnny asked, "What are you two talking about?"

"She thought I was doing unmentionable things last night. And gave me her opinion on it."

Johnny arched his eyebrow at his sister.

"Why do you care what he does at night?"

His words were a cold glass of water in the face, and she had to swallow a couple of times before answering.

"I...I...don't care in the least. But he doesn't have to flaunt it."

"He's not flaunting anything. What the hell is your problem?"

With no reply on her tongue, she stomped up the stairs of the bus as soon as Ralph had unlocked it.

Putting her head in her hands, she groaned.

She had to stop this yearning. It was becoming a large problem, but she couldn't exactly tell Johnny that.

She groaned again.

She was either going to have to give it up or do something about it.

He might be all about the women, but he was also intelligent, sensitive, and funny. Maybe rough around the edges, maybe a bit too private.

Her only recourse was to ferret out some of his flaws so she could keep keeping her distance.

It meant digging deeper because she hadn't found any yet. All the ones she'd harped on had faded away like a puff of smoke.

Where there was smoke there was fire.

The potential there was frightening.

⌒

Lenny and his girlfriend Octavia, were hanging out in the lobby, looking excited when the group arrived in Hartford. Introductions were made and Rissa watched the band amble off soon after to huddle behind closed doors in Johnny's suite. The women cleared out, deciding to find a place to occupy themselves for a couple of hours. Rosie went along for the ride. There were enough of them that she was passed around, loving the attention, pretty much taking up the whole space in the hotel spa.

Rissa found herself next to Octavia, who asked to be called Tay, at the foot bath in the hotel spa, the water flowing into the tub, the tray of polishes in front of them.

Picking up a dark red, Rissa opened the conversation,

"From what I understand, you were here last year."

Tay was perusing the collection of colors on the tray in front of them, her choice a deep orange.

"Yeah. If it wasn't for these guys, I would have gone crazy."

"Not the best tour on record?"

"Not for the band Lenny was in. I had high hopes he'd leave it, then it was a moot point. It fell apart."

Tay placed that one back down and picked up a cranberry color. Rissa had settled on a deep blue.

"What's he been doing since?"

"Picking up gigs, writing, trying to stay busy. He was so happy when he got Luca's call."

"I'm surprised that Luca kept in touch."

"Why? They became pretty good friends."

"When did he find the time? I'm sure Lenny didn't hang out with him after hours."

Rissa could hear the judgment in her voice as she traveled down the road of condescension.

Tay had her head back, her eyes closed as if enjoying the foot bath.

"No, he didn't, but Luca hung out with us a lot, during downtimes. He was kind of at loose ends with Johnny so consumed with Tish. Especially after they got together."

"That's right. His playmate was through playing."

Tay sat up and grinned broadly.

"That downfall was fun to watch. You could tell Luca had a hard time with it."

Rissa tilted her head in question.

"How?"

"He gave Tish an awfully hard time at first. Then…well, it's hard not to like Tish."

Placing her foot on the towel, the pedicurist began to massage her instep.

Tish and Luca hadn't gotten along?

As if musing to herself she said, "They're pretty close now."

"Must be if he's riding your bus. He wouldn't have stepped foot on it last year."

"Why not?"

"He was determined to stay…actively engaged, shall we say, and the married bus had some pretty strict rules about women."

"Isn't that what hotels are for?"

"B.T., before Tish, Luca and Johnny would start scouting before we left. There were just as many women in the hotel lobbies as at the venue. If Luca found someone who interested him, he'd bring her on board to wait with him. It was definitely a singles space."

"Not this time around. At least from what I can tell."

"Gia's already given me a tour. It seems tame. I wasn't sure what I'd find."

"Do you mind riding that one? Lenny will be the only member of the band riding separate."

"I'd ride on the roof if it means staying with these guys. The band is stellar and the guys get along."

"Gia's cool. You won't be the only couple."

After letting the pedicurist know which color she was going with, Tay asked, "Did Luca change buses for us?"

"Yeah, at Johnny's request."

"That was nice of him. But then again, he's a lot nicer than people give him credit for. He's kind of hard to get to know, a lot private in certain areas, an open book in others."

Rissa relaxed as the polish was drying, chewing on what Tay had told her. There wasn't much that was private anymore, at least not for her. She'd uncovered so many different fragments. The only trouble she was having was integrating them into a whole.

If she forgot about the trouble he was causing her nerve endings.

Once the women had finished up in the spa, they wandered around the city.

Tish had stopped outside the hotel restaurant to check out the menu.

"Hey, this looks like a good place. Anyone up for lunch?"

Annie, always hungry now, didn't hesitate. After opening the glass door, she waddled through, the rest of the group following her in.

Letting the conversation flow around her, Rissa sat thinking about Luca as she ate, the way he made friends, kept them, and the glaring omission of women since the first night on the road.

She bit into a slice of pizza, savoring the taste of the pistachio pesto, thinking a bite on Luca's shoulder after a concert just might taste as good. All sweaty male.

She was glad to get her mind off that tidbit when Tish all but cooed, "Oh, this is soooo good."

Twirling the angel hair pasta around the tines of her fork, Tish gave herself another sinful bite before announcing, "I think we need to shop more. This afternoon was great. I'm going to have time to do this again. And again."

After finishing her bite of sirloin sandwich, Annie agreed, "More girl time, for sure."

Tay was enjoying her ravioli, not mixing in the conversation.

Tish asked no one in particular, "Okay, why has Luca taken a break?"

Annie laughed.

"Yeah, what is going on there?"

Rissa felt her cheeks flush.

She liked that fact. She wished he'd done it because of her but that was a delusion she was going to have to shift to reality. She had decided, after much careful deliberation, to give up the infatuation or rather, lustful imaginings about the man of many beds.

A break would mean...? What?

Tish was just finishing up the last French fry on Annie's plate when she eyed the single piece of pizza on Rissa's before snagging it. She wasn't the only one in the family who had scavenger ways.

After chewing she pronounced, "Oh, this is good, too."

Wiping a bit of the pesto off her chin she said, "So Rissa, does it have anything to do with you? I almost fell off the bunk when Johnny told me he was riding with us."

Rissa was taken completely off guard with the question.

"Me? Why would it have to do with me?"

Tish grinned at her sister-in-law.

"I told you...the sizzle."

Needing to keep the heat from spiraling at the thought of him, the lustful imaginings back in technicolor, she reaffirmed her original premise.

"And I told you...dislike."

"You're going to honestly tell me that you don't like him? You guys have been hanging out a lot lately."

Fingering the pool of pesto on her plate, she shrugged her shoulders.

"We've gone jogging. No big deal."

Tish leaned forward, not letting the subject drop.

"And cycling, eating Italian sticks. You looked pretty cozy that day."

Meeting Tish's eyes, she said, "He likes Italian bread. So what?"

Annie sat back, her eyes filled with gallows humor.

"He studies you on the bus."

Rissa's eyes flashed up.

"What do you mean, studies?"

Annie took a sip of her iced tea before saying, "With book in hand, he devotes time and attention to every move you make."

The contents of her stomach began to agitate round and round, up and down like clothes in a washing machine, heading quickly to the spin cycle.

"How do you know?"

Smiling, Annie said, "Because he doesn't turn a page."

Rissa was getting flustered now.

She didn't want him to do that.

Didn't want to feel this heat sliding along her spine at the thought of it.

Annie seemed rattled.

"I hadn't realized it before. He has stopped going out. God, I think it was after the first or second night on the road."

Rissa held her breath, knowing it was true but not wanting anyone else to know she'd been that observant. Or why.

Pretending she hadn't noticed, she asked, "What makes you say that?"

"He's slipped out after the concert with Tim and me twice, he spent one night with Trevor, there was the karaoke night, and not many in between. He's stopped...going out."

Tish's eyebrows arched, her lips pursed.

"I know it has something to do with you, Scalera. Fess up."

"There's nothing to confess."

"You are so doing the Scalera thing. Sniping, insults, then smiles and sunshine. Fire then ice. Exactly what your brother did to me for months."

Annie pointed out blithely, "Weeks. It only seemed like months. Years for some of us."

Tish tapped her finger on the table.

"Don't miss my point here, please."

Turning on her sister-in-law she asked, "What are you doing? And what is he doing back?"

Rissa hesitated, then blinked rapidly, her heartbeat skidding against her chest.

"I'm not doing anything. He's...he's just not what he seems sometimes. It's confusing."

Gia agreed. "He is. Confusing. He used to scare me. Full out intimidating sometimes. But once you break through the shell, he's so different. Dry sense of humor, kind, thoughtful. But please don't tell him I said that. He'd do more than call me a liar."

Annie conceded, "He's definitely been burned. A person doesn't shut down his emotions unless he's got scars. I've told him he needs to be more open. Show his true self. Take a chance on something real. That song he wrote indicates he is doing that. Why now?"

Tish began glaring at Rissa as if she was pressing for a confession.

"I haven't done anything. Honest."

"You don't feel anything for him? That sizzle I feel every time you two are together is all in my imagination?"

She swallowed hard.

"It must be."

Tish wore an earnest expression as if in warning.

"If you do end up moving on this fabrication, you have to remember. He might have a hard outer covering, but our Luca has a soft-mush center."

Becoming impatient with this whole line of questioning Rissa replied, "Yeah, and if those scars Annie mentioned mean anything, he's not going to take it very far. Even if you're right."

Gia asked, "How about yours?"

"My what?"

"Scars?"

Why were they all ganging up on her?

Her voice was thin and reedy.

"I don't have scars. I just have a penchant for picking the wrong men. Just another reason for me to stay away from him."

Tish rubbed her hands together.

"I think we should bet on the outcome here. Twenty bucks says they...do it."

Gia, her smile sly, offered, "I don't think it's a question of them doing it but when...they do the doing."

Rissa squeaked out, "You're betting on my life, here."

"Blame your brother. I seem to be picking up on one of his idiosyncrasies. Okay, date rather than if?"

All the women were in and Rissa just slunk down in her chair.

If she were a betting person, she wouldn't take this one. Odds were too high against.

But when she thought of rippling muscles, soft, full lips, the ache in her belly, she hoped that one of them would be right.

Her curiosity quotient was rising, and she thought tonight wouldn't be soon enough to unravel the mystery that was Luca.

⌒

Rissa had stayed behind with Rosie so Tish could be at the edge of the stage for Lenny's first night with the band. And as usual, as soon as Johnny and Tish returned, she headed down to the bar.

All she had thought about was the earlier conversation, the bet the women had made and whether she could manipulate an outcome.

When his voice cascaded over her from just outside the elegantly appointed barroom, she turned her head to see him standing there, watching her.

"Not done for the night yet?"

"Just wanted to relax after Rosie. She was a grumpy girl who didn't want to go to sleep."

He approached and the humming in her belly started in earnest now, not toning down like she'd hoped.

"Can I join you?"

"I don't own..."

She stopped herself and gave him some truth.

"Yes, I'd like that."

Directing his order to the bartender he said, "A 252 please."

"You got it."

"What is that?"

"Rum and Wild Turkey."

"Hm. Interesting but I don't think it would sit well on top of the tequila."

He chuckled before he said, "Probably not. Maybe next time."

He shot it down and looked up into the mirror to watch her without saying anything.

She was about to make a comment about his self-gazing but noticed he was not paying attention to his own image but to hers.

She swallowed hard when her eyes met his.

The pooling had started again. The pulsing of her body made her want to squirm in her seat to ease it.

"I would have thought you'd still be fighting off the women."

"I sneaked out with Tim and Annie."

Again.

She thought it risky to give credence to what Annie had said earlier, but it seemed like she was right on target. When the overwhelming urge to lean over and touch him got to be too much, she told herself urgently,

"I better go."

"Something I said?"

She shook her head to answer his question as if thoughts of him and how he made her feel would be flung far from her mind...and body.

Swiveling off her seat, she lost her balance, but he was there to make sure she didn't fall over. It hadn't been the drink. She had only had one. Her legs had gone rubbery and had refused to hold her upright. It didn't help that he took his time disengaging from the hold.

"Here, let me help you to your room."

Instead of pulling out of his grasp, she let herself relax into him. She liked how it felt. The coiling arousal was tightening, and the cloud of sensation was making her dizzy. He led her to the elevator, inside and up, the rocking motion keeping her unsteady on her feet.

She eyed him, his body language giving nothing away, and she wanted to pierce his complacency.

What would happen if she pushed him against the wall and plastered herself to his body? Probably nothing. She was so not his type. It made her determined not to give in to the impulse.

But when they reached their floor and he stepped into the hallway she took his hand and led him to an alcove just beyond.

His look was a questioning one.

The crackle of energy that sparked between them gave her the courage to ask, "Would you mind if I satisfied my curiosity about something?"

There was an amused gleam in his eyes, but they'd darkened, the pupils dilated.

"Depends on what you're curious about."

Her eyes remained on his as she admitted, "I saw you outside your room one night."

"And what were you doing outside my room?"

"I had innocently gone to get ice when I saw you with..."

Her head dipped and she was unable to finish the sentence. It made her voyeurism more shameful.

"A woman? Must have been in Portland."

"Yeah. She was pretty brazen with her hands."

"And you'd like to do something that concerns hands?"

"Not exactly."

"What exactly did you have in mind?" His voice was deceptively soft and smooth.

She took a step closer and, with trembling fingers brushed his hair off his face. A streak of lightning moved through her immediately.

"You want to touch my hair?"

"Ssh. I want it out of the way for a minute."

Her finger trailed down his cheek before her hand went behind his neck and she pulled his head closer.

She was a breath away from his lips and she lingered for a moment before pressing hers against them.

Soft, full, sinful lips and she couldn't help pressing deeper into them.

It was everything she'd dreamed it would be and a deep sexual hunger flared in her belly. His scent was intoxicating the feel of his chest against her sent ripples of gooseflesh across her skin.

It took only seconds for it to all die away.

He wasn't participating and it was a crushing blow.

She released him and stepped back.

With what Rissa felt was a lack of emotion, he asked, "Curiosity satisfied?"

Keeping her eyes riveted to his, she admitted, "Not quite."

"Do you need to repeat it?"

"I need you to—return it."

She wasn't sure he was going to grant her wish until he pulled her to him, slanted his head, and laid his lips against hers.

The humming had become a symphony of kazoos, a steady throb that she felt in every cell in her body.

Slowly she wrapped her arms around his back, pulling him closer, not wanting it to end, wanting to be here in the same place tomorrow, doing exactly the same thing.

He apparently didn't feel the same way.

She felt him disentwine her arms from around him and set her back a foot away.

"Now is it satisfied?"

Gulping hard to get the knot out so she could speak, she found her voice still didn't work so she merely nodded.

"Okay, then. Bedtime."

Taking her hand, he led her to her room, helped her with the key, and closed the door to separate them before she could say anything.

CHAPTER NINETEEN

Luca took a step along the hallway, then stopped, needing the support of the wall. With his head leaning back against it, he gulped.

What the hell just happened?

That kiss had set off a rocket in his head that he was sure would explode if he'd let it continue. More like the big bang when energy and matter were condensed into too confining a space. What resulted was a titanic, cosmic explosion.

Like an idiot, he'd stopped it when what he should have done was let the pinwheels of energy spiral. He went with safety rather than pleasure.

Her lips were luscious, ripe with wanting, something that scared the shit out of him. This was not in his plans. She was not the girl of his dreams. He wasn't even sure she liked him. It might have been purely physical; curiosity prompting the move.

She might be a tempting diversion, but she couldn't give him what he'd need in a mate.

Mate?

What the hell was he thinking?

How had he gone from wild nights to domesticity?

Paige.

Her email had set him off in a new direction. The feeling of loneliness had been escalating, expanding without limit, just like the cosmos, growing bigger and wider, forming black holes of emotion. Paige had reached out at the perfect time for renewal.

Being with Rissa would sidetrack him from his goal, upset the order of things.

New York City was only a week away.

It held the promise of everything he had ever wanted or needed.

He made his way the few short steps to his room and barricaded himself behind the door.

His breathing still hadn't regulated.

How was he ever going to get the memory of that kiss out of his head?

After striding to the desk, he booted up his laptop and opened his emails.

He'd reread the ones Paige had sent, re-grounding himself, reminding himself that his future lay there, if it lay anywhere at all.

Sliding his body into the chair, his breathing beginning to normalize, it seized again.

There was a new message waiting for him.

Luca:

I wanted you to know that I won't be coming with any baggage. I miscarried soon after we met in the coffee shop and the father and I had no reason to move forward with our plans. I could never have contacted you if things had gone a different way. I've dated over the years but never found anyone who met my standards. You set a pretty high bar.

I wish my days of rebellion had come before I met you, not during. I was so isolated and protected in high school that when I got a taste of freedom, I abused it.

The last few years have been devoted to getting my career in place. Now it's time to think about my future, a family and all that entails. The one thing I'm sure of is that I need a partner who is my intellectual equal. There are few out there who meet that requirement. Seeing your picture at this point in my life was rather synchronistic, don't you think? All things coming together in the perfect time, space continuum.

I am looking forward to that drink.

Paige

Her message was clear.

He threaded his fingers through his hair, his heart sputtering but the soft explosive sounds weren't due to the email.

They were due to the ineradicable effects of Rissa's kiss, the way her body felt pressed close to his own.

He closed the laptop and sank back against the pillows.

The causal implications of this were significant.

⌒

Rissa stood gaping at the door Luca had closed on them.

Her heart was still palpitating from the kiss, but he'd given no indication that it had affected him at all.

The good thing about following the urge was that she now knew what she wanted from a man.

Bursting rockets, fireworks, a whole colorful, chaotic display of light and sound.

Her whole body had come alive, her senses reeling, her heart pounding, a feeling she had never experienced before.

The downside was Luca didn't want to be that man.

Would she ever be able to find this again?

After stripping off most of her clothes and pulling on a tee, she tumbled into bed, her whole body in spasms. She wanted to feel the full effect, from beginning to completion. The kiss wasn't nearly enough.

Would she be willing to put herself out there again, push her limits, see if he was willing to show her what it was like?

To be completely satisfied.

Would she play the fool for it?

She looked at it from a new angle.

She wouldn't be doing this to please him.

It was obvious she had done nothing to excite him.

She'd be doing it for her own pleasure.

For the first time in a long time, she was going to make a grand sacrifice for herself.

She was in love with him, had fallen with slow and measured slips down that mountainside. His rejection was a foregone conclusion. She'd know that going in, but at least, for the first time, she'd walk away with something of value.

The downside? She'd lose a piece of her heart in the process.

She watched the day dawn from her window, the oranges, purples and yellows creating a palette in the sky. Donning some cut-offs and a sleeveless tee, socks, and sneakers Rissa grabbed her rollerblades and decided she'd head out to a local park to release some pent-up energy. She had lain in bed last night, wanting something she knew she couldn't have, and she'd only gotten snatches of sleep. Blading was better than running, the motion soothing, the connection to nature relaxing.

As she pushed through the door of the hotel, her phone rang. Glancing at the name, she dropped onto a bench outside and clicked on.

Her voice gave away her delight with the caller.

"Hi."

"How's it going?"

It felt good hearing the friendly voice. Kathy Cole was one of her best friends from high school and the one person she had kept in touch with over the years. Accepting the role of bridesmaid at a wedding that was never to be, she had helped Rissa through some of the horrible days that followed the cancellation. Kathy was an analyst for a high-tech firm in Boston, married and living in Beverly. Sometimes Rissa envied Kathy's life.

"I have to admit I'm having a blast."

"Is it getting any easier?"

An image of a tall, lean but muscular build filled her mind and she said honestly, "I don't think about him at all anymore."

"Good, Riss. Your mother knew what she was doing."

She gave a carefree laugh. It was good talking to someone who knew her well.

"Doesn't she always."

"Meet anyone interesting yet?"

"Haven't been looking for that. But I'm sketching everywhere we go, hanging around with one of the band members."

"Which one?"

"Oh. Um, Luca, the bassist."

"Isn't he the one who's single?"

There was a question hiding beneath the question.

"I would hope so. But it's not like that. I'm kind of like everyone's younger sister."

She wouldn't think about the kiss. It might have been coerced but it wasn't brotherly.

"Is that offer you made about tickets still out there?"

"Yes, absolutely."

"I talked to Betsy to see if she wanted to go with me and she's all for it."

"Oh, my God. I would love that. I haven't seen her in years. Now that Tish is staying with Rosie and with my mom coming in to steal some time with her grandchild, I'm free. We could meet and grab something to eat. I'll talk to Johnny about hanging out backstage. That way we won't even have to deal with tickets."

"It'll be just like it was when we were freshmen. Of course, now the guys we drooled over are out of commission, your brother being the main attraction."

"And that idiot Joel."

"Yeah. Is Luca the one who replaced him? I thought it was a guy named Reject.

Rissa cringed. "I refuse to call him that."

Although that was true, the word *reject* flashed in her brain like a neon sign reminding her that she had to resist the urges that rippled over her in waves.

"How is he?"

"Great bassist. Kind of a player, but as he's the last single man standing you can't blame him for taking advantage."

"Bets will love that. She just broke up with someone, can't keep track really and she'll probably love a night with a rocker."

Something strange started in the pit of her stomach at the thought of her other friend coming on to Luca.

With more bite than she'd meant, she said, "No nights with rockers. She'll be there to be with us, not try to seduce Luca."

"Do I detect something about Luca you're keeping from me?"

Struggling hard to keep her voice normal, she said, "Of course not. I certainly don't need another player in my life."

"You would think one's enough in a lifetime but you..."

"I do not."

Kathy laughed. They had talked at length about Rissa's luck with guys. Before Jude, there'd been Randy who was exactly what the name implied. That had ended badly, too.

"Maybe you need a matchmaker."

"Oh, yeah. I'll get my mother right on that. She'd have a field day."

"She really would. Sorry. But that thought is too delicious."

"Not a word to her when you're here or our friendship is over."

More seriously, Kathy assured, "I'll always have your back, Riss. You know that."

She did and would be forever grateful. Kathy was one of the kids who'd stuck with her despite her ups and downs in high school and her mood swings from grief to anger.

"I'll call as soon as I talk to Johnny."

"And I'll give Betsy a call. Let her know."

"Okay. Talk to you soon."

"Bye, Rissa."

"Bye, Kath."

⌒

Knowing that she'd be enjoying a night with her friends soon, the day was even more perfect. She must have bladed close to ten miles, and the warmth of the sun was turning her skin a nice bronze color. Never one to sit out to just bathe in it, she still got a good tan most summers from all her other outdoor activities. A bit sweaty when she got back, she breezed into the hotel to find the band members hanging around in the lobby, signing autographs and chatting with fans. Attempting to scoot by without being noticed, her appearance less than appealing, she had almost made it to the bank of elevators when she overheard one of the women asking Luca for more than his signature.

As she hesitated to hear his answer, he looked up from the bra he was holding and noticed her standing there.

She felt an overwhelming sensation when his eyes connected with hers and it held her to the spot as he told the fan that he was sorry but tonight wasn't possible. Rissa let a breath out that she hadn't even know she was holding.

When the elevator pinged and the doors opened, she broke contact, stepping inside to escape what she knew was a very dangerous indication of things that could come. If she let them.

Leaning against the wall against the shimmying movement, she almost laughed. She was doing it again. Wanting a man who didn't want her. Spending time scheming how to get him to take her to bed was crazy. It wasn't only his sexual drive that would complicate matters but the fact that he was so damn smart. Her D in Biology in freshman year had set the tone for all those meaty subjects that came after. She was hopeless when it came to numbers, equations and multiples.

Why the hell was she even thinking about that?

She wasn't counting on a lifetime commitment, wasn't after that. All she wanted was one night to ease the pangs that were twitching.

Slipping into her room, a couple hours left until she went to get Rosie, she pulled out her new pad. The charcoal moved in a frenzy as she captured the man with a bra in his hand, his head up and his eyes looking at a distant object, suggesting something she knew she shouldn't want.

⌒

Luca exhaled. He knew he should be used to handling women's intimate apparel by now, but it still made him uncomfortable. That he had been holding a bra when Rissa returned, the look on her face somewhat accusatory, had him almost defensive. At least it hadn't been a pair of panties. In his opinion, they were the most offensive. Too personal to let a stranger touch, handle, put his name to. As he scanned the guys, he was assured they were as uncomfortable as he was. How did their wives deal with it so well?

How would Paige handle the craziness?

He knew now, after years of bedding some very inventive women, she was straight laced, a bit proper. Would this offend her sensibilities?

Annie and Tish were great about it, laughing sometimes at the absurdity of it all. Marci had loosened up over the years, and had come to expect this as part of their fame.

He was relieved that the time allotted was almost up.

They devoted an hour to this kind of fan interaction before ending the meet and greet. He used to relish the aftermath, the women fawning over the last man standing. Not anymore. The taste had become bitter. When Johnny gave the nod, he ambled over to the elevator with the rest of them. Joining the guys when they retired from the attention was becoming his new routine. He was tight with them again and preferred their company over anyone else's.

As the elevator door swept open, Johnny asked Tim, "Hey, you remember Rissa's friends from high school?"

"The ones who used to listen to us play?"

"Yeah, Kathy and Betsy. Rissa texted me earlier to see if it would be okay for them to come to one of the Boston shows, hang around backstage to watch us."

"Oh, God. I hope they're over you."

"If not, I think I might know what will stop them in their tracks."

"Shouldn't you rather say who, not what?"

"I never led them on. They were so fricking young."

"Not anymore. They're legal now."

"Kathy's married. Happily, from what I hear so that just leaves Betsy."

"She was the quiet one, right?"

Johnny laughed, thinking about the stories Rissa had just told him about her friend, president of both the senior class and National Honor Society. And how she'd changed.

"From what I hear, she's become a man-eater."

"We'll leave her to Luca."

Luca backed out of the circle as if to decline the invitation but no one seemed to notice.

And when Luca closed his own door, he shut out the world.

⌒

Picking up his iPad, he booted up the sci-fi game he'd gone back to playing. Determined to keep his nights free, to refrain from something that had gotten old, he found the game was helping him keep his mind off other things that might tempt fate.

His fingers moved as the action began and he was once again in a bleak Boston future. His character wore the regulatory Red Sox cap and leather jacket, but he was finding the game to have a somewhat limited progression. There was the usual mix of cybernetics, magic, and fantasy though, so even if it wasn't the best game on the market, he could play with a modicum of skill. It was the kind of fantasy he could work hands on, unlike his growing fantasy about a certain female who he'd coax into bed if his future wasn't so uncertain.

His fingers stilled on the keypad, and he rested his head against the wall, his vision filled with the woman who was stealing into his thoughts much too often lately. A real tomboy who loved rugged sports, she had an earthiness that was extremely sensual. Her breasts were the perfect size for the kinds of games she played, never getting in the way of her skill, and he wanted to know what they'd feel like in his hands. All clean lines and angles, but with just enough plush in the right places. His body seemed inclined to agree with his need to feel her under him and he felt a part of him reach up in pursuit of the kind of pleasure she could provide. He hadn't felt this kind of desire in a long time and wished he could act on it.

Why now?

He'd gone so many years without a tumble into this kind of territory and now...

He couldn't, wouldn't go with this.

If he was going to give up his freedom, it would have to be with a woman who he could talk to about black holes, tectonic properties, the origin of life. Someone whose talents he could respect, whose mind he could admire.

His body surged with electricity as he plugged his thoughts into the woman who caused a chemical reaction that was radioactive and dangerous.

There was something to be said for that kind of a meltdown.

But it would critically endanger any chance for a life-long commitment.

CHAPTER TWENTY

Rissa couldn't believe the whole group made it down to breakfast at the same time the next morning. It was highly unusual. In between bites of pancakes, Johnny told her, "A couple of years back, I went to this rock-climbing center. It was great. You might want to try it before we leave this afternoon."

Tish offered, "Why don't you go with Riss. I'll man the fort. I won't be practicing until later."

His eyes lit up as he looked at his wife. "Are you sure?"

"You haven't played in a while, so go have fun."

Giving her a kiss, he grinned. "Just another reason I can't live without you."

Addressing the group, he said, "Anyone who wants to come can join us."

They all disbursed soon after, those wanting to hit the rock-climbing center agreeing to meet back in the lobby fifteen minutes later.

Dressed in her leggings and tee that would let her move freely, her sneakers hopefully giving her the traction she'd need when scaling the wall, she was surprised at the others who wanted to go with them, Luca being one of them.

Ambling over to where he stood, she stated, "I don't see you as the rock-climbing type."

"Not sure I'll give it a try, but it might be fun to watch everyone hanging from the heights."

Joe, Chappy, Gia, Ralph, and Jett climbed aboard the bus, which would take the group to the facility. It was their mode of transportation around the towns they visited. It saved on taxis, especially when there was a group of them participating.

❡

When Rissa stepped inside and scanned the huge space, eager anticipation flooded through her. There was a monolith center stage, sitting in the middle of a cavernous circle of white, dotted with colorful climbing holds that had volume and outsized shapes for gripping. Various members of the staff were managing ropes for some of the climbers, some beginners, some obviously old hands at moving from point to point. There were dozens of climbers already rappelling up the side of the pillar, and she looked around for a place to ascend without interference.

A staff member came over. "Welcome. I'm Roger."

Looking as if he were doing a mental count he asked, "How many climbers today?"

Johnny, as always, was the spokesman.

"There's seven of us."

As there were eight bodies standing there in the open space, Roger showed his proficiency in math.

"So only one won't be rappelling?"

"Yeah."

With clipboard in hand, he looked down as if assessing who he could pull to work with the group.

"We don't have the staff to accommodate all of you at the same time. If you had called ahead..."

Johnny reassured him, "No problem. We can alternate amongst ourselves."

Holding the clipboard against his chest, Roger said, "You've obviously done this before?"

Johnny reassured him, "Most of us."

Roger was scanning his clip board again, his finger moving down the page. "I have the manpower for two of you. Who wants to start?"

Johnny looked at Rissa with an arched eyebrow.

"If Luca's willing, he can be my belayer. He's strong enough and it will free up someone else to go."

Johnny turned to see if Luca was willing, to hear Luca ask, "What do I have to do?"

Rissa met his eyes and said, "Hold my rope. Make sure I don't fall."

Their eyes held for longer than necessary before he answered, "You trust me to do that?"

Her voice conveyed her confidence.

"Yes."

Trusting him with her heart was another story.

Johnny affirmed, "He wouldn't let anything happen to you, but he'll try extra hard with me in the vicinity. He knows if you got hurt, I'd have to do some bodily damage."

"I guarantee I won't let her fall."

Rissa wondered if there was a double entendre in the simple statement but couldn't quite understand what it meant.

After choosing a double rope hanging against the surface, Rissa stood beside it and climbed into her harness while Luca fastened his. Once her climber's knot was secure, she turned to help Luca with his system, assembled his carabiner clip, and began to loop the rope and push it through the silver device.

"It has to sit straight so you need to keep this loop clean." Glancing up to give him a brief smile, she added, "Piece of cake, right?"

"What are you saying, I'm neat?"

The lopsided smile told her he appreciated her attempt at humor.

His nearness was causing a slight tremor in her fingers, and as she tried to clip the device onto the harness, her fingers slipped, brushing against him, and the heat of that slight touch caused her to snatch her hand away as if it'd been scorched.

"Sorry. Maybe you better do the rest."

He closed the carabiner and tested it before looking to her for further instruction.

With a voice that all but croaked, she went on.

"Now, hold the bottom of the rope in your strong hand. While I'm climbing, you have to keep it taut, so don't let go. As I go up, the rope will become slack, so you need to tighten it again and again so it stays stressed. If I start to fall, pull the slack and hold it. It will suspend me where I am and I can get back to the rock and grips. When I'm done, you'll need to control my speed during the descent by keeping the rope—"

"Close to my body." Now it was his turn to smile. "Physics in action."

Her head shot up to see if he was kidding. There was a smile, but she couldn't read it well.

"Really?"

"Slack and tighten, like a pulley."

"Gee, I never thought of it like that."

"And here you thought you didn't understand the forces of energy."

Her eyes widened in surprise. This was physics? It was interesting how her brain stuttered along while her body put it all together. When he checked her system one last time, examining her harness belt to make sure it was secure, her body seemed to be in tune with another force of nature, one her brain was determined not to give in to.

Needing to get said body out of his range of touch, she chalked her hands and asked, "Are you ready?"

Grasping the rope in his hands, he said, "I am. How about you?"

Johnny had come to stand beside her and challenged, "Bet I can climb straight up."

Jerking on her rope to make sure it was tight, Rissa countered, "You've been here before. You know whether you can or not. I only bet on sure things now."

"I wasn't able to do it before. It's not a sure thing."

Taking a step away, Rissa looked up to study the terrain, analyzing which route to take and which holds to use. It was like a mental puzzle and her brain was sifting and sorting out the pieces that would get her where she wanted to go with the least amount of resistance.

Luca asked, "Making a mental map?"

"Yeah, I have to anticipate height, balance, and reach, figure out the best way up. Sometimes I work backwards. Choose a spot where I want to finish and visually find my way down."

Once she'd sorted through her options, had devised a route, she moved close to the wall.

Lifting her foot, she placed it on the sloper hold and began her journey up. She felt confident, Luca working the ropes well. She could concentrate on her ascent, not the shimmy of an unseasoned hand. It had the makings of one of her better climbs.

She glanced down once to see him watching her. He was standing with feet slightly apart, braced to counter her weight and balance. His eyes were intently focused on her, causing her hand to falter. Tightening her grip on the holds, her muscles tensed, and her face became a study in concentration, her center of gravity perfectly balanced. When Johnny fumbled at the midway point of the ascent, swinging sideways out from the rock, she smiled to herself as Jett tightened the rope to keep him steady until he could regain his foothold. She had just gained another edge. She climbed the route from bottom to top, using jug, pinch and crimp holds, her legs pushing her body from point to point in one continuous flow. She pumped her arm and hooted when she'd reached the top, accomplishing her feat, and Luca had kept her steady.

Luca must have been watching Johnny's reaction because she heard him call up, "You should have bet him."

Looking down, she grinned from ear-to-ear. "I didn't want to humiliate him. He is my brother."

Johnny's head tilted back to take in her success and gave a fisted arm pump in congratulations.

"Way to go Riss."

Working in tandem, their rhythm completely in sync, Luca expertly managed the ropes as Rissa made her descent in a smooth flow of motion.

Once her feet touched the ground, she threw her arms around him.

Feeling the ripples of muscle when she embraced him, her arms around his shoulders, her breathing short-circuited. But instead of bolting back, she forced herself to let them flow under her fingertips. Never once did she doubt, he'd keep her safe, and it was the strength and power in these muscles that had done it.

"Thanks. You were great."

Luca cut short the hug and took two steps back.

And she almost stumbled at the break in contact.

"Sorry. I..."

"You did that like a pro. Poetry in motion."

Swallowing hard, wishing she were still in his embrace, she whispered, "Thanks."

The ache she felt at his distance was the price she paid for falling in love with the wrong man.

Removing her equipment, she returned it to the service area and found an empty corner of the building where she could quietly disassemble. The day had suddenly turned on her. High from their partnership, her successful climb, her body was not only sore in muscles used to stretch and pull but pulsed and tingled in a very private place. Short of jumping him, she wasn't sure how to make it stop.

Luca went to stand in the loft-style viewing area as the partners on the ground switched positions, Joe and Ralph standing beside him. He didn't watch the action. Instead, his gaze was on a woman who stood quietly in the corner, her shoulders drooped, and her lips turned down. He didn't like seeing her so sad, and it felt even worse because he suspected it had to do with the embrace. Or the fact that he'd declined to stay in it. Frissons of pleasure and need had raced through him as he'd watched her body maneuver the ropes. When she'd flung herself at him a jolt of sexual energy had hit him hard and fast. It was something he couldn't move on, couldn't satisfy so he'd forced himself back and away.

At the image of her climbing that wall, her sweet ass so inviting, his body had told him something his mind had neglected to see. She was a very physical being. It played out in everything she did, from jogging to singing. The climb had highlighted her other skills, those of a scientific bent. Her mental notes combined her knowledge of gravity, physics, and anatomy.

It was a startling revelation. He would never have made the connection if he hadn't been watching, questioning, making his own analysis of her options. She'd chosen perfectly, engaging all her muscle groups, showcasing her endurance and fluidity of motion.

She used every one of her senses along with every muscle and tendon and he had a feeling she'd come to his bed with the same energy as she expended on everything else. And he had to make sure that she didn't get the opportunity to show him just what she could do there. He couldn't take the risk of blowing the upcoming reunion. He was going to have to stop playing with fire. Her heat could burn away every intention he had to stay detached, and he knew he'd be left standing in the ashes if he let it consume him.

When he finally got back to the hotel, he took a cold shower.

It had become a necessity to wash away her touch, her scent.

She did things to him that he couldn't afford to feel.

CHAPTER TWENTY-ONE

They had finally arrived home to their city and Rissa's excitement bubbled up.

Every one of them was born and bred in Boston and there had been talk about dispersing to their own individual houses but they'd decided to remain a group. With two sold-out concerts over the next two nights, a new member aboard, cohesiveness would help tighten their sound.

She couldn't be happier, but she didn't want to dwell on the why.

Another perk about being in Boston was that she'd get time with family. With her mother coming in from Melrose, both she and Tish could attend the concert, Celia taking on some grandmother duties being so close by. There would be more of it in the future. She'd promised she'd be descending on the group from time to time throughout the tour.

"No way am I going three months without seeing my *carina, carina* becoming Celia's nickname of choice for Rosie, adding to a long list of endearments that covered the family in love.

Holding Rosie on her lap on the sofa of the sitting room, Celia just sat cooing and carrying on while the others caught up on their lives.

Rissa's younger sister was here to attend the concert. Lana loved her niece but had never exhibited a fondness for children in general. It made everyone wonder whether they were in her future or not. Three years younger, Lana had her life completely together and mapped out. Graduating from culinary school just last year, she had brought what she'd learned into her mother's catering business, and Celia's Cookery had taken a quantum leap in sales and had just been featured in *Boston Magazine* as one of the fastest-expanding businesses in the area.

The sisters gossiped and caught up on all the family drama before leaving for the Boston Garden, which was what Rissa still called the TD Center.

Lana asked Rissa, "So have you hooked up with any good-looking guys yet?"

Rissa flopped into an empty spot next to her mother. She examined Lana, who had taken a seat across from her. She was dressed up, showing off the curves she'd inherited from the female side of the family. Her own DNA had skipped that gene or replaced it with a more angular frame, like her brothers. Looking down at her ripped jeans and tank top, she sighed.

Mentally she stuck her tongue at her sister before answering her question.

"That's not why I'm here. Besides, I've been kind of busy."

"Have you been to a concert yet?"

"Yeah, I've gone to a couple. There is a preponderance of women. If I were into them, I'd have my pick."

"Don't you go out nights?"

"If I'm with Rosie I just go hang out in the lobby once the band gets back. There's not much activity that late at night, so I guess the answer's no."

Johnny interjected, "We actually got a night off recently. Went to a karaoke bar. Seems Riss belted one out."

While fixing the headband she'd pushed on to keep the curls contained, Rissa took a calming breath.

"Let's not get into that, okay?"

"Luca said she left them crying in their seats."

Celia's eyes shot up and she asked, "You were with Luc?"

"No, I was with Johnny and Tish. He was just along for the ride."

Her mother put her attention back on her granddaughter when she said, "He's such a nice boy. You could do worse."

Lana said out loud what everyone else was thinking. "I think she has."

Giving her a sisterly arched brow rebuke, Rissa said as nonchalantly as she could, "I don't really see a lot of difference between them. Both out for a good time and all."

Her mother's brown eyes flashed at her and pointed out, "Luca is not committed, so he can have all the fun he wants without hurting anyone. Jude is a cheating son of a bitch. There's a mile of difference. Besides, from what you told me, Jude didn't treat his mother very well. He didn't take very good care of her."

"It wasn't really his place to do that, was it? He does have a father."

"Elana told me some stories of Luca's childhood. It was sad. He rose above it and became a very nice young man."

Curiosity won out over continuing her surliness and she scooted closer to her mother.

"What did she tell you?"

"Nothing I'm going to share with you. That was told in confidence, mother to mother."

"Did you talk about me?"

"Why? Do you think I shared all my misgivings about who you were with? I didn't. Mostly we talked about the boys, the band, their success, how it's changed them."

Johnny asked, "And how has it changed us?"

"In good ways, believe it or not. We got you back and Luca came out of his shell."

Rissa mumbled under her breath, "Boy, did he ever."

"Don't be disrespectful. I worry about you, Marissa. You have no sense when it comes to men. You always pick the losers."

"I don't always."

"Yes, you do. You wouldn't know decency if it bit you on the ass."

"Ma."

"Now Lana's Rafe? He's a good boy. Respectful, honest, hard-working, honest trade. Jude? He's self-centered, lacking in morals, plays in a speculative trade. Money is where his focus lies and he's too showy for my taste."

She had to admit all of that was true.

Lana was the one who pointed out, "He worked hard, I have to give him that."

Celia gave her opinion on that as well.

"He worked a lot of hours. Or so he said. You really didn't know where he was or what he was doing, though, did you, Marissa?"

She didn't, although she'd come to suspect it was rarely where he said he was.

"You were alone more than you were together. All he gave you was a car, a nice place to live but he took them away without a second thought. He didn't give you honesty or his heart. I would think those things are more important."

Celia was right there, as well.

Lana put her two cents in.

"You need to start looking for someone who's kind, attentive and who can love you for who you are, not what he wants you to be."

"That's not Luca."

And it clawed at her heart. The scratches were beginning to throb.

As if just realizing something of importance, Celia asked, "When did everyone start calling him by his given name? It's about time."

Johnny grinned at his sister and informed, "Rissa suggested that it might be the right thing to do."

Their mother looked up at her older daughter and smiled.

"Hmm. There's hope for you yet."

⌒

When it was time, Jett collected them in the lobby, having taken on the duty of bodyguard for all the Scalera's. Tony and Dennis would be added to the mix later.

As they were boarding the bus, Lana gave Rissa a head-to-toe-perusal.

"You do know you won't attract honey that way, don't you?"

"I don't particularly like honey, so I don't see the problem."

"Rissa, you can't mope around. He isn't worth it."

"I'm not moping. Really, I'm not. And I promise I will get back on the horse soon."

Wriggling her eyebrows so Lana would get the pun, she knew she'd reached her objective when Lana laughed.

"I just want you to be happy. You deserve better than what you settled for."

Becoming serious, looking at a point over her sister's shoulder, she admitted, "I think Ma might be right. I can't seem to pick a winner."

"Are we back to the horse play?"

A semblance of a smile appeared on Rissa's face.

"What did I see in him?"

"A family?"

"Maybe. On paper, he didn't look that bad. Successful, put-together, pretty good-looking."

"It's more than that, sweetie. There's got to be passion. There has to be a spark, which comes from fire, not a piece of paper."

"It was always easy for you. You knew what you wanted to do and dove in. You were never hesitant, and you've ended up with it all."

"But I took care of me first. Figured out what I wanted and didn't let anyone divert me. If a guy didn't like that I worked crazy hours, well, he was out of the equation. You let Jude influence what you thought, what should be important, how you should dress, what topics were worth talking about. You let him try to change you. You are so perfect at who you are. I envied your friendships, your ability to play, your athleticism, your talents. As the baby of the family, I should have felt far less responsible."

Lana had never been the typical youngest child. Much more serious about life than any of them.

"Dad's dying changed all the dynamics. We all grew up pretty quickly."

"Someone had to help Ma with the business. It had to feed all of us. The pension would never have covered it, especially with the way Johnny and Den ate. Quite literally they almost ate us out of house and home."

"But you were only twelve."

"But I loved every aspect of it."

Lana always felt at home in their kitchen, loved trying out new recipes, excelled at the family favorites.

"You always did make a mean cannoli."

Lana gave her a smile and asked in a quiet and serious voice, "What do you love to do? What gives you joy, Rissa?"

She thought about it for a minute. The kids at the preschool, the volleyball team, reading. She loved all those things but the one activity she would go to above all others?

She pulled off the head band, pushed the curls off her face.

"Sketching. I love capturing emotions, thought processes, activity and I never leave the hotel without my materials. But what can I do with that? I can't make money that's for sure."

"As they say, do what you love and the money will come."

"I don't know who they are, but I don't think they'd want to live at home with Ma while waiting for it any more than I do."

"You'll figure it out. Just make sure you stay true to who you are. Don't ever let anyone try to change you again. I, for one, love you..."

Rissa sang the ending.

"...just the way you are?"

"And that voice. Join a band. You'll make money that way, I can guarantee it."

"Wait until you see the way the fans mob the guys. Definitely not for me."

Rissa tucked her arm in the crook of Lana's as they headed for the door.

⌒

Rather than being backstage, Lana and Rissa sat several rows back. Ron had set aside a ton of seats for their hometown concert, and they were sitting with all the other wives, girlfriends, and friends who had been invited. Tony and his playmates were with them, and they had a great time trading insults about the brother who was up on stage. The off-duty policemen couldn't believe Tony's big brother had made it so big.

Rissa sat mesmerized and didn't know how Joe and the roadies did it. From this vantage point, she could see the backdrop they'd assembled. Lightning flashed, thunder rumbled, the lights creating a virtual storm swirling around the four musicians. You could almost smell the rain as it hovered in the clouds, almost feel the electricity in the air. It was an incredible display of genius, and she respected the artistry of the background people the band had around them.

Throughout the concert, as they danced and moved to the music, Lana would point out some guy that she thought was hunky.

"I bet the guys wouldn't mind if you invited someone backstage to meet them."

"Why would I want to do that?"

"It's called flirting."

"I don't flirt."

"It might be time to start."

But there was no one she wanted to approach. Well, maybe one but that would be foolhardy. It would confirm her inability to choose wisely. He hadn't shown a shred of interest, and she didn't want him to reject her advances again. He'd already put her in her place twice. She wasn't going for a third.

It didn't mean she couldn't watch.

He was covered in just a tee shirt and jeans, and she knew what the body beneath looked like, at least some of it, had seen the muscles that rippled, the abs that were firm and strong. He never flaunted it, so she was sure the women who'd gotten lucky were wildly surprised by his physique.

How would it feel under her fingers?

She felt a quickening in her belly that gave her the answer.

Lana, who had seen them in concert before, said "They're playing really well tonight."

"This is home. They give it an extra punch when they're here," Annie explained although she didn't have to.

Gia was gyrating to the music when she asked, as if she didn't want the night to end,

"Where are we going to go afterwards?"

Tish said, "I'm going back to feed Rosie and then we're taking Lana out and show her a good time."

Rissa rolled her eyes. "She's home, for cripes sakes. She doesn't need us to show her anything."

Tish smiled. "Yeah, but she's never been out with the guys before. You know that's a very unique experience."

Rissa returned the smile and said, "If you like stampedes."

Tony interjected, "Yeah, we're hoping to get some spill off."

"Hey, you're taking Ma home, remember. Please don't desert me."

"I can get some phone numbers. Being the drummer's brother has got to have some perks. We look a little alike."

"Very little. You're shorter."

But when she took his arm, she felt the muscles that came from working out for a job that needed muscle.

"The build's the same. Muscles on muscles. You should definitely attract some attention."

Lana said excitedly, "I can't believe we're all together. I haven't been out with you guys in a long time. This should be fun. Tomorrow Rafe's joining us but tonight it's just family."

Rissa's lips puckered in disgust. Another couple she'd have to watch kiss and cuddle.

It seemed to be all around her and it wasn't getting easier to sit and observe.

Maybe she'd just go back to the hotel, hang with her mother.

Then, her gaze went back to a man she wanted to spend more time with, his body something to behold.

Mid-way into the set, when Tim stepped forward to the mic, she knew what was coming and she tingled at the thought. Johnny had mentioned Luca would be singing his first song with the band although he hadn't given out any other information. She had no idea what the song was about, although she didn't think it would matter to the fans.

The noise level amped up a thousand-fold, and Tim's hands went into the air, attempting to get the fans to listen. He shifted his body to give a shrug and smile to the other members of the band before looking out over the vast number in attendance.

John began a drum roll signifying the need for quiet, but it took a couple of minutes before the noise subsided at least to the point Tim could be heard.

"It's so good to be home, in Boston, and we couldn't think of a better place to introduce one of our new songs. Are you ready for a treat tonight?"

The applause started to ramp up again and Tim made another attempt, his hand up in stop fashion and the crowd acquiesced.

"Johnny and I do most of the writing, as many of you know. But we didn't write this one. This one was written by none other than our very talented bassist."

The women in the audience seemed to surge forward, screams piercing the air, the message a potent one.

"After..."

His hands went in the air again, shushing the masses, waiting again for some normalcy. Tim began, "After you hear this, you'll know how he got his name, but as of tonight I hope you begin to call him Luca."

Turning toward the man in question, he offered him the stage.

Screams echoed through the halls, and it was Luca's turn to try to stop the pandemonium. Stepping to the standing mic, Luca began, "I've left the writing up to these guys 'cause they do it so well. I'd leave the singing up to them as well but they're kind of bossy."

The laughter rumbled beneath the women's squeals.

"I'm sure many of you have seen the abundance of pictures from my high school days. It was a rough time for me, but as you can see, things have gotten better. Good friends, great fans like you have made the difference. This song goes out to anyone who has or is still being bullied."

The drums filled the air. The wail of the electric guitar sent shivers running up Rissa's spine.

She sat spellbound, waiting to hear what he had to say.

When Luca's voice floated out, it filled the arena with the same melancholy she quite often saw on his face. It was a good voice, and it wrapped around her like a soft, warm blanket. She didn't understand why he didn't sing more. It didn't have the smooth tenor of Tim's or the raw emotion of Johnny's. But it moved everyone in the place.

And the words stung. They told her what she'd done, how she'd hurt people. Thank God Dennis had intervened, had gotten her to stop. Her eyes pressed shut, blocking out the images of Luca shamed by people like her. Luca hit every note, expressed exactly what it was and what it felt like. He had put himself out there, something he'd said he'd never do, and she wondered why he had this time.

"My God. He's good."

Annie sat with her mouth open as if it was a totally unexpected pleasure.

"The women aren't going to leave him alone now, that's for sure."

"I think he just got some of them to jump the Johnny and Tim ship."

Rissa knew they were right.

And it meant she had even less of a chance to get to enjoy all his gorgeousness. The field had just multiplied by a power of ten.

To erase all doubt, the screams that erupted once the song was finished were deafening.

Luca gave a short wave and stepped back into his comfort zone.

It had taken courage to expose himself like that.

Could she do the same? She'd already done it twice, exposed what she wanted. He'd given her no reason to believe the third time might be the charm.

The powerful rush of emotion told her she just might have to go for it.

The meet and greet was chaos, and Lana stood with her mouth open as women all but assaulted the guys, no exceptions. Rissa laughed out-right at her expression. Many of the women just wanted an autograph but where they wanted the signatures was ridiculous.

"Ew. She wants Johnny to sign her ass?"

"At least she's leaving her jeans on. Some don't, from what I've heard. They call them Moon Junes."

"Come on. He's not that great."

"You're looking at it from a sister's point of view. It's all perspective."

"Riss, that woman just lifted her shirt up...um, she isn't wearing anything underneath. What's Luca gonna do?"

"Watch and see."

Lana's eyes were bulging. Until she saw Luca turn the woman around and sign her tee on the back side. The woman ended up flashing her parts at the rest of the audience.

Lana chuckled. "Smart man."

"One of the brightest."

Lana's head snapped to look at her sister. Her sister's voice held a tinge of adoration, and Lana suspected that maybe he was the reason Rissa wasn't interested in exploring the field of men. "You seem to like him."

Regaining her composure, she said too casually, "Oh, sure. He's a good guy."

Bumping her sister's shoulder, Lana wheedled for an answer, "I sense some chemistry."

Rissa shook her head sure the disappointment was evident in her voice.

"No. That takes a reactive chemical that I don't seem to have."

Lana took her hand and squeezed. "Then he's not as smart as I thought."

"It's not his fault I don't have the ingredients for a thermal reaction."

"I personally think you're a very combustible component."

That drew a small smile.

"You're looking at it from a sister's perspective, not a male one."

Their eyes met and they broke out laughing.

Johnny ambled over, Tish at his side.

"What's so funny?"

Lana and Rissa looked at each other and Lana stated, "Someone actually put their ass in your face. It just seems kind of humorous."

"What was actually funny was Tish signing the other cheek."

"Just wanted her to remember who your ass belongs to."

"Oh, they're gonna start again. I'm out of here."

⌒

Mindlessly, Rissa walked through the throng of people, most waiting anxiously for their turn to meet members of the band. Before she knew it, she was in the same vicinity as Luca, as if drawn magnetically to where he stood. Standing off to the side, she listened to his conversation with a couple who seemed to have a more moderate approach than most. He was amiable, articulate, and she could tell he was sincerely enjoying the interplay when suddenly, his posture stiffened, and the smile faded from his face.

Turning quickly to see what had caused the sudden change in Luca's demeanor, she noticed a man walking slowly toward the bassist, a woman's hand tucked in the crook of his arm.

Excusing himself from the couple he'd been talking to, Luca stood his ground almost braced for the encounter.

"Luca."

His eyebrow arched in disbelief that he'd called him by his given name, but he answered moderately.

"Ryan."

"This is my wife, Becky. Beck, this is...Luca Caroli."

The blonde was obviously excited to be meeting the man and her voice was animated when she said, "It's nice to meet you. The band is great. I couldn't believe it when Ryan said he went to school with you."

He weighed his words carefully, answered honestly, not sure where this was going.

"He knew Johnny and Tim better than he knew me."

Becky gave her husband a questioning look. "I thought you said you were in high school with the three of them."

"I was. But Luca's right. We were never friends."

Taking a deep breath, looking at his wife before putting his attention back on Luca, Ryan continued, "I want to apologize for high school. I was a shit and I..."

He heard his wife's intake of breath but managed to continue. "Look, I know you don't have to accept my apology for the way I acted, but I needed to tell you how much I regret it. You might not believe it, but I've changed."

Luca's stance relaxed a bit, but his arms crossed over his chest as if protecting himself.

"It seems both of us have."

"I know but that's not why I'm doing this. It's not like now you're famous so you're okay. In fact, that song made me feel even worse than I had before. I have kids and one of them is having some problems, word darts, I think you called them. I don't like the fact that I was one of the ones who shot them."

Luca adjusted his stance, a concerned look on his face.

"I'm sorry about that. No kid should be made to feel bad about who he or she is."

Ryan grimaced. "I guess it's payback. I just wish it was aimed at me and not at my son. I think it hurts more this way."

"That's what I've heard."

"Well, that's all I wanted to say. I'll let you get back to what you were doing. Thanks for not taking a swing at me. I would have deserved it."

Extending his hand, Luca said, "Apology accepted. Thanks for offering it."

Ryan shook it in gratitude.

"Maybe my wife and I can take you out to dinner some-time. I'd like to get to know you better. Something I should have done years ago."

"That'd be great. And good luck with your son."

"Thanks. Have a good night."

"You, too."

Luca wore a look of wariness, as if he was waiting for the hidden joke. He was tired and the song had taken a lot out of him. Ryan had been one of the biggest offenders back in high school. A football jock who got his kicks beating people up on and off the field, he'd done his best to make senior year a living hell. He'd succeeded.

"Why did you forgive him?"

Luca looked up, startled to see Rissa standing there, her arms crossed, her face showing her disbelief.

"Why not? He seemed sincere."

"Yeah, but you could have made him feel worse."

"Then I become him and the others. Why would I do that?"

He smiled when Rissa's face scrunched up into a sideways scowl.

"He was a dick back then. He treated everyone like they were scum, even the other jocks."

"Here I thought it was personal. Thanks for letting me know I wasn't special."

"You're too nice."

"Excuse me? Did I hear you right? Did you just tell me I was nice?"

"Yeah but don't be fooled. I've got some scathing remarks in waiting."

"That's more like the Rissa I know and...abide."

"Tolerate, in other words."

"That seems as good a word as any."

She scowled as she backed away, rejoining her sister and brothers who were waiting across the room.

She could no longer refuse to admit it. She wanted to be way more than tolerated.

CHAPTER TWENTY-TWO

Rissa was glad that they chose a club they knew well in their home territory.

Most of the patrons seemed to know them by name and left them alone. There had been a few autograph seekers, but for the most part, they relaxed, talked, laughed, and nursed their drinks.

Rissa sat with her siblings, Luca part of the clan, everyone else spread out among other tables. Terry sat with Joe, Tim and Annie, Chappy and Gia, although there was a lot of table swapping as the night wore on. Tony's friends were enjoying the night, beers in hand as they laughed and joked.

Tony clapped his brother on the back and said, "Hey, Johnny, this was a trip. Thanks for the tickets."

"Glad you enjoyed it. You were the one who gave me the hardest time when I started playing."

"The racket was god-awful. I couldn't escape it anywhere in the house."

"I did love my cymbals back then. You didn't so much. You used to hide my drumsticks on me."

"It was my only defense. When you started carrying them with you, I thought seriously about moving out."

"You were only six."

"Which made it impossible. Although I did pack my suitcase one day and started trudging down the street."

"I remember. Ma made me run after you and bring you back."

"I fought pretty well for a skinny kid."

"You did. I had black and blue marks on my shin for a month."

"Rissa bought me earplugs but they didn't work."

"That was the year you joined little league, wasn't it?"

"Yeah, anything to get out of the house. I used to make Rissa take me to the park until you got better."

"She always had my back."

"Mine, too."

"Our mediator."

Taking a sip of her drink, Rissa smiled at them both.

"Yup, that was me. United Nations."

One by one, the group dwindled down to just her and Luca, although she didn't know how she'd let that happen. Or why he had, either. Switching tonight from her usual order of beer, she'd gone with something a bit more lethal. Conversation between them had stalled, but the looks they were giving each other spoke volumes. The tequila had gone straight to her head, his eyes went straight to her heart, and when his fingers took hers away from her lips and held them, her whole body started to tingle.

She extricated her fingers, the tingles getting too prickly for her own good, and he asked, "Something wrong with my hand?"

"No. It's a nice hand."

"Is that a compliment?"

"It sounds it to me."

"Come to think of it, you haven't insulted me in almost...I don't know...days."

"I'm not going to do that anymore."

He gave her a sardonic smirk.

"Why?"

"Maybe the fact that you had my back at the rock climbing place and...there was that kiss."

"The one I didn't participate in."

She gulped hard and corrected him, his eyes holding her captive.

"No, the one you did."

They stared at each other, the seconds ticking by before Luca asked, "What are you doing, Rissa? What do you want?"

He hadn't let go of her fingers and she let hers curl around his.

"I'm just curious again."

"About what?"

"Um, maybe hands, and other things."

"I can't get involved in anything right now, Rissa. It's not a good time for this."

"Why? It's all I think about lately."

She almost groaned. That was entirely too much information. She was sure he didn't need an FYI on her sexual fantasies.

The smile he gave her was lopsided. "I find that when you want something you shouldn't have, you usually regret getting it."

The tip of her finger began tracing one of the lines on his palm.

"Why shouldn't I have it? It's not like you haven't done it before."

He asked almost casually, "What exactly?"

"Taken someone to bed who...wants to be taken."

He extricated his hands from hers and leaned back in his chair.

"You're different."

She slumped down.

"Yeah. I know. Nothing like the ones you pick out of the crowd."

She was right. He'd never pick a woman like her out of the crowd.

He knew why. She was dangerous, not the run-of-the-mill fan. He should never have let her close enough to feel the heat that emanated from her smile.

"Your brother would kill me."

"My brother doesn't have to know."

Luca's expression turned hard.

"He'll know. Things change. The energy is different. Everyone knew exactly when Tish and Johnny got the job done."

A little too hopefully she suggested, "We can hide it better."

After taking a sip of the light amber liquid, he asked, "What makes you think so?"

Rissa downed the last finger of booze in her glass with one swallow.

"I have a feeling I'm going to be so embarrassed tomorrow by this conversation that I'll hide in my room for a week."

"It doesn't sound as if you're sure you really want to do it. Is it the liquor talking?"

"I'm totally sober. Okay, well, not totally. I couldn't be sitting here asking you...for what I'm asking for if I was totally sober."

The last sip had driven away all inhibitions and she admitted, "You wouldn't even have to...participate...much."

"You plan on doing all the work?"

Her chest tightened when he called it work. It wouldn't be that at all for her. The tightening in another part of her got her to admit, "I don't think it would take much from you to..."

She dipped her head, sorry she was so forthcoming.

"I wish I knew how to flirt. It would be so much less humiliating."

"We'll be playing with fire, Riss."

Her breath caught, a surge of feeling so intense it felt like pain coursed through her. There was no doubt in her mind that it would be the incinerator kind.

"I know."

⌒

It was close to three a.m. when he walked Rissa to her door. He was holding on to his willpower by a thread. He needed her to open it and slip inside, before he did something foolish, but she placed her hands on his chest. He wondered if she could feel the thud of his heart beat beneath her fingers. His hand itched to get beneath her skirt, to touch what was hidden beneath it. He used every ounce of control he had to fight it off until she slid her arms around his neck, moving against him, her breasts scorching his chest.

It almost slipped.

He had to keep his eye on the ball. New York was inching its way closer and he had to stay committed to his course. Rissa was a distraction he couldn't give in to, no matter how much he wanted to.

And he wanted to.

When her arms slid around his neck and she moved her lips over his, his body jerked from the electrical current moving through his bloodstream.

He put his arms on hers and forced her back. "Rissa we're not doing this."

The statement was punched out, his jaw clenched and rigid.

Her look was filled with longing.

"I'm a little bit in love with you, Luca. I just want you to know there would be feeling in it for me."

Anger and frustration ripped through him. Why was she pushing him to do something he knew he'd regret?

Lashing out to cover his own need, he asked, "Is that to make it feel less slutty?"

She bolted back, as if he'd slapped her, hitting her head on the door. "I didn't deserve that."

She was right. She didn't but if he didn't say something to get her to back off, he'd be doing it in the hallway with her. He wouldn't be able to wait the time needed to get to his room.

Logic would have to prevail even if it wasn't representative of the whole truth.

"I won't have the same kind of feeling. Do you still really want to do this? Because I could give you what you want, but will it really be what you want?"

Her cheeks burned in humiliation.

"I don't want a pity fuck if that's what you mean."

Her eyes shifted through each emotion, hurt, pain, and the kind of desire he'd never read in anyone's eyes before.

And it was his undoing.

His hands went to her face, and he held her tightly within them.

"I can assure you it wouldn't be that."

And then his lips were on hers, demanding something from her that she had been demanding from him a moment before. A shot of fire surged through him as she returned the kiss with all the heat flicking at his insides.

His tongue sought hers in hunger, invading the sweet mouth that he'd so longed to taste. And in one swift movement, he lifted her up and she straddled him, never releasing his mouth from hers. Cupping her bottom, he was driven to increase the invasion of her mouth, the feel of her so intoxicating. His hands moved over the curves, his fingers brushing her inner thighs, until they reached the apex where he felt the hot, wet heat of her.

With a ragged breath, he whispered, "If we don't get inside, we'll be doing it in the hallway on the floor, and for as much as I'll take you anyway I can get you, I don't think it would be a good idea."

Her voice was deep and infected with the same kind of need.

"You've got my key."

She had given it to him to hold for her earlier in the evening, not having a purse to keep it in.

Adjusting her on his hip, he reached back and extracted the rectangular card and inserted it into the pad.

As he shut the door with his foot, he reclaimed her sweet ass, so perfect, so much softer than he'd imagined.

"Sorry but these have to go."

And in one deft movement he had ripped her panties with both hands so he could explore all of her.

His fingers grazed her core, and he heard her soft moan, goading him on.

He unbuckled his belt, unzipped his pants, then shimmied them off and they pooled at his ankles. He settled her on his throbbing member, sliding in with ease. She was so wet, so ready for this, and he filled her completely. In mere seconds, she was quivering around him, her spasms creating a force that Einstein would wonder about. And he gave in and let the release come, his head ready to implode in the process.

He was completely spent, and his legs almost buckled, so he dropped onto the bed, never letting her go.

She rested her head in the crook of his shoulder and he felt a perverse need to hold her like this through the night.

"I told you...you wouldn't have to do much."

His heart squeezed in his chest.

"I'm glad you let me come along with you."

She smiled at the double entendre and kissed his neck.

He whispered, his hand straying to the mound still covered by her shirt, "I think we should take it more slowly this time."

Her breathing was shallow, and her glazed eyes implied she was as ready as he was. "I think that would be nice."

"We'll make it last a little longer this time."

She bit her lip her gaze mesmerizing.

"It was kind of quick."

Kissing the corner of her mouth, he teased, "Are you insulting me again?"

Placing her hands on his cheeks, kissing his lips with brush-like strokes, she said, "No. That was my fault. The reality was better than the anticipation, and I lost my head a bit sooner than even I thought I would."

"My head is wondering what the hell just happened."

And he began kissing her again, slowly, letting it build, his body wanting as much as she'd give him.

He kicked off his pants, their bodies still merged, his shaft not willing to abandon the sweet core of her.

His head dipped and he bit at her breast, the cloth material barely a barrier. A shot of desire flooded him, pulsing inside of her as he grew bigger and more engorged than before.

He nibbled on her protruding nipple, but it wasn't enough.

Sitting back down on the bed, he yanked the shirt over her head, releasing her from the restraining bra. And she spilled out into his hands.

He grazed the naked nubs with his thumbs, as she arched back, as if in invitation.

"God, you're beautiful."

And then his mouth was on her again, pulling, teasing, biting, and before he knew it, they were riding the crest again, falling, crashing, drowning in each other.

And it didn't stop for the rest of the night.

Every time she peaked, he took her to another level, as he continued his exploration and savored her every way he could.

⌐

He had crept out of her bed when he heard stirrings next door as Tish and Johnny set about their morning rituals. Kissing her on her temple, he glanced down for one final look. Never had he felt such an explosive coupling.

Never.

Rissa was the heat that would never be extinguished.

But heat wasn't everything.

He'd just made a grave mistake. He had taken advantage of her.

He'd given in to his insatiable need for her body knowing it wouldn't go anywhere.

CHAPTER TWENTY-THREE

Patting the concealer under her eye, Rissa attempted to make it look like she'd slept just a bit and not spent the night making love to a man she'd thought she'd never taste. Sighing, knowing she'd never get rid of the purple smudges, she gave it up.

She shivered at the memory.

For the life of her, she hadn't expected the sex to be...like...that.

No wonder there had never been complaints.

She had wanted to melt into him, had almost become a puddle on the floor.

His tongue had...

"Marissa, are you up yet?"

If her mother only knew she hadn't slept a wink, and the reason behind it, she would have had a heart attack. Or maybe, seeing it was with Luca, she'd be more understanding. She'd never know. What had happened between them last night would stay a secret. A beautiful, shiny secret and it would stay tucked away in her heart. Her curiosity had been satisfied and she now knew what rip-your-clothes-off sex was like.

"Johnny said you got in late last night."

"I did, Ma."

"What were you doing?"

"Um, none of your business?"

When she opened the door that separated them, her mother looked her up and down as she scrutinized her face.

"Why didn't you sleep? I thought you had gotten over Jude by now."

"It has nothing to do with Jude, Ma, trust me."

"Then who?"

"No one."

She almost tripped over the lie.

"I was up sketching all night. You know how I can get."

"You're coming with us."

"Where?"

"Home. I'm making dinner. Now finish getting dressed. We're taking the bus. It seems like the whole bunch is coming."

Tingles resurfaced on her skin. "I think I'll skip it."

She couldn't face Luca after the way they had burned down the room last night. Way too humiliated in how she had all but forced him. And then there were the things they'd done...to each other...

"You most certainly will not. I'll need your help."

Seemed her mother was not going to let her get away with skipping out on.

She gave in reluctantly. Chances were the men and women would be separated, women doing the work, men relaxed, feet up, anticipating the bounty that resulted. One of the traditions, one of the downsides of an old-fashioned Italian family. In this case, it was an upside.

As soon as they boarded the bus, their usual mode of transportation, she couldn't help but feel his eyes on her and she could feel the heat creeping up her neck as she tried desperately to ignore his presence.

When her mother began to assign seats, using the power of the matriarch, she scurried to the back of the bus hoping Celia wouldn't notice.

"Rissa. Here. There are no seats back there."

That busy Italian finger was wagging itself at the seat she'd steered clear of.

What was the bossy old woman playing at? She had an agenda, that was for sure. She just didn't realize yet that Luca didn't want to be part of it.

With resignation, she took the few steps needed to claim it.

She felt a voice that was much too close to her ear and closed her eyes in embarrassment when she heard, "Is there a reason you don't want to sit with me?"

She noticed Celia take a seat behind the driver. Probably to do some backseat driving. But it was safe to talk with her so far away. She turned her eyes to Luca's and then averted them. She could read dismissal.

"I was trying to avoid this."

"What's this?"

"You. Last night. My..."

Her eyes closed as her cheeks heated up. His voice did nothing to ease her discomfort.

"You got what you wanted, didn't you?"

His whispered tone was so measured she was sure she was mistaken about his reaction to her body last night. He'd kissed her with a tenderness that was disturbing, held her close, cradled her against his chest, his heart thudding beneath her cheek. She'd felt something in the way he touched her. At least she thought she had.

"Probably not."

"Are you saying you weren't..." He gave a quick look around to make sure their conversation stayed private. "...satisfied? Because I don't believe you."

Irritation flared. It was okay for him to disregard what they'd done last night, but it was apparent she wasn't allowed the same consideration.

"Believe what you want."

His eyes narrowed, as if doubt was creeping in.

"Are you curious about something else?"

Her heart skipped a beat. She was curious. She wanted to know if it would be as good the next time, if the rockets would be as bright, the kisses as explosive.

It was not something she was going to tell him.

She fixed a smile on her face.

"Yeah. What's a quark?"

He sat back, examining her before giving in to the change of topic.

"Let's see. How can I explain it? Let's just say it's an elementary and fundamental particle of matter. They combine to form hadrons which are made up of electrons and neutrons..."

"Don't overload the system, please."

He focused his gaze on her, and she felt it right down to her elemental particles and figured he couldn't overload her system any more than he had already.

⌢

They ended up moving the party to Johnny and Tish's house, which was more able to accommodate the swelling numbers of people who wanted to sample the Scalera fare. Tony had brought over all the necessary ingredients for their mother's famous escarole pie, the gnocchi and the sauce she always had in her freezer for just this kind of family gathering.

"This kitchen is a cook's dream."

Celia had already inspected the huge space the first time she'd been invited over and was excited about using the high-end appliances and gadgets that Tish hadn't really tested yet.

She might be one fine pianist, but her kitchen skills were in the very elemental stages of development. Kissing her daughter-in-law, Celia said, "You're in charge of the salad. I know you can manage that."

Tish smiled at the woman who had become a mother to her and said, "Yes, Ma. That one I can do."

"Good. Riss you're in charge of the eggplant, Lana you start on the antipasto, I'll get to the pizza."

After wrapping an apron around her middle and washing her hands, the older woman began sautéing the escarole, adding the garlic, olives, and seasonings. The dough was kneaded, and the pan was oiled.

"Hi everyone. Anything I can do to help?"

Delaney had arrived with Dennis and was already pushing her sleeves up to help in any way she could.

"Yes, would you set the table? Get Gia to help you. She shouldn't be out there mixing with the men while there's women's work to be done."

"Do you know we live in the twenty-first century, Ma?"

"Yes, Rissa, I'm aware of that but some things should never change."

All the younger women exchanged glances and knowing smiles and kept busy with the task that had been assigned.

Johnny stepped to the edge of the kitchen, Luca beside him.

"Can we help?"

"No. Get out of my kitchen."

"Technically, Ma, it's mine."

Tish was showing which side of this fence she was on when she said, "And mine. Please do as your mother asked."

Putting her attention back on the lettuce she was pulling apart, Tish suggested, "Go show Luca the picture you just hung. I think he'll like it."

Rissa's knife stopped mid-slice. She knew the picture Tish was talking about. She had given it to her sister-in-law last month after she'd finished it.

Hearing the front door opening, Celia looked at her eldest son and said, "There's Paul. See if he needs help with the bread and pastries first."

"He's here? I thought he caught a homicide?"

"He did. But he's good and lady luck was on his side. They've already arrested the suspect. He finished the paper-work late last night so he could be here today."

While Johnny went to do his mother's bidding, Luca stayed behind. He was standing too close as she dipped the eggplant slices into a pie pan filled with egg and milk, before breading them and transferring them to a pan. Wiping her fingers on the *moppina* around her waist, she worked at the pieces as they turned a golden brown.

He couldn't help asking, "You can cook?"

Rissa looked up from her task and smiled. "Have you met my mother?"

He returned the smile, licking his lips in anticipation. "My mother and sister used to do this when I was growing up. It's one of my favorites."

She watched his tongue slide over his lips, and the throbbing started again. It seemed she was helpless and at his mercy as she thought about the night they'd spent in each other's arms, where he'd given as good as he'd gotten.

Johnny interrupted her growling need and nodded his head at Luca.

"Got something to show you. This way."

Rissa watched them walk away towards the rotunda where Tish's baby grand sat majestically in the middle of the room.

⌒

He glanced back to see that Rissa had gone back to her assigned job.

For as much as he'd maligned himself for his actions last night, when Celia had forced Rissa to sit with him, he'd felt the same kinetic vibration that had him falling into bed with her. He might not like the fact, but he couldn't deny she did some incredibly strange things to his system. It was as if there was a cosmic inevitability about their bodies being tangled together. As if everything that went before led here. The aftershocks of their cataclysmic union were still reverberating through him, and he was finding it hard keeping his hands from touching her, in some small way, to see if the sparks were still spurting for her, too.

From what she'd said on the bus, he might not have satisfied her as well as he'd thought he had.

He'd left her earlier than he'd wanted. There had been no time to taste her again, the stirrings in the next room screaming for him to get out and away. He didn't want to risk her brother finding out what they'd done.

Johnny was pointing to a picture hanging on the wall over the fireplace and his eyes shifted to take it in.

"Rissa gave this to Tish as a birthday gift. I think it captures her spirit pretty well."

Luca felt a magnetic pull and was soon not two feet away from the sketch of Tish at the piano, playing. It was enhanced by watercolor and truly spoke to the essence of the pianist, revealing what the audience felt, saw, and heard when Tish used her magic on the keys. It also revealed Rissa's expertise and talent.

"This is amazing."

"Yeah. I've got to somehow convince her to stick with it. I've even thought about contacting a gallery and arranging to have her work showcased."

He finally pulled his attention from the painting and put it on Johnny, a small smile playing across his face. "Um, good luck with that."

"What would you do?"

His hands burrowed deep in his pockets. "I'd contact a gallery and have her work exhibited."

"Knowing she could possibly stop speaking to me for a year or so."

"You'd be too busy selling her work to notice."

Johnny walked towards the painting to take a closer look and then faced Luca; indecision still written on his face.

"When we get back, I'll see what I can do. I don't have a lot of knowledge about this kind of thing."

"Start by calling around to some of the galleries. I can ask Val to look into it."

"Would you? That would be great. Then we just hit the ground running when we're done touring."

Luca laughed.

"You've got the running thing right. How far do you think you'll have to go to get away from her?"

"I'll tell her it was you who came up with the idea."

"I wish you wouldn't. We've moved from dislike to...tolerance. I don't want to take a step back."

In any shape or form.

"Yeah, what up with that?"

"Don't know."

"Sometimes I get the feeling she likes you. Really likes you."

The yellow lights started flashing a warning.

"We have had some memorable moments."

Giving Luca a sidelong glance he asked, "What kind of memorable moments?"

Knowing mentioning last night was not smart, he gave Johnny what he wanted- platonic examples.

"The day we went cycling, the day at the rock-climbing place. I think she enjoyed them."

Visibly relaxing his shoulders, Johnny grinned.

"This has been a stellar tour. You're hanging out with us a lot more, my sister's here, we've been well received. And you gave us that song. I want another one soon. You need to start living up to your potential."

"Ryan apologized for being a dick in high school."

The smile on Johnny's face faded.

"I didn't know what he was going to do when he asked where you were. I watched the exchange ready to step in but when I saw you shake his hand, I figured he might have said something along those lines."

"Rissa thought I should have held the grudge."

"That you didn't says something about you, not Ryan."

"It's in the past. I'd like to leave it there."

"I don't think I've ever formally apologized myself."

"You have, repeatedly. I don't know why. You were never part of that bunch."

"I should have stopped it."

"When did you begin seeing yourself as superhero?"

Walking to the doorway, flipping the light switch back off, he said, "I've always had visions of grandeur."

"Seems to have worked out for you. You've lived up to the hype."

"I'm not the only one. Let's go eat, Super Nerd"

"Shit. I left my cape back on the bus. How will they ever distinguish between us?"

Johnny slapped him on the back as they were called into the dining room. The Scalera culinary masterpiece was ready and waiting.

The table was soon filled with family and guests. Beer and wine flowed, music blared, and conversation was easy and relaxed. Rissa was serving, had been recruited as waitress, dishwasher, and gopher and was relieved that the time spent with Luca was short and sweet. She wasn't sure she could sit and talk to him, watching his lips move, knowing how they tasted and felt. Thankfully, she had to eat on the run, stuffing her face with the Italian cuisine when she'd get a moment to breathe. Twice she'd stopped and stared as he talked to Marci who was sitting beside him, had to hold herself back from asking Marci to move so she could sit there just to hear his voice, maybe sample those lips again, her body leaning in without thought until the sounding alarm in her brain had prevented another embarrassing moment.

She had to stop giving in to these urges. She was becoming addled-brained.

Staring into space, her thoughts not where they should be, she was surprised when her mother came up to squeeze her cheeks. "Thank you. You were very helpful. But we are not finished yet. Can you please clear the table?"

"Yeah, fine. Sorry."

Patting her face, Celia smiled and said, "Such a good girl *gazzella*."

Luca looked up and smiled.

"Gazelle. It suits her."

"Yes. It does, Luca. She's beautiful, swift and graceful. I have a nickname for each of my children."

"Doesn't every Italian mother?"

Rissa couldn't hide the smile, or the twinkle in her eye. "It's better than *capretta* which is what she calls my sister. Means little goat."

"She always raced around this way and that."

"And bleated before she could talk."

"Hey, I heard that."

"Why do you use animal names?"

"John was *dita*. Not an animal. It means..."

"Fingers."

"Yes, his were always so busy."

Rissa couldn't help to complain like she always had about Johnny's nickname.

"But with Johnny it would be *dita mio*."

"He was my first born. He was the first to take a piece of my heart. You, my middle child, my first daughter, took the center."

Celia held Rissa's face in the palm of her hands and kissed her forehead, having to stand on tiptoes to do it.

An overwhelming sense of tenderness washed over her at her mother's words. "Ma, you never told me that before."

There was a look of disbelief on her face. "I had to tell you?"

"You seemed closer to Johnny, Lana..."

"I attended every one of your games, every one of your tournaments..."

She stopped mid-sentence, a look of regret on her face.

"I know that changed when your father died. After that happened, I needed different things from each of you. I counted on you more than anyone. You were the one who kept us going, kept us tethered, brought life into the house. I needed that as much as I needed Lana's help in the kitchen. I'm sorry you didn't know that."

Tears collected in the corners of Rissa's eyes and she brushed them away before they had a chance to fall. Having a place in her mother's affection was all she'd ever wanted. Knowing she did snapped pieces of her broken heart into place.

"Ma. I love you."

"Good, now clear the table. We've got to serve the dessert and coffee. Your brother warned me that all the food had to be digested by the time they hit the stage."

Marissa smiled. Her mother was known for words of wisdom but not sentimentality. Now that it was said, Celia was anxious to get back to what she did best.

Feed the masses.

⌒

Luca watched while Rissa cleared the dishes, the dish towel around her waist, worn and well-used. When she had leaned over him to gather up his plate, he'd breathed her in. She smelled like her mother's tomato sauce, and he'd noticed she had a smudge of it on her neck. His immediate inclination was to lick it off, taste the sweetness, nibble on her small ear, go lower...

Shifting in his seat, he was beginning to think this was a losing battle.

All he'd thought about for the last twelve hours was the way she fit. Or the way he did right to the hilt. Even after he'd returned to his own room, all he'd thought about was the texture of her skin, the way she smelled, the colors that burst inside when they... Nothing had relieved the ache, the swell, the throb.

Would it be so bad to have a couple more nights like that? With no expectation for anything more. Never putting himself in danger of falling headlong into her. He'd tell her up front they didn't have a future. Leave the decision in her hands.

Glancing up again as Rissa placed the platter of Italian cookies on the table, her arms lean and well defined, he knew it would be a big mistake.

One he was almost ready to make.

When Rissa got back to the hotel, she showered and changed. Kathy and Betsy were arriving soon, and she wanted to be dressed and waiting when they got there. Perusing her belongings, she wanted to amp it up a bit tonight. Kathy would be in a dress, a bit too feminine for her liking, but she had a feeling, after the stories Kathy had told her, that Betsy would be dressed to kill, and she wanted to at least keep up appearances. Not that she thought she'd be competing or anything. As she'd told Kathy, she was going to make sure Betsy stayed out of a certain bed tonight.

She had picked up a skirt while out shopping with Tish last week that she thought might work. It was like a stained-glass mosaic in navy, beiges, pinks, and browns and came to mid-thigh due to her height. Tucking in a navy cami and wrapping the belt around her waist, she modeled the outfit in front of the bathroom mirror. Bending in to get a closer look, she decided to apply a bit of makeup just to enhance the bronze color she'd earned from her time out in the sun. Her hair had a natural curl that she left free to adorn her forehead and twirl around her ears. Slipping on the blue ballet flats she'd bought on the same shopping spree, she was satisfied with the overall effect. The only things that seemed to be missing were some curves, the ones Betsy would be flaunting in everyone's face later in the evening.

It would have to do.

As she passed into the adjoining room where her mother was once again holding Rosie, John was just coming out of his bedroom.

"Whoa. What's the occasion?"

Tish was right behind her husband, as usual, and complimented her. "I knew that was perfect for you. You look great in it."

"Thanks. I'm glad you talked me into it."

"That's my wife. The humble glamor queen. I don't think anyone would believe she's so into clothes."

"I like looking nice. Is that such a crime?"

"I have to admit, there are times you look kind of criminal."

"It keeps you in line, doesn't it?"

"It keeps my mind in one anyway."

"Oh, would you two please knock it off. It gets kind of sickening sometimes."

Johnny pulled both Tish and Rissa into a hug and laughed. "Two of my favorite women."

She extricated herself and smiled at him. "I think there's four, but who's counting."

She noticed when Johnny glanced in his mother and daughter's direction and could see his heart overflowing with love.

"Yeah, four."

Gathering up her purse, Rissa called out, "Break a leg. And play well, please. I've got friends I want to impress."

"You've got the passes?"

"Right here." She patted the purse hanging loosely over her shoulder. "I'll see you later."

Just as she got off the elevator, her friends were walking in through the revolving doors of the hotel. Kathy was dressed in a simple dress with a floral design. Betsy, on the other hand looked almost totally out of place with the two of them. The difference between this Betsy and the one from high school was like night and day. Gone was the conservative clothing and in its place, was a caramel-color two-piece dress. It had an overlay top that created a bare triangular midriff. It nearly hit her upper thigh and the dress hugged her ass like a kid glove. Chunky strap heels added several inches to her frame and Rissa's heart sank. Here was buxom and smart all in one package. She just might be forever sorry she had agreed to this.

Joe's whistle gave her a heads-up that some of the group had started filtering down. They would straggle into the lobby a few at a time until the buses were ready to leave for the arena. Rissa turned, her eyes seeking out the man she didn't want anywhere near the threesome and couldn't help but notice Luca's eyes widen as he approached.

She gulped past the sob wanting to erupt.

Charlie, a member of Mechanical Devices, was the one who asked, "Can you introduce us, please."

"Oh, right. Charlie, Joe, Rambler, Luca, Terry, these are my friends, Kathy Cole and Betsy Hogan."

Betsy stepped forward toward Luca, who didn't move a muscle.

"I'm looking forward to spending some time with you guys tonight. This should be a lot of fun."

When Luca took a miniscule step back, Rissa's heart did a rhumba.

She didn't know how he managed it, but he was suddenly standing right beside her. She was almost able to breathe again. He didn't seem to be taking Betsy's bait.

"Are you coming with us for the set-up?"

It was as if he were whispering in her ear, his voice soft like a purr, and then his arm brushed hers, the spark ready to ignite. The one she was getting used to when he was anywhere near her. The one she was trying so hard to ignore. She'd gotten what she'd asked for, a night of intoxicating sex. There had been more than just a flicker of fire. The smoke alarm had gone off.

"No. We're going to grab something to eat and then head over."

She heard the breathiness in her voice when she answered. Could he read her thoughts?

When his fingers tapped against hers, she thought he might be signaling he could, and her heart skipped a beat.

Meeting her eyes, he said, "I guess we'll see you then."

CHAPTER TWENTY-FOUR

Rissa had begun to argue about the benefits of taxi over Uber but too late to do any good. Betsy used her app, and they were picked up and taxied across town in record time, arriving at the restaurant across the street from the music venue to claim the last available table, with a view of the street. Within ten minutes of their arrival, the popular tavern had a line out the door.

"See, if we waited, we would have been standing back there instead of sipping our wine here."

"I'll give you that. I've heard some sketchy things about the service, so I don't use it."

After glancing around the place, as if scoping it out, Betsy put her attention back on Rissa and asked, "What happened to you? You used to be fearless."

"I'm beginning to think that was a misconception...on everyone's part, mine included."

Betsy studied her. "Hell, you never backed down from a challenge and some of them were pretty risky. Like the day you punished that guy for hassling you?"

Kathy laughed at the memory. "When you opened that locker door in his face, I thought he was going to deck you."

Rissa smiled when she remembered the guy's face after getting a flat of steel against his nose.

"I saw the move in a movie my mother was watching. Or was it Lana? I didn't think it would work, but I was done with his bullying."

Betsy signaled the waitress, her wine glass in need of a refill as she asked, "What happened? I heard you were complacent with that asshole you were engaged to."

Kathy must have shared with Betsy more than she'd let on. Kathy was the only one she vented to. It seemed now she shouldn't have. Then again, what did it matter anymore? The subject had been deleted from her life.

"I don't know. I think I had a lot more self-confidence back in high school. You both knew what you wanted to do and did it. I've been at such loose ends since graduation."

Both the techie and statistician had done well for themselves. But then they were the smart ones. She was an artist and jock. Neither led to a successful, financially rewarding career. Unless you went pro. She wasn't that good.

Betsy finished the bite of ahi tuna and stabbed at a potato. With the fork half-way to her mouth, she asked, "Why didn't you accept the softball scholarship at Northeastern?"

Rissa slumped back in her chair, took another sip of the icy brew.

"Because I had no idea what I wanted to major in."

"That's what college is for. To figure things out."

"I thought art school would be a better fit."

"It should have been. You had a lot of talent. I'm sure you still do."

Rissa told them about her brother's suggestion, described what she'd been doing since beginning the tour, and they were both excited for her.

Betsy sighed.

"To think we knew them when."

Kathy laughed.

"Sitting in Johnny's living room, just hanging out. You never had so many friends in your senior year in high school. After the band played at the Fall Ball all the girls wanted to become your new BFF."

Betsy added, "It was satisfying seeing them so dejected when you turned them down."

"If I remember correctly, she told them to fuck off. Which reminds me, I bumped into Felicity last weekend. She married a stockbroker, had a big rock on her finger and a couple of kids. Being mean didn't dim her prospects."

A passerby jostled Betsy's chair, bumped her elbow, causing some of her wine to spill on the table. Mopping it up with her napkin, she said almost defiantly, "I realized a few years back that good girls finish last."

Kathy said defensively, "Hey, I like my life."

"You're the exception."

"Rissa's doing okay."

"Not really. Whose fiancée calls off the wedding one month before the date? At least he didn't leave you standing at the altar. That would have been even more humiliating."

Kathy's face expressed the shock that Rissa felt. "When did you get so...mean girl?"

Betsy seemed to have lost her discretion along with her...discretion. They had been such good friends once. Betsy had been the good girl, studious, shy, conservative. Today all resemblance to that person was gone. But she was right. It would have been far more embarrassing if Jude had let it get that far.

Betsy glanced from one friend to the other and then dropped a bomb. "It happened to me."

Both other women were incredulous and said, "What," at the same time.

Kathy's voice echoed her surprise.

"I didn't even know you were engaged."

Betsy took a sip of wine.

"It was when I was living in Ohio, where I went to college. I met him senior year. The wedding was set for a week after graduation. The ceremony was small, so I didn't have too many witnesses to his disappearing act. I was left holding the bouquet, as you might say. I didn't tell anyone. It was too embarrassing. I'm over it enough that I can share that part of my life, at least with friends."

"What the hell happened?"

"He left me a voice message which I retrieved later. Told me he wasn't ready to settle down. Wanted to sow some wild oats. He thought I was too uptight to get down and dirty."

"I'm so sorry, Betsy."

"Being a good girl didn't get me anything so now if I see a fine piece of flesh, I go for it. And Luca is one fine piece. And you'll get to draw all that yummy goodness. I'd have him do a nude."

Images of a well-muscled torso streaked through Rissa's mind, so she choked on her response.

"Get in line. You'll see just how many women want a piece."

"I plan on doing just that."

The Cuban sandwich had lost its taste as that thought settled like lead in her stomach. There wasn't anything she could do to stop it, not without making a complete fool of herself.

But when they got to the venue, that's exactly what she did.

Rissa took the first opportunity that came to her and pulled Luca by the hand to a hidden corner of the backstage area.

Amber eyes twitched with amusement, "Curious about something?"

"Is that now going to be a running joke every time I ask to speak to you privately?"

He fingered a curl at her ear and chuckled. "Probably."

The two times she'd come on to him out of curiosity, he'd been hesitant, so she wasn't expecting him to be so playful.

Biting her bottom lip, she took a deep breath before blurting it out. "I just want to warn you about something."

Inching his head closer to hers, he whispered, "What?"

His proximity was not making this easy. Her breathing was coming in spurts now, and she wasn't sure the information would come out as casually as she wanted it to. Like one friend to another instead of hopeful candidate for an upcoming selection process.

"Betsy told us at supper that she's going to make a play for you."

Crossing his arms over his chest, he chuckled.

"I figured that one out all by myself."

"Um, she's only after you because...she wants..."

"Bragging rights?"

Her eyes flicked up to meet his.

"Yeah."

Tucking a recalcitrant curl behind her ear, he said quietly, "Why else do you think the women come on to us? Okay there are some who think they can get us to settle down, get married, fulfill the daydream of catching the rock star. But mostly it's to see how we are in bed, how big our penises are, how well we use them. One woman wanted a picture of my junk to show her friends."

Her face felt flushed. Must be the heat from his finger as he swept her hair back. Definitely not the word he used or what it implied. She could give a reference on the latter. He used it quite well and the size was something to write home about. Not that she'd let her mother in on that one.

Was she like all the others after all?

With all coherent thought gone, she muttered a vapid, "Huh?"

Now the twinkle was back in his eyes. "There's a lot more pressure on us to perform than you thought, isn't there?"

Her anger at his ego would have flared just a few weeks ago, but tonight there was another part of her that got there first.

"You're okay with it." Putting some bite into her words she offered, "Sorry, I thought..."

He was back to caressing her hair, his hands fingering the loose strands back.

"Thank you for your concern but if I had any desire to climb into bed with Betsy, I'd know what I was climbing in for."

Backing away from him, the furnace he'd stoked blazing hot inside, she almost tripped over her own feet trying to get away from him.

⌒

He watched her stumble away, still chuckling.

Did she really think he couldn't read the signs of a come-on, one that was so flagrant it was almost offensive?

More importantly, did she really think he'd want to spend a night with Betsy instead of her?

A thought flicked in and he didn't like it much.

What kind of man would sleep with a woman's friend?

Even if Betsy called to him tonight, he'd never do that to her.

She couldn't think too highly of him if she thought that.

Just another reminder that what they had was pure lust.

Nothing more.

And yet, she had come closer than anyone to seeing beneath the surface, of seeing him as he was.

Her sketches told him that much.

And when he was on stage, he could feel her eyes on him. He'd glance up and find her there, in his sights looking at him like...a piece of candy.

Those soft brown eyes would burn in intensity; her lips would part slightly as if in invitation.

She wanted him as much as he wanted her.

But that's where it had to end.

As they returned from their night out, Kathy laughed at the crazy life they lived.

"I wouldn't have believed it if I hadn't seen it with my own eyes. Don't they get tired of it all?"

"Not so much now. They've cut down the touring part so it's just a couple of months here and there. This is where it gets kind of scary. The fans can be pretty possessive."

"They were throwing underpants onto the stage. And bras. I think even Betsy was dumbstruck."

Searching the crowd that was still milling in the hotel lobby, Rissa began to get physically agitated.

"Where is Bets?"

"I don't know. I haven't seen her recently. She was talking to Luca on the bus earlier. Maybe she went off with him."

Nooooooo. No. Nooooo.

She had hoped her target for the night hadn't been the man she wanted, the one she knew she shouldn't have.

Well, she'd had him, but she knew she wouldn't hold him.

Now Betsy. There was a woman who could hold any man.

Except the one who left her at the altar.

That had shocked the shit out of her. But it didn't change the facts. Marissa Scalera was not Luca's dream woman. And there was no changing to make it so. It made him an unhealthy choice for her to make.

But Betsy was not a healthy choice for him to make either, at least from her perspective, and she was going to make damn sure he didn't.

Relieved when Kathy said, "Look I've got to go. I brought my own car, just in case this happened, and I have got to get home. The kids will have me up at the crack of dawn. Thanks, Rissa. It was great. Text me when you get back, okay?"

She already had a foot in the direction of the elevator when she replied, "I will. We'll hang out some night."

"Sounds good."

With Kathy barely out the door, Rissa ran toward the bank of elevators, hitting the up button again and again until the doors slid open, cursing herself and what she was doing. The verbal assault continued down the hallway as she argued over what she was doing, reminded herself of how embarrassed she'd be tomorrow, especially if she found what she expected.

But it didn't deter her from her mission. In fact, it only made her hurry her steps until she was facing the door. And knocking on it. Loudly.

If he didn't answer right away, she'd leave.

Well, if it took him a couple of minutes to answer, she'd leave.

Maybe she'd have to break down the door and then leave.

He couldn't screw someone with the door gone, could he?

Maybe he would.

Unless she refused to leave and stood in the empty doorway.

She jumped when his voice carried through the door that was already a splintered pile of rubble in her head.

"Who's there?"

"Rissa."

It sounded like there was a frog in her throat from both sides of the door.

Luca opened it a crack and asked, "What are you curious about now?"

Wanting to shove the door open and show him, she took a step back instead.

"Is Betsy here?"

His eyes narrowed. His expression told her he was the one curious now. "No. Why?"

"Um, I was...just looking for her."

"And you thought she'd be here?"

"I thought...it was a...possibility."

His smile faded, as if something bothered him.

Like maybe you banging on his door to interrupt his...

"And if she was?"

Okay, she hadn't gotten that far.

Yes, she had. She was going to take Betsy down. That would have really played out well. Did she think Luca would just stand there and watch?

Talk about being addle-brained.

And tongue-tied because now she didn't know what to say.

Luca helped her out and asked, "Why do you think I'd sleep with your friend?"

"I...She's...pretty smart and...she's got some...pretty nice...attributes. I..."

His arm was leaning against the door jamb, his expression one of mild amusement. But the heat in his eyes told her a different story.

"I hadn't really noticed."

With the way he was studying her mouth, she was beginning to feel enough heat to vaporize her and sounding as dumb as she felt, she muttered, "Huh?"

She wondered if he was playing with her, giving her back a little of her own medicine. Not quite believing he hadn't noticed Betsy's flagrant assault on the male species in general, on him specifically, she searched his eyes to find the truth.

Giving her somewhere else to look, he provided, "I think she's with Charlie. Give the band a couple of years and she can say she shagged him when."

He watched her eyelids drop closed and thought he heard her take a deep breath.

"Sorry to bother you. I'll...let you get back to...."

Opening the door wider, he stepped into the hall and asked, "I thought your opinion of me had improved. At least I hoped it had. Do you really think I'd do that? Sleep with your friend. After last night?"

"I...I..."

"I've never known you to stutter before. Are you, all right?"

Then he pulled back, his eyes meeting hers, lingering there.

Her eyes dipped down as if she were ashamed of what she was going to say.

He waited, his chest constricting in anticipation of what it was.

"It...happened before."

His finger tilted her face up so he could read what was there.

He didn't like it.

"I'm sorry." His words were soft and low.

"Don't be. I had only gone out with him a few times. It was more my pride than anything."

"But it still hurt."

She nodded her head, biting her lip, still not meeting his gaze.

His fingers were playing with her hair. It seemed he was always tucking a stray curl behind her ear. It never failed to elicit a streak of lightning that shot through her.

"I hope you dumped him. And the friend."

"I didn't have to. He dumped me."

His heart stuttered. He knew what it felt like to be rejected.

She had put herself in the firing line, knowing it could very well have happened again.

"What are you really doing here?"

She raised eyes filled with a sad resignation. "I didn't want to share you with her. It would have made last night less..."

"Personal?"

"Maybe that's the word. I don't know the word for this. I didn't want to hear her version, and she would have crowed about it, bragging rights and all. It would have somehow diminished my own."

"And that was?"

He heard her inhale a deep breath before letting it out slowly.

"Too big to talk about."

His thumb was brushing her bottom lip, the fullness soft and silky.

"For me, too. It would have been a good reason to decline her invitation."

A slight smile tipped her lips up.

"It seemed more like an assault."

Should he tell her she was the assault on all his senses? Pure sheet lightning, vivid colors, a spectrum of light.

And he wanted to feel it again. Tonight.

This minute would be good.

His head dipped for an intended kiss, but before he could reach his mark, his phone rang in the background.

He didn't move.

The adrenaline rush was still spurting.

His fingers touched her face and she trembled. When his knuckles brushed her cheek, she stepped mindlessly up on tiptoe and pressed her lips against his, entwining her arms around his neck, pulling him closer.

His hand wrapped around her hips and she could feel his full arousal, pulsing against her. His fingers inched up her skirt, and she could feel them probing a part of her that was begging for more, something that had never happened until now, until this man.

Alarm bells started ringing right along with the bells, whistles, and fireworks that were exploding inside of her.

But before he could pull her into the room, the hotel landline began screaming for attention.

Swearing silently, he stepped over and picked up the receiver.

He mouthed the word *Johnny*.

"She's here. Wait a minute."

"No. Just tell her to get back here now. My mother won't leave until she says goodbye...What's she doing there?"

Watching her reaction to his lie, he said, "We met in the hall. She was just telling me how much her friends enjoyed the show."

"Oh, okay. I thought I was going to have to kill you or something."

"I'm not the big, bad wolf, Johnny."

"I know but you're not the marrying kind either."

He sobered at that thought.

He was beginning to feel the tug of a family. That was the reason he was meeting with Paige.

Looking up, as he put the receiver down, he stared at lips he wanted to reclaim. His fingers twitched to touch silken skin. He did neither.

"Your mother's waiting for you."

Her eyes closed and her lips curved into a rueful grin.

"Of course, she is. Thanks for covering for me. I guess I'll see you tomorrow."

He didn't let either of them off that easily and he lost the fight with his conscience, his body struggling with what this meant.

The kiss in the aftermath was singed with heat and he cursed himself for giving in to the urge.

All the discipline and intention he used to brag about having seemed to have vanished into thin air.

CHAPTER TWENTY-FIVE

Backing out of the doorway, her mouth throbbing, her core keeping the same rhythm, she raced down the hall and knocked frantically at her brother's door.

Her mother was standing just inside, Paul hovering nearby.

"Where were you? You had to know we were waiting to say goodbye. It was good seeing Kathy and Betsy again although I never would have recognized Betsy in that getup. She should meet a nice boy and get married."

Taking a step closer, Celia began inspecting her daughter.

"Your face is the color of paste and your eyes are glassy, as if you're in shock. What's the matter with you? Are you sick or something?"

"No. I...I'm just tired."

"You're shaking like a leaf. Here, sit down."

Celia took hold of her shoulders and all but shoved her down on the couch.

"Do you want some water?"

Celia's hand was on her forehead, her hands cupping Rissa's cheeks.

Johnny was by her side in one stride. "Ma's right. You look like you've seen a ghost."

"No ghost."

Just a quivering mass of jelly. She still couldn't believe she had knocked on Luca's door looking for Betsy. The shaking had started as soon as he'd put his hand on her. Then when he'd kissed her...she had come apart in his embrace.

Wanting more, needing more.

This was so unlike her. She'd never craved a man's touch before. Wanted it more than breath. That's what she felt for Luca and it was beginning to scare her.

There was a centrifugal force at work here, compelling her to do things she just didn't do.

Her eyes flickered from her mother's concerned expression to her brother's.

Tish's voice came out of nowhere. "Did Betsy end up with anyone tonight?"

"Um, Charlie."

Johnny looked surprised. "It seemed she had her sights set on Luca. He didn't..."

The word came rushing out like an expletive.

"No."

Johnny's eyebrows arched. "Would that have bothered you?"

Fiddling with her still-trembling fingers she finally replied, "Not in the least."

Refusing to look at her brother, her eyes set on Tish who was wearing a satisfied smirk.

Johnny's hands went to his hips.

"Is there something I'm missing?"

Tish reiterated what she'd been harping on.

"He's gone celibate."

"I think that's a bit extreme. He says he's taking a break."

Celia clapped her hands over her ears.

"I don't want to hear this."

"Sorry, Ma."

Rissa squeaked out, "Don't you guys have to get going?"

"I think you're coming down with something."

"Ma, I'm fine. Just tired."

The adrenaline high of facing Luca was beginning to wear down, and her whole body was feeling the effects. All she wanted was to climb into bed and pull the covers way over her head.

And stay there until the tour was over. Unless there was a chance of...

"Okay. If you're sure."

Then lifting the burden of motherly concern onto Johnny's shoulders, she said in a firm voice, "I'm counting on you to take care of her."

"You know I will Ma."

Patting his cheek, she purred, "You're a good boy, *ditto mio*. I will trust you."

As Paul and Celia stood at the open door, ready to leave, Johnny said, "I'll text you tomorrow, let you know that she's fine."

Following her towards her bedroom, Tish asked quietly, "Is there something you want to tell me?"

"No. I told you, you had it all wrong."

"I don't and you will. I just have to figure out how to get it out of you."

Closing the door in Tish's face, she leaned against it.

How was she going to keep her feelings hidden?

She was acting out of character, weepy, anxious, love crazed. If he gave her any indication at all that they could have another night together, she was going to take it, no questions asked.

If Tish found out, someone would win big.

⌒

Luca stood by the closed door.

He'd done it again. Leaned in for a kiss that he knew was dangerous.

Rissa was a powder keg, and he was the fuse, or was it the other way around? It was hard to distinguish. He had been all in with the "no" his mind was shouting, but his body was in direct opposition, and it had won hands down.

Hands.

She had busy ones often tinged with charcoal, always brushing them off on a towel she kept nearby.

He'd ripped her panties off last night.

He'd never done that before, but he'd never felt the need to get inside a woman that desperately.

What did it mean?

He rubbed his face and groaned.

No one had ever affected him like that before.

No one.

He'd been a virgin until college and the culmination of years of waiting must have intensified his need. Perpetual horndom had been the result of the initiation. Acting like rabbits for the first few months, he concluded that he'd reached the height of passion in Paige's arms.

Was that the underlying hypothesis? Had he postulated the right theory? Had he really loved her?

He'd been young and inexperienced. Had he misinterpreted physical satisfaction to mean love instead of what it really was? A libido well satiated?

Over the years, he'd gotten it anywhere he wanted, and it had been great.

It had healed his underdeveloped ego, his low self-esteem.

But what he had with Rissa was different from anything he'd ever had before. It wasn't only the sex but the banter, the easy companionship that added an explosiveness that was beyond the pale.

But the sex...was indescribable.

As soon as their bodies merged, he was close to the edge. He had to fight to keep control. Shit, it happened even before that, otherwise he'd have had control enough to take her panties off slowly, deliberately. He wouldn't have to rip them off to satisfy the urgent need.

She was a combination of so many things, all athletic grace, child-like innocence, creative artist, earth mother. With a hint of recklessness that was almost endearing.

In a way, she reminded him of himself, all the opposites fighting for domination.

She had ridden him hard and well but there was incompleteness to it. He wanted the foreplay they seemed to skip, wanted to savor every minute. He wanted her back so he could take his time, bring her to another peak, taste her sweetness, fill her completely.

Was he unconsciously conducting a scientific experiment, with his heart and perhaps even his soul, the data points? He'd never succeeded in a lasting relationship before. What if it was Rissa who added the unexpected phenomena that resulted in success, a crucial ingredient that had never been there before? She'd blown his original hypothesis out of the water with one fucking kiss.

Was Rissa the key or his downfall?

It looked like she would be one or the other, and his skills as a scientist had nothing to do with the outcome.

He threaded his fingers through his hair. There were two options here.

The first was to burn the sheets until the damn conflagration was over. The second was to stay the hell away from her.

He closed his eyes, the feel of her lips on his, an addiction he wasn't sure he could fight.

That left only one thing to do.

⌢

The next morning, to shake off the too-hot-to handle feelings, Rissa decided to spend the morning, sketching. The bus wouldn't be leaving for Providence until later in the day and for as many times as she'd hung out in her city, she'd never gone for the express purpose of getting the street scenes on paper.

With her backpack hanging loosely from her shoulder, her hand on the door lever, she did a mental checklist to make sure she had everything she needed. Being immersed in visions of lips and other body parts wasn't helping.

She jumped when she heard the sharp knuckle rap on the wooden panel.

Once her heartbeat regulated, she opened it.

Luca stood on the other side, looking delectable, in jeans and a blue knit shirt, his hair a shimmering mass of ebony.

His nearness made her head swim and her throat constricted, so she stood, mute.

"Where are you going?"

A warning voice whispered for her to be careful.

"Not sure yet. I was just going to wander and see where I ended up."

He smiled easily.

"Can I join you?"

She stammered, "Why? I...I thought we weren't going to pursue...this."

"I don't remember having that discussion."

Had she gotten it wrong? She could have sworn he'd told her he couldn't do this. She'd worked all night to get it through her head.

Now?

"So, you're in, thinking about being in, refining your decision...what exactly do you have in mind?"

She held her breath waiting for his answer.

"I'm not thinking about anything more than wanting to spend the day with you. Is that a problem? Do we need a life plan?"

She fought to control her disappointment. Expecting anything more than this would have been foolish. While studying him, she waffled back and forth over his request. For as much as he might be good company, he'd be a major impediment to her focus.

Being honest, hoping he'd back away, she told him, "I plan on working as I go."

He didn't.

"I thought you knew by now that was fine with me."

His answer was further confirmation that he was exactly the kind of man she wanted to be with. Shrugging her shoulders, figuring that was her problem not his, she said, "Okay. Suit yourself."

They spent the time wandering around, stopping periodically for her to sketch some of the historic landmarks. He seemed more impressed with her art than bored, watching intently as she scribbled across the page, sometimes his chin resting on her shoulder so he could get a bird's- eye view of what she was doing.

He had clasped her hand in his as they meandered down the street, the sidewalks less crowded this time of day.

"I'm glad you've decided to show your stuff to Jessica."

"I'm going to work on some of the pictures this afternoon."

He stopped, met her eyes with his. "Can I watch?"

She pulled him forward, not wanting to become spellbound.

"You're a big distraction in a hotel room."

Not that he wasn't out here in public.

"I promise I won't talk. I'll bring a book over and read. I've been wanting to finish the one I started the first day of the tour. I don't seem to spend much time in the hotel room anymore."

The smile he gave her was disarming.

"Talk about distractions."

"Are you complaining?"

Her heart always beat a little faster at the thought of lying in his arms. It was picking up steam.

Leaning over, he kissed her cheek, reassuring her, "Not in the least."

Closing her eyes, she let the quake at his nearness have its way. Her life plan hadn't worked out, so why did she think a long-term goal meant permanency? She was going to allow herself to enjoy pleasure in the moment.

⌒

They returned to the hotel, stopping by his room to get his book.

"I'm not coming in. I have work to do and..."

"One step in and the afternoon might go up in smoke. Is that what you're saying?"

"I'll be waiting down the hall. Knock on the door when you get there."

Her blood was pounding, and it would be so easy to give up her art this morning and pursue other pleasurable activities. She let the signs of a firestorm hang in the air. She had a free morning, and she was going to put her energies into something constructive.

"I'm going now."

He patted her on the ass and sent her on her way, promising he'd be there soon.

She entered the empty suite. Her brother and Tish had gone to their house for a morning of quiet comfort. Tish could practice on her own baby grand; Rosie could sleep in her own crib.

The quiet was almost a soothing balm. Was she getting used to being alone? Maybe all it took was being in the company of such chaos for silence to become something to be appreciated.

She unpacked her watercolors, brushes, filled a glass with water and sat at the low table in the center of the sitting room, her legs tucked underneath. She wanted to get the paint on early so they had time to dry, something that was imperative before stacking them away again.

The knock told her Luca had decided to join her. She hadn't been sure he would. She also wasn't sure she wanted him here.

He moved into the room, walking over to inspect what she was working on. "They're very good, Rissa."

When she looked up into his eyes, she thought she read something, but like those science books she was still trying to muddle through, his language was undecipherable.

His presence wasn't as disturbing as she'd thought it would be. There was something about him that was calming.

When he wasn't doing strange things to her body.

She heard him move to the chair, and she put her focus back on her work.

Riffling through some of her most recent sketches, she chose one that she'd done of Tim. They'd been on the bus, and he was laughing at something. He had a great smile and it was on full display. Staring at it, she needed to figure out how to enhance it, what spaces to leave white, what to color as shadow. So intent in her concentration, she only became aware of Luca's perusal when she could feel his breath against her neck as he leaned forward to see what she was doing, his closeness settling around her.

"That's a great one of Tim. Not too many people see that side of him. I think it will surprise a lot of his fans."

"Annie had tried a joke, which as you know is not really her forte, and he just burst out laughing when she couldn't get the punch line right. He looked almost boyish. It was kinda cute."

"What are you going to do with it?"

"I can't decide whether to leave it as is, glaze it, or fill it in with color. I think the starkness of the black and white makes it more visually appealing."

"While you figure it out, I'll just keep quiet and read."

He crossed his leg over his knee and settled back and she let his presence fade into the background.

Along with using the proper techniques she'd learned in school, there was also a sixth sense that helped make the artwork come alive. It seemed to come from some emotional place inside her. The sketches themselves defined a concrete subject, the colors added dimension, created an illusion, enriched the drawings with an almost sensual aspect. Or was she just seeing everything through a sensual prism these days, especially with him so near?

She thought she'd be confined by his presence, but for some reason, she intuitively knew which colors to mix, how to apply them, how to balance the ratio between water and paint. It was as if he freed her from all constraints, all while making her feel safe to follow her instincts and she became completely absorbed in the applications. Time flew and before she knew it, she had completed almost a dozen pictures and, more importantly, was pleased with the results. Straightening her legs, she stretched them out while keeping her seat on the floor and swiveled her head to work out some kinks.

Luca leaned forward and began to massage her shoulders, his thumbs pressing against the column of her neck before moving to the tendons in her back and she issued a groan of contentment.

"Oh, this is heaven."

He scooted down behind her, his legs alongside hers under the table, his hands continuing to work magic on her tired and sore muscles.

And then his hands traveled to the front of her, her breasts cupped in his hands, his lips on her throat and his member throbbing against her back.

His voice was thick with wanting.

"Do you like this?"

She gave a small moan.

"I think it's called foreplay."

"Is that what we're doing?"

"If memory serves me, yes. It seems I've lost the art somewhere along the line."

She leaned her head back and allowed him to continue his exploration of her body, his hands sure, awakening a pool of desire that she could do nothing but drown in.

Getting to his feet, his hands under her arms, he pulled her with him and slowly led her to her room, where he continued to stroke, pet, nibble, and bite until they moved from foreplay to the skyrocketing main event.

CHAPTER TWENTY-SIX

"It's okay Rosebud. Don't cry. Mama will be back in a little while."

Johnny was wearing a path in the carpet, rubbing his daughter's back, trying to get her to settle down. Tish was gone every day for a couple of hours, practicing on whatever piano they could reserve for her, but Rosie must have known the timetable down to the second when her mother usually returned. Today there had been a break in the routine and Rosie just wasn't having it.

Tim was pacing right along with father and daughter.

Luca watched the exchange between the two men, shaking his head.

"Do you think she's hungry?"

Johnny's voice held a tight knot of agitation.

"I just fed her an hour ago and she drank it all down."

"Her diaper need changing?"

"It's only been ten minutes since her last change."

Luca got up and strode to the door.

"I'll be right back."

And when he returned, the men were still pacing, still questioning what they should do to get Rosie to calm down.

Luca held his iPod and port in his hand. Plugging it in, he set it up, and soon strains of classical music filled the room.

Rosie's shaking sobs slowly turned into mews of pleasure.

The piano keys did their magic, and the small snores announced that Rosie had succumbed to sleep.

"Good call."

"I was hopeful."

"Don't put her down," Tim ordered.

"As long as we leave that playing, she should be okay."

"Keep walking her around. I don't want to go through that again."

"This will be you next year. Get used to it."

Johnny shot Luca a glance.

"I should be surprised that you were the one to come up with this, but you're so coolly logical it doesn't surprise me at all. I wonder if you'll be as clear thinking when it's your own."

Luca was sitting in one of the chairs, his leg crossed over his knee, but it bounced with a hidden energy.

"Won't know that for a while or...ever."

"Don't want kids?"

"Someday, I think. Maybe."

It would mean bringing down the walls of his defenses to let a woman through.

"You've never told us why you left school. Not that I'm not grateful you did, but there must have been a reason."

He always shot down these types of questions, always evaded, ignored them. Maybe it was time to part with some of the truth. Especially now that he was meeting up with part of his past. Glancing from one man to the other, Luca gave a short and succinct answer that he hoped would mollify them.

"A woman. An impulsive mistake. The need for radical change."

Johnny stopped, his hand still patting Rosie's back with gentle strokes, and studied him. After a moment of what looked like thought, he said, "So if this woman hadn't...done whatever...you wouldn't have quit school, learned the bass, grown your hair, radically changed, or joined the band."

After his summation, broad smile appeared on his face.

"Can I have her number? I'd like to thank her."

Breath sniffed out his nose as Luca snickered.

"I hadn't thought of it like that."

"Well we wouldn't be who we are without you. You being some hot-shot scientist wouldn't have been good for Thunder."

Tucking his hair behind his ear, he paused. Johnny was the undisputed leader of the band, an energy system all on his own, and to have him say Thunder wouldn't be the same without him was almost humbling.

"I'm sure you would have found someone else. Probably had someone else already lined up who could play even better. I always figured you'd taken me on because of a guilty conscience."

"I have to admit that was part of it. But there was something about you that I thought would be a good fit for us. You had a good head, no ego, weren't into illegals, and I figured you would complement our personalities."

Johnny held Rosie's small body relaxed against his chest, looking out into space as if contemplating something. His eyes finally settled on Luca.

"I can't see you as impulsive."

"Doesn't happen often. In fact, there was only that once."

He couldn't call what he'd done with Rissa, impulse. It was more than that. Out-of-control need came to mind.

"Learned your lesson?"

"In a big way."

"Nothing would make you jump off a cliff?"

Tim, a smile on his face, joked, "He'd be too busy analyzing how far down he'd fall, the wind velocity, the spatial vector capacity..."

"The what?"

"I don't know. It sounded scientific, didn't it?"

"Very NASA."

"I read they're hiring astronauts", Johnny said, then added, "I was thinking of applying."

Luca pointed out the obvious.

"And be away from Tish and Rosie for months or years? I don't think so."

"Oh, maybe not then. I can't be away from them overnight."

"Maybe we could send Terry. He can follow orders well."

Luca gave him back one of his own phrases. "He wouldn't know how to calculate the spatial vector capacity."

Johnny grinned.

"That's a great term. I think you should discover or invent something so we can use it."

"I'll get right on it."

Johnny and Tim began a discussion on it.

"What kind of equation would it be?"

"I think it should have pi in it somehow. Very few know what to do with it."

"I like pie."

"No Johnny..."

"I'm kidding. I know what it is, at least in a very abstract way."

"Shut up you two. You're showing your ignorance."

"No, we're not. We're just highlighting your genius."

"Can't do it. I have no ego. Remember?"

"You really don't. But nobody really knows that but us."

Wanting to extricate himself from this line of conversation, he asked, "Where is Terry?"

"I'm not sure. Joe said something about a boat tour."

Johnny asked, somewhat surprised, "What is up with you and Joe anyway? You're here with two old guys with a kid and Joe's on a boat tour?"

"Feeling our age."

"Oh, yeah, you're all of twenty-nine. Older than dirt."

"Some days it feels that way. Don't you remember? You were in the same place last year."

"Yeah, but I wasn't admitting it was because of Tish. Is there something you're not admitting?"

Is there? Or is it just a longing for something more?

"Nope."

"If you weren't admitting it, that would be your answer."

"You had the tooth and nails gripped in your hands, fighting them both. I'm not fighting anything. Just need a break from all the lust."

Just then Luca spotted a book sitting on the table and he leaned forward and picked it up.

It had to be Rissa's. He couldn't see Tish reading a book about the universe.

Sitting next to it was a sketch pad and he was far more curious about that than her reading material. Although he'd have to think about what that meant.

"Do you think she'd mind?"

Johnny looked up, checking on who the who was, noticing the spiral notebook in Luca's hands.

"Not if you're the one who suggested she have it bound. She'd have to assume you'd check it out at some point."

"I feel like I'm invading her privacy."

"Hey, she left it out. That makes it public domain."

He opened to a sketch of him, and he fell back against the cushion, not believing what he was seeing. Then he began flipping the pages and everyone was more personal than the next.

In one, he was playing, his head bent as if looking at his finger action, his booted toe up as if he was keeping time to the music. His face was in shadow, his hair hanging in his face, his tee shirt soaked at the underarm, the backdrop his amp. The next page showed him laughing with Tim, his eyes crinkled at the corners, his facial expression revealing the moment of something humorous that transpired between the two. The next he was cycling along the stone-edged path in Burlington, his hair away from his head as if the wind was having its way, the satisfied smile as if he was truly enjoying the adventure. He found himself sketched on page after page, in various poses, his face displaying various emotions: reflection, seriousness, intensity, confusion. He was shaken by her ability to see him, every facet of who he was, all the conflicting aspects he tried to funnel into one coherent whole. He wasn't sure he wanted the world to see this. It had taken too much effort to hide these parts of himself that she had been able to read so easily.

"They're good, aren't they?"

As if horrified, Luca exclaimed, "They're all me."

Johnny laughed. "That just must be her Luca journal. She seems to have one for all of us. Even the women. It's been interesting watching her work. She gets almost frenzied while she's doing it."

It should have been a relief to know he wasn't the only one she was capturing on paper, but the images were so expressive, so revealing that he had a hard time thinking beyond what was in his hand.

Had she gotten under his skin? Gotten inside his head?

How had that happened?

He had pushed her away at every turn. Well, not every way but in too many for her to have figured him out.

He noticed the book again, the definitive one on the universe written by one of his favorite scientists.

What game was she playing?

He dropped the sketch book down on the table a minute before she returned, chatting with Tish, bags weighing heavily at their sides.

He slipped out without saying a word, hoping to get the picture of her body out of the landscape of his mind. She wore a slip of a dress, pale shade of pink, that might have hit mid-thigh. She seemed to be dressing up more, not always in cut-offs and tees but adding more feminine things to the mix. He'd been mesmerized by her long legs and there was a hot, steamy flash of them wrapped around his waist while his hands cupped her bottom, exploring what lay beneath. She'd had her arms around him, and he felt her breasts against his chest, the nipples extended and poking into him.

Taking off had been for self-preservation.

Once they'd arrived in Providence, he shut himself away in his room. He sat staring into space, thoughts filled with Rissa, her sketches, the sex, and a way to extricate himself from a very dangerous precipice.

When his sister called, telling him she and Ken were waiting for him in the lobby, he'd been surprised. They'd arrived earlier than he'd anticipated, or he would already be dressed and waiting but the afternoon had gotten away from him.

After throwing on his jeans and yanking one of his silk shirts off a hangar, he buttoned himself up, tucked himself in and headed down to the lobby. As soon as he saw his sister, his body transformed itself back to mild-mannered brother and he went over, enfolding her in a hug.

"It's good to see you."

"You, too. These tours are much too long."

"This year it's only a couple of months here and there. I've got more down-time than I know what to do with."

"You need a family..."

"Let's not go there, okay?"

With her pursed lips and her silence, he got what he'd hoped for.

"I couldn't get you a room on our floor but you're only one up. Let's get you registered. Then we can grab a cup of coffee, catch up."

It was too late in the day for a meal, but he wanted to hear about the wedding plans and what was going on in their lives. Ken had become a rock for the family Luca left periodically and he liked him a lot. It made it easier to leave them behind for months at a time.

As Luca turned around to head to the registration desk, his eyes were drawn to the figure sitting in one of the chairs. Her legs were curled under her, her sketch pad on her lap, charcoal in hand.

Every cell in his body went on alert, the hairs on his arms tingling.

As neutrally as he could, he offered, "That's Johnny's sister. Come on, I'll introduce you."

He noticed Rissa scramble up as soon as they began their approach in her direction, gripping the pad in her hands more tightly.

"Rissa, I'd like you to meet my sister, Val, and her fiancé, Ken Moura."

Rissa smiled and reached out to shake Valeria's hand and then stopped mid-way.

"Sorry. My hands are a mess."

The grey smudges were displayed when she held up her hand.

Instead, she offered a smile and said, "It's nice to meet you. Luca has spoken highly of both of you."

Patting him on the back, Val said, "He's such a good brother. We love yours. He's one of our favorite people."

"Yeah, Johnny has that effect on most everyone."

"You look like him."

Luca glanced at Rissa, smiled, and said, "Not really. Different shape eyes and nose...among other things."

He was just paraphrasing her words although he made a point of not mentioning her boobs. The thought of how they felt in his mouth alone caused a mutiny, and he felt the rise of the Rissa flag coming to full mast.

Smiling back at him, Rissa said, "We get that a lot."

Their eyes held for a moment before Val asked, "What are you drawing?"

As if noticing the weight in her hand, Rissa brought the pad up to her chest and hugged it.

"Oh, I do some sketching. I like to people watch. It gives me subject material for practice."

"Don't let her fool you. She's very good. She just doesn't think it merits using."

Val smiled. "The only thing I can do is draw a straight line, but I need a ruler. I love going to art museums, wish I had just an ounce of their talent."

Rissa straightened her posture.

"I guess we all want something we don't have. Grass being greener and all."

Val asked, "What's your favorite medium?"

With animated gestures, Rissa described her work.

"Charcoal, chalk, sometimes oil pastels. I've got a lot of nervous energy and the quick strokes help me release some of it. It's busy work, and you can finish it in just one sitting. I used to paint but it's a more time-consuming process, and I don't get the quick fix I need with it."

With sincerity, Val said, "I'd love to see them some time."

Luca met Rissa's eyes. "We've suggested she collate them and publish a book. You know, something like, *On the Road with Thunder*. I know our fans would love to see how she's captured moments in our daily lives. We'd sell it at our merchandise table."

Giving Rissa a fixed stare he added, "I'd have veto rights just to make sure mine aren't caricatures."

Val's eyes widened.

Luca was also surprised. Instead of taking it humorously as he'd intended, Rissa seemed affronted.

Rissa answered softly, "I haven't done that. Wouldn't. There are too many ways to draw you. You have so many sides, so many layers."

Val pointed out, "No one sees the real him most of the time. Of course, it doesn't help that he keeps it hidden."

Luca reminded his sister, "I'm standing right here, Val."

But it didn't stop her from continuing.

"There were so many years..."

Luca cut her off in the middle of her sentence with a look that expressed his unwillingness to discuss that topic.

After deciding coffee wouldn't cut it, Luca derailed the conversation and said, "Let's get you checked in. Then we can go to the bar before I have to leave for the show."

Val asked, "Will you join us, Rissa?"

Her eyes met his as if asking permission to say yes. There was also a simmering heat that he should have expected.

His voice was a bit husky when he told her, "Some of the guys wanted me to let them know when Val got in. They'll be coming down, so you're more than welcome to join us."

"Thanks. I'll go and wash up and meet you there."

His eyes followed her, and he was still reeling from what she'd said. He's seen for himself that she'd drawn him in a myriad of ways, which meant she'd watched him. They hadn't been caricatures but something much deeper. She'd seen layers. Sides. It was scary that she could see into who he was. He hadn't given anyone the time to expose the real him, didn't trust what they'd do with it, but it seemed she was burrowing her way under his walls.

And she had still fallen into bed with him with passion and abandon.

Was this what it was supposed to be like?

Intimacy?

Knowing what lay beneath the surface and accepting, cherishing what it was?

He glanced back up just as the elevator doors were closing, perplexed by the powerful hold she was beginning to have on him.

⌒

Rissa was appalled at the number of smudges that were on her clothes. Changing had become a priority, so she riffled through her bag to see what she'd brought in from the bus with her. Yanking out a piece at a time, once she'd exhausted her choices, she groaned.

Why hadn't she packed any of the new things she'd bought with Tish? Instead, she'd just carried her tote in with leftovers. Going through the pile now heaped on her bed for a second time, she silently cursed herself for not bringing anything that seemed appropriate.

She couldn't wear the skirt she wore the other night, again. The memories of it bunched around her waist as he entered her had her breath vaporizing.

After pulling every article of clothing out of her bag, she had to settle for her distressed jeans. By choosing a black spaghetti-strapped tee with some ruffles she hoped she'd offset the casual with a bit of fancy. Once she'd showered and changed, she studied herself in the mirror, cursing.

She was primping, for goodness' sakes.

For what?

A man who could bring so many other women into the bed with them that she'd fall right off the edge.

Enough.

But before she turned away, she reached out for the palest of pink lipsticks and quickly applied it. *Moron* was all she could say to the image in front of her.

Hurrying to the door, not wanting Luca to change his mind, she rushed down to the bar, hoping she had given them enough private time.

Taking a few deep breaths, she entered the hotel restaurant.

In the dim interior, she could barely make out where they were but then Luca stood up and beckoned her over. She was the first out of the Thunder crowd to arrive and cursed her anxiousness in wanting to be with him again.

Fumbling with a chair, he offered Rissa a seat.

"Here sit down. What do you want to drink?"

Val and Ken were seated at the table, a glass of wine in front of both, but that wasn't her drink of choice. Wine seemed more refined, but she could never get used to the taste. Her preference was chugging beer from a bottle.

Tonight, she'd be a little more urbane.

"A Sam, please. With a glass."

Both women watched the man walk away towards the bar before Val put her attention on Rissa.

"I hear you're somewhat of an athlete."

Tucking an unruly curl behind her ear, Rissa dipped her head.

"Yeah. Some people get the brains, some get looks. Some get athleticism. I got to wear the gym shorts."

Luca tipped the glass and poured the brown ale into it before setting it down in front of her. He shook his head as he took his seat. Rissa really didn't know that she was both smart and pretty.

Addressing his sister, he asked, "How are the wedding plans coming?"

"Good. We just finished setting the menu, ordered the cake, and we're almost finished with the flower order. Have you decided who you'll take yet?"

He shouldn't have been surprised that she threw that question in, and he gave her the same reply he had every time.

"It's two months away. I will."

The frostiness in his tone told her that subject was off the table.

But she wasn't his older sister for nothing.

Meeting Rissa's eyes, she explained, "He's giving me away. I want him to attend with someone who will appreciate the significance of that. Not some fan who will be there merely because of who he is."

Trying to deflect her serious posture on the subject he joked, "That's such a ridiculous phrase. It makes it sound like you're a commodity I couldn't sell...so I gave you away."

Rissa could feel some underlying tension but didn't really know what was causing it. She didn't know what to say, so she let the air settle around them until Val picked the thread of conversation back up.

"He's walking me down the aisle. Is that better?"

"Yes, as a matter of fact it is."

Placing her hand on his, she squeezed. "I'm glad it will be you."

Drawing Rissa back into the conversation she said, "Even if our father was alive, Luc would be doing the honors. Marlan Arcila left when I was just a kid. Luc wasn't even born yet."

"Oh, I'm sorry."

"Unless your Marlan's representative, don't be. We got through it and we're closer because of it. He died from complications of cirrhosis of the liver when I was ten."

"Wait, isn't your last name Caroli?"

Taking a long swig of beer, Luca explained, "Yeah, Mom put her maiden name on my birth certificate and legally changed hers and Val's when the divorce was finalized."

"Oh."

Rissa couldn't imagine how hard it would be knowing your father didn't even stick around for your birth. Being rejected even before you were born had to have side effects. No wonder he had accepted the name so easily. But he hadn't let it define him. He had come out of it on top.

She flushed at how proud of him she was.

Like she had a right to be. Like what did that even mean?

Deep in her thoughts regarding Luca, another layer exposed to light, she almost missed Val's request.

"So maybe you can come to the wedding as Luca's date. When I look at the pictures years from now, I want to see someone who I can think of fondly."

The gruffness in his voice held a warning. "Val..."

Fingering the top of her wine glass, Val didn't look at him when she observed, "You seem to be friends."

Rissa peeked out from her lashes, wanting to see Luca's expression at Val's implication. It wasn't encouraging.

She didn't heed her own voice demanding she not move forward with the plan.

"Tell you what. If you're not dating anyone by the time the wedding rolls around, give me a call."

"Luca hasn't dated..."

He looked pointedly at his sister and interrupted. "Does that satisfy you?"

Val hesitated before answering.

"Yes, actually it does. Thank you, Rissa. Johnny and Tish will be there as well, so you won't feel like an outsider."

"I'm sure it will be a lot of fun but I'm also sure Luca can find his own date."

The thought of that completely undid her. She didn't want to think of him with another woman right now although she knew in her heart that what they had done the other night wasn't a sign of a permanent attachment. A flash, a spectacular light show, or maybe more a flash in the pan than an eternal flame.

CHAPTER TWENTY-SEVEN

At what felt like the crack of dawn, Rissa's hotel room phone rang, waking her out of a deep sleep. Fumbling with the receiver, she answered with a yawn, "Hello."

The voice on the other end had her sit up quickly, wiping her eyes open and awake.

Val?

"I'm very sorry to have awoken you but I was wondering if you would have a cup of coffee with me in the cafe."

"Um, now?"

"As soon as you're able. I talked Ken into having breakfast here, but I'm not sure how much time he'll give me."

"Let me throw on some clothes. And if you don't mind, maybe brush my teeth."

"I'll be downstairs waiting."

She jumped out of bed, taking a brief glance at the clock, which glaringly told her it was ten past eight in the morning, giving her only maybe four hours of sleep. She raced around the room trying to put herself into some semblance of order, along with her mind. She'd been unable to get to sleep again last night, tossing and turning for hours, trying to figure out what Luca was so adamantly trying to hide.

And she knew he was hiding something. His voice had been tight, and he'd cut off his sister numerous times.

Why would Val have asked her to meet with her?

Those thoughts followed her down to the restaurant and into the room where she found Val and Ken sitting at a table against the window.

Sliding into a chair, Rissa took the carafe of coffee and poured herself a cup. "I need this first."

Ken scowled when he said, "I want to apologize now for what Val wants to talk to you about. I'm not convinced it's a good idea and I don't think Luca would be pleased."

Looking deep into Rissa's eyes, Val asked coolly, "Are you involved with my brother?"

Clearing the cobwebs out of her brain, still half-asleep, Rissa asked, "What?"

"Are you involved...."

"I guess I did hear you right. And the answer is...no."

Slumping back against her chair, Val hid her eyes behind the fingers of one hand.

"I could have sworn..." She braced her arms on the table. "There was certainly some kind of chemistry between you. He hasn't seriously dated anyone since his engagement ended while he was in college, and I was hoping..."

Rissa's mouth had slackened and she was visibly shaken by the revelation. He'd been in love with someone to the point he asked her to marry him? In college?

"Luca was engaged?"

He'd mentioned that college had been easier than high school, that he'd gotten better at relationships, but...engaged?

Was that what he was hiding?

But why?

Unless it was another painful part of his past.

"Not in the real sense of the word. He was willing to marry someone...out of some sense of...I don't know what exactly but I'm glad Paige left him before he could do something else so radical."

Was...Paige the cause of the scars he carried? Annie had suggested that someone had hurt him badly.

"What happened?"

Ken placed his hand on Val's arm, warning her not to give away too much of Luca's story.

"Luca had a very tough time in school. Kids can be mean and they were merciless with him. There's only so many times you can see a loved one with a black eye or torn pants before you start thinking about retribution. We lived in a pretty run-down section of Boston until he was in high school. I got a decent part-time job while I was in college, and we moved to Melrose. I was hoping high school would be better but...I don't know what everyone had against him. Maybe he was too sensitive, maybe just too damn smart. He's off the charts for genius and kids can be...cruel."

Rissa took a sip of her coffee, anger building inside, but she didn't say a word and let Val continue.

"Luca didn't date, for obvious reasons. When he got to college, well, he seemed more comfortable. He began to develop friendships, he was happier. When he began seeing someone his freshman year, I was happy for him. I met her once and she seemed well-suited, smart, and cultured. I had hopes for them. In the end, she hurt him badly."

Her look was stone cold and Rissa shivered slightly.

"She's the reason he left school. When...the dust settled, he had already dropped out and refused to re-matriculate. He barricaded himself in his room, started playing bass, hid from the world really, wasting his talent, or so I thought. Still don't know where he got those brains, and I was pissed he wasn't using them."

"What a bitch."

Stunned that she had said that out loud, she looked up. "I'm sorry."

"You don't have to apologize. I feel the same way."

"I thought maybe he dropped out because it was so expensive."

The thought that he dropped out because he couldn't cut it had never even crossed her mind.

"He was there on a scholarship, but I would have worked two jobs to keep him there. I stopped talking to him for a couple of weeks, finally got over myself, and realized he needed my support more than ever. He eventually got a job bartending and waiting tables at a local restaurant and kept up with the bass. Before I knew it, his hair was long, he rarely dressed in anything but jeans and tee shirts, and he had joined a band. Different life than I'd anticipated for him."

Rissa wasn't sure she wanted to know all this. It made the longing more intense. She was hurting for him, the boy he was, the man he had become.

"Why exactly are you telling me all this?"

"Paige...has reached out. I found the message on the band's website, but I haven't told him yet. I was hoping that if you were together, she wouldn't be able to pull him back. I love my brother very much and I want to see him with a good person, someone I can trust. I don't trust her. He's been trying to measure up to some un-quantitative standard, one that she set, and I don't want her messing with his head again."

Rissa held her tongue.

She wanted the same thing as all the others, just another woman who wanted to find a way into his bed.

"I'm truly sorry he was hurt. I know how that can feel. I recently got out of a disturbing relationship with a man who couldn't seem to keep his...*pecker in his pants seemed the inappropriate phrase here*...promises to me. Even if there was something between us, I'm looking for a real commitment next time around."

Val's tone was chilly and her words contradictory.

"Luca will make a wonderful partner, husband. You seem to make him happy."

"I'm sure he will make a good husband, but not for me. He needs someone more intellectual. I don't meet that standard, and if he does get to the point he wants to settle down, he'll be looking for that. After what I went through, I want to be the only woman in the relationship and in the bed, not a diversion until someone better comes along."

"You're beautiful, talented, and from I can tell, you have a good heart. What else could a man want?"

"Thank you for that but he needs someone he can talk to, discuss his passion with. What I have to offer wouldn't compensate for that."

Val looked disturbed by the information, but she gave Rissa a wan smile.

"Maybe you're right. If we could keep this conversation between us, I would appreciate it. Luca wouldn't approve of me sharing his dirty laundry."

"For what it's worth, Luca has a good head on his shoulders. Whatever he decides will be right for him. He's got his career and he's made lasting friendships. I know Johnny loves him like a brother."

"And I will always be grateful Johnny gave him the opportunity he did. And you're right there. He loves what he's doing. I've come to understand he might have gone to college to satisfy me, not him. He loves science and he's so smart I thought it would be best for him. I might have been wrong to force the issue."

"I'm sure he'll find the right woman someday."

"I know he could if he gave himself the chance. For so many reasons in his past, he believes he would never be first choice for someone."

"I can think of thousands who would pick him first."

"Yes, but for who he is or who they think he is?"

She thought it must be sad that none of them could trust that a woman could love them for who they were rather than their celebrity.

"I know Johnny used to worry about that, too. Then he found Tish. He had no doubt that she loved him and couldn't help but be swept away. It might happen that way with Luca. Some woman will sneak under his skin before he ever knows it happened."

"I just hope he trusts her enough to give it a chance."

"Me, too."

It was said without conviction because she didn't hope for that at all. Unless it was her.

Ken seemed a bit more relaxed than at the beginning of their coffee.

"Are you ready to go, Val?"

"Yes."

Taking Rissa's hand, she thanked her. "I guess I've got to trust you with what I've told you. I don't think Luca's told anyone the whole story about Paige. Ken's right. He wouldn't be too pleased with me for sharing part of it."

"I promise. Your secret is safe with me."

"Our mothers got on very well in Italy. I hope we can get them together sometime in the future."

"I'm sure my mother would like that very much. Maybe when you're back from your honeymoon."

"But before the holidays. I hope I see you at the wedding, Rissa. I'll keep my fingers crossed."

"Good-bye."

Rissa watched the couple walk down the street through the window, then sank back against her chair.

There were parts of the story Val had left out. Rissa could feel it. But she had no idea how to connect the dots. Had Luca really dropped out of college because Paige dumped him? It didn't seem a good reason for something so extreme. Escaping from a life that seemed to cause him nothing but grief might have been a valid reason though. Val said he'd dropped out of the world, not only school. His re-invention of himself was total. A small smile appeared.

He was still a scientist at heart, serious, logical. The smile tipped downward when she thought of the underlying sadness that she saw clearly in his eyes.

"Who are you, Luca?"

There were so many oppositional aspects to him. For someone who hadn't fit in anywhere once, he fit in everywhere now.

⌒

She ordered breakfast after Val and Ken said goodbye, but the food was sitting uneaten on her plate.

"Hey, I've been looking for you."

The voice went right to her heart, and when she looked up, his eyes held hers in a spell.

"I'm here."

"I see."

Before sitting across from her, he asked, "Do you mind?"

"Not at all."

"Sorry about last night. Val can be somewhat pushy when it comes to..."

"Yeah, I know the feeling."

Italian families consumed their young.

Taking her fingers in his hand, he said, "I think we need to talk."

She readied herself for the dump. Not that what they had was a relationship of any kind, but she still felt vulnerable. The sex had been so good she'd hoped...that it could last a little bit longer anyway. Now that Val had confided in her, she knew there was no chance in hell he'd choose her. He'd already set things in motion for a new start. It wasn't with her.

"I think we have a problem here."

The frustration in his voice confirmed what she knew was coming. She was the problem. Now he wanted to extricate himself.

She wanted to beat him to it. Pushing away a pang of regret, she said lightly, "I don't know what you're talking about. We had great sex. A fling just like you're used to..."

He sighed and leaned forward, his head almost touching hers.

"That's not the problem, Rissa."

She felt a quiver before asking, "Could you be more specific then?"

He was holding her hand and the flutters in her stomach started a descent.

"We seem to have some kind of off-the-chart chemistry."

Her stomach tingled. What was he saying?

A sprig of hope blossomed.

"Kind of unexpected, huh?"

"Very. The thing is....it can't go anywhere."

The blossom turned to dust, and she extricated her hand, clasped it to the other in her lap. She should have known, did know, but to hear it put as bluntly was a heart-stopper.

"I told you before I'm not in a head space to make it more than what it is."

"I appreciate your honesty. I haven't had the courtesy of that in the past. Let me assure you that I didn't have any hopes for forever, Luca. I was enjoying it for what it was."

There was sad expression on his face, as if he didn't like what he was saying any more than she did.

"It would be stupid for us to keep enjoying it."

When she didn't respond, the lump in her throat too tight, he asked, "Right?"

It would be stupid. Self-abasing. She'd moved away from that need over the last few months, and she couldn't allow herself to fall back there.

Her eyes met serious and brooding amber.

"You've been honest with me, so I'll be honest in return. I wish...this thing between us was more than just physical. I knew in my heart it couldn't happen. You saying the words out loud confirms that."

She felt the hitch in her voice before she heard it.

"I can't repeat my mistakes. I can't stay with someone who doesn't want me."

His arms reached out to her, but she scooted her chair back so he couldn't reach her. His elbows rested rejected on the table.

"You have that wrong. I want you but..."

Sitting back in his chair, he dipped his eyes to his fingers.

"I...Someone is meeting me in New York City. An old friend. I haven't seen her since college but she reached out. We've been emailing each other and..."

Paige.

"You're thinking of going back with her?"

His eyes flashed up in surprise.

"How do you know we dated? I said a friend."

She closed her eyes and took a slow, calming breath. "A friend wouldn't cause you to say what we have between us has to stop."

His elbows were back on the table, his face imploring.

"I haven't seen her in years and we had a pretty rough patch at the end. I haven't made any commitments, I haven't put myself on a shelf, but I need to see if there's anything there."

Raw grief settled in her heart. Rissa forced the words passed the lump in her throat. "Then we stop what we're doing."

⌒

"It would seem to be the smartest thing to do."

He reached out and fingered a curl before tracing her cheek with the digit.

"I told you smart was overrated."

She sniffed out a laugh. She had dreamed about being crushed in his embrace one more time. It wasn't going to happen.

"You did."

"So that's it."

"I think it's for the best."

At least her best. She couldn't continue to sleep with him knowing she would never be who he wanted.

She was stuck just watching his mouth move, his shoulders filling the fitted white shirt with well-defined muscle, his hand caressing a coffee mug the waitress had brought over and placed in front of him. in a way that made her envious. His fingers were long, and she knew they were nimble, making music with only four strings.

Finally lifting her eyes, she fell right into an amber gaze. Her insides melted and the air evaporated, making it hard to breathe. Unable to maintain the contact without completely coming apart, she pushed her chair out and walked toward the exit, needing to be outside, where there was more oxygen and less Luca.

Once in the clear, fresh summer morning, she took a breath to quiet her nerves, castigating herself for even thinking this would work.

He was meeting an old girlfriend in New York. She was glad she didn't know this nugget of information when she was talking to Val. She wasn't great at keeping her expression neutral and she might've given something away that Luca wanted kept secret.

Had he reached his saturation point?

Was she one of the women who'd helped him get there?

Then his voice was near her ear, his breath close and warm.

He fingered a loose hair behind her ear as he asked, "Why did you walk away?"

The heat from his finger caused a rumbling inside, and it wouldn't take much for it to peak and explode.

Dipping her head away, she mumbled, "Was there anything else to say?"

She fumbled her words and he arched his eyebrow.

His finger was back under her chin and he raised it so he could look in her eyes. "Do you want me to stay away from you?"

She shivered as he appraised her for an answer. "Yes," she whispered.

Without another word, he led her out to the bus, her bag already aboard.

⌒

He sat on his bunk and watched her.

Last night he'd wanted to knock on her door, stood outside for interminable minutes.

What had stopped him was the need. It was too strong, too big. She was an explosion waiting to happen and any chance of a future would be blown to bits.

So instead, he went back to his room, the regret stifling.

Now, his eyes consumed her as she sat cross-legged on her bunk, flipping through her sketches. Jessica, the merchandise queen, had loved the idea of a book. She'd told Rissa to put some pages together and she'd look them over, see if it was something she thought would sell.

That's what was keeping Rissa's hands busy.

She was so intently focused, he watched without distraction, her brow furrowed, her skin flawless, her lips ripe, her boobs defined beneath her tank top.

He wanted her.

Wanted to be inside her, her soft, silky, and oh-so-wet center where he felt so at home.

She'd told him to leave her alone, but could he?

Could he convince her to go for another couple of nights? It might be all they had. He wasn't sure it was enough time to extinguish the fire but they could test the hypothesis, see if it was possible. If he were another kind of man, she another kind of woman he might have taken the time to see where it went.

She was creative, fun, sexy, with a figure that could make him sweat.

Which was a complete surprise.

He'd always gone for curvier women but he'd found lean to be much more assessable. His palms grew moist as he remembered what she felt like, how her breast fit his mouth perfectly. Little had he known that less could be so much more. Her nipples had come alive under his tongue's ministrations and he wanted to taste them again, consume rather, her whole mound fitting into his mouth as he sucked and played. He could splay her middle with his hands, and her athletic body could contort into positions that unsettled and enflamed him.

He was walking a dangerous line but one he wanted to walk until he fell off.

He just hoped she wanted the same thing.

Unsure as to whether he could give her up right now, he had to find a way to persuade her to keep this high-wire act in play.

CHAPTER TWENTY-EIGHT

She felt his stare, felt heat ignite in the center of her belly and because she couldn't help herself, she glanced over and time stood still.

His eyes held hers, the deep amber burning her skin, telling her he wanted another night beside her, inside her, touching her in places that still throbbed.

The problem was, she'd ended it. Told him to stay away from her, and she meant it but what she read in his eyes would lead her to take another night.

She wanted it with something akin to obsession.

To taste him, to feel the rippled muscles under her fingers, be the instrument he played so well.

Because he was everything she had ever wanted and more.

She hadn't known there was more until he'd slid himself into her and every particle in her body had ignited.

If she had any reservations about her past relationship being over, the coupling she'd had with Luca had singed it off the pages of her life.

What she'd had before was tepid, disappointing at times, tedious.

With Luca, it was immediate incineration.

She went up in smoke at a look, a kiss, a touch, never mind the actual moment he entered her.

She could give herself one more night if she was willing to take it.

Hartford was the last stop before New York City.

She would gladly make a fool of herself for this man, without regret.

Something she'd sworn she would never do again.

⌒

Johnny had ambled up the aisle, the bus moving down the exit ramp towards their destination.

"There's a science museum here in Hartford, isn't there?"

He directed the question to Luca, and she listened for his response without looking up.

"Yeah. Why?"

"Might be a good place to spend some of our down time."

"Why?"

"Going with you might be interesting. You can explain things as we go along and it might give Rosie the stimulation she needs to stay entertained. What do you say? This afternoon?"

"Sure, why not? How about you, Rissa?"

She couldn't look at him. The urge to go, be with him was too strong.

"I'm not sure. I should be working on the book."

He entreated, "You have to come with us."

Her eyes shot him a look of defiance.

"I don't have to do anything."

He stood and walked over to her bunk, his rangy body doing strange things to hers. He leaned in so she was the only one who could hear what he had to say.

"There's something there that I'd like to show you. Please, come with us."

Without breaking the spell he'd cast over her, she nodded in reply just as the bus pulled up to the hotel.

She enjoyed the easy bantering back and forth that began once they got underway, and the volume increased as they stood in line waiting to buy tickets at the Hartford Science Center.

"Why haven't we ever been to the Boston Museum?" John asked.

Luca laughed. "Speak for yourself. I've been dozens of times."

"Why didn't I know this?"

"You never asked?"

"Why wouldn't you have told us?"

"What's there to tell? I visit museums. Now you know."

"Have you ever been here?"

"A couple of times. I meant to come last year but we had some stuff of major proportions going on, so I decided to skip it. Your head wasn't on right for a while there and then you had left us in the lurch going in search of the holy grail."

Rissa thought that must have been when John went running after Tish, leaving Chappy in charge of the drum kit.

"Oh, yeah, that would have been my fault."

"Yes. It would. Seems fitting that you're the one who suggested going today."

As they entered the building, they stopped to check which exhibits they wanted to see. The first level was devoted to anyone under the age of seven, so they opted to hit the stairs and see what was on the next floor up. Naturally they were drawn to the Wild Music exhibit, the whale song pulling them into the room. There was a jamming room where people could compose and play their own music.

He was getting a kick out of the guys. They looked like kids, wandering from one section to the next until they came to the sign that read, FORCES OF MOTION.

Rissa smiled at him and asked, "Can you design a race car?"

The smile was open and friendly, not tremulous. Had she so easily accepted the fact that they were over before they even began?

The one he returned was only half-hearted.

"I don't know. I never tried."

Johnny wasn't going to let Rissa run the show, so he called out, "Hey, they have a sports lab here. Want to use the ski simulator?"

Rissa stopped to think about it for a minute, before replying.

"We're the only ones into sports, Johnny. Let's just keep looking for something that might interest everyone."

Tish said, "I didn't know you could ski."

"Yeah, we learned when we were kids. Rissa kept it up, I think."

He looked at his sister with a questioning arch to his brow.

"I haven't skied in years."

"Afraid that I'll do better?"

"No way. I can ski rings around you."

"Bet money?"

"You're on."

Tish could only laugh at the two of them. "Nothing like a little sibling rivalry?"

Luca was smiling as well. "This ought to be entertaining."

Going up another level, the Scaleras all but raced to the game, Johnny beating Rissa out by a step. "Ha. I go first."

Crossing her arms across her chest, she gave him a sly smile.

"Fine. Then I get to see what I have to do to beat you."

Johnny's eyes grew smaller, as if he were analyzing her strategy. Shrugging it off, he stepped up to the machine and turned it on. Within seconds he had done a somersault right onto a highway.

"Ha, you not only wiped out, you're dead. My turn."

"Not yet. Let me have another try."

"Not happening, big brother. Watch and see how the big girls do it."

Reluctantly and somewhat petulantly, Johnny backed away so Rissa could take his place.

Luca leaned against one of the pillars in the space, wanting to have a front-row seat for Rissa's slalom run.

As if really on skis, Rissa bent her legs, swooshed from side to side, mentally balancing herself.

Without warning Johnny pushed the power on, hoping she wasn't ready. Anticipating just such a move, Rissa carefully made her descent down the hill. Gliding, her body going from right to left, she moved gracefully through the snow, turning from front to back, glazing off a boulder to make it back onto the course. Beginning to gain confidence, she started hotdogging, skiing backwards, somersaulting successfully before going back to forward movement.

Tish was patting Johnny's shoulder hoping to make him feel better about his sister's much better run.

Johnny hooted as Rissa took a tumble down the slope, bouncing off a granite rock, and was in a much better mood.

"Wipe out."

"But I won hands down."

"My somersault was better."

"Your somersault killed you. I'm banged up but will live to ski another day."

His fingers found a sensitive spot on her shoulder blades and pinched.

"Ouch. Stop."

He was laughing outright. "What else can we do? This is great."

He was like a little kid as he wandered from one activity to the next.

"Hey, they have car races using brain waves. How does that work?"

The question was directed to Luca but he just shrugged his shoulders as if he didn't know the answer.

Johnny challenged, "I bet I can beat you."

Raising her eyebrows, Rissa laughed. "Yeah, right. Your brain waves are going to beat his? Don't think so. Do you really want to be two for two? In losses, that is."

Without making it seem as if he were the only bright one in the bunch Luca explained, "It doesn't have anything to do with brain power or intelligence. It has to do with brain waves."

Johnny asked, "And everyone has them, right?"

"Unless they'd somersaulted onto a highway and smashed up their head."

Rissa burst out laughing.

Terry, not wanting to be excluded said, "I want a chance to do something."

Johnny gave in rather easily. "Then you go head-to-head with Luca. I'll sit this one out."

Tim and Annie had just returned from grabbing something to eat and were coming in at the tail part of the conversation. Tim asked, concerned, "Terry might be at a bit of a disadvantage, don't you think?"

Luca countered, "Then why don't you race with him. I'll try to explain what's going on."

"What are you trying to tell me?"

Luca slapped his back. "Nothing more than I'm not explaining it again and I'd rather watch than compete."

Rissa stifled a chuckle but when Luca flashed her a smile, she soberly melted into it.

As soon as they were done, Tim winning the competition although not understanding why, Luca checked his watch and said to Rissa, "Come on, it's time."

Turning to the rest of the group, he said, "We'll meet you back at the hotel."

Rissa noticed Tish pull on John's arm when he was about to complain just as Luca took her hand and guided her to another part of the museum.

"Where are we going?"

"The planetarium"

"Stars?"

"Yup."

"It's what you studied in college?"

"Not exactly, but close."

"Cosmology."

"Yes."

"Which is what exactly?"

"It combines observational astronomy with particle physics."

"English?"

"I was studying the evolution of the universe."

Shit.

How deep would someone have to be to keep up with him?

He was as complex as the big bang theory, that was for sure. She knew the term but couldn't get beneath the surface of what it all meant.

Luca was the same type of phenomena.

There was a tinge of disappointment in his voice when he said, "You'll be bored."

"God, no. I just won't understand it all very well."

He smiled easily as they made their way to the waiting area. "Not many people do. It doesn't mean you can't appreciate the night sky."

"Stars?"

"And recognizable planets. There's a show this afternoon that gives you a live tour of the current night sky. I thought...Maybe you couldn't care less."

"No. I'd love to see it. I started reading a book about it. I got lost in the third chapter, when the author was explaining how Venus got so hot."

"That takes a bit of background. I saw the book you're talking about in the sitting room one day. It's a good one, but a bit...scientific for the average person."

"It's dry reading. I'm more into visuals. When I began getting lost in the explanations, I had Lana order me the DVD. She gave it to me when she came to see you guys play in Boston. I've been watching it during my downtime, sometimes on the bus. I'm enjoying it."

"The old or new version?"

"I don't know. The narrator is someone named De Grasse Tyson."

"The newer version. He's one of the best. I heard him speak once, try to catch his appearances whenever he's on air. He brings a lot to the table. He deciphers a lot of the science jargon for..."

"People like me?"

"For people in general."

"I have to admit, I see it from a more artistic point of view. One of the photographs at the beginning of the show looks like something that Georgia O'Keefe might have painted. I never realized the universe was so beautiful. Music and art combined."

"You're right. Kepler believed that the speed of every planet corresponds to musical notes. Their motion brings a unique harmony to the whole."

"Who's Kepler?"

"He lived in the 1500s, defined three laws of nature that still stand, and ended the succession of scientific astrologers by becoming the first astrophysicist."

The usher was unclipping the rope, telling them it was time for the show. As they moved forward, she glanced at him sideways and said, "I'll be asking more questions. I can't even pick out the North Star in the sky."

"Hasn't anyone ever told you there's no such thing as a stupid question?"

"I used to tell my students that all the time...but to be honest..."

"Okay, so maybe there are, but not today."

They made their way to a couple of empty seats, and she sat listening to the intergalactic music that swelled in the space. She craned her head to look up at the blank white screen, anticipating what it would look like when the show started. Luca was holding her hand, his body at ease, his lips curled into a smile.

He was in his element here and comfortable grace settled over her as well.

A voice penetrated the silence, introducing the presentation, and then the overhead dome was filled with sparkling dots of light. What looked like a ninja star, a galaxy of stars, came hurtling toward her, and as it filled the screen, the guide told her it was the Milky Way.

She was fascinated with the planets, the description of dark matter, but it was the colors of the universe that pulled to her. As an artist, she felt in pigment hues, and as Jupiter and Saturn spiraled in space, she was stunned at the immensity and vibrancy there.

They lived in a limitless world, galaxy, universe, and she was blown away by the grandeur.

She leaned over to whisper in his ear, "I can understand why you wanted to dedicate your life to this."

It was such a complex and beautiful subject.

And through the prism of theater, the visuals satisfying her learning style, she followed along from the big bang to current-day exploration. She might not know why Venus was red but she understood the concept of an ever-expanding universe, where twinkling stars lived millions of miles away, that galaxies could explode, leaving a dust storm of light and atomic energy, and black holes might be the doorway to other dimensions in space.

Captivated by the show, she let all conversation lull, asking all her questions once they exited into the sunlit afternoon.

"You could have asked me questions while we were watching, you know. I wouldn't have told you to be quiet."

He had a lopsided smile on his face, and she was jolted by the reminder of what she'd said to him at Tish's concert last year, telling him to shut it while Tish was playing.

Closing her eyes, she whimpered.

"I'm sorry about that. Your voice..."

She looked up to meet his eyes.

"...sent shivers down my spine and it kind of pissed me off."

He sputtered, "I spent the rest of the concert feeling put in my place because you liked my voice?"

"What do you mean, put in your place?"

"My mother taught me manners, please, thank-you, that sort of thing, but I never learned the intricacies of social situations. When you told me, I was being rude that night, I thought I was being rude. I took you at your...word. I haven't opened my mouth in any of Tish's concerts since."

"Well, the la-di-da people keep their mouths shut, and once Tish begins, I kind of forget to talk, I get so caught up but it's not rude to ask a question. It was rude of me to scold you like I did."

She fell into his eyes and when he asked, "So you like my voice?" she leaned in to kiss him.

"Among other things."

"I didn't expect you to..."

"Want another night? I shouldn't. Neither should you, not with what you told me."

"I told you I haven't made any commitment there. If you go into this with your eyes open, I'm not hurting anyone."

He was wrong.

He'd be hurting all of them but it didn't matter.

She wasn't doing this for him, she was doing it for her. Giving herself the gift of his body. One more time.

CHAPTER TWENTY-NINE

They slipped into his room.

The hallway was quiet and there had been no spectators.

As he pulled her head close for a kiss, he asked, "Can we take this slowly?"

He chuckled when she said, "Not sure."

Flinging her shorts and panties onto the floor after he took them off, he admitted, "Me neither. I don't know what I was thinking."

They groped their way to the partially naked state they needed and were quickly riding the crest of their desire as hard as they could before they peaked and came, crashing together.

It was a good thing she'd never gone off the pill. They never would have made the necessary pause to get the damn rubber on.

They had grunted that right before the first time.

He'd said, "Condom."

She'd said, "Pill."

And the conflagration had continued without another word.

As they lay entwined, he kissed her temple. "We'll never get to do this the normal way."

"Isn't this normal?"

He was kissing her now, more slowly, more measured.

After sliding the tank over her head, he unclasped the bra and let her breasts spill out into his hand.

"So beautiful."

Her breath stuttered.

No one had ever told her that before. It wasn't just the words. Luca made her feel that way, in the reverent way he touched her, which lessened her inhibitions, the caresses making her squirm with need.

"No, you don't. Slowly. I want to take our time."

She gave in, knowing it would be their last, letting the mounting frustration grow, the throb growing with each kiss, each nibble as he made his way down her body.

Arching up, his tongue tangling with her nipple while his thumb brushed her other lips, the stab of pleasure was almost pain.

Her hands roamed his body as she tried to keep from exploding under his hand, her fingers in his hair, down his neck to his shoulders, down his hips, around his buttocks, the feel of him against her fingers so excruciatingly good.

His moan told her he was almost ready to acquiesce to her need, his lips coming up to take hers in his own, their tongues stroking, stoking the flames that seemed to be increasing in intensity until he thrust hard and deep, her own cry of possession driving him deeper still. His lips pressed her head into the pillow, as he drank long and hard, his breathing as labored as her own.

And then she could feel him tense, and she let herself go, riding the waves with him, his mouth never surrendering hers, his thrusts fulfilling her in ways she never knew existed.

He rested his head on her chest, the light kisses continuing as he fought for breath.

When he wrapped her close to his side, with a pressure that spelled deep-seated feeling, her arms went around his middle and her head lay quietly against his beating heart.

The muted ring from his phone alerted him to the time.

"Shit. I've got to go. They've probably been waiting for me in the lobby."

He sprang up from the bed and began stuffing himself into his clothes.

"I'm not even going to have time to change."

"Sorry..."

He strode over to where she still lay in the bed, liking how satisfied she looked, knowing that it was he who'd put that look on her face.

"I'll knock on your door after the concert. We can pick up where we left off."

After kissing her, he lingered, ran his hand up her thigh.

She felt so good.

Made him feel...as if they were meant to be together.

She cupped his chin in her hand, the look on her face scaring him.

"No. This was it. One final time for posterity."

"What do you mean? We have another night."

"No, we don't. You made a promise to someone, and it wouldn't be right."

"Rissa, it might not even..."

"Luca. You've already chosen her over me. I won't take second place again."

He pulled her into his lap, buried his face in her neck, inhaled her scent.

Had he done that?

It hadn't been his intention. He'd made the choice before the tour even started. Before Rissa had come to him, opening herself up, setting him on fire.

He held her closer, not wanting to admit she was right.

"You have your mind set on another type of woman." Her voice was soft against his cheek. "If it doesn't work out with you and...whoever, you'll still be looking for your fantasy. I'll still be me. I want to be with someone who wants *me*, with no doubts or lingering reservations. I won't allow myself anything less. Kiss me good-bye and then go."

He sucked in a shallow breath as her fingers threaded through his hair, her face a breath away, her lips settling on his.

He felt hot and tight, the same primal urge pushing him for more.

Giving in to it, he took her lips in savage need, his tongue plunging into the soft interior of her mouth, his hands roaming her still-naked body, his heart beating so hard he thought he'd die from ecstasy.

She eased away from him but he grasped her hand. As she pulled away, the tips of their fingers were the only part touching. It had become a Morse code of sorts. Letting her know he was having a hard time leaving her.

It didn't change her mind.

Gathering up her clothes, she didn't give him the courtesy of a backward glance as she made her way into the bathroom to dress.

His fingers itched to be touching her again, his body feeling the loss of her heat and fire.

His phone vibrated. He couldn't take his eyes away from the door.

He stalled for time, knowing that when he went out the door this thing they had would be over.

Thing?

Was he that unwilling to give a name to what they had together?

He could describe her in detail, define her to a T, but had no word for the combustible way they came together.

He could feel worry lines crease his forehead.

If he couldn't define it, how would he know what he was losing when he walked away?

⌒

She waited until she heard the door click shut. It seemed endless. It gave time for hope to spring up again, that he'd changed his mind.

See that she was what he needed, wanted, but when she stepped out, she found an empty room.

The bed sheets were tangled, his discarded tee shirt was lying on the floor, his glasses resting on the side table.

Drawn to them, she picked up the black, square-rim, thick-lensed glasses. She'd seen him wearing a similar pair in some of the photos on-line. When he was younger.

She closed her eyes.

What would he look like in them now with his hair long, his ear pierced?

She'd never know. They'd never spent the entire night together. They'd never wake up to hidden yawns, bed hair, morning breath, bathroom runs, glasses.

She'd never have the chance to be that intimate with him.

She sunk down on the edge of the mattress, placed the glasses back.

Damn him for wanting something else. Didn't he see how good they were for each other?

She did.

Her mother had told her what to look for and she'd found it. Someone who encouraged her to be...her. The night she'd lost herself in that song, the day in the museum, his compliments on her sketching. He didn't even seem to mind her competitive nature, smiled at how hard she fought to win.

And the sex was exactly what her friends had touted it should be. Intoxicating.

She dragged herself up, looking around one more time.

She was drained of emotion and walking away was a brutal but necessary reality.

Her appointment with hurt had been set from the beginning of the tour. If she'd known, would it have stopped her from jumping headlong into his bed, following the urge to taste his sweetness?

Probably not.

She was glad she'd gone with the compulsive need, but she wouldn't hang on.

A man either loved you or he didn't.

Luca didn't.

That simple.

Trying to make it so was a fruitless endeavor.

It was over.

She picked up her backpack, wishing it could be different, but there was nothing she could do to change the fact that it wasn't.

At least it was on her terms.

She wouldn't change herself, wouldn't settle for being second best. Wouldn't hang around for the scraps he might throw her way. No more contortions to be accepted, to be loved.

She walked out of the room, closing the door firmly behind her.

⌒

It was after midnight and Luca was out walking the streets of Hartford.

The show had run long, and he was too restless to hang around waiting for the bus. Against Lou's advice, he made his way through the crowd, wanting to be alone. The emptiness left in the wake of Rissa's decision, was an aching wound. Essential to his well-being was the night-time sky, the moon a faint sliver in the darkness to keep him company.

No one could touch him out here.

It had been that way since he was just a kid, sitting outside his house, observing the brilliant points of light that rested in the inky stillness. His hunger to learn about his place in the universe was the beginning of a lifetime obsession. It began with Sagan, who he'd read in the library stacks when all his work was done. Sagan, Kepler, Copernicus, Ptolemy, Isaac Newton, each a scientist blazing trails for others to follow. It'd kept him focused, kept him alive. Proved to him there was a purpose for everything, a place for everyone. It took him years to find his.

Or was he still looking?

He wanted to feel Rissa's hand in his but couldn't see a future there.

Shoving his hands in his pockets, he leaned against a building, his eyes raking the sky for some answers.

He groaned.

He'd effectively shut her out, so he wasn't sure what kind of answers he was looking for.

Pushed her away by telling her...the truth.

What did he think she was going to do once his admission was out there? Stick around?

Take the nights they had left and spend them wrapped around him, all while knowing he was making plans with someone else?

He pushed himself off and away, continued along the sidewalk, the streets still bustling with taxis, drivers, pedestrians.

He had no plan.

There was only the possibility of....

What?

Did he really envision a life with someone from his past, now that he was in such a different place?

He might be her intellectual equal but he was no longer emerged in science. He'd found another facet of life that appealed to him.

Could she speak to him in this new language?

Would he have anything to say to her that would sound profound?

Struggling with the gravity of the situation, he was being pulled down by a heavy weight that now rested on him.

As a scientist, he had to find the right questions to ask, the right data to apply to the experiment. It should be based on logic, not emotion.

This was more a quantum physics experiment, one of thought. Schrodinger's superposition that a cat in a box was both alive and dead came to mind. The result was based on what might or might not occur, what choices were made in any given moment. The outcome was cast when the box was opened.

He had Schrodinger's box in his hand.

He wouldn't know if the past was dead or alive until he opened it.

He'd know soon enough.

Would Rissa give him one more day before he lifted the lid?

He never got a chance to talk to her before the women left on another all-girl's outing. She'd ignored him on the short ride into the city, then run off, her pack bobbing against her back, her eyes cast down and away from him. What made it more difficult was that she was sharing a room with Johnny and Tish, so he couldn't seek her out there.

Had she requested it or had been booked that way?

Was it her way of letting him know she meant what she said?

If it was, he wouldn't be able to talk her into spending the day with him.

He'd gotten used to her lively conversation, her enthusiasm for life, her child-like heart making everything she touched golden. Her smiling face, devoid of artifice, was one of the things he'd miss about being with her. There was howling grief raging inside of him when he thought of the other things he'd miss. He laughed more easily when in her company, shared more of his past, revealed bits of himself he always kept close.

She'd made the last couple of weeks less shallow, more real, significant.

Why did he feel he needed someone who was his intellectual equal, someone with whom he could discuss those things important to him, who could understand the fundamental elements of the universe? When Paige had said something similar, it had sounded arrogant, pretentious, as if they were somehow a cut above the rest.

As a member of a band, he'd learned that everyone brought something to the music. Johnny might be more conversant through lyrics and percussion, but they needed Tim's voice to express the underlying power of the sound. Without the other key ingredients, the bass and lead guitar, there'd be nothing to support the score. There would be no harmony if they all carried the same talents. The band worked because of their differences.

He scrubbed his hands over his face.

His aching heart and empty arms told him something he didn't want to hear, but his decision had been made. Now he had to learn to live with it.

Going in search of Johnny, he'd decided to take him up on his offer to hang this afternoon. He'd initially declined. Keeping the affair secret was not in character and increasingly difficult. Johnny was the one he talked to, not that he had given him the full story of his past. He couldn't broach the subject of Rissa, but he wanted to be with a person who reminded him of her. He'd have to choke back the truth, pretend that all was well, but it was worth the discomfort to hear the same kind of laugh, see the same kind of sparkle.

"Thanks."

Johnny was handing the driver the fare and stepping out.

When Luca didn't move, Johnny yelled, "Hey, come on. Where are you?"

Luca mumbled and followed his friend into a small shop at the corner of the street.

He was surprised. The place was clean, could have been any kind of shop. A glass showcase sat against the wall; a leather sofa offered a place to sit and wait. He'd never stepped foot in a tattoo parlor because he never had any desire to write things on his body. The only one of the four that didn't have any ink on him. Johnny had several, Tim had a couple, including an A within a heart, and Terry had the most, a veritable art show all over his arms and back. Today Johnny would be adding another.

One of the artists came out from the back and instantly recognized them.

"Raging Thunder. I love it. You came in last year. Glinda, wasn't it?"

"Good memory. Today I want to add my daughter's birthdate."

"You and Glinda had a kid?"

"Yeah. She's magic just like her mother."

He turned to Luca. "Shit, man. You're the bassist. I play one myself. You're one of the best out there."

"Thanks. I appreciate the compliment."

"What can I do for you, my man?"

"Not sure. I'm still thinking about a tat."

"We have a book over there you can look through. You might change your mind while you wait for your friend."

He wasn't going to tell him he doubted it because he had gotten an idea. "Can I watch? See what's involved?"

"If your friend says you can, I have no problem with it."

Johnny nodded his assent and added, "Sure."

As Luca sat and watched the artist work, the needle steady in his hand, the date of Rosie's birth etched on Johnny's forearm, he almost wished he could ink something for Rissa. She had crawled so far under his skin it seemed only appropriate that she be on the surface in some way. A reminder of what they'd had together.

But what?

Some symbol he could see on his chest when showering, changing, hanging out that spoke to the memory of her.

A pickle?

He smiled at the thought but shook his head. That would be too blatant.

A paintbrush, a piece of charcoal?

The soft hum of the machine rattled him, but Johnny didn't seem fazed by the needle or what it was doing to his arm.

"Are you going to get one?"

"I've never been into body art."

"You're the only one who doesn't have a bit of ink on you."

"For a reason."

"Which is?"

"Too...raw."

"There's got to be something. Something science-y?"

"Science-y? I'm not sure that's a word."

"Start a trend."

It gave Luca an idea, a symbol that only he would know the meaning of.

When he described what he wanted, the artist shrugged his shoulders and made the design before inking it just over Luca's heart.

Johnny scrunched his face, narrowed eyes peering at the three ovals, each pierced with a black dot, a larger one at its center.

"What the hell is that?"

"It's the symbol for a proton."

The particle with an electromagnetic force. A positive force.

Which is how he thought of Rissa.

"Huh?"

"You said to get science-y."

"You're weird."

"I know."

He was almost getting comfortable with it after all these years.

For the first few minutes in the cab ride back, there was silence between them.

Then from out of the blue, Johnny asked, "Is there something going on between you and my sister? You're almost joined at the hip."

The question threw him off, and he stammered out the lie he'd been practicing. "Not in the way you're thinking."

"Where did you end up going when you left us yesterday?"

Luca looked out the window, not wanting Johnny to read what was in his eyes.

"The planetarium. She's interested in the cosmos lately."

"I noticed her reading the book, caught her watching a show on it. It's another reason I thought...you know, that you two were...getting close."

Luca turned from the window, stared at Johnny, baffled.

"What does her reading material have to do with it?"

"My sister's always been a people-pleaser. She tends to immerse herself in whatever the guy she's with likes. She never seemed overly interested in science before."

"Johnny, your sister is a physics major in every way. She's just beginning to understand that her athleticism uses every scientific force known to man."

"Like what?"

"Gravity, space, relativity, resistance. I could go on."

Luca could hear Johnny tapping his fingers against his thigh.

"I never would have thought you two would find anything in common but I was wrong. You seem to enjoy each other's company."

His pulse began throbbing. Visions of her body creating an overwhelming need.

If Johnny knew the extent to which they'd enjoyed each other's bodies, he'd probably cream him.

He all but croaked out, "We do."

A couple of minutes passed in silence.

Then Johnny said, "She's creating some great stuff."

Luca glanced over to see pride shining clearly in John's eyes.

"She is."

"You're bringing out her creativity."

"I don't know about that. That seems to be a part of who she is."

"She's bringing you out of your shell."

Luca laughed at the idea.

"I have a shell?"

"You do. I've never met anyone so private. You hand out parts of your life like breadcrumbs we need to follow."

He was going to deny it but knew Johnny was right. "I've had to be. It's how I survived."

"I know that better than anyone. But we're your friends, Luca. We'll always have your back. Being who you are shouldn't be so tough, not with us anyway."

"I know. The problem is I haven't really changed much since high school. I'm still that nerd from the wrong side of town."

"You were never the problem. Who you were back then was nothing short of courageous."

"Yeah, that's why I buried myself in the stacks at the library."

"You proved that every time you walked down the damn hall. I'm beginning to realize you're just as vulnerable today as you were back then. The shell helps you hide that."

"The shell being...?"

"The adulation, the women. I did the same thing."

"You did it for a different reason."

"Same game, same result."

"What?"

"I played the game not wanting a family. I ended up isolated, bored and lonely. You play it for acceptance but you're as isolated as I was."

"How the hell am I isolated?"

"You are so damn remote. As if nothing can touch you. I think my sister is touching something and if you're like me, it's going to scare you to death."

"If nothing can touch me, then I hardly see your sister having any impact on my life."

The taxi was pulling up to the hotel and they both got out from opposite sides.

Before going their separate ways, Johnny made one last remark that got Luca's attention.

"That's what I thought, bud. And I almost screwed up the best thing that happened to me. Don't make the same mistake."

CHAPTER THIRTY

Her heart hadn't been in shopping with the women, so Rissa had gone off on her own.

Not able to pull off happy and playful, she grabbed a cab and headed towards a place that held pain and grief...and hope.

Walking toward the hallowed ground where the twin towers had once stood, she could hear the water rippling and pooling, could almost smell the acrid smoke as it gushed upward from the blazing inferno. The trees added grace and a sense of symmetry to the area and stood as guards to protect and defend.

She didn't dare go into the heart of the memorial, her own heart heavy, couldn't bear to read the names etched in bronze, so she tucked herself in a corner and watched the solemn faces, felt the underlying grief as people passed her by. Then began to sketch.

It was the one way she could work the spiraling pain through her. Her hand busy, pouring all emotion onto the page.

She had started believing that he cared about her.

That he enjoyed being with her.

When he had told her about meeting someone...Paige, if she had to make a guess, after the concert tomorrow night, her heart shattered, cutting her to pieces.

She'd held it together long enough to enjoy one more night in his arms.

And then...she hid in the bathroom so he couldn't read what was in her heart.

It was full of him.

Her fingers worked furiously, purging disappointment, sadness, regret, yearning.

She was in the exact same place she was just months ago, dumped and without a job.

What the hell was wrong with her? Why couldn't she read the underlying message in a person's actions.

Don't tell me, show me.

Well, Luca had done that by showing her the door.

Where did that leave her?

Her hand stilled and she looked around. This place was the scene of the most catastrophic assault on American soil, but something had risen out of the ashes.

Here was a memorial that encapsulated what was lost by remembering it.

It was the same site but repurposed.

She might be in the same place, but the road ahead didn't look as bleak.

She had declined the invitation to hang around in case things didn't work out for him.

For as much as she hurt, she would face it, let it burn away in its own time, making room for a new beginning.

Maybe she'd drive up to Oswego, see Dr. Aalmers, talk about enrollment.

But was that what she wanted?

Her soul was calling her someplace else. She didn't want the constraints that school put her under as a student. Having the freedom to sketch anything she wanted, anywhere she wanted these last few weeks, had given her a sense of weightlessness, choice no longer a burden but a blessing.

She'd have savings after the tour, her brother paying her generously. She'd have the book to work on, collate, sell. Maybe she could even afford her own place to live, a small one, on the outskirts of the city. It could be a new start.

An apartment, a career she loved, at liberty to live by herself with no one telling her what to do or how to do it.

The direction was crystal clear.

It pointed north.

Home.

As soon as the tour was over.

For now, she had to find a place to recover.

She couldn't face the coming nights, knowing what could happen before they were over.

That Luca would touch someone else the way he'd touched her, fingers nimble, calloused, tantalizing skin with their finesse, filling someone else the way he filled her. Completely.

Maybe they'd be able to take it slowly.

Let it build, ripple.

Foreplay.

And as the picture of another woman all but possessing him invaded her mind, a numbing sensation took over her whole body, her limbs shaking, tears burning.

Her head ached.

The breakup with Jude should have felt like this. She'd spent almost three years with the man, not a couple of weeks.

How could it hurt this much?

Brushing the unshed tears away, she swallowed hard.

Jude had been right. She was needy.

She needed Luca in her life, in her heart, in her bed.

Wanted to cling to him and the love he'd brought her.

He was the one who'd encouraged her to be herself, but she wasn't what he wanted.

She was going to have to learn how to spend the rest of her life without him.

Maybe she was reckless after all. She'd handed Luca her heart and he'd filled every square inch of it.

⌒

Luca paced his room.

He'd gotten a confirming email. Paige would be waiting for him after the concert.

His future was right at his fingertips.

But there was something niggling away at him.

The time.

Since he got back from the tattoo parlor, the minutes had moved so slowly, he thought he'd never be able to get through the day. It wasn't anticipation that was pounding in his blood, but the agonizing reality that Rissa was no longer part of his life.

What was he doing? Why was he taking a step back? What was the fucking hold?

He hadn't even liked it there.

He'd built walls to stay on the other side of it.

It was Rissa who'd come close to dismantling them, prying at brick after brick, with every look, smile, touch.

How was he going to live without her?

He needed another night, another smile, another kiss. Then he'd be able to move forward.

He picked up his phone and texted her.

Have 2CU

He wanted to spend the day with her, in her arms, wrapped around her body. He wanted to wake up to her tomorrow, make tender love...love?

That wasn't what he was feeling.

It was lust, pure and simple.

She wasn't the woman for him. A diversion while he waited...

For what?

His past to come crashing back on him, like a tsunami whose waters receded before gushing forward, sweeping away all in its path?

He fingered the tattoo. It was a spectral signature on his chest. There was another one on his heart.

Both were Rissa's.

She was a whirling magnetic field, tendrils of light, smoky appearance, or more like a pulsar that flashed waves of energy that glowed. He was the shattered remnant of that massive cosmic explosion.

All night long, he sat in the chair overlooking the parking lot, waiting for her to text him back. Time, space, and light were conspiring against him. He was light-years away from a discovery. It had already happened; he was just beginning to feel the effects.

He moved slowly to the window, the dawn telling him he'd almost made it through to a new day, his mind still a jumble of missing pieces. He saw Rissa climb into a cab.

His fingers touched the glass, wanting to touch her face, see her smile.

His heart lurched inside of him.

What the hell had he done?

⌐

She told the driver to drop her at a good place for breakfast.

It didn't matter where, she just needed to be away from the hotel and any chance she'd bump into Luca.

He'd texted her late yesterday and she'd almost given in and texted him back.

He wanted to talk, anywhere, anytime and he missed her.

It had taken all her discipline not to give in to the urge to see what he had to say.

Because it didn't matter.

He was already taken.

By a ghost from his past, the one thing she couldn't compete with.

Didn't want to.

She'd spent too much wasted energy trying to hold on to a man. The men might be completely different, but they had one thing in common. They each wanted a trait in a woman that she didn't have.

Looking at it from a new perspective, it was their loss, not hers.

She smiled at her shiny new outlook even if it was blurred by sadness.

When the cab driver dropped her at a midtown eatery, she hoisted her pack and went through the door. Seated at a booth, her coffee cup in her hand, she glanced around, putting her people- watching skills to work.

It was busy for this early in the morning, the sun newly risen. It's what she loved about a city. It didn't sleep and neither did the people.

Life pulsed, energized by the promise of a new day.

There were a few hours to go before the Museum of Modern Art opened, and she was excited at the prospect of losing herself there.

Her phone vibrated and she snuck a peek at who was calling.

Luca.

She swiped ignore and the call went to voice mail.

⌐

Why the hell wasn't she answering?

You know why and you can't blame anyone but yourself.

He was standing at the curb of the hotel when a cab pulled up asking him if he needed a ride.

Leaning down he asked through the open window, "A cab left here about ten minutes ago, picked up a woman with a backpack. Can you find out where it dropped her?"

He pulled a fifty out of his pocket and handed it over, just in case the cabbie needed some motivation. It helped.

He heard the name of the restaurant, squawked over the wire, and before the voice faded away, he was in the back seat, the driver already knowing his destination.

He didn't waste time dawdling once he arrived. Striding in, he scanned the interior, his eyes falling on the woman he was after.

He took the steps to where she sat.

"I've been trying to reach you since yesterday."

He slid into the opposite side of the booth, his arms leaning against the table, his fingers seeking hers.

She placed her hands out of reach, in her lap.

"And I've been ignoring you. What about that don't you understand?"

Her voice was cold and restrained.

"Rissa."

Just the sound of her name on his tongue aroused him. He was hard-pressed not to steal a kiss, a touch but he avoided temptation clasping his hands together in a prayer grip.

"We have a free day today. I was hoping we could spend it walking around the city. You could sketch, I could watch..."

A shimmering wave of exasperation shone in her eyes.

"You want to be buddies, now? I'm not good enough to date, but I'm a great pal to hang with?"

"You'd be a great woman to date..."

"Just not for you. You're too smart, too educated, too much a science geek to be with someone like me. I get it. I knew from the start that it would never amount to anything. The sex was great, the planetarium was fun. Now, we move on."

That was the problem. He couldn't seem to do that.

"You've got as many brains and talents as I do. You just use them differently so don't put yourself down."

"I'm not doing that. You are. You're the one with high expectations. I don't have what you're looking for. End of story. Will you please go now and leave me alone?"

"I don't want to lose our friendship."

Her voice went soft, almost a whisper. "We were never friends, and we can't go back and start over."

"We became friends."

"No, we became lovers. There's a difference."

His agitation was building. He was lost in a labyrinth of need and desire and couldn't find his way clear.

She was taking money out of her wallet, leaving it on the table, gathering her things and sliding out of the booth.

"Have a good life, Luca. I hope you get what you're looking for."

As soon as she left the diner, Rissa swung left, not knowing where she was going, just knowing she had to get away from here, Luca, the way she felt about him. Trying to get her bearings, she moved to the side, and pulled out the map of the city she'd taken from the hotel. Her finger followed the street she was on, first one direction, then another. The park was nearby. She could spend some time there, waiting for the museum to open, waiting for her heart to stop aching for something it couldn't have.

He sat there, his head in his hands.

With nowhere left to go, he returned to the hotel but not to his empty room. Even though Rissa had never stepped foot in it, her absence was tangible.

He knocked on Johnny's door. There would be vestiges of Rissa there, traces of her that might ease the loneliness.

Johnny opened the door and then left it to him to enter. "Come on in. Rissa isn't here."

He stood there, inspecting every corner.

"I know. She's...out in the city."

Johnny went over to the room-service cart, poured himself some coffee and raised his cup as if to ask if Luca wanted some.

Luca shook his head.

After taking a sip, Johnny asked, "How come you're not together?"

He felt awkward. This was not a subject he could discuss with his friend.

All he could offer in the form of explanation was, "She wanted to work, said she wanted to be alone."

Tish had come out of the room, Rosie awake and alert in her arms.

"Hi Luc, Where's Riss?"

The awkwardness continued. Why the hell had he thought this was a good idea?

"We are not joined at the hip no matter what Johnny thinks. We do our own thing now and then."

"Okay. Sorry. We've gotten used to you two being together."

The thread of anger that was snarling since Rissa had gotten up and left him in the diner snapped.

"Well, don't."

Johnny's eyebrow arched. "If you're going to have an attitude, take it someplace else."

Tish shot Johnny a look that told him to stop. "Did you two have a fight or something? Should we be worried about her?"

"No. She knows what she's doing. She's fine."

"You're not."

"I'll be fine. Off days put me...off."

He spied the book sitting on the table. She had it out again. Maybe she'd gone back to it after the planetarium exposition. Walking over to it, he asked, "Think she'd mind if I borrow this?"

"I don't know. Don't you have your own books to read?"

"I do but I haven't read this in years and I'm in the mood for Sagan."

Tish was the one who responded, "I can't see the harm in it, as long as you get it back to her."

"I promise. If she wants me to, I will."

Rissa was probably done with science if her efforts to understand it were for him.

After entering the silence of his room, he spent the rest of the day skimming the contents. It was always one of his favorite books, and it never disappointed. Along some of the margins were scribbles, question marks, as if Rissa didn't understand the premise. His name was in others.

Did it refer to something she wanted to ask him a question about it, or did the passage remind her of him? The phrase "suns with companions" was circled, as was, "two stars that orbit one another, close enough to touch."

What he could have told her about that was the energy that birthed the universe was star stuff, all the chemical elements released into the cosmos from the inner, fiery core of the stars, through stellar explosions. He could categorize her as that same glowing energy, his life rebirthed from the magnetic burst of power that came from their joining.

Flipping through more pages, he found a scrawl about how the night sky was alive with patterns, the word underlined. It was those patterns that prompted the names of the constellations, the Big Dipper, Pleiades, Canis Major, Orion, the stars creating a dot-to-dot sequence that fed the imagination.

He read on, skipping over well-read portions about space and time travels, reading in depth the chapter that always called to him about the lives of the stars.

He bolted up, an aha moment awakening a dormant cell. He knew the facts but he hadn't assimilated the information before. Maybe he'd never had reason to.

How had he forgotten that attraction came when there were two opposing charges, the proton and electron? It was the combination that held an atom together, yin and yang, complement halves of the whole. When the charges were the same, they repelled, and it took a force of nature to hold them together.

Rissa was his proton.

He almost laughed out loud. She was also a force of nature.

Either way...

His eyes shot to the clock on the bedside table.

It was time to stop looking back, clinging to a past he didn't even want.

Rissa was the big bang of his life. He was ready to risk it all, step to that precipice. He was standing on the edge of forever. It was Rissa who was there with him, not a ghost from his past.

He had to get moving.

He had to wade through a deep black hole to get there.

CHAPTER THIRTY-ONE

Luca was banging on the door.

Johnny's door.

When it opened, Luca pushed past him, heading in the direction of second room off to the side. "I came to see Rissa."

"She's not here, Luca."

"Is she in the lobby? I didn't see her when I came in."

"She's on her way to the airport."

Johnny glanced at his watch.

"Probably already there. She's going home for a few days."

"What? Why?"

"She said she has to figure some things out. With Ma and Paul coming in this weekend, she said she'd have the alone time to do it."

"But this late? Why didn't she wait until tomorrow?"

"I asked the same question. I didn't see a point to midnight travel. She just mumbled something about needing to be gone tonight, took her backpack and left. I still don't understand."

It was clear to Luca.

She thought he would be with the chosen one. He'd realized almost too late who that really was.

⌐

He only hoped her heart was big enough to forgive him.

"Why are you here looking for her? You were talking to some chick after the show. I thought you were back in the game."

"The game's over. She was a former girlfriend, the woman who caused the impulse that set my life on a different track."

Johnny's eyes shot up to meet his.

"That was her?"

"Yeah."

"Is she the reason the game's over?"

Luca's mind was not on the topic at hand, but Johnny kept asking questions.

"Why are you looking for Rissa if you're back with your ex?"

"I'm not. It's over but Rissa mustn't have gotten my text."

Or didn't want to talk to him, which was becoming a real problem.

"Who? Rissa? What are you talking about, dude?"

He spun away from the conversation heading to the door.

"My awakening."

It had come in a blinding rush of sights, sounds, textures and colors. All belonging to Rissa.

"I fucked up and I need to make it right."

"What does that have to do with Rissa?"

"I don't have time to explain. I have a plane to catch but...hopefully I'll get her to come back and we can both tell you."

He spun away from the door, patted his back pocket, making sure he had his wallet. He flew out of the lobby's glass door, signaling for a ride. He threw himself in and gave one simple directive.

"Airport."

"Which one?"

"Shit. I don't know."

Punching in the number he wanted, he waited for Johnny to pick up.

When he did, Luca barked out, "I didn't ask what airport, which flight. She must have told you."

"She did. What the hell's going on?"

"Seems I'm a one-woman man just like you, after all."

"My sister? When the hell did this happen, Caroli?"

"It will all become clear soon enough. Can I have the information, or do I have to scour the airport looking for her?"

"If you're not going to tell me what's going on, I should make you work for this."

"You could do that. I'm hoping you won't."

There was an agonizing pause and then Johnny bit out, "JFK Delta. I think it's Flight 1722."

Luca barked out the information and hung on to the seat, willing the cabbie to go faster. He didn't have much time left, grateful that the concert had been an early one.

When the cab had come to a stop in front of the terminal, he threw some money at the driver and raced into the airport.

He approached a ticket counter, the blonde woman behind it giving him a smile.

"Good evening, sir. What can I do for you?"

"I wanna buy a ticket."

"What's your destination?"

"New England."

He only needed the ticket to get through security, but he couldn't exactly say that. Not with NSA at every corner of the terminal.

He reached into his back pocket and pulled out his wallet, then Amex card.

She gave him a look that suggested she was wary of his motives.

"You'll have to be a bit more specific than that."

"Look, give me any ticket you want. Manchester, Boston, it doesn't matter."

"We have a flight leaving for Boston at 11:10. But it's just about ready to board so you'll have to hurry."

A flash of urgency hit him.

"I'll take it."

"Any bags to check?"

"No."

"One way or two?"

"One way."

He was becoming impatient now, his fingers tapping firmly against the counter.

Once the ticket was printed and he was on his way towards security, he was almost running again.

Whipping off his shoes, his watch, pulling everything out of his pockets, he dumped it all in the tray and rushed through the archway, collecting everything and fumbling to get it all back in place.

As he scanned the gate numbers for the one he wanted, his mind was numb, his heart racing.

He went up and down each row of seats in the waiting area, taking in each face, each body but was unable to find her. Turning around left then right, he scoured the area for a flight screen that would tell him what other airlines had a plane leaving for Boston. He had to find her. Wasn't leaving until he did. Would use the ticket he held in his hand if he had to. There was no way he was going back to the tour without her.

Without at least talking to her.

She might not be able to forgive him for thinking he wanted someone different.

He was going to lay it all out, put it all on the line.

His heart, his mind and his body.

Closing his eyes against the eventuality of a bad outcome, he felt his heart slam in his chest.

Still in the throes of his self-inflicted misery, he felt a spurt of electrical current and looked up to see her coming in his direction.

Her head was down as she checked her phone, her face ashen. Her eyes carried the evidence of sleepless nights.

Taking her in while she continued in his direction, he was overcome with a feeling so strong he thought he'd die from it.

And then she looked up and saw him, stopping short not three feet away.

"Luca."

"I have to talk to you."

She began walking past him and moving toward her gate.

"There's really nothing to say."

Keeping up, he insisted, "Yeah, there is."

"Then there's really nothing I want to hear."

Faltering a step, the hesitation taking her several steps away from him, he called out,

"Rissa I'm sorry...I was blind and stupid."

She stopped and turned toward him, tilting her head to the side, her lips pursed.

"Didn't it work out?"

How did he explain it? Would she even believe him if he tried?

"I didn't take the time to find out."

Why had he let her get this far away?

"You didn't meet her?"

"No, yes. Only to tell her it was a mistake, that I...."

"You didn't make up your mind up in time to cancel."

It wasn't a question, just a foregone conclusion, and she was right.

"I tried texting you but you never responded."

"If I had, what would you have told me?"

"That I didn't like what I was feeling, didn't want to lose you."

"I'm still me, Luca. Messy, competitive, artistic. I have an insatiable curiosity about the world and the people in it, but I'm not book smart, don't know the meaning of quark."

"I explained it."

"I'll let you think you did if it's important."

"It's not. Important. I don't care. Being with you is. I thought I wanted safe, comfortable, a meeting of minds. I don't. I want alive, chaotic, a meeting of souls. Being with someone else would have meant what we had was nothing, when it was everything."

"Everything?"

There was hope in her eyes, which sent it spiraling through him.

Maybe she hadn't given up on them.

Her lids fluttered closed as if she gave too much away. Like she always did. Her heart written so plainly on her face, a face that made his heart lurch, enflamed his senses.

He's the one who held everything in. Didn't give anything away. Snagging her arm, he placed his hands on her shoulders trying to keep her in place.

"Please. Give me five minutes."

He wasn't sure he could cover all the ground he wanted, needed to, but it would be a start.

She attempted to escape from his grasp.

His grip was like iron.

"No. I need to tell you some things. When I'm done, if you want to walk away, I can't stop you."

"You can't stop me now."

He hung his head, knowing he couldn't. Not unless he wanted to force her, and then he'd have security all over him. Looking back up and into her eyes he admitted, "No, I can't. But please...there are some things I need to say. Let me explain."

Taking her hand, he began to lead her to a row of seats hoping she'd follow him. There was a little resistance at first but then he felt it fall away.

Helping her to take a seat, he crouched down so that he could still hold on to her, his fingers entwined with hers.

"There are some parts of my life I've kept locked away. They hurt too much to talk about, and I didn't want to stir it up. My past has a bearing on how I totally screwed this up."

Kissing the hand in his, the soft skin a balm to his fevered senses, he went on.

"In college, I started going out with this girl. Her name was Paige. She seemed to like me, something I couldn't believe at the beginning. She was pretty, smart, anyway...we moved in together sophomore year. I had to work a lot more hours to afford the rent but I thought...well, it was the first time someone seemed to like me enough to be with me like that. Things seemed to be going all right then...she changed, started doing things totally out of character, or so I thought. She wanted frat parties, motorcycle rides, she began smoking weed, getting drunk. I didn't want to spend my life partying every night, so we spent more and more time apart. She told me I wasn't much fun. I was too serious, too studious, too earnest."

Bringing her hand up to his mouth again, he held it there and paused.

His lips pressed against her fingers, giving him the courage to go on.

"She cheated on me, got pregnant, moved out. It shouldn't have come as a surprise, but I was blindsided. I spent so many years hiding, I thought I had learned how to keep myself safe. I let my guard down and paid. Then, after struggling to regain my balance, she came to the apartment, apologized, begged me to take her back. I thought I loved her, so I asked her to marry me. When she said yes, I quit school and began looking for a job."

He glanced up to see her expression and there was a play of emotions that crossed her face.

Was it anger, hope, fear?

Was she listening? Did she care?

He continued.

"She was livid. Wanted to know how I was going to support us all with only a high school diploma. She tried to convince me to stay in school, told me her father would pick up my tuition, pay the bills, but I couldn't agree to it."

His brow furrowed; the tell-tale signs so easy to read now. She hadn't loved him. She'd needed him but it had to be on her terms.

"Paige dumped me as soon as she convinced the father of her unborn child that I wasn't good for them. She told me over coffee, the prospective dad sitting next to her. It wasn't the kind of guy I expected her to be involved with, the kind she'd been chasing. He was part of her moneyed crowd, someone I met the summer we were together. After she told me, he started talking. He told me that Paige would not marry me, and that there was no way his kid was going to be raised by poor white trash. They got up, leaving me with a broken life. I had quit school for nothing. I was out of the relationship with no idea what I was going to do. I thought she'd destroyed me. I was angry for a long time."

"Luca, I'm so sorry..."

"Don't be. I survived just fine. But it's why I've lived my life the way I have. I never intended to let anyone else in."

"How would seeing her have changed that?"

His fingers massaged his cheeks. "It wouldn't have. It was such a jolt when she emailed, apologized, told me she'd made a mistake. It was like I had to prove to her that she was right. I thought she was the type of woman I needed and it was coming together after all these years."

He began to caress her cheek, the softness tantalizing.

"Then my world blew apart. You snuck in, got under my skin, and I didn't even see you coming, didn't know which way to turn."

The overhead loudspeaker announced that her flight was boarding, but he kept her hand in his, hoping she'd stay to hear him out.

Easing into the seat next to her, he brought her hand up to his heart.

"I barely got through the first day without you. My heart felt hollow, like it had been carved out. That's why I tried so hard to find you. When you got into the cab, I couldn't just watch you go. I had to run after you. I was taking another risk, one that had a much higher chance of failing."

"Why were you willing to marry her?"

The question she asked wasn't the one he'd expected but he answered her without even thinking about it.

"I knew what it was like having your father take off before you were even born. I didn't want the kid going through that."

"I should have known that's what it was. I thought it was because you loved her."

He stopped and studied her face, those beautiful eyes, full, soft lips.

"I didn't even know what that word meant. I see the world in different colors when I'm with you, experience life in ways I've never experienced them before. I trust you completely with who I am. You're the one I want to spend the rest of my life with."

Silence stretched between them, and he didn't know what else to say, wondered if he'd told her too much or not enough. Had he even told her what he'd meant to?

Taking a breath, he began, and the words came out easily, convincing in their truth. "I love you, Rissa. So much and so deep I didn't know what to do with it. I can't believe I was willing to do nothing."

Smiling, trying to lighten the moment, she whispered, "You get around to participating a little, eventually."

He squinted his eyes at her. "A little?"

Her fingers were on his face, stroking him back to life, her smile making his heart lighter than it had ever been.

"Okay, you seem all in after a while."

"I was that, in more ways than one."

Fingering her cheek, he said, "Last night was the worst night of my life. I missed you so much I couldn't sleep, couldn't eat. The bed was too empty without you there. I never want to go through another night like it again."

Her thumb brushed his bottom lip, the sparks shooting through him tantalizing, promising.

Touching her finger, he said, "If I had a ring, I'd ask you to marry me."

Her breath caught in her chest. Wanting that with all her heart she offered, "In some parts of the world, they skip the ring part."

"I need to tell you something first. It might be a deal breaker."

Fear crept into her eyes and he wished he hadn't put it in such dire tones.

"Remember that first day, when I yelled at you about your car?"

"How could I forget?"

"Well, I called Val as soon as we got on the road. There's a new Honda waiting for you at Tim's."

Her irritability was hard to miss.

"You bought me a car?"

He squeezed her hand, needing her to understand it held no strings.

"It's in your name. I have the keys back at the hotel Val gave them to me the night she was here."

Panic was imbedded in her words.

"Why did you do that?"

He kissed her hand, placed it over his heart.

"Val got in a pretty bad accident when I was a kid. I didn't want to risk the same thing happening to you."

"Luca."

"If you answer yes to my question, we'll be getting married. What's yours is mine so I can drive it anytime I want."

"You drive a Saab. Why would you want to drive a Honda?"

"Just saying I could."

Going from the crouched position to down on one knee, he held her hand and asked, "Will you marry me Rissa. I want...no, I need to spend the rest of my life with you."

When she threw her arms around his neck, his heart began to beat solid and steady. He stood, bringing her with him, so they could get as close as humanly possible.

Whispering in her ear, he hoped to take away the hurt he'd caused her.

"There's never been anyone for me but you. I'm sorry it took me so long to see it."

He could hear the applause of a couple of women who were sitting beside them, watching and apparently listening.

When his eyes returned to Rissa's he asked, "Are they right? Did you say yes?"

Leaning in, she breathed the answer into his lips and kissed him.

He deepened it, hundreds of electrochemical impulses sweeping through him. She was the essence of all he loved, and he'd never let her forget it.

CHAPTER THIRTY-TWO

Rissa stood looking at her reflection in the master bedroom's mirror. She'd needed ten minutes of quiet, her heart near to bursting, and her family had acquiesced once they knew it wasn't cold feet prompting the solitude.

The interior of the room was in the background, beautifully decorated, Luca's clean lines combining with her artistic color scheme, and she still couldn't believe it was her home.

Nor could she quite believe it was her wedding day.

But the woman in the looking glass was dressed in white, the gown accentuating her thinness, the applique of sheer lace over a silk underdress, feminine yet simple, with an extension at the bottom that would train out as she walked down the pink runway that covered the lawn.

To meet Luca.

She felt beautiful in it. Smiling she wondered if the feeling came from him, because he always made her feel that way whether she was in a dress, a pair of cut-offs or her paint-smeared leggings.

The last few months had been such a whirlwind that she'd barely caught her breath yet.

Once he had proposed, her life had taken on a new dimension, although there'd been still a few worries to get through before she could finally relax into his love.

It'd taken almost a month to get the ring on her finger. They'd gone shopping in a couple of major cities on tour, but she couldn't find one they agreed on. Until Colorado.

She looked down at her beautiful, round three-carat diamond set in a square frame filled with baguettes. There was a bit of filigree on the band, which was kind of girlie, but she had loved it and hadn't taken it off since he'd slid it on her finger.

There were a couple of other tests, and although they'd caused some tense moments, they had passed them.

The Honda he'd purchased had been waiting at Tim's house just like he'd told her.

Still a bit unsettled over it, wishing she could bring something of material value to their relationship, she'd taken the keys tentatively.

"What's wrong, Riss?"

"I still...I wish you hadn't done this."

She watched his face cloud over, anger beginning to surface. Pointing to the rusted car parked beside it, he said, "I can't let you drive that thing home. If I couldn't before, there's no way I'm doing it now. If anything, ever happened to you..."

She stepped up to him, her finger on his lips to silence him.

"I know. And I love you for it. I just feel like I'm not bringing anything to this...not even a decent car..."

"You're going to have to get used to having a lot of money. A lot of money. Half of what I have is yours. More if you want it."

She reached up to kiss him, lightly.

This wasn't the time or place to put something into it. There wasn't anywhere to disintegrate into each other. But she let him know, "I just want you."

As he hugged her close, his heart beating steadily beneath her cheek.

"That's why you can have more than half of what I have. I've waited my whole life for someone like you. You can have it all."

She kissed him before stepping back to admire the Honda.

He unlocked the car and handed her the keys.

She folded her body behind the wheel.

She inhaled the newness of the leather seats, found her stations on the radio, programmed her Blue-tooth, and then she looked up to see him smiling as he waited patiently for her to be ready.

If the car hadn't been an indication he had money to burn, the house would have provided all the additional evidence she needed.

She stood and stared.

It was beautiful. And big. A bit asymmetrical with bay window, dormers, painted grey with darker-colored shutters and a red front door. He had given her some of the details describing the chef's kitchen, the sunroom, finished basement, where a gym was set to go, but she hadn't thought it would look like it did.

Once inside, the hitch in her breathing continued.

As she turned in a three-hundred-and-sixty-degree circle in the kitchen, taking in the white cabinets, stainless steel appliances, raised island with quartz countertops, her mouth must have been ajar, giving away some of her tentativeness.

Luca took it to mean something different. His old melancholy expression returned to his face.

"Do you want me to take you home?"

Swallowing hard, wondering if he had changed his mind already, she asked plaintively, "I thought I was home."

She saw his features relax but then she heard him declare, "Then you don't like it."

"Luca, I love it, but it wouldn't matter where we live as long as I'm with you. It's just so grand. It may take a me a little while to get used to it."

He crossed the distance that separated them and he held her tightly, letting his heartbeat settle back to a normal rate.

"Being on tour is like living in a bubble. I've been a little nervous that once you were back..."

"Me, too. But we've got to start trusting each other. That we're in this for life and that how we feel won't change."

"I never expected it to be this good."

"Me neither."

She pushed away just enough that she could look him the eye and said, "But, Luca, I hope you don't expect me to clean this thing. It would take me a whole week to get through it before I'd have to start again. I'd never have time for anything else."

She would never again give up what was important to please a man, even this one. The difference was, he wouldn't expect her to.

"I've already talked to the woman who cleaned my old house. She'd going to give us three days a week."

"Have I told you today how much I love you?"

"In so many ways."

But before they ate some of the food Val had stocked for them, they took the loving to a physical place in the only piece of furniture they owned: a bed.

⌒

The next week was spent buying furniture to fill the space. He had cancelled the delivery of all the pieces he had chosen before the tour, wanting her to feel like it was her home as well. And while out, he drove to a shop in an artsy district and used a key to get in.

She looked at him quizzically and asked, "What's this?"

"After Johnny showed me the sketch you made for Tish, he talked to me about finding you a space to paint, to showcase your work. I was going to have Val look into it for him, but once we...got together, I figured if you were going to get mad at someone for doing it, it might as well be me. You are extremely talented, Rissa, and I couldn't think of a better wedding gift."

He studied her gaze, wondering aloud, "Is the wedding still on?"

There were tears in her eyes, so he wasn't sure if she was pleased or getting ready to run.

"You can't keep doing this. I can't reciprocate in any way, shape, or form."

Tipping her chin up, he thumbed away the tears. "You saved my life. You helped me become whole again. I could never begin to try to repay you for that. Let's say we've made an investment. In you. We can't lose."

Her lips found his and the shop got a christening, and she was grateful that the previous tenant had left a long table that accommodated them. Still not needing much in the form of foreplay, they were soon back out on the street with the rest of the day spent making plans.

⌒

Luca adjusted the morning coat in the mirror of a bedroom down the hall from Rissa.

His fingers were steady as they fiddled with the cravat, before making sure the ring was in his pocket. Not in a million years would he have expected to be getting ready for his wedding. The most surprising thing was he couldn't wait to make her his wife, slide that ring on her finger, have children with her.

Although his heart had almost stopped beating when they had talked about that. Johnny had made the comment the band would need an extra bus next time out with all the spouses and kids being added. Tish had asked Rissa, who was sitting on his lap at the time, if they had talked about having kids.

When Rissa had said she wanted to wait, he'd thought for sure she was implying that she wanted to give the marriage a chance, to see if it was going to hold before getting pregnant.

He knew his voice had sounded funny when he asked her why, and he hadn't been prepared for her response. "I want to spend some time just with you for a while. Would it be okay with you if we waited a year before starting a family?"

He had captured her lips with his, the scar tissue on his heart being erased one small kiss at a time. They hadn't had nearly enough time together, but he would probably be able to say that fifty years from now when they were celebrating their golden anniversary.

Val peeked her head in. "May I come in?"

"Of course."

"You look so handsome."

"A bit different than when I'm on stage, that's for sure."

"I am so happy for you. I had hoped..."

"I know. The day I called you to tell you I had a date for your wedding you sounded like you didn't trust me. There was concern in your voice."

"I thought it might be...Someone reached out to you on the website..."

"I know and I understand why you didn't tell me. I'm glad it happened, though. I began to see what I wanted versus what I thought I wanted."

"Rissa is perfect for you."

"Yes, she is."

Cosmic inevitability.

"I could tell she loved you the morning I talked to her and I felt I could trust her with who you were. She said you were looking for a different kind of woman."

"I'm better with rocket science than human emotion."

"That's never been true. You just shut all emotion down. Rissa got you to unlock your heart. You smile more, laugh more...give of yourself more."

Opening her small purse, she extricated a silver key and handed it to him. "Here. The papers were signed Thursday. You are now the proud owner of a house on the outskirts of Florence."

"How did you get the key so quickly?"

"They overnighted me a set."

"We can use it on our honeymoon?"

"Yes. Although I don't know why you had to buy it before you saw it. I could have worked something out so you could stay there to get a feel for the place."

"It was an artist conclave once. The views have got to be good. I wanted her to be able to paint there if she wants to. We can change the interior but not the location."

"I found a woman who'll go in and freshen it up for your arrival."

Cupping his face in the palm of her hand she said, "You are going to make the best of husbands Luca. I always knew you had this kind of love in you. With all those women throwing themselves at you I didn't think you'd give yourself the chance to find it."

He laughed, proving his sister's point that he did it much more frequently now.

"I just needed the right woman to throw herself at me."

"What are you going to do with that?"

"The women? I can't help the swells, but I can control what I do with them."

"And you are okay with that?"

"Val, I'm more than okay with that. Knowing Rissa will be waiting for me after a show...well, let's just say I can't even see other women."

Something Johnny had said once. He could never figure it out...never knew anyone could feel this much love for a person.

Johnny came back in the room and asked, "So, you ready to take on my sister?"

Val kissed her brother's cheek before leaving the men alone but heard the commitment in her brother's voice as she walked away.

"For a lifetime."

"Good luck with that. She can be a bit reckless at times."

"I've seen firsthand how reckless she can be. She recklessly put her heart on the line for me. I can't do anything less for her."

"Good. That means I don't have to have the talk where I say if you hurt her, I'll have to dismember you. Am I right?"

"You're right but the detective you call Paul already gave me that warning. Only he added no one would find my body."

"Good man that step-father of mine. Now I don't have to put the band at risk."

Tish was standing outside the door, Rosie in her arms. "We're just heading down to our seats, but Rosie wanted to come and say welcome to the family, Uncle Luca."

Johnny was the one who looked as if he'd just been hit with something hard.

"Your kids and ours will have the same blood. You really will be family."

"That a problem?"

"Only if yours lord the brain thing over ours."

"Johnny, I'm not the only genius here. You've got the drums and can develop music like no one I've ever met, the mind of a true artist, just like your sister has. And Tish, well, her fingers are golden when it comes to the piano. Our kids will be...our kids. Smart, artistic, talented in some way, and we'll love them no matter what. Right Rosie?"

She gave him a smile that would one day melt young men's hearts.

Tish turned toward the doorway.

"I'll let you get back to your man talk. See you down there."

Johnny kissed both females and then took his place beside the man who'd be his brother-in-law, and they made their way down the stairs, and out to the garden.

⌒

Lana knocked on the door. "Okay, your ten minutes are up. I've got to get that veil on and you've got to go meet Luca. He's already standing there with Johnny. Don't make the poor guy wait."

And once the floor-length veil was attached, she walked down the stairs where Paul waited in his rented tux, Lana fixing the train as she did.

"You look beautiful, Marissa."

"Thank you, Dad."

Tucking her hand into the crook of Paul's elbow, she made her way to the pink silk runner that carpeted the lawn, never taking her eyes off the man standing there with a definite look of appreciation on his face, with the look of love she'd been waiting her whole life to see.

As the strains of the music filtered out over the audience, Rissa began her walk down the aisle, thinking of a quiet place she could escape with her new husband for the short amount of time it would take to satisfy another one of those Luca urges.

About Faith

Faith O'Shea is a contemporary women's literature writer who loves writing about strong women and the friendships they build. She throws in a little magic, a little romance, and develops unique personalities, and what you get are characters who come alive on the page. She's found that strong women need more than a happily ever after.

Faith lives in a small town in Massachusetts with her husband Jeff, dogs Cooper and Molly, and Isis, the Egyptian feline queen. Her children live close and are a big part of her life. In her spare time, she reads, walks Coop, dabbles in all kinds of cooking, and takes time to play with her grandchildren.

You can visit her on Facebook and Twitter or find her through her website at www.faithoshea.com.

THIN BLUE LINE

After her father's death on a routine domestic abuse call, Lana Scalera swore she'd never marry a cop. No way was she wearing widow's weeds before her time. That she fell for a marine, seemed workable. He'd be home and out of danger once his tour was up, no longer the yellow dot on the enemy's target.

When Zach Taylor is shipped home from Afghanistan with severe injuries, there to comfort and help him through the grueling hours of rehab is his pen pal and sounding board. He wanted more than friendship now that he was back and would do anything to get her to say yes to the ring.

When Zach rejoins the police department, Lana makes good on her promise. No way was she going to lose him to a bullet. He was out although her heart was still hell-bent on changing her mind. What would it take to convince her that death wasn't the worst that could happen?

CHAPTER ONE

Lana Scalera was sitting outside her parents' house, waiting for her mother, the sun not even peeking out of the January sky yet. They had a lot on their agenda today and their commercial kitchen beckoned. She looked over to the door, expecting her to run out any minute, her bags of staples swinging from her arm.

What was taking her so long?

Celia was the one who'd called, insisting she be here at this ungodly hour, the to-do list having multiplied overnight. There was probably a method to her madness, this time of year not one of Lana's favorites. Yesterday's family dinner, replete with birthday hats and streamers had done nothing to alleviate the ache and yearning her memories evoked. The cassava cake from her favorite Italian bakery was still untouched, taking up space in her refrigerator.

She honked the horn again, her fingers tapping on the steering wheel, and glanced up to see Paul in the doorway, beckoning her with a wave of his hand. While mumbling about being late, about the full day of cooking ahead of them, she pushed the clutch in, put the car in reverse, yanked on the emergency brake, and ran the short distance to the house. She slid through the opening, Paul stepping out of the way to let her in.

She went on red alert almost instantly. His expression was somber, and her heartbeat went into overdrive. She'd lived through something like this before and it had changed her life forever. She couldn't afford to have it happen again. She glanced in her mother's direction, hoping her instincts were wrong, but the look on her face did nothing to quiet her nerves. The twist of pain in the region of her heart sucked the air right out of her lungs.

She knew what they were going to tell her, why she was here.

If it were a more family-inclusive disaster, she wouldn't be the only one standing here. Her brothers and sister would be with her.

When Paul pulled out a seat at the table and said, "Sit, please," she collapsed into the chair, clasping her hands together to stop the trembling. Her heart was now beating like a horde of wild horses, trying to outdistance the impending doom.

Paul's silence was making it worse, so she stuttered out, "Tell me already. What...happened?"

The voice was gruff as Paul scratched out, "It's Zach."

She'd braced herself for this, or thought she had. Panic like she'd never known before welled in her throat. Her blood rushed and dizziness consumed her. It was hard to form the words, but she had to know.

"Is he..."

Paul was quick to reassure her. "No. He's alive."

Her eyes fluttered shut at that small miracle.

"But..."

Paul had taken a seat beside her, reaching out to hold one of her hands.

"He was beat up pretty badly last night, or should I say early this morning. He got out of the operating room an hour ago. He's stable but critical."

She felt the prick of tears as they filled her eyes. What was growing in the pit of her stomach was a scream, a primal one, directed at Zach, at whoever did this to him, his supervisors, the superintendent.

The noises in her throat sounded odd to her own ears as she gasped for breath.

"I knew this would happen. Didn't I tell you..."

Paul remained calm in the face of her agitation.

"Lana, he didn't go looking for this."

She replied in a small, frightened voice, "He doesn't have to. These things find him. I told you I couldn't deal with this. I...I hope he doesn't expect me to visit him."

She'd sat by his bedside once before, coaxing him back to health. It had gotten her a heart full of pain.

Paul said slowly, "I know very little at this point. He's in recovery. I'll be going over later to check in."

She'd gotten up, begun to pace, a finger in her mouth that she chewed with vigor.

"What are his odds?"

She stopped, held her breath, waiting for an answer, not wanting to care, but needing to know if he was going to live or die.

"The doctor thinks fairly good considering his constitution."

He'd been a Marine. Still boxed, still lifted weights. Apparently still had a death wish.

She pressed her palms into her eyes, holding back the pinpricks of tears that threatened.

Her mother, who was hovering nearby, closed the distance. Her voice was soft and gentle. "Lana, I think you—"

Lana threaded her hands in her hair as anger sliced through her.

"Don't Ma. I walked away for a reason. This reason. I don't have any inclination to walk back into it."

Celia took her hands. "Lana, he's in bad shape."

"His choice, not mine." Her voice quivered.

Now there was a bite in her mother's tone. "You're going to tell me you don't care about him at all?"

Lana stared right through her.

Yes, she cared. She cared too much. It was the reason she'd cut him out of her life.

Putting trembling fingers to her forehead, she announced, "I can't work today."

As she raced back out to her car, she whispered in a ragged voice, *I'm sorry, Zach. I can't do this. Not again.*

On auto pilot, all her thoughts on the man in the hospital, she drove home, pulled into her parking spot, and sat staring into space, not remembering how she got there.

There were too many images of him in her head, his smile, his rugged features, his broken body. The one she'd helped him rehabilitate after his last brush with death.

He was one of Boston's finest. The truth, according to her, was far different. He was a hot-dogger, with a freneticism that was un-reined and undisciplined, who did everything he could to get himself killed. One of these times he'd succeed.

A ripple of fear coursed through her, along with a ripple of something else she didn't want to name.

Once inside her condo, she ranted and raved at him as she cleaned, scouring everything, from top to bottom, the nervous energy needing an outlet.

⌒

Zach could hear sounds, murmurs, the beep of the heart monitor announcing he was still alive, felt a nurse checking his pulse and he forced his eyes open. Then closed them again. His mother and father were here, along with Lana's stepfather, Paul Catalano. He should be glad. No one liked dying alone, but the one person he needed to see had stayed away and he knew the reason. He'd been here before. Not the same room, but the same hospital, hurt, tattered, and in pieces. She'd helped him regain his focus back then, got him through the pain of recuperation and rehabilitation, made him laugh even as she cried. He'd seen to it that she was no longer part of his life and he'd proven her instincts correct with this latest disaster.

He swallowed past the lump in his throat, allowed the pain to have its way. Maybe he deserved it.

His mother sat by his bedside, and he felt her take his hand.

He licked his lips, tried to get the words out, but failed. His jaw hurt like hell, his body hurt like hell, but he had to ask.

He pushed the question out, his voice hoarse. "Does she know?"

"I told her this morning." Paul's voice sounded as if he were underwater, the reverberation pounding in his head, one of Johnny Scalera's drum solos going full out.

⌒

He rasped out, "And?"

He noticed Paul glance over at his parents before he admitted, "She's not coming. Said she couldn't."

He could feel his mother's tension in the way she squeezed his hand, but she remained silent on the issue, and he was grateful for that one small favor.

The nurse, who must have been hovering close by, announced, "I'm sorry but you're all going to have to leave. He's only been out of surgery for a couple of hours, and he needs to sleep."

He felt his mother's kiss on his forehead, heard his father's strong voice telling him they'd be back, before he opened his eyes to see the look of regret in Paul's. His lips were pressed thin, as if he wanted to offer some hope.

"Maybe she'll change her mind."

With a clenched jaw, Zach suggested otherwise. "We all know where she stands. She won't. Just remind her that I'm alive."

"I will. You take care."

Zach gave a brief nod, talking too painful.

He heard the door open and close, and he was finally alone, alone with the thoughts that could undo him.

When he'd been laying in the alleyway waiting for the grim reaper, there was only one thought that rushed his mind in waves, one word he'd said over and over. *Lana, Lana, Lana...*a mantra that focused all his thoughts in one place. Left bleeding and broken, he hadn't been sure he'd survive this time, thought he'd never see her again, never hear her laugh, never see her eyes sparkle when he walked in the door, never feel her muscles tighten around him.

Had he cried out her name with that last kick, the one he thought would finish him off? It wouldn't surprise him. He'd seen enough soldiers on the battlefield cry out for someone at the moment before death. Most called for their mother. But then most had been boys who hadn't lived long enough to find a love deeper than that.

⤙

He'd loved her down to the bottom of his soul, but he'd found out the hard way that her love hadn't been as deep as he'd thought.

It was ironic that the assault had come when it had. Last night, his body had been broken. Two years ago, to the day, his heart had been.

It was also ironic that he'd fought with everything in him in Afghanistan during his last battle, and in the alleyway where the thugs had jumped him, but he hadn't fought as hard for the one thing that really mattered to him.

Fact was, he hadn't fought at all. It was the first time in his life he'd simply walked away.

What had that told her? That the job *was* more important than her? That if he couldn't have it his way, she'd have to choose?

Well, she had, and he'd spent the last two years looking back. He still was.

As he drifted in and out of consciousness, the flashes of the past adding to the physical pain, he decided it was way past due to go to war for the woman who was more important to him than his life.